THE HUMAN FLIES

HANS OLAV LAHLUM is a Norwegian crime author, historian, chess player and politician. The books that make up his crime series, featuring Detective Inspector Kolbjørn Kristiansen (known as K2) and his precocious young assistant, Patricia, are bestsellers in Norway.

Hans Olav Lahlum

THE
HUMAN FLIES

Translated from the Norwegian by
Kari Dickson

PAN BOOKS

First published in the UK 2014 by Mantle

This paperback edition published 2015 by Pan Books
an imprint of Pan Macmillan, a division of Macmillan Publishers Limited
Pan Macmillan, 20 New Wharf Road, London N1 9RR
Basingstoke and Oxford
Associated companies throughout the world
www.panmacmillan.com

ISBN 978-1-4472-3276-6

This translation has been published with the financial support of NORLA.

Originally published in 2010 as *Menneskefluene* by Cappelen Damm, Oslo.

1 3 5 7 9 8 6 4 2

A CIP catalogue record for this book is available from the British Library.

Printed and bound by CPI Group (UK) Ltd, Croydon, CR0 4YY

Visit **www.panmacmillan.com** to read more about all our books
and to buy them. You will also find features, author interviews and
news of any author events, and you can sign up for e-newsletters
so that you're always first to hear about our new releases.

Dedicated to my late aunt

DAGMAR LAHLUM (1923–99)

*the double agent – a human fly whose war experiences
and subsequent fate were the inspiration for this
historical crime novel*

DAY ONE

Murder Mystery in 25 Krebs' Street

I

In 1968, 4 April fell on the Thursday before Easter. At lunch, I marked the not-so-insignificant three-month anniversary of my move to a new, larger office at the main police station in 19 Møller Street by eating a piece of cake on my own. The date is generally remembered as the night when civil rights campaigner Martin Luther King was shot and killed on a hotel balcony in Memphis, Tennessee, unleashing a wave of racialist strife across the USA.

Of lesser interest to the history books, but of greater significance to my own life and that of those affected, was a murder that took place at almost the same time in a flat in Torshov, on the east side of Oslo. Thursday, 4 April 1968 was one of those days when the phone at home in my flat in Hegdehaugen rang late, and an impatient voice promptly asked if he was talking to 'Detective Inspector Kolbjørn Kristiansen'. It was just before eleven o'clock in the evening when the out-of-breath police constable Asbjørn Eriksen phoned to report that an elderly man had been shot and killed in his flat in 25 Krebs' Street. The circumstances were 'highly unusual', according to the overwrought Eriksen. I had always regarded Eriksen as an unpretentious and level-headed constable, so I felt the excitement surge through me even before he mentioned the victim's name. It was only a matter of seconds after he had said, 'It's Harald Olesen!' before I was out of the door and in the gathering dark, racing towards my car.

In 1968, Harald Olesen was not what one might today call an A-list celebrity. Months could pass between mentions of his name in the national press. But for those who had been young in the years immediately after the war, the image of his hawk-like face and gaunt body was still the portrait of a hero. Harald Olesen had been a well-known Labour Party politician in the 1930s. However, it was not until he was almost fifty that he became a household name as one of the legendary heroes of the Resistance. Olesen himself was extremely reticent about his experiences during the war, but this had in no way served to diminish the at times fantastic tales of his bravado as a leader of the Resistance in his home region. After the war, he was given the opportunity to serve as a cabinet minister and sat on the Council of State for four years. Following this, a couple of senior positions in the civil service ensured that he remained a familiar face and name until he retired in 1965, at the age of seventy. Now, three years later, the former hero of the Resistance and cabinet minister had been shot and murdered – in his own sitting room.

When I drove home at around one o'clock that night, having spent a couple of hours inspecting the scene and taking witness statements, I rather reluctantly had to admit that PC Eriksen's conclusion still held true. We had a body, a crime scene and an indisputable murder, but not only did we not have a motive, a weapon or a suspect, we had no idea how the murderer could possibly have fled the victim's flat after firing the fatal shot.

II

Viewed from outside, 25 Krebs' Street was a rather ordinary three-storey brick tenement building in Torshov. The elderly caretaker's wife who met me at the entrance told me that it had been sold and done up three years before. The improvements included a simple lift in the stairwell and bathrooms in all the flats. Otherwise, the building was more or less as it had been when it was built in the 1920s: big, grey and hard. It struck me that both the building and the caretaker's wife could have been taken straight from Oskar Braaten's novel *The Wolf's Den.*

The drama that unfolded in 25 Krebs' Street on the night of Thursday, 4 April 1968 had quite literally started with a bang at a quarter past ten. A shot was fired in the right-hand flat on the second floor that was heard all the way down to the ground floor. Olesen's closest neighbour from Flat 3B was about to mount the stairs, but at that moment was having a neighbourly chat with one of the other residents on the ground floor. When they heard the shot from Mr Olesen's flat, they both ran up the stairs immediately. The door to Flat 3A was locked and there was not a sound to be heard from within. A couple of minutes later, the pair were joined by a man from the first floor, who had left his wife and baby son in the safety of their flat and run up to the second floor. Then the caretaker's wife came panting up the stairs. One of the residents on the ground floor was wheelchair-bound and therefore came up in the lift after several minutes. The last of the eight adult residents, a young Swedish woman, remained bolted into her flat on the first floor until the police rang the doorbell half an hour later.

Meanwhile, the neighbours out on the landing could only open the door to Harald Olesen's flat once the caretaker's wife had arrived with the key. After some discussion, they decided not to cross the threshold until PC Eriksen arrived half an hour later. Their fears of a shootout soon proved to be unfounded. There was no sign of a weapon in the flat, or any form of life. Harald Olesen was lying in the middle of the sitting-room floor with a bullet wound on the left side of his chest. The bullet had gone straight through him and was lodged in the wall. Otherwise the flat was in every way the same, as far as the caretaker's wife could remember, as it had been the last time she was there – with no sign of the murderer or murder weapon.

The very fact that the gun was missing of course disproved any theories of suicide. However, there was no evidence that another living person had been in the flat, or any indication of how the murderer might have left the scene of the crime. Harald Olesen lived in an ordinary two-bedroom flat with a bathroom and kitchen, but no balcony. The thirty-foot drop down to the pavement made the windows an unlikely escape route. Any ideas of fire ropes or mountaineering equipment being used to escape floundered on the fact that the windows were closed from the inside.

In other words, the front door remained the only feasible option. If the murderer had managed to get in, he or she could surely have got out the same way. The door had a snib lock, and the safety chain was not on. The most pressing question therefore was, how had the murderer managed to leave the flat in those few seconds between the shot being heard and the neighbours arriving at the scene? And the second question was, how on earth had the murderer left the building? The second floor was the top floor and the only way down was either the stairs or the lift. If the murderer had taken the stairs, he or she would have met the other neighbours on their way up. The first two neighbours at the scene gave each other an alibi. Any suspicion of a conspiracy between them was groundless given that there was no murder weapon and insufficient time before the other residents appeared. They were all agreed that the lift had been standing on the ground floor both immediately before and after the shot rang out. The lift was empty when the caretaker's wife hurried past and when the wheelchair-bound resident on the ground floor opened the door a few minutes later. And it was impossible to imagine that anyone had succeeded in using the lift to sneak past the neighbours on their way up and then managed to get past the caretaker's wife, who was by the entrance.

From half past eleven all available police officers helped to search the flats and building from top to bottom, without finding the weapon or anything else that might help to clear up the murder mystery. The caretaker's wife had been given four hours' pay to clean the victim's flat the previous weekend and had used her time diligently. With the exception of her own fingerprints, the only ones found in the flat were those of Harald Olesen.

Meanwhile, I pondered the possibility that the murderer had actually never been in the flat, but had fired the shot from another building. This theory was, however, flawed, as it would appear that Harald Olesen had been sitting or standing in front of a solid stone wall without a window when the shot was fired. And if that did not make things difficult enough, all the windows in the room were still intact.

So, apart from the presence of a dead man with a bullet wound in his chest and the bullet lodged in the wall behind him, there was no sign of drama in the flat. Harald Olesen was lying on the floor in the sitting room by a coffee table that was set for two. He had drunk from one cup and left his fingerprints on it, whereas the cup on the other side of the table was untouched. It would appear that Harald Olesen had been expecting someone for coffee and cake, but there was nothing to say who had visited him – or whether the invited guest was the murderer.

The remains of a meal of meatballs were still standing on the cooker and by the sink. There was milk, bread and cheese in the fridge for tomorrow morning's breakfast. The radio on the kitchen table was plugged in. A Vienna Philharmonic Orchestra record lay ready on the turntable. Death had obviously come suddenly to Flat 3A in 25 Krebs' Street.

By one o'clock on the morning of 5 April 1968, it was clear to me that there was nothing more to be gained from staying at the scene of the crime. I left one constable on guard on the second floor and another on the street outside the building. I asked the pathologist to send me a report as soon as possible, and requested copies from the census records and police records for all the residents of 25 Krebs' Street. Then I sent everyone there to bed, but asked that they stay at home in the morning to be available for questioning.

It was already clear to me on the night of the murder that the murderer was in all likelihood one of the deceased's neighbours. There was nothing to indicate so far that anyone else had been in the building that evening. Fortunately, I had no idea how difficult it was going to be to find out which flat the murderer had come from.

DAY TWO

Seven Neighbours – and a Blue Raincoat With No Owner

I

I got up unusually early on Friday, 5 April 1968. By half past six I was seated at the breakfast table engaged in a fascinating discussion with my reflection in the coffee pot. We promptly agreed that this was a case I should not allow to be taken from me by the more senior detectives. They could be trusted to give me all the dull tasks, while they themselves took all the glory for solving the case. Fortunately, my boss usually came to work before them. And on that day, I even beat him to it. When he unlocked his office at the main police station in Oslo at a quarter to eight, I was already sitting ready in the corridor.

The commanding officer was a broad-minded man in his sixties who understood that it was important to encourage hard-working young men with inflated ambitions. He had, in fact, mentioned on several festive occasions that he himself had been just such an overambitious young fellow until his fiftieth birthday. It was therefore no surprise that he now found my enthusiasm and interest in the case to be praiseworthy. He agreed that it was certainly of no disadvantage that I had been the first inspector at the scene. And by the time the clock struck eight we had shaken hands and agreed that I would lead the investigation on my own and that the scope of my authorities would be extended in order to do so. I nodded hastily that I would of course seek advice from him and other more experienced colleagues should it be necessary. Then I strode confidently into my first murder investigation, intoxicated by the belief that it would bring me both honour and glory.

The Friday papers had little to report regarding the murder in 25 Krebs' Street. Two of them carried a small notice about the murder, and one hinted, without mentioning any names, that the deceased was 'a well-known and highly respected citizen with a background in the Resistance movement'. During my brief pit stop at 19 Møller Street that morning, the switchboard could already confirm that the media's interest in the case was growing rapidly. Before leaving for Krebs' Street, I therefore dashed out a short press release. First and foremost, it stated clearly that I had been given overall responsibility for the murder investigation. In addition, the press release confirmed that it was former cabinet minister and Resistance fighter Harald Olesen who had been shot and killed in his home in Krebs' Street on the evening of 4 April, but in light of the ongoing investigation no further comment would be forthcoming.

On my arrival at the scene of the crime on the morning of 5 April, I began at the obvious starting point: a tidy little care-taker's table just inside the front entrance. The caretaker's wife who sat there was called Randi Hansen and was a small, plump, grey-haired woman in her early sixties. She lived in the caretaker's one-bedroom flat in the basement. Her husband normally worked there as the caretaker, but, she informed me, was away that week. Their children had moved out many years ago, so she generally sat alone at her post in the entrance, a few steps down from the flats on the ground floor. She looked after 25 and 27 Krebs' Street, alternating between the two, as well as managing all telephone calls to and from both buildings. As fortune would have it, she had been sitting in 25 Krebs' Street on 4 April. She promised to stay at her post until the investigation had been closed.

Randi Hansen proved to be an exceptionally diligent individual who had noted everyone's comings and goings that afternoon and evening. As with most caretakers' wives, she knew the residents and their daily routines relatively well.

The caretaker's wife was careful to point out that she only sat in this building every other day and that sometimes she was ill or had to leave her post for a few hours. However, she believed that her impressions of the residents and their activities were fairly accurate. I saw no reason to doubt this, but immediately noted that there was a 50 per cent chance that any visitors or incidents might pass unnoticed. Furthermore, from her position by the entrance it was not possible to see the doors to the flats or the hallway, even on the ground floor.

The murder victim, Harald Olesen, had lived on the second floor since before the war. As a cabinet minister, he had been one of the most famous people in this part of town and the pride of the street. In his later years, he had lived the quiet life of a pensioner, but still came and went with some irregularity. The caretaker's wife had seen him together with many a national politician and well-known Resistance fighter over the years, but less often more recently. Visits from his relatives were also less frequent since his wife's death five years ago. The caretaker's wife thought that he had found it very hard to accept that he was a widower, despite outward appearances. With the exception of shopping trips to the Co-op on the corner, Olesen had started to go out less and less. He was a friendly and correct man who always greeted her with a nod as he passed. If he had laundry to be done, or required any other extra service, he always asked politely and paid well. The caretaker's wife had never noticed any tension between him and the other residents. In fact, she found it hard to imagine who on earth would want to kill such a kind and respected pillar of the community.

Olesen's neighbour on the second floor was an American by the name of Darrell Williams whom the caretaker's wife believed to be in his early forties. He had been living there for no longer than eight months, and the rent was paid by the American Embassy. The caretaker's wife had never actually asked what he did at the embassy, but thought that he held a senior position – she described Williams as someone who was 'always well dressed and no doubt important'. He also spoke very good Norwegian after only a few weeks. Darrell Williams went to work first thing in the morning and often came back late in the evening, but never brought home guests.

Miss Sara Sundqvist lived in the flat below Olesen. She was a young Swedish student who had been there since the start of the academic year in August, and had surprised the caretaker's wife with flowers and chocolates when she moved in. Sara Sundqvist was well dressed and elegant. At times she perhaps seemed distant, but always smiled and greeted her. Miss Sundqvist took her studies very seriously and lived a rather regulated life. She usually left between eight and nine in the morning and came home between three and five in the afternoon. During the first few months, one or more of her fellow students had sometimes come to visit. They always behaved impeccably and left well before eleven.

Sara Sundqvist had clearly charmed the caretaker's wife, and yet there was something about her face that led me to believe that she was hiding something. A rather stiff expression that remained when she went on to talk about the young husband and wife, Kristian and Karen Lund, who lived in the flat to the left on the first floor. They were a friendly and helpful couple who seemed so very much in love, even after the birth of their first child. The Lunds had moved in two years ago as newly-weds and now had a son who was just over one. Mrs Lund was twenty-five years old and the daughter of a factory owner from one of the most desirable parts of Oslo. Her husband was a couple of years older and was the manager of a sports shop in Hammersborg.

A taxi driver lived in the flat to the left on the ground floor. Konrad Jensen was in his fifties and was not married. The caretaker's wife had heard from one of her nephews, who was also a taxi driver, that Konrad Jensen drove one of the oldest taxis in Oslo but still managed to negotiate the city's many confusing side streets more quickly than most of his colleagues. Konrad Jensen worked hard and often long hours. Otherwise, he only went out to the odd sports event. As far as the caretaker's wife could remember, he had never received any visitors in the twenty years that he had lived there.

The caretaker's wife opened and closed her mouth a couple of times after she had spoken about Konrad Jensen. Again, something unsaid was left hanging in the air. I had no idea what, but for the moment there was no need to push the caretaker's wife any further on it.

The final resident lived in the ground-floor flat to the right and was a wheelchair-bound man by the name of Andreas Gullestad. He was around forty years old and, as far as the caretaker's wife could understand, was a rentier who lived on his inheritance. This must have been fairly substantial as he was always elegantly dressed and lived an apparently carefree life, with the exception of his physical handicap. Despite his difficulties, he was always in good humour and friendly to anyone he met. He had moved here from the better side of town three years ago, after the building had been done up. As a result of an accident shortly before that time, he was now dependent on a wheelchair, so was happy to find an easily accessible flat on the ground floor. Gullestad was the only person, apart from Harald Olesen, who had accepted the property owner's offer to buy the flat.

Andreas Gullestad's sister and niece sometimes came to visit, but otherwise he lived a quiet and perhaps rather lonely life. He sometimes ventured out onto the street in summer when the weather was good, but in winter preferred to stay indoors and often asked the caretaker's wife to do his weekly shopping. He paid her generously for this and always presented her and her husband with gifts at Christmas and on their birthdays. As far as the caretaker's wife could understand, Gullestad was unable to move around without a wheelchair, but he still seemed to have use of his upper body and arms. And there was certainly nothing wrong with his head: he was an exceptionally intelligent and knowledgeable man.

Fortuitously, the caretaker's wife had not only been sitting at her post all afternoon and evening on the day of the murder, but had also made note of the residents' comings and goings. Harald Olesen had himself been out to the shops in the morning, but had come back around midday and then stayed at home for the final ten hours of his life. No one had phoned him. The only registered phone calls of any interest from the weeks before his death were several calls to and from his lawyer at the firm Rønning, Rønning & Rønning.

As far as the other neighbours were concerned, the wheel-chair-bound Andreas Gullestad had as usual been at home all day. Mrs Lund had stayed in with her young son. According to the caretaker's wife, Mr Lund had left at around eight in the morning and not returned until nine o'clock in the evening. The only phone call to the Lunds' flat was when he called home around four hours before that. Sara Sundqvist had gone out to a morning lecture at half past nine and come home again at a quarter past four. Darrell Williams had gone out just before nine in the morning and come back just before eight in the evening. Konrad Jensen was working a late shift that week. He left in his car around midday and came in the door only a few steps behind Williams. The only resident the caretaker's wife had registered leaving the building again later was Darrell Williams. He had gone out for an evening stroll at five to ten and returned fifteen minutes later.

The caretaker's wife had not seen any strangers in the building on the day of the murder and it was highly unlikely that anyone would have managed to sneak past without being seen. Only she and the residents had a key to the back door. Everyone else had to come in through the front entrance and past her. And on Thursday, 4 April she had been able to see the back door more or less constantly for the six hours prior to the murder.

Before I left her, I asked the caretaker's wife whether she had noticed anything unusual from her post, especially in the hours before and after the murder.

'There is one thing,' she replied, and got up. She indicated that I should follow her into a small back room.

On the table was a large blue raincoat with a hood and a red scarf.

'I found both of these on top of the rubbish bin by the back door this morning. I've never seen any of the residents wearing either the raincoat or the scarf. Both items look more or less brand new, and they both appear to have been washed before they were thrown away, because they are still damp. I didn't see anyone throwing them away, but they were not there when I went to throw out some leftovers early yesterday afternoon. That's certainly worth mentioning, isn't it?'

And I had to agree with her. It was definitely unusual enough to mention that someone had thrown away an almost new and recently washed raincoat on the very day that there was a murder in the building. The blue raincoat was immediately added to my list of questions to ask the residents.

II

So, Darrell Williams lived in Flat 3B. He was a large, dark-haired American with a firm handshake and an unexpectedly pleasant voice. He showed me his diplomat's passport, which gave his age as forty-five, though he looked younger. He was at least six foot tall and no doubt weighed well over fifteen stone, but still had little surplus fat. He spoke remarkably good Norwegian, with only the faintest American twang.

When telling me about himself, Darrell Williams explained that his slightly unusual Christian name was due to his Irish ancestry. His grandparents had emigrated to the United States in the 1870s, following the Great Famine. He himself was born and raised in New York, and was the son of a well-known lawyer. Darrell Williams had given up his own law degree in order to sign up for military service after America joined the war, and took part in the Normandy landings in the summer of 1944. The following year, he had come to Norway just after its liberation as a young lieutenant in the US delegation. He soon found himself a Norwegian girlfriend and a post in the American military mission and stayed on in Norway until the spring of 1948. He had learned Norwegian back then and had so many fond memories from that time that he had, nearly twenty years later, applied for a vacant position as attaché at the embassy in Oslo when the opportunity arose. In the intervening years, he had pursued a career in the military and risen to the rank of major, before making the switch to diplomacy in the early 1960s.

In answer to my question regarding his civil status, Darrell Williams's smile was relaxed and full of self-irony.

'I got married in the USA in 1951, but the high point of the marriage was when we split up three years later. It resulted in too many arguments and no children. My wife claimed that she left me for a certain man, which would appear to be untrue as she then went on to marry someone else, and to have a child with yet another man!'

The diplomat spoke openly of his disastrous marriage. As a single man with no children, the diplomatic service had allowed him to fulfil his childhood dream of seeing more of Asia and Europe. Over the past decade he had been posted to a number of embassies, but could, 'with his hand on his heart', honestly say that he had never seen a capital as beautiful as Oslo.

The embassy had both organized and paid for the flat. And Darrell Williams had no complaints about it, only that due to long working hours and official dinners, he was not here very much, so he did not know the other people in the building particularly well. Williams thought the caretaker and his wife to be 'orderly and helpful'. The handicapped man on the ground floor was 'a very cultured and friendly man' who spoke good English and could discuss Jack London and his other favourite American authors. The young Swedish student also seemed to be 'nice and knowledgeable' in the few conversations that Williams had had with her. The taxi driver on the ground floor was a perhaps 'a simple soul' and kept a very low profile, but he was interested in football and other sport, so Williams exchanged the odd word with him now and then. They had stopped for a chat about the forthcoming Norwegian Cup game when they bumped into each other by the stairs on the night of the murder.

The American had barely spoken to the young couple on the first floor, so only confirmed that they seemed to be 'unusually happy and full of the joys of life, even for newlyweds'. On the night of the murder, Kristian Lund had swung through the front door only a few steps ahead of him. Williams had touched his hat, as was his wont, and received a friendly 'good evening' in return. That was about the extent of the contact between them: brief but never unfriendly.

Darrell Williams remembered Harald Olesen's name well

from the years 1945 to 1946 and had been quite excited by the fact that he now lived in the same building. Shortly after he had moved in, he had taken the opportunity to knock on his neighbour's door and was well received. But during his visit and on a couple of later occasions, Williams got the impression that something or other was weighing on Olesen's mind and he did not wish to burden him further. Olesen had continued to greet him with a friendly smile all the same. However, it had struck Williams more than once that the old war hero was becoming an increasingly isolated and dejected old man.

Williams had not seen Olesen alive on the day of the murder. He had been to a dinner party and did not come home until around eight. After his evening stroll, he had been talking to Konrad Jensen on the stairs for a few minutes when they suddenly heard a gunshot on the second floor. Williams had instinctively started to run up the stairs, with Jensen at his heels. They did not meet anyone on the stairs, nor did they see anyone else in the hallway when they reached the second floor. They rang on Olesen's doorbell several times without any response. A minute or two later, Kristian Lund had also appeared, closely followed by the caretaker's wife. The caretaker's wife had then gone back down to get her keys and to call the police, as they had not heard a sound inside the flat. While she was doing this, Gullestad had come up in the lift. The five of them had discussed whether or not they should open the door, but had agreed to wait until the police arrived. They neither heard nor saw any signs of an intruder in the building, and it was not possible that anyone could have sneaked past them.

Williams could not recall ever seeing a blue raincoat in

25 Krebs' Street, not on the day of the murder or previously. He responded openly and honestly to my question regarding firearms: 'I had a .44-calibre Colt revolver and a .36-calibre pistol with me when I came to Norway, but everything seemed to be so safe here that I sent them both back to my home in the USA a few weeks ago now.'

Strictly speaking, he did not have a licence, but I saw little reason there and then to pester a man with an American diplomat's passport with minor details such as that. The house search the evening before had shown that Williams, like all the other residents, did not have a gun in the building on the night of the murder. But all the same this did not strike him from the list of possible suspects.

III

Sara Sundqvist proved to be a slim and unusually tall young woman who waited for a moment or two before opening the door and then kept the safety chain on until she saw my uniform. Despite being around five foot eleven, she could not weigh much over nine stone. I felt that her wrists and arms could snap at any moment, but despite her dangerously tiny waist, her figure was in proportion and her bearing elegant. And even though her expression was drawn and anxious, one could not help but notice her feminine curves. The apparently demure and high-necked green dress only served to emphasize a pair of shapely breasts.

Sara Sundqvist was very serious and slightly shaken by the murder, but still struck me as being sensible and trustworthy. She spoke grammatically correct Norwegian, albeit with a gentle Swedish accent. She gave Gothenburg as her hometown, and her age as twenty-four. She had come to Oslo to study English and philosophy the previous August, and had found the flat through a newspaper advertisement posted by the owner. She used her Swedish student grant and money from her parents to pay for the rent, but also worked in the university library a few hours a week in addition to her studies.

Otherwise, Sara Sundqvist told me that she spent the bulk of her days studying, but did do some amateur dramatics in her free time. She generally went out very little in the evenings. And on the evening in question, she had been at home alone and was in the kitchen making her evening coffee when the gunshot rang out. She had heard it clearly, but thought that perhaps something had fallen onto the floor. She was later frightened by the commotion out in the hall and had decided that it was safest to remain locked in her flat until the police knocked on the door. Although she had not seen any of the drama herself, it had been 'an extremely frightening experience'. In line with her statement from the evening before, she said that she had not left the flat after she came home at a quarter past four.

I was certain that the young Swedish woman probably smiled more on a warm sunny day and that her gaze was steadier than it was now. I found it easy to accept that a murder in the same building would be very frightening indeed for a foreign female student.

Flat 2A had some rather cluttered bookshelves, crammed with Norwegian, Swedish and English books, but was otherwise the flat of a tidy young woman. And apart from some kitchen knives, there was no evidence of any weapons in her flat either. She was momentarily baffled when I asked her if she had seen anyone in a blue raincoat, but then replied that she had not seen anyone in such a garment in the building, not yesterday or before.

Sara Sundqvist said that she had only spoken to the now deceased Harald Olesen briefly on a couple of occasions. He seemed to be a very friendly, if quiet and correct old gentleman. She had made efforts to be on first-name terms with the caretaker's wife and the other people in the building, and had nothing negative to say about any of them. However, she could not claim to know any of them very well. 'The Lunds, of course, only have eyes for each other and their little boy, and the others are all men who are a good deal older than me.'

There was nothing dramatic about Flat 2A and its tenant, and both struck me as being trustworthy. It was with some hesitation that I refrained from striking Sara Sundqvist from the list of suspects.

IV

According to the red heart-shaped nameplate, Kristian and Karen Lund lived in Flat 2B. With their thirteen-month-old son peacefully asleep in his cot, they came across as the epitome of a young, happy couple. And though they smiled every time they looked at each other or their son, the sombreness soon returned when they met my eye. Kristian Lund was a blond, stocky man of around five foot eleven who no doubt was normally relaxed and charming. However, he was now visibly shaken by the situation. He repeated several times that a murder in the building was of particular concern to someone with a wife and child, and that he was not at all sure whether he dared to leave them alone while he was at work until the murderer had been caught.

Neither Mr nor Mrs Lund could for a moment imagine that anyone in the building was behind the crime, so the murderer must somehow have managed to get in from outside. They only had good things to say about Harald Olesen. At times he might appear to be a bit lonely – he was after all a pensioner living on his own – but he was still an elegant man of vigour. The Lunds had never seen any guns in the building, and certainly not in their flat. The key words 'blue raincoat' meant nothing to them.

Regarding her own background, Karen Lund could tell me that she was the daughter and only child of a factory owner from Bærum. She had met her husband on an 'otherwise rather boring course at business school' and had worked for a fashion retailer for a while before getting married. Kristian Lund came from a lower class and was the child of a secretary and single mother from Drammen. There was a rather emotional moment when he commented that 'My father could be anyone and I no longer want to know who he is.' His mother, whom he had much to thank for, had died of cancer the year before, only days before the birth of her first grandchild. Kristian Lund was a qualified manager. He smiled smugly for a moment when he told me that his marks from business school were 'better than expected by anyone other than myself'. He had received several 'very attractive' job offers recently, but was happy in his current position as the manager of a sports shop. His wife added in support that her parents were delighted with both their son-in-law and their grandchild. On the whole, she seemed to be far calmer and less shaken than her husband.

Following my visit with the Lunds, one rather mysterious question remained unanswered, which was, when had Kristian Lund actually come home on the evening of the murder? His wife was in no doubt that he'd come home at nine o'clock precisely. He had come in the door just after the start of *The Danny Kaye Show* on television, which started at five to. Kristian Lund explained that he had had to stay behind on his own in the shop as there was bookkeeping to be done, and that he had left there at around a quarter to nine. This was in line with what the caretaker's wife had noted, which was that Kristian Lund came home at nine o'clock. But this did not accord with another small and rather confusing detail, which was that Darrell Williams claimed to have seen Kristian Lund come into the building while he was chatting with Konrad Jensen a whole hour before.

Kristian Lund's anxiety regarding the situation increased when I mentioned this. He repeated several times that he did not get home until nine o'clock. If the two neighbours said otherwise, they must either be wrong about when they came in themselves or have confused him with someone else. His wife immediately came to his aid. She added with great sincerity that she had the world's most reliable and honest husband, and that he had phoned home several hours before that to say that he would not be back until around nine. I hastily played down my question and withdrew, tactfully, to mull it over.

My next stop was again the caretaker's wife at her post by the front entrance. She furrowed her brow and insisted that 'Kristian did not come home before nine o'clock yesterday evening.' Her writing was absolutely clear with regard to the time, and she had jotted down the residents' names in the order that they came home. 'If Kristian came back before Darrell Williams and Konrad Jensen, then it's strange that I wrote his name on the line below them,' said the caretaker's wife. I had to admit that that sounded reasonable. And furthermore, the caretaker's wife had logged the telephone call mentioned by Mrs Lund when Kristian Lund called to say he would not be home until around nine.

When I looked at the caretaker's wife's neat and simple list, I found it hard to believe that she might have made a mistake. But there seemed to be no reason to doubt that Darrell Williams had both seen and greeted Kristian Lund by the entrance an hour earlier. And so the Lunds were not struck from my list of suspects either.

V

More drama lay in store in the left-hand flat on the ground floor. Konrad Jensen was a short, middle-aged man dressed in a red sweater and gaberdine trousers. He confirmed that he worked as a taxi driver and had his papers at the ready, which showed that he owned the older Peugeot model with a taxi light that was parked on the street outside. Konrad Jensen informed me that he had lived in his flat since 1948, and that, as he was unmarried and had no children, he had lived alone all his adult life.

Konrad Jensen's hair was turning from black to grey. And in the course of our conversation, his unshaven face also seemed to turn from frustration to despair. His answers got shorter and shorter, and he became increasingly morose in response to my routine questions. Yes, he had definitely come home from work at eight o'clock, a few steps behind Kristian Lund and Darrell Williams. Yes, he was certain that Kristian Lund had gone into the building just before him. Yes, he had been standing by the stairs discussing a football match with the American at a quarter past ten when they heard the gunshot on the second floor. And yes, the two of them had immediately run upstairs and waited outside the door. Yes, Kristian Lund, the caretaker's wife and Andreas Gullestad had also come up in the course of the next couple of minutes. No, he had never seen a blue raincoat here in 25 Krebs' Street.

Then all of a sudden he mustered the courage to raise his voice a little.

'I might as well tell you myself because it will come out sooner or later all the same. I supported the Nazis and was a member of the NS during the war, and served a six-month sentence for it from 1945 to 1946. I joined the party before the war and worked as a driver for the Germans after 9 April 1940. I've never denied any of it. But that is the extent of my crimes. I've never amounted to anything much, for better or worse.'

As is only reasonable, I looked at him in a new, more critical light.

He added hastily: 'I never met Harald Olesen during or after the war, and I have nothing whatsoever to do with his death. In fact, his death is the worst thing that could happen to me.'

Then, after a short pause for thought, he carried on in his slow, morose manner: 'Everyone will automatically suspect me. It won't take many days before the papers write that I'm a Nazi and then I'll be a moving target. I've struggled with that ever since I got out of prison. I've had to change my name twice already, from Konrad Hansen to Konrad Pedersen and then to Konrad Jensen. But there's always someone who knows someone who knows and I always end up being called "Konrad Quisling". There's still people who won't get in my taxi because they've heard I was in the NS, but that's happened less and less over the years. Now it will all get worse again.'

Konrad Jensen got up slowly from the sofa. He went over to the window and pointed down a side street. 'That's my car over there. Not new, and wasn't the best in the world when he was new either, but he's still working, and I know him better than any person. My car has been my most loyal friend. I know it's childish, but I like to call my car Petter, after a friend I had when I was a lad. Petter Peugeot and Konrad Jensen, a couple of wrecks that have got old together and know the streets of Oslo better than most.'

His face was bitter when he continued. 'I turned fifty in February, but celebrated on my own, a modest meal in a restaurant. I don't want anything to do with the old NS people, and it's not easy to make other friends. My mother and father died a long time ago, and I don't have much contact with my brother and sister. I last heard from my brother in 1940, when he'd borrowed money at an exorbitant rate so he could pay back a loan I'd given him. My sister sent a card for my fiftieth birthday that contained all of seven words and came four days late!'

I did not find these personal and familial frustrations of any particular interest. So when Konrad Jensen stopped for breath, I took the chance to ask about his relationship with his neighbours.

'Not much to tell there either. We pass in the hallway, say a few words about practical things. The caretaker and his wife of course know about my background from the war. They never mention it, but don't say very much else either. Olesen must have known about it. He was already living here when I moved in, and had no doubt heard from one of his war cronies. There was never a confrontation, but there wasn't any contact either. He never said a word to me, and I didn't dare speak to him. He always seemed so scornful whenever we met in the hall. I have to admit I didn't like Harald Olesen, but I had no reason to kill him. His death will just make things worse for me, especially if the murderer's not caught quickly.'

He was silent for a few seconds, then ran quickly through the other flats. 'The American on the second floor moved in quite recently, but he speaks good Norwegian and seems to be nice. I chat with him about sport and the like whenever I get the chance. The cripple is a polite man and always smiles and says hello, but seldom anything else. He's been rich and smart all his life and so naturally is not interested in me. The couple on the first floor got married relatively recently and so still live in their own bubble. They've occasionally asked me to drive them somewhere when they need a taxi, to and from parties and things like that, but we haven't really talked much then either. They're young, with so much to look forward to and so many opportunities, and I'm an old man going round in worn circles to an untended grave.'

When I mentioned Sara Sundqvist, Konrad Jensen suddenly started to laugh, albeit a short and bitter laugh.

'It's ironic, really, isn't it . . . given my background, that I should end up here two floors under a famous Resistance fighter and one floor below a Jewess. In a way, she's even above me now. I don't like it. But she's very quiet and doesn't cause much fuss or conflict.'

I had not heard or seen anything to indicate that Sara Sundqvist was Jewish and immediately asked if he was sure. I was treated to another burst of Konrad Jensen's bitter laughter.

'If there's something I know more about in this world than driving cars, it's how to recognize a Jew when I see one. You can see it in the nose and hair and eyes. I am absolutely certain that she is a Jew.'

Konrad Jensen was obviously not used to having an audience and was now on a roll. He tried to be quiet for a few moments, but then carried on.

'I know it's not wise to talk openly about this, but those of us who were in the NS were proved right when it came to Stalin and his Bolshevik friends. Even leading politicians in the Norwegian Labour Party admit that today. And one day we'll be proved right about the Jews as well. I didn't want the Jews to be killed; I just wanted them gone. It's a good thing that they've got their own state on the other side of the world, and I hope that most of them will go there. It's best for them, best for us all.'

He nodded at the ceiling and lowered his voice. 'But to be fair, she doesn't make much noise or cause any trouble for anyone. I don't know if she has any Nordic blood in her veins as well – you'll have to ask her about that yourself.'

This was followed by silence. He no doubt realized that I was not listening out of sympathy and the bitterness returned.

'There's not much more to be had for you here, unless you're looking for a scapegoat rather than the murderer.'

Which was not the case, and I had the answers to all my questions for now, so I bid Konrad Jensen farewell as politely as I could. Once out the door, I immediately noted him down as the primary suspect.

However, I did then go back up to the first floor and knock on Sara Sundqvist's door. She opened it just as cautiously and slowly as before, but her smile was broader when she saw me this time. I apologized and explained that I had forgotten to ask her about her family background. After pausing for a few seconds, she replied that her parents were Jews who lost their lives during the war. As far as she was aware, they had no other children, and she knew very little about the rest of her Jewish family. She had been fortunate enough to be adopted by a couple in Gothenburg who were teachers, and they brought her up together with their own two daughters.

It did not seem necessary to ask her for any more details at the moment. But I did somewhat reluctantly have to admit that Konrad Jensen was not entirely unreliable, and that Sara Sundqvist was of some interest to the murder investigation. And that the mystery of when Kristian Lund had in fact come home on the evening of the murder was becoming ever more intriguing.

VI

It took over a minute before Andreas Gullestad opened the door to Flat 1A. When it was finally opened, the man who looked up at me from his wheelchair was friendly and all smiles, and I was immediately shown into the sitting room with an open hand. Andreas Gullestad was a fair-haired man who gave his age as thirty-nine years old. His sedentary life had left him slightly overweight, which reinforced his natural jovial character. I guessed that he would be fairly tall if he could stand up. His voice was bright, and his vocabulary bore the hallmark of a cultured background. He did not appear to be overly shaken by the murder, just rather pleased to have a visitor.

'Welcome to my humble abode, O honourable detective! I have been waiting for you to come and am more than happy to contribute what little I can to solving this frightful crime. Can I offer you some tea or coffee?'

He had set the table for two and had the water on the boil, so I said yes to a cup of tea. The choice of teas was generous, and very much in keeping with the atmosphere in the flat. Andreas Gullestad's home was an oasis of colour and calm, with paintings on the walls, overflowing bookshelves, a television set and luxurious furnishings. Sitting comfortably on a cushion in his wheelchair, my host appeared to be reconciled with his fate. He was remarkably philosophical, even in relation to the ongoing murder investigation in the building.

Gullestad told me that his previous home had proved to be 'somewhat impractical' following a 'very regrettable' accident four years ago that left him paralysed from the waist down. And with a small, self-deprecating smile, he added: 'I had never, not even in my worst nightmares, ever considered the possibility of living east of the river.'

Nevertheless, he had taken to the flat instantly and had not since regretted buying it. It was important for him to have a ground-floor flat in a building with low thresholds and a lift, and what was more, he had been pleasantly surprised by how helpful everyone else was here. The deceased Harald

Olesen had always been friendly and polite, and it was an honour indeed for someone who had been a child during the war to live in the same house as such an old hero from the Resistance. Gullestad could not imagine that anyone in the building was capable of murdering Olesen, and nor did he think that any of them would have the motive to do so. He believed that the murderer must somehow have managed to get in from outside, though he could not explain how.

Gullestad also mentioned that the caretaker was perhaps a little too fond of the drink, which obviously had a considerable effect on his wife. But when he was sober, the caretaker was a handy man, and his wife was always helpfulness itself. Darrell Williams was the most recent incomer. He had accepted an invitation to coffee and made a very 'favourable' impression. But being two floors down, Gullestad did not know much of what went on on the second floor. On the other hand, he had very good relations with the young couple on the first floor.

As far as Konrad Jensen was concerned, Gullestad was aware of his 'deeply unfortunate' affiliations during the war and wished to make it clear that he deplored them. But he was able to overlook these old sins as long as Jensen's behaviour now gave no grounds for complaint. Jensen had almost certainly not had an easy time of it during the war, and seemed to be both lonely and disillusioned. All the same, Gullestad could not imagine that he was a cold-blooded murderer. The young Swedish lady had also accepted an invitation to coffee shortly after she had moved in last August, and had then, as later, been 'utterly charming'.

Gullestad paused for a moment and sucked thoughtfully on a sugar lump. Then he added in a very quiet voice that 'at the risk of being indiscreet', he should perhaps mention something with regard to Miss Sundqvist that may be of relevance to the investigation. Although he had never seen her with a boyfriend, or heard her mention anyone, he was under the impression that there was a man in her life. Gullestad's bedroom was directly under that of Sara Sundqvist, and the sounds he heard from there would indicate that she occasionally had 'very enjoyable and lively visits'. He had only heard this in the afternoons between five and seven, never at night. So it would seem that Sara Sundqvist had an admirer who only visited her in the afternoon and did not stay the night.

Andreas Gullestad was swift to reply that he had no guns in the flat, and had not seen evidence of one in any of the other flats. But he sat deep in thought for a few moments in response to my question about the blue raincoat and then answered gravely: 'I definitely did not see any blue raincoats in the building on the day of the murder, but there was a day last summer when I saw an unknown man here on the stairs in a large blue raincoat with a red scarf over his face.'

Naturally, I was extremely interested in this information and asked for further details. Gullestad concentrated hard for a minute or so before answering.

'I am fairly sure that I saw a man in a blue raincoat here last year. It struck me as odd as it was nice weather that day, with no moisture in the air, and I speculated for a while who the mysterious man might be visiting. The exact date escapes me, but it may have been the Whitsun weekend. For a while I wondered if it was perhaps in connection with a carnival or some other festivity, but I'm afraid I don't remember much more.'

I could not quite let this unexpected glimpse of the man in the raincoat go and asked if he was sure that it had been a man. Gullestad took a moment to reflect before he answered. He certainly seemed to be a conscientious and reflective witness.

'I believe so, as the person seemed to be rather tall, but I would not like to swear to it. I only saw him in passing, and it is not always easy to know what a raincoat like that might be hiding.'

Andreas Gullestad told me that he himself was originally from a small place near Gjøvik in Oppland. And despite the early death of his father, he had had a very privileged childhood. Following his mother's death when he was twenty-five, he had inherited his father's fortune, which was so substantial that, if his consumption was moderate, he could live well on it for the rest of his life. He had deposited most of it in the bank and invested the rest in stocks, which thus far had provided a 'very tidy' profit. The accident that had left him disabled had of course been a shock and marked a dramatic change in his life, but it had, nonetheless, been less catastrophic for him than it might have been for many others. As there was no pressure to earn a living, he had previously studied a bit here and there in his twenties, and had otherwise lived a very pleasant life. With another small, self-deprecating smile, Andreas Gullestad commented: 'And now I largely just sit here all day with the television, the wireless, my books and the newspapers. But sadly, that is also what I did in my previous flat, before the accident. The main difference is that these days I pay for someone else to do my shopping without feeling guilty.'

Before letting me go, Andreas Gullestad asked if it would

be 'acceptable' for him to go to visit his sister in Gjøvik at the weekend, as planned. There were some 'family matters' that needed to be discussed, and his sister and niece were now no doubt concerned about him and keen to hear more about the situation. He assured me that he would return on Sunday afternoon and gave me a telephone number where he could be reached in the meantime. I saw no reason not to let him travel.

My visit to Andreas Gullestad's flat left me with the impression that he was the least likely of the residents to have anything to do with the murder, but that he may still be hiding important information all the same, whether consciously or unconsciously. Of most interest was what he had told me about seeing the man in the blue raincoat, especially as he had also mentioned a red scarf without any prompting. I noted that other pertinent questions were the identity of Sara Sundqvist's secret guest and how he managed to get in and out of the building unnoticed.

I immediately went down to the caretaker's wife and asked her again about the blue raincoat, only this time I asked if she could recall having seen a person wearing such a garment in the building. The caretaker's wife dutifully thought about it for a minute or so, then emphasized that she could not be certain, but that she may possibly have seen a man in a similar coat here last summer. In which case she had only seen him in passing in the hallway or on the stairs. She thought perhaps she was mistaken, as she had not seen anyone like that come in or go out. But she may of course have been out shopping or doing something else at the time.

Once again, I went and knocked on Sara Sundqvist's door and explained that I had unfortunately forgotten to ask how often she had visitors. She replied that she had occasionally had friends round, but not for several weeks prior to the murder. She had seen less of her fellow students in recent weeks, as they all had exams approaching. She replied negatively to a direct question as to whether she had a fiancé or boyfriend, adding in a quiet voice: 'In the eight months I have lived here, no one has ever stayed overnight.' With the information from Andreas Gullestad fresh in my mind, I nodded my acceptance of the latter without actually believing the former. Sara Sundqvist's elusive afternoon guest remained a minor mystery.

VII

The technical reports lay waiting on my desk back at the main police station, but as yet provided no answers. The pathologist could definitively lay to rest any theory that the gunshot came from another building. Harald Olesen had been killed by a single shot fired from a .45-calibre Colt revolver at close range. The bullet had passed through his heart, causing instant death. There was no indication that Olesen had been injured in any way before being shot. And according to the pathologist's report, this could have happened at any time between eight o'clock and eleven o'clock, but that was of less interest, as the statements from all the neighbours gave us the exact time of a quarter past ten.

The information about Harald Olesen in the census rolls really only confirmed what was already known. He was born in 1895 and was the son of a well-known pharmacist from Hamar. Harald Olesen married in 1923, and remained married until the death of his wife forty years later. She was the educated daughter of a shipowner, but had been a housewife all her life. Olesen had an older brother and a younger sister, who had both died before him. As his parents were long since deceased and he had no children himself, his closest relations and presumed inheritors were a niece and a nephew who lived in the west end of Oslo. Olesen had moved several times in the interwar years, but had stayed at the same address in 25 Krebs' Street since 1939.

Konrad Jensen was the only resident in the police records. He had indeed served six months for treason from 1945 to 1946, but had no other criminal record.

There was no information in the census rolls about the American Darrell Williams or the Swedish Sara Sundqvist, and on the whole, they simply confirmed what the Norwegian citizens had told about themselves. There was nothing new to discover about Konrad Jensen and Karen Lund. The only interesting additional information about Andreas Gullestad was that he had taken that name four years previously, and before that had been called Ivar A. Storskog. The rest of the information was, however, what he himself had told. His father had been a wealthy farmer from Oppland who owned substantial amounts of land and forest, and had died in 1941, aged only forty-eight. His mother had died in 1953. Andreas Gullestad had never been married or had any children, and his closest relative was indeed an older sister in Gjøvik.

The most interesting revelation in the census rolls was in relation to Kristian Lund. His father was simply recorded as 'unknown', and his mother was a secretary from Drammen. Kristian Lund had, however, either not known or not wanted to tell me that the very same mother had been a member of the NS from 1937 to 1945. She had had several secretarial positions with the occupying forces during the final three years of the war. The protocol from her trial for treason was attached and showed that she was sentenced to eight months in prison after the war, but was released after four months due to good behaviour and out of consideration to her young son. According to the census rolls, he came into this world in Drammen on 17 February 1941 and was his mother's only child.

As a result, I concluded that of all Olesen's neighbours, Kristian Lund was the first that I should talk to again. But none of the residents had any known links to Harald Olesen that might give them a motive for murder, and the day had given disappointingly few breakthroughs. Darrell Williams's impression that something had been bothering Harald Olesen seemed plausible in light of the murder, but we still had no idea what it was. And for want of any better clues, I decided to spend the next day trying to establish what it was that had been bothering the murder victim in the last year of his life.

After a couple of attempts, I finally managed to get hold of Harald Olesen's nephew on the phone. Joachim Olesen was an economist by profession and worked as an adviser in the Ministry of Finance. He had been waiting for a phone call from the police and immediately offered to come down to the main police station with his sister the following morning at nine o'clock to be interviewed. In the meantime, I asked for the name of the deceased's doctor and bank, which he gave without any hesitation. Two brief telephone conversations later, it transpired that the doctor was himself on sick leave and the bank was closed due to an inspection of accounts.

I had to admit that I felt none the wiser when I drove home alone the evening after the day of the murder. As I had few better leads, I listed the former NS member Konrad Jensen as the main suspect. As with all the other residents, though, he lacked not only a motive and a weapon, but also the opportunity. I still had not the foggiest idea where I might discover any of this.

In short, I was not looking forward to reading the morning papers on Saturday, 6 April 1968 with any sense of joy or optimism. It was dawning on me that the opportunities afforded by having sole responsibility for this murder investigation were great, but that my fall from grace could be equally great. I still had no idea that the case would bring me face to face with the most calculating criminal I have ever met, but also with the most remarkable person I have ever had the pleasure of working with. Meanwhile, I brooded over the case alone, fruitlessly, until I fell asleep.

DAY THREE

The Princess of Erling Skjalgsson's Street – and Her Sensational Discoveries

I

Saturday, 6 April 1968 started earlier than expected. I had set the alarm clock for eight, but was woken by the telephone a quarter of an hour earlier. The caller was patient and the phone continued to ring until I had struggled out of bed and answered it. I immediately recognized the deep and commanding voice on the other end.

'I do apologize for disturbing you so early on a Saturday morning, but this may be of considerable interest to you. Am I speaking to Detective Inspector Kolbjørn Kristiansen?'

I confirmed that I was he as I tried desperately in my still sleepy state to recall where on earth I had heard that voice before. Fortunately, I did not have to wonder for long.

'This is Professor Ragnar Sverre Borchmann. First of all, may I congratulate you on your most recent promotion. I hope, however, that we can still be on first-name terms and that you remember me as a guest in your childhood home?'

I most certainly did. Professor Director Ragnar Borchmann was an industrious and renowned university friend of my father's. He had not been a frequent visitor to my child-hood home, but had always caused quite a stir when he did come.

'I'm calling about the tragic murder of Harald Olesen. And while I do not wish to raise false hopes, I think I may possibly be able to help in the investigation. It is of course entirely up to you to judge whether you feel it is worth your while, in relation to following up other important leads.'

If the truth be told, I did not have many other important leads and at this point was willing to listen to any reliable person who might be able to move the investigation forward. What is more, I was keen to hear pretty much anything that Professor Director Ragnar Borchmann might have to say. But above all, I was extremely curious as to what he may be able to tell me about the case. So without further ado, I said that I would be more than happy to put aside some time to meet him, for example between eleven and twelve.

'Excellent. Eleven o'clock precisely it is. For reasons that will become apparent, we will have to meet here at my home, but I would be happy to send a car for you should that be necessary.'

I replied politely that it would not be necessary, double-checked that the address was still 104−8 Erling Skjalgsson's Street and promised to be there at eleven precisely.

II

As expected, the newspapers had a much bigger spread about the case today. They all carried photographs of 25 Krebs' Street, and most of them had old wartime pictures of Harald

Olesen on the front page. The headlines varied from 'Resistance Hero Murdered in His Own Home' to 'Unsolvable Murder Mystery in Krebs' Street'. The name of the detective inspector leading the investigation was fortunately mentioned in favourable terms à la 'apparently very capable young detective'. One of them had even included the fact that I was known as 'K2' among my younger colleagues and that I was said to be a man who could deal with major challenges and dizzying heights.

The newspapers made depressing reading for the remaining residents of 25 Krebs' Street. The deceased's neighbours remained anonymous, but the address and photographs would make it easy enough for anyone interested to identify them. The papers would be disheartening reading for Konrad Jensen in particular. Several of them carried the news that the residents of 25 Krebs' Street included a previously convicted Nazi. No one gave his name. One of the main newspapers did, however, mention that the previously convicted Nazi now worked as a taxi driver – and printed a photograph of his parked car.

Harald Olesen's nephew and niece were in their forties and gave an immediate impression of prosperity and reliability when they came into my office at nine o'clock. The niece, who was tall and blonde, was called Cecilia Olesen and worked as an office manager for the Oslo Cooperative Housing Association. Her brother was the same height, somewhat darker and more serious. With regard to his civil status, Joachim Olesen said that he was married and had two children under school age. His sister had been married and had a daughter, but had taken back her maiden name following a divorce. The niece and nephew both said that they had had good, if sporadic, contact with their uncle. He had withdrawn somewhat following the death of his wife, but still had relatively regular contact with the family. He had spoken very little about the other residents in the building.

The niece and nephew were also both of the opinion that Harald Olesen had been downcast of late, but believed that this had a natural, medical explanation. After a Christmas party the year before, he had told them that he had been diagnosed with cancer and may not live to see next Christmas. So the news of his death was not entirely unexpected, though obviously the circumstances had been a shock, and a blow to the whole family.

The niece and nephew had both understood without anything having been said that they were his closest relatives and could therefore expect a substantial inheritance. They had, however, never wished to ask about it, and he had not said anything explicit. He had inherited a large amount of money from his father and had never been a big spender, despite earning well for many years himself. The family therefore had reason to believe that he was a very wealthy man. They had only received a short and businesslike message from their uncle's lawyer stating that in accordance with the deceased's wishes, the will would be read at the law firm's offices six days after his death, more specifically on Wednesday, 10 April at midday.

I made a note about the cancer, which was the most important new piece of information from the niece and nephew. The other important piece of information was that Harald Olesen had the year before asked for the family's permission to work on his own biography. This was prompted by a request from a young history student by the name of

Bjørn Erik Svendsen. Without prying too much, the niece and nephew had later understood that the book was underway and that Harald Olesen had had several open-hearted conversations with his biographer and also given him access to parts of his archive.

The niece and nephew had nothing more of any relevance to tell. I said goodbye to them around ten and promised to inform them as soon as there was anything new to report in connection with the murder investigation. The history student Bjørn Erik Svendsen was added to the top of my list of people to contact as soon as possible. It struck me as odd that I still had not heard from him two days after the murder. Fortunately, this little mystery was quickly cleared. It transpired that a message from a woman who had called as she absolutely had to talk to me was from a certain Hanne Line Svendsen, and she was Bjørn Erik Svendsen's mother. She said that her son had gone to an international socialist youth conference in Rome, but had been informed of the murder by telephone and telegram. He was expected home late on Sunday evening and would come to the police station first thing on Monday morning. Bjørn Erik Svendsen had said, on a very bad line from Rome, that it was possible that he had some important information about Harald Olesen's early life and would of course make this available to the investigation. I reluctantly accepted the news that Mr Bjørn Erik Svendsen could not be contacted before Monday morning. I tried to see it as positive that new information regarding Harald Olesen was on its way to Norway.

In the meantime, I called the law firm Rønning, Rønning & Rønning. The Rønning I needed to speak to, Edvard Rønning Junior, was unfortunately not in the office. According to his secretary, he had flown to West Berlin a couple of days earlier. The secretary apologized and sheepishly explained that there were 'several indications' that Rønning Junior was going to meet one or more personal friends in Central Europe, but no one knew where he was going from the airport. When he had called the office about another case on the Friday morning, he had of course been informed of Harald Olesen's death. Rønning Junior had immediately explained that Olesen's will had recently been 'reworded' and, in accordance with the explicit wishes of the deceased, would be announced six days after his death.

Rønning Junior had promised that he would personally be present to read out the will in the law firm's offices at midday on Wednesday, 10 April. He would send a telegram 'as soon as possible' with a short list of the people the deceased wished to be present at the reading of the will. If the police contacted the firm, he had asked that they be informed that the most recent version of the will was responsibly secured, that all the formalities were in place and that we were welcome to come to the reading of the will on Wednesday. He had then said that he had to 'rush to an extremely important meeting' and hung up. Unfortunately, the will was not to be found in his office, and the telegram had not arrived yet. Thus the firm could only apologize that they could not be of any further help in the investigation. Rønning Junior was 'an exceptionally talented young lawyer, and rigorous with regard to formalities and discretion on behalf of his clients', the secretary concluded apologetically. I had no problem in believing her, and saw little option other than to ask Rønning Junior to contact me immediately if anyone should speak to him before Wednesday morning.

Harald Olesen's doctor was still on sick leave, but was willing to answer questions on his private phone. Having tussled briefly with his conscience, he felt that he could make a pragmatic exception to patient confidentiality, vis-à-vis the police, with regard to a patient who was in fact already dead, as was the case. He then confirmed that Olesen had been diagnosed with bowel cancer about a year ago. This had spread more rapidly than expected in recent months and Olesen had been told in December that the end might be only a matter of months away. Olesen had received this news with admirable dignity. He had remained seated, pensive, and then said that he had some important issues to consider and sort out before it was too late. The doctor thought this was quite a natural reaction and had not enquired as to what these might be.

The bank where Harald Olesen kept his account was closed. During a search of his flat, however, several documents had been found that answered most of the questions I would have asked of the bank. Olesen had apparently been a very organized person. Statements from the past five years were in a file in one of the desk drawers. These confirmed that Harald Olesen had died a rich man. The most recent statement was from March 1968 and showed a balance of just over a million kroner. What was more striking, however, was that the statements from 1966 and the first part of 1967 showed even greater wealth. Over the past six months, the sum in Harald Olesen's account had fallen by at least 250,000 kroner, even though his civil service pension should have been more than enough to cover the outgoings of a widowed pensioner. And the strange thing was that there were no documents in the drawer that could shed any light on where this money had gone. The sum appeared to have been paid out in three large cash withdrawals. Harald Olesen had initially taken out 100,000 kroner in October 1967, then 100,000 in February 1968 and a further 50,000 one month later.

I immediately envisaged two possibilities. Either Olesen had started to bet or make risky investments in his old age or he had paid out a large amount to one or several people. The latter seemed to be more likely, and it then was natural to assume that the murder may in some way be linked to blackmail.

It was frustrating to feel that the investigation was receiving ever more important information while I was no further forward. However, it was now the back of half past ten and time to solve the only mystery that I could guarantee would be cleared up today, which was what Professor Director Ragnar Borchmann had to offer that would help to solve the murder of Harald Olesen. I pondered this as I drove to 104–8 Erling Skjalgsson's Street, without making much headway there either.

III

At well over six foot and close to twenty stone, Ragnar Borchmann was quite literally one of the most imposing characters I had met. But it was his personality and intellectual capacity that were most imposing. Ragnar Borchmann was the only son of a consul and director from one of Oslo's most well-known families. He had inherited his father's business empire, but ran it more or less as a hobby. His working hours were spent as a professor of economics, and he had a long list of books on his CV and an exemplary reputation. At the age of sixty-four, Professor Director Ragnar Borchmann was now, I dare say, one of the richest men in Oslo and one of the most admired intellectuals in Norway.

But Ragnar Borchmann had carried a great sorrow for many years. I first heard about this when I was ten. One Saturday evening, in sheer delight at the end of the war, he and his wife sat up late with myself and my parents. Both guests showed a touching interest in me, my schooling and future opportunities in life. Before I went to bed that night, my father said to me: 'There are many things that I may envy about Ragnar Borchmann, but still I am the richer man. Because I have you.' In his early twenties, Ragnar Borchmann had married a girl from a very good family who was also at the start of a promising academic career. The couple always appeared to be happy and harmonious, but they remained childless. A sorrow settled on them, which seemed to weigh more heavily on him. By 1948, Ragnar Borchmann was forty-four years old and had amassed an impressive legacy of books, property and money, but he did not have an heir, and it seemed had no prospect of getting one.

My childhood was spent in a decidedly upper-class home where strong emotions were seldom displayed in public. I can only remember seeing Mother and Father cry on one occasion – and then it was with tears of joy. One day in July 1949 I came home from school to the news that the forty-three-year-old Mrs Caroline Borchmann was expecting a baby. It was only then that I understood how heavily their childlessness had weighed on the Borchmanns and their immediate circle. I have never seen joy and anticipation emanate more than it did from the middle-aged couple that summer. I went to their daughter's christening together with my parents in January 1950, as did around 250 other 'close friends' from the capital's cultural, financial and intellectual elite. It was jokingly said that Oslo had never seen the like since the crown prince's christening in 1937, but then that also seemed fitting, as we were, after all, talking about an emperor's daughter. Choosing a name for their only child was obviously no easy task for two parents with such illustrious names on both sides. In the end, they settled on Patricia Louise Isabelle Elizabeth Borchmann.

'The Borchmann girl' had been reading books from the age of four, if my parents were to be believed. She was eight when she read her first Ibsen play. At the age of ten, she appeared on the front page of one of the national newspapers, without wishing to do so, under the headline 'Super-Intelligent Director's Daughter Challenges Single-Stream Comprehensive Schools'. The problem was that the school principal, with backing from the Ministry of Education, would only agree to move her up one year, whereas her parents and the teachers believed that jumping three would be more valuable. The following year, Patricia Louise I. E. Borchmann appeared in the newspapers again, but this time on the sports pages, under headlines that ventured 'The New Sonja Henie?' The reports also mentioned that she was one of the nation's rising stars in shooting, having achieved several high scores in the national youth championships.

One winter day in 1963, my mother and I met Patricia Louise and her parents on our way home from the skating rink. Professor Borchmann dominated the conversation, as always. However, in the course of his analysis of the day's news – the future of the new Gerhardsen government following the Kings Bay Affair – the impossible occurred. Not only was he corrected in his review of the facts, he was also challenged in his analysis. And what was even more astonishing was that he took it with good humour, admitted his mistakes and even patted his critic happily on the head several times. This made a deep impression on my mother and me. 'We'll be hearing more about that girl,' my mother said, as we watched them continue on their way.

Unfortunately, I only remember the episode and my mother's words in light of the tragedy that would colour it forever. That was the last time that we saw Mrs Borchmann alive, and Patricia was never to skate again. A few days later, one of the Borchmann cars skidded on the black winter ice at a crossroads, resulting in a full-frontal collision with a spinning articulated lorry. The driver and Mrs Borchmann, who was in the front, were killed instantly, and the passenger in the back seat, Patricia Louise, was still in a coma five days later, fighting for her life. I have been told that two nights in a row the doctors declared that she was not likely to live to see the morning. Ten days after the accident, the newspapers carried a small notice that her condition was no longer critical, but the damage would probably be permanent. That was the last thing that anyone wrote about Patricia Louise I. E. Borchmann.

I later heard from my mother that Patricia was paralysed from the waist down and had been taken out of school. Her father in his despair sought advice from a number of leading doctors, and in pure desperation also took her to see an old healer in Lillehammer and a younger healer in Snåsa. There was no chance of a recovery, so Patricia would have to live with the prospect of deterioration looming over her for the rest of her life. After that I had heard nothing more of either her or her father. Until he called early on the morning of 6 April 1968 to offer some unexpected help in solving the murder.

The facade of 104–8 Erling Skjalgsson's Street, where Ragnar Borchmann had both his home and business empire, was just as impressive as I recalled from my visits as a boy. The enormous building went by the name of 'the White House' among friends and acquaintances, because of its colour. The three separate houses had been joined by Ragnar Borchmann's paternal grandfather, who now stood on a plinth in the cavernous hallway outside his grandson's office. It struck me that entering the Borchmann household was like going back in time to the 1930s.

Professor Borchmann's secretary showed me the quickest way to the director's office. The staircase, with its twenty-three steps, was almost as long as I remembered from childhood. And when I reached the top, Ragnar Borchmann was by and large almost the same as well. There was a sombreness to him that I did not recognize from before, but his back was as straight, his hair and beard as black, his handshake as firm and his voice as powerful as I remembered.

'Welcome, and once again congratulations on your recent promotion. I am absolutely certain that you will rise to this challenge. Now, shall I call you Kolbjørn or Detective Inspector Kristiansen?'

I assured him that I would take it as a compliment if he chose to call me Kolbjørn, but to be on the safe side, I would continue to call him 'Professor Borchmann'. He smiled, but did not object.

'First of all, I must apologize if I have lured you here under false pretences, but it was with the best of intentions. Sadly, I have nothing to contribute myself. I of course met Harald Olesen on and off over the past few decades, but saw less of him more recently. If you have not done so already, you should talk to Supreme Court Justice Jesper Christopher Haraldsen regarding the war years and Party Secretary Haavard Linde about politics and the party. But other than that, I am afraid I am of very little use to the case.'

I had not yet got as far as talking to either of the grand gentlemen mentioned, but he was absolutely right that I should contact them. So it was still a mystery as to why I was sitting here. Borchmann saw the confusion on my face and carried on hastily.

'I am aware that this is both unorthodox and somewhat irregular, but it is Patricia and not me you should be talking to.'

My confusion was in no way diminished by his next comment – in the form of a totally unexpected question.

'Have you ever met a person whose thoughts are constantly one step ahead, faster and more profound than your own? It is a fascinating and yet frightening experience to look in the eye of someone who, quite frankly, is more intelligent than you will ever be. You feel you are in good hands and helpless at the same time.'

I nodded vaguely. I did not like to say in so many words, but I knew that feeling only too well. For example, I felt it every time I spoke to Professor Director Borchmann.

'Of course you have. I have perhaps felt it less often than others, but I too have experienced it. Unless the discussion involves my specialist areas, I experience it practically every time I talk to my eighteen-year-old daughter now. She not only reads twice as quickly as me, be it in Norwegian, English, German or French, she beats me hands down in the speed and quality of her comments on what we are reading. It frightens me a little, but also makes me tremendously proud.'

I felt extremely uncertain and was not sure of what to say, or how, so I kept my mouth shut. The professor continued without pause.

'Nothing has interested Patricia more in recent years than unsolved crimes. She has read dozens of books on the history of crime, and at least a hundred detective novels. She has on more than one occasion predicted the outcome of big criminal cases on the basis of what she has read in the papers. She is particularly interested in the murder in Krebs' Street. Partly because Harald Olesen was a friend of the family and partly because of the extraordinary circumstances surrounding the case. She has questions and comments that I cannot answer – including an entirely plausible solution as to how the murderer managed to leave the flat. But for all I know, it is perfectly possible that you and your colleagues have solved the mystery already and will shortly be making an arrest . . .'

He looked at me in anticipation. I tried to shake my head without appearing to be desperate.

'In that case, I would be immensely grateful if you could discuss the case with Patricia for a short while, in all confidentiality of course. It need not take more than fifteen minutes of your time, and could be of considerable assistance.'

I thought quietly to myself that perhaps mandatory limits should be introduced for how highly a father could praise his child, but by now my curiosity about young Patricia and her world had been piqued. And I was no less curious as to how she had solved the mystery of the murderer's disappearance, while I had found no solution. So I gave a friendly smile and replied that I would be more than happy to set aside fifteen minutes or so in all confidentiality to test the theory.

Professor Borchmann smiled, pressed my hand and, without further ado, rang a bell. A young, blonde maid in her twenties appeared a few seconds later. 'Please show my guest into Miss Patricia Louise in the library straightaway,' the professor said. Then he turned back to the paperwork on his desk with characteristic efficiency.

IV

Patricia Louise Isabelle Elizabeth Borchmann now lived in a tidy and serene little kingdom one storey above and a garden away from a grey and busy street in Oslo. She was sitting waiting at a table set for two, in the middle of a room that was larger than many of the gymnasiums that I have been in, surrounded by more books than in all the private libraries I have ever seen.

Young Patricia was in no way physically impressive. I guessed she would be a good head shorter than me if she could stand up, and her body was so slight that she could barely weigh more than seven stone. The family likeness with her father was undeniable. It was there in the black hair, but more than anything in her stern face and unwavering gaze. I couldn't recall having seen a young girl with such a strong face – or any woman, for that matter.

As if by some unspoken agreement, we did not shake

hands. I just nodded, and she pointed brusquely to a large armchair directly opposite her. She herself was sitting in her wheelchair, with a television set, as well as a wireless and stereo player, within reach. The table between us was large and obviously necessary. To her left was a telephone of the very latest model. In front of her, there were three ballpoint pens and a notebook, as well as a pile of at least six of that day's newspapers. Judging by the selection of papers, Patricia Louise I. E. Borchmann was open-minded and non-party political: she read everything from the reactionary *Morgenbladet* to the communist rag *Friheten*. On the right-hand side of the table lay three books, with bookmarks. The one on top was a French book, the title of which I could not understand, the one in the middle appeared to be a university textbook on sociology, and the one on the bottom was a collection of short stories in English by Stanley Ellin, of whom I had never heard. There was a large jug of water in the middle of the table, as well as a pot of coffee and a pot of tea.

'Welcome. I am extremely grateful that you can give me a few minutes of your time. Do you have any particular preference when it comes to refreshment?'

I swiftly declined.

'In that case, that is all for now, Benedikte. I will ring should there be anything else.'

The maid bobbed a silent curtsy and quickly retired. Patricia Louise I. E. Borchmann was a lady of principles and discretion. She did not say a word until we were alone in the room. Then, like her father, she got straight to the point.

'I don't want to waste any more of your undoubtedly precious time than necessary. The picture given in the papers of the residents of the building is somewhat incomplete, so if

I am to say anything of any value, I may need to be updated. The newspapers all mention the unsolved mystery of how the murderer could escape the flat undetected. The windows were closed and locked from the inside, and there were no broken panes to indicate that the shot came from outside. The door has a snib lock, which means that the murderer could have left the flat and locked the door behind him. But the other residents were at the door so soon after the shot that no one could have escaped that way unnoticed. Is that, in brief, a fair description of the mystery as to how the murder was committed? And is it still an unsolved problem for you and the investigation?'

I nodded quickly – twice. The Borchmann family obviously had a talent for giving simple, brief synopses and clarifying critical issues.

Young Patricia seemed to grow in her wheelchair. She chewed thoughtfully on the inside of her cheek for a moment before continuing.

'This is a variant of the closed-room mystery, but not of the most difficult kind, as the security chain was not on. As Sherlock Holmes says, "When you have eliminated the impossible, whatever remains, *however improbable*, must be the truth." The murderer obviously left through the door, so in reality, there are only two possible ways in which that could have happened.'

I listened in fascination to her determined, self-assured voice. She was clearly excited and took the opportunity to take a couple of sips of cold water before continuing.

'The first solution is very much like one of Agatha Christie's best-known novels, in which all the characters have, for various reasons, conspired to kill the victim. In which case, you shouldn't place too much emphasis on the other residents' statements.'

I had hoped for something more realistic, which must have been obvious. She hurried on, without stopping for a drink.

'But that kind of plot definitely works better in English novels than in daily life in Norway, and does not seem very likely in this case. There would also be a considerable risk with so many people involved, and the residents seem to be a very mixed bunch. If we let go of our paranoia and shelve the theory of a major conspiracy among the residents, there's really only one possibility left.'

I stared at her with renewed interest, my thoughts racing as she poured and drank another half-glass of water. And yet her question was completely unexpected.

'Have many of the other residents complained about being disturbed by the baby on the first floor?'

Patricia smiled briefly and a touch condescendingly when she saw the confusion on my face, before continuing swiftly.

'Or, more to the point, does sound travel exceptionally well in 25 Krebs' Street? Does the building have unusually thin walls and good acoustics?'

I started to get a vague idea of where she was going, but I still did not see how it would end. I thought about it, then shook my head. None of the residents had complained about the baby making a noise.

'But then how can a shot fired from a revolver in a flat on the second floor be heard clearly as a loud explosion in the hallway two storeys below?'

It was a good question. A very good question in fact, one

that I should have thought of myself. But before I had time to understand its full significance, her voice broke my thoughts.

'Interestingly, the residents, press and even the police have all made the same classic and logical mistake. If you hear a gunshot and then shortly afterwards find a man who has been shot, it is easy to conclude that he was killed by the shot that was heard. Logical, but not necessarily true. In other words, Harald Olesen did not die from the shot that the other residents heard at a quarter past ten. He was killed by another, less audible gunshot that was fired earlier in the evening, presumably using a silencer. Wouldn't you have used a silencer if you were going to shoot a man in his flat and had every intention of getting away unnoticed afterwards?'

Of course I would. It was painfully obvious when she explained it so clearly and simply, and it grieved me that I had not seen it before. However, a glaring question did occur to me soon after.

'Then where on earth did the shot that they all heard come from? We have searched Mr Olesen's flat and all the others with a fine-tooth comb and have found no evidence of a radio transmitter or surveillance equipment.'

Patricia smiled again. 'I guessed as much. And that shows that we are dealing with a remarkably well-planned murder that was carried out by an exceptionally cold-blooded murderer. But did there happen to be a record player in Harald Olesen's flat, with a record on the turntable?'

That hit me like a well-aimed punch in the solar plexus. I had seen and made note of the record player and record, but not understood their significance. I nodded and wiped my forehead dry. It was embarrassing that Patricia had seen so much here in her own closed room that I had failed to see, despite several visits to the scene of the crime. And I now discovered that she could also apparently read minds.

'It's strange how often it is easier to see the connections when you are sitting with all the elements in tidy order, without any interference or impressions from the scene of the crime. But the notion of using a sound recording to alter the time of a murder is familiar enough, from one of Agatha Christie's earlier novels in particular. Now, if you go back to 25 Krebs' Street and play the record that is still lying on the turntable in Harald Olesen's flat, I would gladly bet my wheelchair and half my inheritance on the fact that you will sooner or later hear another gunshot.'

I didn't offer to take her up on the bet. I fortunately had no need for a wheelchair, and I unfortunately would never have as much money as half her inheritance. What is more, I did not for a second doubt that she was right. I mumbled my thanks and stood up to leave. She called for the maid straightaway. While we waited, Patricia wrote down a number on a piece of paper and handed it to me.

'This is the direct number to my telephone. I would appreciate it if you could call me once you have confirmed my theory about the record player. Then we can see if there is any more I can help you with.'

I vaguely registered that we were already on more informal terms, and that it felt completely natural, despite the somewhat grand-old-days feel of the Borchmann home. I nodded, tucked the slip of paper carefully into my wallet and silently and obediently followed the maid out. I still felt as though I had been hypnotized by the time I reached the car, but understood keenly enough that my apparently unsolvable murder mystery had taken a great leap forward towards a possible conclusion.

V

When I arrived at 25 Krebs' Street around two, everything appeared to be as calm as before. The caretaker's wife was sitting in her place by the door and immediately let me into Harald Olesen's flat. There was no sign of any of the other residents. I had some new questions for a few of them, but for the moment there was no room in my head for anything other than Harald Olesen's record player.

The record player was still there, with the recording by the Vienna Philharmonic Orchestra on the turntable. With a pounding heart and shaking hand, I carefully lowered the needle. I expected the label to be fake and the record to be soundless at the start, but I had another shock in store when an irresistible waltz immediately filled the room. The volume was nearly on full, and the record was obviously real enough. So now I expected that the music would fall silent and the gunshot would ring out at the end of the record. Having turned down the volume, I waited with growing anticipation for a gunshot that never came. The needle lifted and returned to its place without further drama once the final bar had been played.

To begin with, I was disappointed. Then I laughed, despite the setback it meant for me, as the cocksure Miss Patricia's creative theory had not held. I put the record on again and increased the volume before going over to Harald Olesen's telephone and dialling the number on the slip of paper in my wallet.

Patricia picked up the phone before the second ring. I could actually hear her surprise, prompted by the music, and so talked louder than necessary to drown it out.

'I am in Harald Olesen's flat and have turned on the record player and listened to the whole record. And as you can hear, it seems to be a red herring.'

There was silence for a moment on the other end of the line. It is possible that Patricia doubted herself and her theory for a matter of seconds, but it certainly did not last long.

'But that *has* to be it. There is no other credible solution. Is the record player free-standing, or is it part of one of these newfangled stereo systems with a cassette player?'

I glanced quickly over at the record player and was immediately gripped by uncertainty. The record player was indeed part of a big new stereo system with a cassette player – and there was a cassette in the player. Patricia's response was as quick as a flash when she heard this.

'Then the cassette player *has* to be the answer. Play the cassette that is there, but turn down the volume in order not to terrify the whole building if – I mean *when* there is a gunshot. Call me again when you have played the cassette. But of course, if there is no gunshot on the cassette either, there is no need for you to waste any more time in calling me again.'

Thus spoke Patricia Louise I. E. Borchmann – without drawing breath. Then she put down the phone without saying goodbye.

I looked at the stereo, full of doubt, but then turned off the record player and rewound the cassette to the start. The cassette looked genuine enough, and the German writing promised Beethoven's Ninth Symphony. It seemed to take an eternity to rewind. When it had finally rewound to the start, I reduced the volume by a couple of notches and sat down to wait for the cassette to crank into action. It started, as expected, with Beethoven's Ninth Symphony. I immediately wondered if this was the most valuable use of my time. However, the music stopped with a loud click after only a couple of minutes. The cassette then crept forwards as slowly as could be for the next twenty-five minutes. At first, I paced around the room, but as the tape got ever closer to the end, I moved ever closer to the large loudspeakers of the stereo player.

I expected the tape to stop at any moment when suddenly there was another muffled click, followed by a loud gunshot.

Despite having turned down the volume, it exploded like an atomic bomb in my ears. I jumped and then watched paralysed as the cassette stopped. I stood there for five minutes, puzzling over whose hand might have started this tape recording the last time it played.

When I eventually managed to pull myself together and phone back, she answered the phone on the first ring. 'Was the gunshot at the very end?' she asked.

I mumbled a subdued 'yes', an even more muffled 'congratulations' and a somewhat louder explanation that the gunshot was right at the end of a cassette of Beethoven's Ninth Symphony. I could almost feel the receiver quiver as she breathed out.

'Thank goodness for that. I was almost starting to get worried. Remember to check the cassette and stereo player for fingerprints, but do not be disappointed if there are none. We are dealing with a particularly Machiavellian murderer.'

I replied that that was quite clearly the case, but that it did help to know how he had escaped and to have adjusted the time of the murder to nearly twenty-five minutes earlier. This seemed to confuse her somewhat.

'Hold on a minute. Firstly, I am not at all certain that the murderer is a he, and secondly, where did you get the twenty-five minutes from?'

I smiled to myself that I was ahead of her this time and informed her that the cassette had a playing time of twenty-five minutes. I waited for the 'aha' exclamation, but instead got only a small sigh of relief and another ruthless question.

'But we have no evidence that the murderer put on the cassette immediately after he or she carried out the murder, do we?'

And of course I had to admit that we didn't. The murderer could in theory have waited for as long as he – or she – wanted in the flat before starting the cassette and leaving. Equally, the tape might have been wound forward so that the murder took place only minutes before the gunshot. Suddenly, it became of far more interest that the pathologist had only been able to narrow the time of death down to between eight and eleven. Patricia and I promptly agreed that any of the residents who did not have a watertight alibi for the period from eight until ten past ten must be seen as potential murderers. We also quickly agreed that I should return and discuss the situation with her before talking to the neighbours again.

VI

Half an hour later, I was back sitting in the library at the White House in front of Princess Patricia. She was nibbling happily on a large carrot, like an unusually self-satisfied rabbit. With the carrot in her left hand, she wrote down key words at perfect speed with her right, while I sipped my tea and repeated the neighbours' statements. It occurred to me more than once that this was a breathtaking breach of standard investigation procedure, which could cause enormous problems for me should it ever get out. But it also struck me as unthinkable that either the father or daughter would ever let the secret slip. My childhood trust in the Borchmann family was deeply ingrained. Furthermore, I firmly believed that there was more help to be had here. And last of all, I had to admit to myself, and mark my words to myself alone, that help may be needed if Harald Olesen's clearly cunning murderer was to be caught.

Patricia proved for the first time to be a good listener, as she patiently heard out my long account of what had been found in the case so far. Several times I noticed a twinkle in her eyes, but when I made signs of stopping, she motioned impatiently for me to continue.

'That was very interesting and informative on certain points,' she said, when I had finished, sometime around four o'clock. I chose to take that as a huge compliment.

'So, who killed Harald Olesen?' I asked pointedly.

She gave me a small smile as she shook her head apologetically.

'Investigating a murder when the perpetrator is unknown

is in many ways similar to painting a portrait. On Thursday night, we had a blank canvas, but have now managed to sketch a few characteristics, which will then lead to more. Even though it may all become clear soon, it may still take a considerable amount of hard work before the face is distinct enough. Despite the adjusted timeframe, it remains hard to see how the murderer could get in before the murder without being seen – or escape afterwards. Given what we know, he or she can still only be one of the other residents. But we have to keep our options open. As the murder took place sometime between eight and ten past ten, everyone who was in the building – with the exception of the baby, of course – had the opportunity, in theory.'

I looked at her and hesitated, but then ventured a slight objection.

'Don't you think we can rule out the man in the wheel-chair?'

She shook her head and pushed back her own chair.

'Not at all. Nothing that we know thus far rules out the possibility that a man in a wheelchair, who is otherwise healthy, might have committed the murder, alone or in collaboration with others. You must ask him in more detail about how he came to be in a wheelchair and just how serious it is. Even the caretaker's wife, until proven innocent, is a potential murderer.'

Patricia was on a roll now and carried on tirelessly.

'So, in the spirit of Agatha Christie, the main question therefore must be, who stood to gain so much from Harald Olesen's death that they murdered him? And by extension, why was there a need to kill him now – when he did not have long to live anyway?'

'Perhaps the murderer did not know he was ill?' I suggested.

Patricia nodded, but then shook her head.

'That is, of course, perfectly possible, but I still believe that it is more likely that the murderer knew about the illness, and that, paradoxically, was the very reason why things had to happen fast.'

Naturally, I could not resist asking why. I was not entirely sure what sort of answer I expected; it definitely was not the one I got.

'Because there was no murder weapon at the scene of the crime.'

Again she smiled at my confusion. Her smile seemed to me to be a rather arrogant and unlikeable side of her nature, but I was too interested in what she had to say to give it any further thought.

'I have to admit that the conclusion is somewhat speculative, given there are so many unknown factors, but it is very odd. If you had found a murder weapon near the body, the case would probably have been interpreted as an obvious suicide. Leaving a weapon behind would have been a far more obvious choice than this advanced idea involving the stereo player. The fact that the murderer did not use the option of leaving the gun behind would indicate that the murder was committed earlier than planned. The only other explanation I can think of is that the murderer wanted to demonstrate that it was a murder and not a suicide. No matter what, the question as to why it happened now is currently almost inseparable from the question of why it happened. His will and the money that was missing from his account are obviously both of great interest in this connection. You should follow up both questions as soon as possible after the weekend. In the meantime, I suggest that you ask the neighbours if they can provide the investigation with information regarding their finances. It will be of considerable interest simply to see who answers "yes" or "no" to this.'

I nodded, and immediately followed up with a new question.

'Do you think that this is essentially about money?'

Patricia thoughtfully nibbled on her carrot for a minute or so before answering.

'The money may be decisive, but I think it is a lead more than a solution, and that this is about something more important and more serious. In any case, there are already several clues that point back to the war.'

I thought to myself once again that people who claimed that money was not important for some reason always seemed to have plenty of it. But before I could decide whether to mention it or not, she pushed on to new heights.

'In short, I do not think we are looking for someone who functions normally. I believe we are looking for a human fly.'

Despite the fact that my knowledge of zoology is perhaps better than average, I have to confess that this was an unknown species to me – and I certainly did not understand why she was talking about it now. Having wracked my brains for a minute or so, I had to swallow the bitter pill and ask what she meant. She attempted to give an apologetic smile, without much success.

'I am sorry – I wasn't thinking. It is a concept that I made up myself and have used so much since that I forget that it is not something that other people understand. But I do think that it may be relevant here. There are a good many people who at some point in their lives have experienced something so painful and traumatic that they never get over it. They become human flies and spend more or less the rest of their life circling round what happened. Like flies round a rubbish tip, to use a simple analogy. I think that Harald Olesen himself, behind his suit and mask, was in fact a human fly. And I have a strong suspicion that he was killed by another one.'

I now understood what she meant – and immediately saw a possible link to my own preliminary theories.

'Which would point to Konrad Jensen?'

Patricia wagged her head thoughtfully before answering.

'Yes and no. At the moment, Konrad Jensen is the most obvious human fly among the neighbours. But I suspect that he is not the only one, and I for various reasons doubt that he is the right one. It would be more plausible that he was the murderer if we could find a direct link between his background in the war and Harald Olesen's.'

I had to agree with what she had said so far. And it suddenly occurred to me that I should ask what her thoughts were regarding the blue raincoat. She lit up when I mentioned it and gave me a much longed-for compliment.

'You are absolutely right – it may be crucial. Once we have established who threw the blue raincoat away, I think we will be hard on the heels of the murderer. The problem is that it was not found until Friday morning. And I am sure that you did not go through the residents' wardrobes on Thursday evening in search of a blue raincoat?'

This was my opportunity for a welcome small victory.

'Of course we did not search their wardrobes for a blue raincoat that we knew nothing about, but I think we can say with reasonable certainty that it was not to be seen in any of the neighbours' flats late on Thursday night. No one has made a note of a large blue raincoat, and it would not be particularly easy to hide something like that in the event of a house search.'

For a moment I thought that Patricia was about to get out of her wheelchair. For about thirty seconds her eyes flashed and her body tensed.

'Brilliant,' she almost whispered. 'It is still not a determining factor, but may prove to be.'

I waited for further explanation, but soon realized that this would not be forthcoming. So instead I asked what she made of the neighbours' statements. This time she was quick to answer.

'There are still an extraordinary number of secrets in that building. The fact that all those people have ended up in the same building is suspicious in itself. The American diplomat is perhaps strangest of all, but the student from Sweden, rentier from Oppland and millionaire's daughter from Bærum do not really belong on the east side of the river in Torshov either. Some of them may have ended up there by chance – that goes without saying – but that is certainly not the case for all of them. In fact, I suspect that only one of the residents has been completely open and honest so far.'

She stopped abruptly, no doubt knowing that I would ask who. When I did, she gave me the most tantalizing smile and tore a page from her notebook. With her left hand hiding the page, she dashed off some words before folding the paper. Then she rang the bell for the maid. While we waited, Patricia beamed at me with the most disarming and innocent smile.

'Please forgive my somewhat eccentric behaviour, but it is a shot in the dark that may be wrong. And if that is the case, my speculations must not be allowed to bias your ongoing investigation.'

As soon as there was a knock on the door, she stopped the conversation and held the folded sheet out to the maid.

'Please put this in a sealed envelope and send it to Detective Inspector Kolbjørn Kristiansen at Oslo Police. You will find the address in the telephone directory. Send the letter this evening on your way home.'

Benedikte looked from Patricia to me, obviously confused.

'Benedikte, do not try to think for yourself, as it has never been very successful. Benedikte should just do as she is told and then everything will be fine,' Patricia instructed, in a harsh voice.

The silent Benedikte nodded apologetically, took the piece of paper and hastily withdrew. I felt the episode to be uncomfortable, even though this might be the way they normally spoke to each other. However, I already had more than enough problems without interfering in internal communications in the Borchmann household.

Patricia waited before saying any more until the door was safely closed behind Benedikte.

'The post has already been collected today, so the letter will not be sent until Monday, which means that you will not receive it before Tuesday at the earliest. It may be that I have made a mistake, but it will be interesting to see whether my theories today tally with what happens between now and Tuesday. I would be very surprised if some of the residents had not decided to amend their original statement quite substantially by then.'

I remembered one of the loose threads that I was struggling to tie up and immediately drew her attention to it.

'Kristian Lund is perhaps one of them. What do you make of the discrepancy as to when he came home on the evening of the murder? It's three against two, and I am really not sure who to believe.'

Suddenly, Patricia burst into loud, mischievous laughter.

'Perhaps I should not laugh. That is another story, but it may of course still prove to be important. If you think about it, it is not necessarily three against two in favour of Kristian Lund. The fact that his wife confirms that he came through the door at nine o'clock does not necessarily contradict the claims from the other two that he came in the front door an hour earlier. The only person to support his claim that he came in at nine is the caretaker's wife, who you said seemed to be bothered by the situation. I think you should have a serious talk with her about it, then I think that it will be cleared up soon enough.'

I promised to do so, without entirely seeing the point.

'But where was Kristian Lund in the meantime, then? He could hardly have used all that time to get from the front door to the first floor.'

Patricia laughed again – just as loudly and mischievously as before.

'If that were the case, he would be even less able than Andreas Gullestad and myself combined. If Kristian Lund did come back at eight o'clock, he could in theory have been in any of the other flats in the building. In practice, however, there are really only two possibilities. One is extremely serious, and the other extremely embarrassing – and both are of great potential importance to the investigation.'

I stared at Patricia, more fascinated than ever. She gave me her most coquettish smile and on purpose munched the rest of her carrot at a very leisurely pace before continuing.

'The first and more serious possibility is of course obvious . . . Kristian Lund was on the second floor in Harald Olesen's flat. For reasons he cannot or does not dare to share with us. It is quite possible this is the case, but the second theory is more probable.'

My patience was in danger of running out. And it certainly did when she found this to be a suitable moment to conjure up another raw carrot and take another couple of pensive bites. My suppressed irritation at being teased by those more intelligent than me at middle school suddenly flared up again.

'So where was Mr Lund between eight o'clock and nine o'clock according to your second and more embarrassing theory? Could the young Miss Borchmann be as kind as to let the head of investigation know?'

My sharp tone made Patricia frown for a moment. Then she smiled disarmingly again, but still with a mischievous undertone. Suddenly, she was just like any other normal, gossipy eighteen-year-old girl on a school trip.

'According to my second and more embarrassing theory, he was of course on the first floor. In the bedroom of Flat 2A, to be precise – on top of Miss Sara Sundqvist!'

She burst out laughing again, this time presumably at the expression on my face.

'It fits suspiciously well, does it not? It would explain her mysterious lover, and the remarkable fact that he has never been seen by the caretaker's wife, or anyone else for that matter. It would also explain why Kristian Lund stubbornly denies in front of his wife that he came back any earlier.'

Of course it fitted suspiciously well. Including the reaction of the caretaker's wife, now that I thought of it. The only thing it did not explain was why I had failed to recognize the possibility myself. And why the caretaker's wife had lied. Kristian Lund had an increasing number of awkward inconsistencies to explain, even though I still could not bring myself to see the anxious young father as a cold-blooded murderer.

In wrapping up, Patricia agreed that it would be prudent to inform the press of the change in the time of the murder and the story behind it on Sunday, once I had confronted the neighbours. She said that I was 'right' that it was a better idea to increase pressure on the murderer than to give a false impression of safety. Secretly, I was more worried about what people and the media might think or believe if more days were to pass without any visible breakthrough in the investigation.

On Saturday, 6 April 1968, I left the White House around six o'clock in the evening. In stark contrast to the situation some twenty-four hours earlier, I drove home that evening secure in the knowledge that Harald Olesen's murderer would be caught and face punishment sooner or later.

Just before I left, however, I made an error of judgement that bothered me for the rest of the evening. As I got up, I thought that I should perhaps emphasize the seriousness of the case to Patricia.

'I have been entirely open with you and trust that you will not abuse that. You must never mention the content of our conversations to another living soul, with the exception of your father perhaps, if necessary.'

She gave me the most injured look I have ever received from a woman – and that, sadly, says enough in itself. Then she added, in a bitterly grave voice: 'But my dear Detective Inspector . . . who on earth would I tell anything to?'

Ashamed, I glanced around the large room in which she sat so visibly on her own among all her books. Then I mumbled an apology and said thank you, before following the perpetually silent maid from the room. By the time I crossed the threshold, Patricia had already taken the book-mark out of the book that was on top of the pile and was munching demonstratively on a carrot, without having deigned to say a word.

When I went to bed at the end of the third day of the investigation, I was far more optimistic about the future outlook of the case, influenced by my meeting with Patricia. But I was also aware that we were on the trail of a particularly cunning murderer and that the road to an eventual arrest might be long. I had no idea, however, that it would take a further six days of high drama that resembled a bizarre game of chess between Patricia and the murderer – without them even being in the same room or in direct contact.

DAY FOUR

The Residents Refine Their Memory

I

On Sunday, 7 April, my working day started at Krebs' Street around ten o'clock. I had, however, phoned to warn of my arrival and said to the caretaker's wife that I needed to speak to her. So there she was sitting dutifully at her post, even though it was early on a quiet Sunday morning. She waved and smiled as soon as she saw me, but already from a distance I thought I could detect some uncertainty and fear in her movements. As planned, I got straight to the point.

'Giving false statements to the police in criminal cases is called perjury and is a serious crime that can result in a prison sentence or heavy fine.'

There was little doubt that this hit the mark. The caretaker's wife stared at me, paralysed, her face chalk white and her jaw twitching. I carried on swiftly.

'*But*, as there are as yet no official written statements in this case, and it has been a very demanding situation for you, we may be able to overlook a little confusion at the start, if you now give me a complete and true account of when the residents came home on the evening of the murder . . .'

The caretaker's wife pulled herself together with impressive speed and immediately started to talk like the clappers.

'Thank you so much. I have been so worried, and regretted night and day that I didn't tell you the truth straightaway. But as you said, it has not been an easy situation for me, as I had written on the list that Kristian came home at nine, and I had sworn to Kristian that I would say that it was right if anyone asked. How could we know that it would be the police who came and asked? And I was so sure that Kristian had nothing to do with the murder. So then I got all confused and simply didn't know what to do, so I thought it would be best just to stick to what I had written down and promised. The fact that Kristian sometimes comes home earlier need not really affect anyone apart from him and his wife.'

I immediately used the opportunity to impress a little more.

'And the young Miss Sara Sundqvist, of course.'

The caretaker's wife had got over the worst of her shock and gave a fleeting smile before she continued.

'It is incredible how much the detective inspector has already managed to discern. Yes, of course, but Miss Sara is such a charming and kind young lady. She has nothing to do with the murder; I'm absolutely certain of it.'

Her smile broadened before she carried on. Before she even started to talk, I guessed that she was dreaming about her own days of young love.

'I noticed it, in fact, before I knew anything for sure. Sara seemed to fly down the stairs; her back was straighter and her smile brighter than before, so even an old croney like me could guess that there must be an unusually handsome man involved. I made the connection one morning when she came running down just after he had passed on his way out. The next morning, she came down unusually early, but stood waiting outside on the pavement until he came. And the next day again, she came first and he followed only a couple of minutes later. So then I knew that something was happening. I said nothing to either them or Mrs Lund, naturally. It was none of my business, and I didn't want to make trouble for anyone.'

I nodded my understanding.

'So far, well and good. Except then you started to falsify the lists and to lie to the police. But perhaps that was not your own idea?'

The caretaker's wife shook her head firmly.

'No, no, I would never have thought of anything like that myself. It was Kristian who came to me at the start of the following week. It was so touching; he was so open when he told me that he was head over heels in love with Miss Sara and had started an affair with her. He said that it was difficult and he had to think hard about what he should do. In the meantime, he asked me not to say a word to Mrs Lund about what I might see or hear, or to anyone else. I promised that I wouldn't. But then he asked me to lie if anyone asked directly whether I had seen anything suspicious, and to write on my lists that he came home an hour later on the days when he called and told his wife he would be late. I put my foot down. Not to gossip about things that are none of your business is one thing, but I have never wilfully told a lie . . .'

There was a small silence between us.

'And then . . .' I prompted.

She nodded.

'And then he took out his wallet and said that of course

my help deserved a little reward. He thought that perhaps one hundred kroner a month would do the trick, with two hundred in advance as it was nearly Christmas. He took out four fifty-kroner notes.'

The caretaker's wife sat thinking, without saying a word. A couple of tears rolled slowly down her wrinkled cheeks. Then she got up heavily from the chair and indicated that I should wait a minute. 'I have a couple of photographs I need to show you,' she mumbled, as she went past.

A few minutes later, she came back with two framed photographs in her hands. The first was an old, yellowing black-and-white wedding picture of a smiling young couple. The man was tall and dark, the woman a head shorter and much rounder.

'That was in spring 1928,' she said quietly. As if that explained it all.

'The Labour Party had just formed their first government and the future looked bright. A lot of people asked me then, and over the years that followed, how I had managed to find such a good man as Anton. And he was back then: handsome, hard-working and reliable in everything he did. Everything was rosy for the next twelve years. He had a job; the children managed to avoid tuberculosis and grow up. We never complained, despite the long working hours.'

'And then . . .' I said again, still unsure of where this was leading.

'Then the war came and Anton joined the Resistance. He asked me first, but I couldn't say no when that was what he wanted and the country's future was at risk. I have asked myself a thousand times since how life would have been if I had put my foot down and said no. As it was, his life was torn apart by the war, though we didn't realize it at the time. My Anton was one of the ones who survived the war but could not live with the memories when peace came. He started to have nightmares and problems sleeping, which led to more cigarettes and more and more alcohol. I told you that he was away and you didn't ask any more questions, but he is actually in hospital and won't leave until he is in a coffin. I have told him so many times over the years that with the amount he smoked and drank, either his lungs or his liver would take him from us before he was sixty. He is sixty-two now, but it will be over in a few weeks, thanks to his liver and his lungs. If you need to talk to him, you should not put it off longer than necessary.'

She looked down for a moment, then quickly continued.

'I know what you are thinking: why am I sitting here when my husband is in hospital? Well, it is partly that I have never liked hospitals. But most of all, it is because I can't bear to see him. He is just a shadow of what he once was, and the only thing left in his life is pain. I always go the minute they call and say that he wants to see me, which is not very often, but it won't make it any easier for us when it happens either. One of us has to keep things going, for the sake of the children and the people here. So that is why I would rather sit here with this old photograph. I want to remember him as he once was, not as what he has become.'

The tears were streaming down her cheeks now and I did not know what to do to stop them. I waited for a couple of minutes and then pointed tentatively to the other picture. It was a more recent photograph of an easily recognizable older woman and four dressed-up children sitting on the floor smiling, in front of a Christmas tree and a pile of presents.

'Anton's life went to pieces after the war, and with it so did mine and our family life. And in last few years the fight has only got harder. He struggled to do his work, and every kroner he could get his hands on went on cigarettes and booze. Christmas and New Year have always been the highlight of the year, as all our children and grandchildren come here, and out of consideration to them he managed to stay relatively sober for those few days. But last autumn, I was at my wits' end. We owed money and I had no more friends I could ask for a loan. I desperately needed eighty kroner to pay off the most urgent creditors before Christmas and a hundred more for the Christmas presents and food. I had no idea how I was going to get hold of even fifty kroner. I had nothing left of any value that could be pawned. And then, like a miracle, Kristian stood right here and gave me four fifty-kroner notes. So I swallowed my pride and accepted it. It felt terrible to peddle lies for Christmas and I cried myself to sleep more than once. But then the grandchildren could celebrate Anton's last Christmas with him, with better food and bigger presents than ever before. And I comforted myself with the thought that people had accepted hush money for worse reasons.'

I looked at the picture of the caretaker's wife with her grandchildren and realized that it was true that many other people would certainly have accepted dirtier money for far more dubious reasons than that. So I told her the truth – that on a personal level it was very easy to understand and that we could no doubt overlook the legal implications, as long as it was simply a matter of amending an oral statement. And on the condition that we now and in the future were told the truth and nothing but the truth. The caretaker's wife was mightily relieved and crossed her heart and promised to do so.

'The fact that your husband was active in the Resistance during the war is new to me. Was he in contact with Harald Olesen at the time, do you know?'

The caretaker's wife beamed at the thought of the old days and gave me a proud smile before continuing.

'But of course I know. It was in fact Harald Olesen who asked my husband to join. I can still remember them shaking hands on it, at the kitchen table right here. I helped a bit myself later on. On several occasions we hid refugees in the cellar, until Olesen found a way to get them over the border to Sweden. Anton was just one of many helpers at the time. Harald Olesen was always on the go and managed to build up a big network between here and the border. I have often thought that he must have been a remarkably strong man to not only have coped with all that responsibility during the war, but also to have managed to live with the memories of everything he had experienced.'

I realized that we might be on to something interesting now – something that could lead to a motive for murder.

'Given the way things turned out later, did you or Anton ever direct your frustration at Olesen?'

The caretaker's wife shook her head adamantly.

'We never felt any ill will towards him. How could we? It was the war, and how could anyone know what would happen to Anton later? We were proud to live in the same building as Harald Olesen, even though we lived in the basement, three floors below him. Even in the past few years, Anton would always pick up and drink less whenever he spoke to his old hero. Olesen never really understood how bad things were with Anton, but he did realize that life was difficult in the basement. And he gave us more and more wonderful presents for our birthdays and Christmas each year. Harald Olesen was a good man, always was, and I haven't got a word to say against him and cannot understand who would murder him. I cannot think of anyone from the war who might be of importance to the murder, but maybe my husband knows more.'

I nodded. The caretaker, Anton Hansen, who was currently in hospital, was someone I needed to talk to as soon as possible. I only had one crucial question left to ask his wife.

'But what about Mrs Lund? Did you never think of her?'

'Of course I thought about her and the baby, and more than once it struck me that what he was doing was an enormous betrayal to them both. But Kristian is a good man, someone who has worked his way up. He works long days and has no doubt found it difficult to live up to the expectations of his parents-in-law. The only time her parents came here, they looked at me and the building in disgust. And Kristian took such good care of his sick mother – the last time she was here, he more or less carried her in. He's never had a father, you see, so it's not been easy for him. There is not a bad bone in his wife, and she is very sweet with the child, but she has never been denied anything she wants in life, and she has no idea what it is like to have an alcoholic husband or to grow up without a father. Kristian would have to do something very wrong for me to side with her against him. I have thought many a time that he would be far better suited to the hard-working Swedish student than the doll that he's married to who has never had a problem.'

I thought to myself that the class war was still alive and kicking, at least in this basement flat in Torshov. And that the more I learned about the residents, the less relations on the stairs were what they seemed. The caretaker's wife and her 'absent' husband could also be far more significant players than I had at first assumed.

The caretaker's wife smiled sadly when I said that as a matter of procedure, I would have to see all the residents' bank books, including hers. She got up heavily and pulled a worn red post-office savings book out from a drawer and handed it to me.

'There is not much to brag about there for a lifetime's savings, but it is more than I had when Anton was still at home,' she said, with a tired, tight smile.

I had to agree with her after a quick check. According to her post-office savings book, the caretaker's wife from the basement had forty-eight kroner in her account, and that really was not a lot to boast about for a hard-working life. All the same, she had managed to save what little she could over the past few months. Five months previously, her balance had been four kroner. Wherever the 250,000 kroner that had disappeared from Harald Olesen's account in the past year had gone, it certainly was not concealed in this savings account.

I had thought of going up to the Lunds to ask a few questions and then on to Sara Sundqvist, but the caretaker's wife had noted that Kristian Lund had driven to work around nine, after ringing his secretary and asking her to meet him there, even though it was Sunday. On his way out, he had commented that he was behind with the stocktake and needed some time to himself to think. After a hasty consultation with myself, I decided that Kristian Lund was the next person I should speak to. So I asked the caretaker's wife to phone him at work. I told him in brief that I had to talk to him as soon as possible, and it would perhaps be just as easy if I came to see him at the sports shop. There was silence on the other end of the line before he took the hint and replied that that would be fine. I told him I would be there in about a quarter of an hour, and he assured me that his secretary would keep an eye out for me and open the door.

II

The sports shop where Kristian Lund was manager was airy and modern, with double doors and a large display window facing onto a well-frequented street. It crossed my mind that a position as manager here was no doubt well paid and a good springboard for furthering a career in business, but I did not have time to reflect on this. Kristian Lund's secretary turned out to be a petite blonde of about twenty-five and appeared at the door within seconds. Her body was slim and firm, as was the hand that she held out when she told me brightly that her name was Elise Remmen and that 'our darling shop manager' was waiting for me in his office. I followed her shapely back through the shop and down a long corridor of office doors. Elise Remmen enthused that the sports business was on the offensive and that this chain was leading the competition, so several other shops had recently moved their administration here.

On this Sunday, however, it was only in the shop manager's office that the light was on and the door was open.

Kristian Lund stood waiting with his hand held out over the desk. I struggled to recognize him at first. Secure in his own work environment and with the murder now a few days past, he suddenly gave the impression of being a well-built, relaxed and solid man I could trust. Had it not been for the fact that I had met him before – and had he not been caught in the act of lying.

Kristian Lund held his mask well while his irritatingly nice secretary was in the room. She asked whether I would like a coffee or a tea and smiled so invitingly that I almost said yes. Kristian Lund then informed his secretary in a loud, clear voice that this was simply a matter of routine questions in connection with the murder of his neighbour and asked her to close the door behind her and carry on with the stocktake. She chirped 'of course' and flew out of the room, closing the door gently behind her.

As soon as we were alone, Kristian Lund changed character. His eyes became sharper and his movements more tense. This reinforced my impression that he was quite the human chameleon, with a talent for changing his appearance according to the circumstances.

Neither of us wanted to start the conversation, so we each sat there contemplating the other for a couple of minutes. Kristian Lund fished out a cigarette and lit it. It was like a fencing duel in which neither of us wanted to make the first advance, though one of us would have to eventually.

'So, how can I help you today?' he asked, in the end.

I instantly took the opportunity to launch a frontal attack. 'First of all, I would like to know why you lied about your mother when we last spoke.'

A twitch rippled across Kristian Lund's face. Then he shook his head a couple of times.

'Hmm, lied . . . Well, perhaps I didn't tell you all that I should have done. I realized that afterwards, that I should have mentioned that she was a member of the NS and was sentenced for treason after the war. A good detective such as yourself would of course find that out. But I didn't think that my mother's views during the war had anything to do with the murder case, which seemed complicated enough as it was. And what is more, I am fed up with the fact that I, even after my mother's death, have to answer for things she did in her youth. I have tried to separate my life from it, and that has not always been easy!'

Suddenly, there was a trace of the same bitterness in Kristian Lund's voice that I had heard in Konrad Jensen's.

'I do not deny that my mother was once a Nazi, and that she worked for an inhumane regime whose ideology I deplore, but to me, she was never a Nazi; she was just my mother. And not many I know have a better or kinder mother, especially given all the problems she had after the war. We lived with my grandparents for three years before my mother got an underpaid job as a cleaner. I don't know how many times I heard or saw people shout abuse at her on the street. And I, who was not even born in 1940, was eleven before I made a friend who was allowed to ask me home. Things did get better after that. Two friends came to my twelfth party, five to my thirteenth and nine to my four-teenth, but there was always a shadow that Mother could not shake off. When I was confirmed and my mother stood up alone in church, several of the parents booed.'

He shook his head in indignation – and continued to let off new steam and old hurt.

'I swore that I would never allow myself to be broken, but instead would show everyone what I was made of. And I have succeeded. My success was Mother's only triumph after the war. She was persecuted and struggled with various complexes for years. And when the worst of it was finally over, she got cancer, thanks no doubt to all the cigarettes: I grew up in a cloud of smoke.'

He looked at his cigarette with sudden disgust and stubbed it out aggressively in the ashtray on his desk.

'I keep trying to stop, but it's not that easy . . . You must excuse us if we seem a little nervous at the moment – it has been a difficult winter. Just as things were starting to settle after my mother's funeral and the christening of our boy, this murder happens. Mother fought bravely to the end, but was unlucky. Her last wish was that she would live long enough to see and hold her first grandchild. She lived four weeks longer than the doctor said she would, but our baby was born too late – by only three days. It has been an extremely demanding and painful time.'

I found all this very interesting and wanted to deal with some more details about Kristian Lund's situation, which was without doubt not easy.

'Do your parents-in-law know about your mother's history?'

Kristian's laughter was as unexpected as it was short and bitter.

'I dreaded telling them for a long time, but it was not a problem – and there was no reason for it to be. My father-in-law is worth over four million and earned at least three-quarters of that trading with the occupying forces during the war. His companies broke all records in terms of turnover and profit. But do you think he was sentenced or abused by anyone after the war? Oh no, no one dared to reproach a factory owner from Bærum. A single mother from Drammen, on the other hand, was fair game for anyone. It is a shameful story. But I still do not see what my mother's sad fate has to do with the murder of my neighbour.'

I nodded, trying to be sympathetic.

'Nor do I, really. But I would like to know more about your father, if only to ensure that it has nothing to do with the case.'

He laughed again and shook his head firmly.

'That won't be easy. Apparently no one other than my mother knows my father's name, and she is dead. That was the only bone of contention I had with my mother. I understood from a comment she once made that it was someone that she had had a relationship with for some time, and that it could not have been anyone else, but she never told me his name. I nagged and nagged her when I was a teenager. When things were at their worst, I refused to talk to her for a month because she would not tell me. But Mother was stubborn. The only answer she gave was that he had betrayed her and had never cared about me, so it would only make things worse if I knew who he was. Then, when I was around eighteen or nineteen, I said that I agreed with her and seldom asked after that. I tried to convince myself that if that was how he had behaved, he was not the father I would want anyway. But it remained a big question in my life, particularly when I went to business school and was the only one in the class who could not ask his father for money.'

This was becoming more and more interesting. The question of Kristian Lund's father was yet another little mystery that I wanted to clear up.

'And you have no idea either?'

He shook his head.

'I spent a lot of time thinking about it in my youth. Physically, I am fair like my mother and look very like her, so there was not much to be had there. But one of my science teachers once remarked that with a smart brain like mine, I must have an exceptionally intelligent father. I lived on that compliment for a long time, and it was true. My mother was attractive when she was young, and always kind, but she was not particularly intelligent. She helped me with my homework when I was small, but was not of much help once I had finished primary school. Whereas I was top of my class in practically every subject, certainly in middle school. So it is highly likely that my father was – or is – an intelligent man. But otherwise, I have no idea. I was conceived sometime around May or June 1940, so that leaves a number of options. It could have been a German soldier, a Norwegian Nazi-sympathizer or some other Norwegian. My mother and grandparents spoke very little about that time later, so I do not have much to go on. Nowadays I try to think about it as little as possible. And I hope it is of no relevance to the murder case.'

I nodded.

'We both hope so. But we also have to talk about a certain young woman who lives – and was at home – in the building in which the murder took place, and whom you definitely lied about when we first spoke together.'

The reaction was instant. There was a flash in Kristian

Lund's eyes. With a slightly shaky hand he lit a new cigarette and took a couple of puffs before he answered.

'I know what you are talking about. Was it the caretaker's wife or Sara herself who told you?'

I shook my head.

'Neither of them. I drew my own conclusions based on the information I had, and probability.'

He nodded with approval.

'Impressive of you and reassuring for me. I am beginning to believe that you will indeed find the murderer. But that has nothing to do with the murder either. It is, of course, information that may be of some importance in terms of alibis and the like, and I apologize for lying, but I have got myself into rather a sticky situation. My wife does not need to know anything about this, does she?'

I agreed, but added quickly: 'On the condition that it is of no relevance to the murder. And that you now give me a better account, which is more honest than the last one!'

He nodded vehemently. It appeared that Kristian Lund had no problems talking about deeply personal things. My impression that he was somewhat egocentric but also an intelligent and socially gifted person was reinforced.

'I realize that the fact that I am having an extramarital affair with a woman who lives next door does not inspire confidence. Especially as I have such an attractive, good wife and a sweet little boy. I am afraid the explanation may take some time.'

I indicated that I was in no rush. Kristian Lund's life was something that interested me more and more. He nodded gratefully, leaned back in his chair and thought for a few moments before starting.

'It started sometime last year with a rather generous dose of good old-fashioned desire.'

He sat in silence for a moment. Then his face tightened before he carried on in a self-pitying vein once again.

'But in fact it all goes back to my mother and my childhood. For many years I was the boy who none of the girls wanted to touch or admit that she liked. By the time I turned seventeen, I had still not kissed a girl. One experience in particular left its mark, even though it was completely innocent. When I was fourteen, we went on a school trip and all the boys in the class got a goodnight hug from one of the girls. Except me. "There are limits. Even for hugs," she said with a cold, sarcastic smile. Everyone laughed. I cried all night and swore that one day I would be a success. Then when I was eighteen, everything suddenly changed. I played in a band and was the star of the football team. I had accumulated such a vast lack of intimacy that I exploited my advantage for all it was worth. The girl who refused to give me a hug when we were fourteen was one of several who then lay moaning under me when she was nineteen.'

He broke into a smile. It was obvious that this episode was one of the better memories from his youth.

'I am certain there was an underlying need for self-vindication and revenge on my part, but also physical desire. I was an active young man with a strong libido. Young women soon excited me more than football matches. But then I got older and wiser, and my hormones settled. The atmosphere at business school was more mature and serious, and after I met Karen, I never touched anyone else. Until . . .'

The word hung in the air for a moment before he finished.

'Until Sara stood there one day, glimmering on the stairs,

and said that she had just moved in. I felt a surge of excitement and desire stronger than ever before.'

He leaned over the table towards me.

'You are further from those days than I am, but you must at least once have stood slightly too close to one of those annoyingly beautiful temptresses between seventeen and twenty-three . . . who appears to have unwittingly tightened her belt too much, undone three buttons on her blouse and be standing a bit too close. With a provocative smile that seems to say that you can see this much whenever you like, but no more.'

I waved him on without answering. I indeed had stood too close to at least one young lady who fitted that description. And I noted that we were now on very familiar terms.

'No girl provoked me or turned me on more when I was a lad. Sometimes I lied and made promises that I had no intention of keeping, even when I was sober. I believed that if a girl was giving out mixed messages, she had to accept that the opposite party might do the same. So I played the game, and gained more than I lost, I would say. Certainly, more than once they got a taste of their own medicine and were left crying in their own trap. Sara gave exactly that impression when she stood there in front of me. She was older, taller and more dignified in a way, in her long black dress with only two buttons open at the neck. But her smile had the same teasing, tempting effect, and the impact was all the greater because she otherwise appeared so respectable and intelligent. Her smile seemed to say that no one had been here before and being the first would not be easy. It felt like an open challenge as she stood there no more than an arm's length from me, with her perfect curves under wraps. I have always been attracted to tall, dark women, and suddenly here I was facing my dream woman who was taller and darker than any I had met before. So I fell hopelessly in love, right there on the stairs, with her soft hand in mine. I found myself thinking, as I had in my youth, That smile is going to change and that dress is coming off!'

Talking about his conquests obviously put Kristian Lund in a better mood and he continued his story briskly. I saw no reason to interrupt him as yet.

'A couple of hours after that first encounter, the worst of the shock had died down. But when my wife fell asleep, I lay awake beside her for hours thinking about the beautiful and tantalizing Sara. The following morning, when I was about to drive to work, she so happened to come out at the same time as me. So I played it instinctively, asked where she was going and said that I needed to pop by somewhere close to the university, so perhaps she would like a lift. Her smile was even more provocative than the day before and she immediately got into the car. We hit it off straightaway and had more to talk about than expected. I extended what was already a very long detour by adding a couple of extra turns, so I was almost half an hour late to work. I blamed the unexpected heavy traffic, which was as close to the truth as I could get. The next morning, I left home twenty minutes earlier in the hope that she would pop up again. An unusually beautiful young woman was waiting impatiently for me by my car. Two long, slim feminine legs dressed in tight denim trousers that emphasized her great shape, stamping on the pavement to keep warm. She nodded and gave me the most irresistible smile when I appeared by the car. I smiled back, got in behind the wheel and indicated that she should get in beside me. And off we drove together – as if it was the most natural thing in the world. I think it was when I saw her standing there on the second day that I knew that I would win – if I wanted to win and played my cards right. So I carried on playing the game, inspired. I drove her to the university and mentioned when I would be leaving the next morning. The second day, I got a hug, and on the third, a kiss on the cheek.'

He fell abruptly silent, but then continued happily when I asked him what had happened on the fourth day.

'It all started as a bit of fun and a way of switching off during a very difficult period when I had too much to think about. It was only a few months since my mother had died. I was probably annoyed with my wife, who only thought about our boy and not about me. It was also a busy time with long days at work. The idea that a woman as beautiful as Sara might be interested in me gave me a boost. So a few days later, I let slip that my wife was taking our son to visit a friend in Bygdøy that afternoon. Sara gave me a knowing smile and suggested that I take the opportunity to come by and have a coffee with her. I am still not sure how far we had thought of going, but the invitation to coffee was our last chance to turn back in time. Sitting in the car, I could have said that it might not be appropriate. Or I could have not knocked on Sara's door after I had driven my wife out to Bygdøy. But once I had crossed the threshold, and she stood there with her enticing smile, wearing the same dress as the first time we met . . . there was no going back. We had some coffee and then some wine and we sat on the sofa, but soon we were intoxicated by each other. Somehow we managed to lose our inhibitions after only two glasses of wine. I remember that she sat on my lap and I tried to whisper that we had to stop this now or her dress would end up on the floor and I would be on top of her before we knew it, but my intention was hardly to warn her off. The next thing I remember is that both her dress and the smile had disappeared and she was lying almost naked, moaning on the bed. I had no awareness of anything other than the two of us, and my only desire was to get her knickers off. And when they slid down her thighs . . .'

A dreamy expression slipped over Kristian Lund's face. For a few moments he sat behind his desk lost in his own thoughts. Then he smiled with momentary self-irony.

'Even if one of us had wanted to, it was by then far too late to stop, both mentally and physically. Only brute force could have held me back, and it would have required handcuffs and a horde of constables. It was wrong, of course, thinking of my wife and baby son. But strangely enough, I have never regretted it either. She is far stronger than she appears, both physically and mentally. It was wilder than anything I had experienced in the bedroom before. To feel my tall, dark dream woman underneath me, minute after minute, until I finally collapsed exhausted with a loud groan, was truly the greatest love and triumph I have ever felt in my life. It felt as though I really was the first to be allowed in, and to scale such dizzy heights. Which is what she told me later, and I do believe it was true.'

I waited for a continuation that never came. Kristian Lund remained in his dream world for a while longer.

'And then . . .'

He looked up, distracted, at once accusing and apologetic.

'Then we lay there shamelessly naked for a few hours more. We smoked and talked about life and love, until I looked at my watch and discovered that I should have picked up my wife in Bygdøy five minutes earlier. Fortunately, Karen accepted my excuse that I had lain down for a while and lost track of time without question. Though in many ways, it was in fact true . . .'

He gave what I assumed was meant to be a disarming smile, but I would not be sidetracked.

'But this was not on the day of the murder, was it?'

He immediately understood what I meant and shook his head with a grave expression.

'No, not at all. It was on 12 November last year. I went to bed with my wife as normal that night, but slept very little. My mind was elsewhere. At first, I thought I could avoid Sara for a few days in the hope that it would pass, leaving nothing but a sweet memory. I tried getting up half an hour earlier than usual the next morning, but there she was again, waiting. I thought I might explain to her that we could not carry on meeting, but instead the opposite happened. In the course of the journey, I realized that she was the great love of my life, in both body and mind. It was the first time that I had not only fallen in love with and been physically attracted to a woman, but also felt that we shared a destiny. The love of my life was right there in front of me, living in the same building. Two days later, I was in her bed again. And since then I have bitterly regretted the fact that I was already married to someone else when I met her. Sara would of course like me to marry her, but understands that it is not easy to leave a wife and child.'

'And in this case, you would also be leaving a rather large sum of money, would you not?'

I had expected an angry outburst, but instead he gave a crooked smile and gently shook his head.

'A very large sum of money to be more precise. My wife is an only child and my father-in-law is a canny businessman who has used every opportunity given to him during and after the war effectively. And I must admit that the thought has crossed my mind. Those who say that money means nothing have not grown up poor. But now I have a well-paid job and good financial prospects. So, in fact, it is not something that weighs heavily in this case. In some ways, Karen's father's wealth makes it far simpler. She will never suffer financially, no matter what I do. Sara, on the other hand, lives on a student loan and what money her adoptive parents can afford. I have realized that if I am to let her go, I must at least give her a decent sum to help her on her way.'

Kristian Lund sat pondering for a while before carrying on. And I thought to myself that I could not recall having ever met such a romantic cynic before.

'It is heaven and hell at the same time. I have everything – the great love of my life with Sara and domestic bliss with my wife and son. But every day I am torn between them, and live in constant fear of being discovered. It is an unbearable existence that cannot go on for much longer. In the meantime, I simply keep brushing the problem to one side. The greatest risk was that the caretaker's wife would notice. She is always there, and is both alert and wise. But we understand each other well; she reminds me of my deceased mother. Things are tight and she is in constant need of money, like Mother. So I reached an agreement with her that would give me an alibi, should my wife, or anyone else for that matter, start prying. Of course, I had little idea then that it would be the police who came and asked the questions.'

So far, everything was in perfect accord with what the

caretaker's wife had told me, but Kristian Lund still had one more question to answer.

'We have now confirmed that Harald Olesen was killed earlier in the evening than first assumed. The gunshot that was heard was from a cassette tape, and Olesen was killed at some point between eight and ten o'clock that evening. How does that sit with your alibi?'

Kristian Lund rolled his eyes and thought for a moment.

'I declare myself guilty of adultery and lies, but absolutely innocent with regard to the murder of my neighbour. I guess I do still have an alibi of sorts. Not only the caretaker's wife, but also Darrell Williams and Konrad Jensen saw me come in at eight, and Sara could also confirm that I was in her company from then until nine o'clock. I dare say that there was a minute or two between the time that I left Sara and came home to my wife. But surely it would not even be theoretically possible for me to have entered Harald Olesen's flat, committed a murder and left again within that time?'

I nodded rather vaguely.

'Hardly. But I am sure that you do understand the uncertainty here. And we cannot simply rely on the statements of two women who both have potential motives for helping you.'

He nodded in agreement.

'I do understand that, and also that I do not appear to be entirely trustworthy. I should have told you about Mother and Sara. But even though I have lied to you, and even though I am not proud of some of the things that I have done in my life, I could never kill another person. And as far as the murder of Harald Olesen is concerned, I have a clean conscience. I was just as shocked and baffled as the others when

I heard the shot. In addition, it must still be hard to see any motive for me to murder him?'

I had to agree with that, but his question reminded me of something I had almost forgotten.

'That certainly seems to be the case. However, I must still ask that you and all the other residents let us check any bank accounts you have.'

Kristian Lund jumped and immediately looked more wary. He sounded exasperated and almost aggressive when he replied.

'I am sorry – I do not understand why that is necessary. What could you find in my account that could be of any relevance whatsoever to the murder?'

I felt that I was getting very hot now. I gave him my most piercing look and replied curtly: 'I am afraid that we cannot divulge that for technical reasons. All I can say is that we are routinely checking the accounts of all the residents.'

For a few seconds Kristian Lund looked deeply perplexed. Then he shook his head in irritation.

'I must say that I feel that this is becoming too personal. And I have work to do, so I am afraid that I will not be able to answer any more questions this morning. I would just like to point out that I know nothing about Harald Olesen's murder. And in my vulnerable position, it is hurtful that you do not believe me. I will consider the situation and discuss it with my wife, but for now I am afraid that I cannot give you access to our bank accounts. In the meantime, you may think whatever you like is the reason for this.'

I really had no idea what to make of either Kristian Lund or his accounts, but I realized that I was going to get no further with him here and now, and had more than enough to be getting on with. So I asked him to stay in the office for the next couple of hours, without phoning anyone at 25 Krebs' Street, and got up to leave.

The young Miss Elise Remmen was standing beaming right outside the door and showed me out with great efficiency. And it must be said that as I followed her as she sashayed through the shop, I did wonder how well she actually knew Kristian Lund. He seemed to have a highly developed and enviable knack of keeping the company of attractive women. But I chose only to exchange pleasantries about sport and sports equipment with Elise Remmen, rather than ask troublesome questions about her boss. It suited us both. She twittered away, happy as a lark, and said I would be welcomed back whenever I had the opportunity. If my thoughts had not been caught up in a murder investigation, I may well have been tempted.

With the exception of his reluctance to allow me access to his bank account, I found Kristian Lund's revised statement to be relatively credible. All that remained was to establish what the other residents in 25 Krebs' Street, in particular the young Miss Sara Sundqvist, might have to add to their earlier statements.

III

When I got to 25 Krebs' Street, I made a brief visit to the Lunds' flat first. Karen Lund was at home with her young son, and both were in a splendid Sunday mood. Mrs Lund listened to my story of the stereo's secret with an open mouth, while her son was obviously less impressed and babbled away happily. It was swiftly established that, given the circumstances, it was now technically possible that Karen Lund could have carried out the murder before her husband came home at nine. She assured me, however, that she was not capable of murder, and that if she was going to carry out a murder, she would certainly have to make sure she had a babysitter first.

There was not much more to be had there, and I have to admit that I stayed no longer than strictly necessary. It felt awkward standing with the carefree Mrs Lund, now that I knew her husband was not the loyal family man she believed him to be. As she followed me to the door, I faced a bit of a dilemma when Karen Lund asked if the misunderstanding regarding when her husband had come home on the evening of the murder had been cleared up. I avoided saying anything definite as best I could by replying that there was no longer any doubt that he came home to the flat at nine o'clock on the evening in question. She seemed to be relieved to hear that and smiled brightly. I found myself wondering whether Mrs Lund really was as simple and happy as she seemed, or whether she might have a more serious and dangerous side.

More drama awaited on the first floor. Sara Sundqvist was still visibly shaken by the case and smiled very tentatively when she opened the door to me. However, now that the worst of the shock had passed, she had put on her black dress, leaving the top button undone, and I immediately understood how Kristian Lund had felt when I sat down beside her on the sofa. Her beauty was gracious and could undoubtedly be extremely tempting if she so wished.

It appeared that Kristian Lund had kept his word not to call. To begin with, Sara Sundqvist had very little to add to her previous statement. She was obviously taken aback when I told her about the stereo player, but smiled and complimented me on solving the mystery of how the murder was committed. She then had to admit that she did not have an alibi, as she had been at home from a quarter past four until after the body was found. And she had seen or heard no mysterious movements out in the hallway.

Sadly, she could not tell me much more about her parents. Her adoptive parents had been told only that they were a young Jewish couple, originally from Lithuania, with no other known children. Her parents were registered as dead in 1944, but no further details were recorded. She had been given the names Felix and Anna Marie Rozenthal, born in 1916 and 1918 respectively. Her own given name was Sara Rozenthal, and she had been born in 1943. But her adoptive parents had been given no other details, either about her parents' disappearance or about how she ended up with a Swedish adoption agency in Gothenburg in 1944. She had wondered about it a lot in her youth. Following her twenty-first birthday, she had tried to find out more, with no success. She was told that there was no more information recorded anywhere, and as far as anybody knew, her parents had never been registered as domiciled in Sweden. She had gradually learned to accept the uncertainty surrounding her parents, tried to live her own life and regarded her kind adoptive parents as her only parents.

Her eyes slid over to the window as she spoke.

'But as long as one does not know what happened or have a grave to go to, one can always daydream that they are still alive, somewhere,' she added, in a quiet voice.

When I mentioned her bank account, she hesitated at first

and then asked with a furrowed brow why I needed to see it. She responded swiftly to my reply that I could not answer that for reasons relating to the investigation. Rather reluctantly, she gave me a small Swedish bank book that showed a balance of 55,623 kroner. I allowed myself to comment that it was no mean sum for a student with no other income. She informed me then that she had first inherited some money from her adoptive grandfather and then received a whole year's student grant in March, which together totalled 50,000. This did not sound improbable, and given that she had produced her bank book straightaway, I decided to accept the explanation for the time being.

'However, we do, unfortunately, have to talk about your close relationship with one of your neighbours,' I said in a sharper tone.

She paled and froze for a few seconds, and then asked how I had found out about it. I replied in all honesty that it was thanks to a wise analysis of known facts. I added that Kristian Lund had since been forced to admit the relationship, but that there was no reason for his wife to know about it – on the condition that she now gave me a complete and truthful account. Sara Sundqvist sighed with relief and regained some of her colour.

'In many ways, it is a good thing that you found out. It has bothered me tremendously that I lied so much to you about it,' she said, and moved fractionally closer to me on the sofa. She paused pensively for a couple of minutes. I let her take the time she needed without pressing. It was starting to dawn on me that she was a reflective young lady who did not like to make important decisions without thinking them through.

'I hope you will be kind and not judge me too harshly. I have given considerable thought to his wife and son, and do feel bad for them,' she admitted.

Then she was silent again.

'But . . .' I prompted, after a few moments.

'But I can live with it. And in any case, she has almost everything: two parents, a child, lots of money and no worries about the past or the future. I deserve him more than she does. Kristian and I have both worked our way up from a difficult start in life. And she would probably be happy with any handsome and rich man, whereas I can only be happy with him.'

I resisted the momentary temptation to ask why she was so fond of Kristian Lund. She told me of her own accord: 'It was not planned. It all started with a little social flirtation, of which I have had many without it leading to anything else. But this time it did. The flirtation spun out of control – in a wonderful way I have never experienced before. Suddenly, there we were one afternoon when his wife was away, without me quite realizing what was happening. But I have to take my fair share of the responsibility, as well as him. And I am ashamed to say that I do not regret it one bit, rather just hope that it will continue and that he will leave his wife. It is still a rollercoaster of highs and lows. I go to bed every evening with the hope that in the morning he will tell me that he is leaving his wife, and wake up every morning with the fear that today he will tell me that he is staying with her. Every time the doorbell or telephone rings, I jump and imagine that it is his wife and that all hell is about to break loose. I realize that it is not easy for him either, as his son is so young. But all is fair in love and war, and this is the one great love of my life.

So I hope and believe still that he will choose me. In the meantime, I can scarcely think of anything else, day or night. Things cannot go on like this, I thought the day before the murder, and it has not got any easier since.'

I nodded in agreement. Whatever one's view on the morality of it, it was very much in line with Kristian Lund's account.

'Could you please explain to me what it is that you like so much about him?'

To be fair, the question was not strictly related to the murder case, but I was increasingly curious about the phenomenon Kristian Lund and was still struggling to understand the various people involved in the case. Sara Sundqvist had definitely opened the way for heartfelt confidences now and carried on with enthusiasm.

'He is everything that I have ever dreamed of in a man. There is the physical aspect, obviously. I have always been attracted to blond men of my height, and he has just the right physique and is so elegant. So I thought he was the most handsome man I had ever seen the first time I saw him. But I still would not have fallen for him if he had not also proved to be the nicest man in the world. He is intelligent, hard-working and kind. The fact that he has a wife and son in a way makes him even more reliable and trustworthy. He is the first person that I feel has truly understood me. Of course, we are very different in many ways, but we still understand each other so well. Probably due to our similar backgrounds from the war, I think. He has grown up without a father, and I have grown up without either of my parents.'

I understood what she meant. I actually felt my sympathies torn between the mistress and the wife living as they did, side by side on the first floor of 25 Krebs' Street. The latter appeared to have few admirers here, other than her young son. The same was apparently true of the next person I was going to visit.

As I walked down the stairs, I pondered whether the ever more mysterious Sara Sundqvist had been aware of the fact that I too was a blond and well-built man of about her height.

IV

It took about ninety seconds from the time that I rang the bell at 1B until the door was opened. And I was soon to discover why. If the former member of the NS Konrad Jensen had been disillusioned and morose when I first visited him, he was now fearful, if not terrified. To begin with, he only opened the door a crack to ask who it was, and on hearing my voice, it took another whole minute before two scared eyes appeared. He rushed to lock the door behind me, putting on the safety chain before following me into the sitting room. Here he sank down heavily onto the sofa and hid his face in his hands.

'Did you see Petter?' he asked suddenly, in a choked voice.

I shook my head, having no idea what he meant. Konrad Jensen took his hands from his face, but stared blindly into space before continuing.

'He's parked on the second street to the right, and last night someone wrote, "Nazi murderer," all over him, the caretaker's wife told me. And this morning . . .'

His voice broke and he needed a minute to compose himself.

'This morning, she came and told me that someone had

battered him with a sledgehammer! All the windows have been smashed and the body bashed. This is the end for Petter. It would cost more to repair him than to buy a new car. You'll have to have a look at him this evening, if you think there's anything to be gained by it, because as soon as the insurance folk get here, it'll be the scrapyard for him. I can't bear to see him like that.'

The tears welled up in Konrad Jensen's eyes. It seemed that the damage to his car was more of a shock than the death of Harald Olesen.

'I know it's pathetic for a grown man to cry over his car, but Petter was the only person I could trust, if you see what I mean. When he goes to the scrapyard, I won't have any friends. I'll wait to get a new car until this is all over, otherwise the same thing will just happen again. And I daren't go out at the moment. I've been shopping at the Co-op for twenty years now, but on Saturday, the caretaker's wife came and told me that they didn't want to see me in the shop anymore. A number of customers had threatened to go elsewhere if they saw me there. My life is crashing around my ears, just when I had finally managed to get some kind of control!'

I promised to take a look at the car before I left and ask a constable to look into this act of vandalism. Konrad Jensen nodded with resignation, and sounded a touch calmer when he continued.

'Thank you. I only hope that you find the murderer before the Resistance people or some young louts find me, or before life in here simply becomes unbearable!'

I tried to calm him more by saying that there was surely no reason to fear for his life and body. At which Konrad Jensen hauled himself up from the sofa. He dragged his feet out into the kitchen and came back with a small bundle of letters.

'Well, I haven't received any private letters since the card my sister sent for my fiftieth birthday, but yesterday, I suddenly got seven, and they're not pleasant reading.'

He was absolutely right. The letters were not pleasant reading. The senders of all seven remained anonymous, without signature, and they all took for granted that Konrad Jensen had murdered Harald Olesen. Four of them could qualify as aggravated harassment, and the other three were plain murder threats. Having seen them, it was not hard to understand why Konrad Jensen did not dare to show himself on the street.

I immediately offered to post a constable by the front door, if that would make him feel safer. This prompted an unexpected moment of emotion. Konrad Jensen started to cry when he took my hand.

'Thank you so much. I never thought that I would hear a policeman offer to guard Konrad Jensen, or imply that Konrad Jensen's life was worth anything. But it's the way things are. I'll have to make sure not to go outdoors and be very careful about who I let in. If my time is up, it will stop, with or without a policeman standing guard at the front door. But it is not a very nice feeling. I always thought that Petter and I would go together, so now that he's gone, I feel that I'm close to the end too.'

I felt an overwhelming urge to cheer him up a bit – and to get on with the investigation. So I used the opportunity to tell him about our breakthroughs in the investigation and the mystery surrounding the stereo player. Konrad Jensen congratulated me, but found it unsettling that such a calculating murderer was on the loose. He repeated three times that it was definitely not him who had planned it, but recognized that the adjusted time of murder meant that he too was now without an alibi.

To my question regarding his bank account, he replied with a fleeting, humiliated smile that he had nothing to hide. He had inherited little more than 2,000 kroner from his parents and had scrimped and saved the rest from his earnings of around 1,000 kroner a year. Konrad Jensen's post-office savings book showed a total balance of 12,162 kroner.

'Given the rise in prices, most of that will now go on a new car. So there goes my dream of watching the football on television one day,' he added with a heavy sigh.

The question of what Konrad Jensen was actually doing out in the hallway when he met Darrell Williams on the evening of the murder was apparently more complicated. He chewed his lip before finally answering.

'Nothing at all. I just popped out into the hall because I saw through the window that the American was coming in and hoped that he would stop to chat about the football if I was there. Pathetic perhaps, but true.'

And I believed him. Konrad Jensen was a sorry figure of a man, but he told the truth – as far as I could tell thus far.

Then suddenly he became bashful and hesitated a few times before he said something that I had not expected in the least.

'When you asked if I had met Harald Olesen during the war or earlier . . . I may possibly have answered incorrectly.'

I fixed him with gimlet eyes. He held up his hands in defence.

'It was through no fault of my own. I thought you wouldn't believe me if I told you what I saw, and it's hard to be certain. It might sound strange, but I thought you would just laugh.'

I had started to get used to the fact that Konrad Jensen both thought and spoke slowly and awkwardly, but once again he came round to the matter at hand without prompting.

'I said that I had never met Harald Olesen during the war, which is true, but I think that I did meet him once just before the war. And if that is the case, it was at an NS meeting, of all places.'

This time his pause for thought was a sore test of my patience. He was absolutely right: it did sound rather odd.

'Or to be precise, outside an NS meeting. There was a party meeting in Asker in the summer of 1939 at which Quisling himself spoke, and I was there, loyal as ever, you see. An unusually attractive blonde woman a few years older than me was standing in front of me in the queue, on her own. So of course I took the chance to go in right behind her and sat down next to her. Tried to chat to her before the speech, but only got short, disinterested replies. I understood only too well that her mind was set on another and that I was no great temptation, in any case. All the same, I followed her out in the hope that I might be able to catch the same bus. But of course I didn't get the chance. She was picked up right outside by a somewhat older man in a large car. I remember thinking enviously that there was someone who had everything I wanted in life: a big, fast car and a beautiful young blonde. I only caught a glimpse of him through the car window. But when I saw pictures of Harald Olesen in the newspapers after the war, I immediately thought, Crikey –

that's the same man who picked up the beautiful young woman from the NS meeting. And I had the same thought a few years later when I first met him here, on the stairs.'

I listened to the incredible story with growing bewilderment. Konrad Jensen gave a deprecating shrug when he had finished.

'I said it was strange, and for many years I refused to believe it myself. I've never mentioned it to anyone before now. But no matter how strange it sounds, I am more or less certain that it was in fact Harald Olesen behind the wheel in the car. And then when you appeared and asked if I had ever met him before, I thought that I should mention it to you.'

I nodded in agreement.

'You were absolutely right to mention it, and I take it very seriously indeed. But it would be almost impossible to prove or disprove now – unless you have a name for this woman.'

He shook his heavy head.

'No – unfortunately, I have no idea what she was called. I've never seen her again, before or after, or I'm sure I would have remembered. Thought I knew most of the young NS members in Oslo: there were not many of us at the time.'

'What about the car – do you remember anything about it?'

Konrad Jensen lit up for a moment.

'Yes, I knew all about cars, even back then. It was a large and quite new black Volvo. I'm pretty sure it was a 1932 or 1933 model. My greatest dream was to be able to buy something like that at some point.'

As I was leaving, he added: 'I think you can strike off the caretaker's wife and the cripple. In addition to myself, of course. Not many left then if the murderer lives in the building. I'd put my money on the Jewess, and then the American – even though I like talking to him about the football. But it's really not easy to say, so you've got a hard job ahead of you.'

I certainly agreed with the latter, if not necessarily the former. I no longer had a clear main suspect, and Konrad Jensen seemed to be falling down the list.

V

Darrell Williams filled the entire doorway. His smile was as broad and his handshake as carefree as the last time we met. But even as I crossed the threshold, I had the feeling that this would be a more contentious visit. I had jotted down a few important questions that I assumed would prove a critical test of the American's diplomacy skills.

The story about the stereo player seemed to make less of an impression on him than on the other residents. He praised me for having uncovered such a cunning murder plan, but added that he had heard of similar sophisticated plots in the USA. Quite apart from the fact that he lacked a motive and a weapon, he admitted with a disarming smile that he too was now a potential murderer. He had, as the caretaker's wife had noted, come home at around eight and had sat alone in his flat with a book until five to ten, when he had gone for a short evening stroll through the quiet streets of Oslo, and on his way back in had stopped to discuss the football results with Konrad Jensen. He had not seen anyone other than Konrad Jensen out in the hallway that evening until they were outside

Harald Olesen's locked door and the other neighbours came running.

So far, the conversation was pleasant. However, when I asked whether his Norwegian girlfriend from 1945 to 1948 had a name, Darrell Williams stiffened.

'Well, of course she did,' he said, without a hint of a smile. 'But I have no idea whether she still has the same name and have no intention of looking her up. I have nothing to do with this murder and cannot see what my sweetheart from the war might have to do with it either.'

I said that I would be grateful to know her name all the same, before drawing any conclusions. He replied curtly that he did not want to give it to me – at least, not here and now.

The conversation then went from bad to worse. After the question about his girlfriend, Darrell Williams was on his guard, even before I asked about his bank account. He had no doubt that it was a routine question that we asked everyone and emphasized that he had nothing to hide personally. However, he did find it 'very uncomfortable' and, following a brief pause for thought, said that he would have to discuss it with the ambassador before he could possibly give me his bank books. It could otherwise create a precedent, the consequences of which were hard to foresee. I attempted a witty reply, saying that the practical consequences would hardly be significant if Americans in Oslo only had to give access to their bank accounts in the event that a Norwegian Resistance hero was murdered in the same building. But there was definitely no place for humour in our conversation now; he shook his head in agitation without so much as a twitch of the mouth.

I did not expect to get an answer to any more questions, but finished my list as planned all the same. First, I asked whether he was aware of the activities of an American intelligence organization called the OSS in Norway and other countries during the war, which later went on to become part of a new American intelligence organization called the CIA. Darrell Williams's eyes immediately darkened. He straightened himself up in the armchair and replied that as a diplomat with full security clearance, he of course knew of the organizations and their contribution to the fight against communism. My follow-up question as to whether he himself had been involved with either of the organizations prompted a monotone one-sentence reply that embassy staff were obviously instructed to give in response to this kind of question regarding their work. 'Neither confirm nor deny,' he said.

I had no answers as to whether Darrell Williams was in any way connected to the murder or not, but I did now know that he had another less pleasant face than the one I had seen on my first visit. He sat in the armchair focused and on guard for the remainder of the conversation. It occurred me that, despite his size, he reminded me less and less of a bear and increasingly of a tiger preparing to pounce. When I asked whether it was usual for the embassy to accommodate staff in flats in Torshov, Darrell Williams replied that he had not heard of any other cases, but that he was no expert in the embassy's accommodation policy and there were doubtless many factors to be taken into consideration. He had been offered this flat and had no objections as he found both the standard and location acceptable.

The two final and most critical questions remained. Darrell Williams was now so tense that I was mentally prepared for him to leap up at any moment. As a precaution, I inched my chair away from him before I dropped the bomb.

'Have you ever killed anyone?'

Darrell Williams remained seated, but his eyes bored into me for several seconds. I was certain that he would refuse to answer, in accordance with some diplomatic law or another, but having given it some thought, he answered with impressive composure.

'That is a personal question that does not involve anyone else, so I will gladly answer it. As a young soldier, I volunteered to serve at one of the front lines as we advanced towards Paris in the summer of 1944, following the Normandy landings. I can clearly remember the faces of two people that I know I killed. One of them was a young, fair German soldier, the other a dark-haired young Frenchwoman. I will never forget their faces, but I don't see them as often as I used to now and can live with it. They both had a swastika on their sleeve, and both had been given the chance to surrender. We were fighting in the service of our country, putting our own lives on the line in order to liberate France and the other occupied countries from the tyranny of Nazism. I have never regretted taking part.'

He sat quietly for a moment before continuing.

'They are the two that I know of. We were involved in countless chaotic exchanges of fire that left many people dead, so I can't promise that there were no others. But it was another time in another country, during the bloodiest war in history. I have not killed anyone since the war, and I have never killed a Norwegian.'

'But if it was in the service of your country and for a good cause, might you also kill someone in Norway?'

Darrell Williams sat in silence again. A pensive expression stole over his face before he answered.

'I realize that it would not be believable were I to say no, as I am still an officer in the service of my country, as I was back then. But I repeat that I have never received any such orders after the war, and have no idea as to who might have murdered Harald Olesen.'

He looked me straight in the eye when he said this and I was inclined to believe him. He too would have to be added to the list of people who I did not think had killed Harald Olesen, but who may have done it all the same. The list was starting to get quite long.

Darrell Williams followed me out and then made an unexpected conciliatory move out in the hall. He commented that this was not an easy situation for anyone. I was undoubtedly under tremendous pressure following the mysterious murder of a well-known hero from the Resistance, and he was in service on another country's territory and had to adhere to strict protocol. Given that, he would of course do whatever he could to help solve the murder. If I gave him a couple of days, he would check with his superiors and hoped that he would then be able to answer more of my questions. I enquired, almost jokingly, whether his 'superiors' meant the 'ambassador'. Darrell Williams answered in the same tone that his 'superiors' for the moment meant his 'superiors'. We shook hands and were almost friends again. He was right, of course. This was not an easy situation, either for me or for anyone else in the building. By now it was four o'clock and I still had one more person to visit.

VI

Andreas Gullestad had obviously returned home on Sunday afternoon as planned. He beamed up at me when the door eventually opened. I found myself wondering whether he was simply like that or whether another less friendly face lurked behind this jovial mask. And I intended to test that now, as soon as we were sitting comfortably in the sitting room with cups of tea in our hands. We started with a chat about his trip. He had had a pleasant visit to his childhood stamping grounds and thanked me once again for allowing him to go.

Andreas Gullestad was also astonished by both my astuteness and the murderer's cunning when I presented him with the secret of the stereo. He 'unfortunately' had to confess that he too had been alone in his flat from eight until a quarter past ten on the evening of the murder, and given the adjusted time of murder, he could no longer be struck from the list of potential murderers either. He had nothing new or exciting to tell about his neighbours' movements out in the hallway.

As to the question of money, he replied without hesitation that he had nothing to hide. He pulled out two bank books and a tax return from his desk, which confirmed his total wealth to be 800,000 kroner. He informed me that he had inherited this from his parents. They had left him both money and woodland, which he had got a favourable price for later. Most of the money was now safely deposited in an account, and the rest had been invested in stocks. He had spent some time on his investments and the shares had so far given such a favourable return that he had not needed to use any of the interest on his bank accounts to cover his living costs. The flat was paid for, and his daily expenses were not high.

When I mentioned his name, he immediately threw up his hands. He had realized after my last visit that he should have mentioned it, but had not telephoned as he did not think that it was of such great relevance to the investigation. The change in name from Ivar Storskog to Andreas Gullestad was linked to the fact that he was now handicapped. He told me that four years ago he had been 'regrettably careless' when stepping out onto a pedestrian crossing and had been knocked down by a young driver. The injuries were not life-threatening, but as a result of a spinal injury, he was now dependent on a wheelchair. He had accepted his lot with grace, but wanted to make a clean break from his previous life. He fortunately did not have to rely on government handouts, as he had money enough. He had decided it was a suitable time to change his name and had settled on his mother's maiden name, Gullestad. He was christened Ivar Andreas and had often been called Andreas by his mother and sister, so the change in his first name was not so dramatic.

When I asked about documentation regarding his injuries, he pointed without hesitation to a drawer that should contain some newspaper clippings about the accident. Which it did. Several national papers carried notices about the accident involving Ivar Storskog, and he was later interviewed by one of them about his handicap. 'If you disregard the almost illegible doctor's signature, there should be a doctor's certificate at the bottom of that pile of papers,' he said. Which also proved to be true. I apologized that I had to ask, and he assured me

117

that he understood perfectly well, 'given the grisly nature of the case'.

Probing questions about his finances and handicap seemed to make no dent in Andreas Gullestad's unrelenting good humour and friendliness. However, all this drained from his face as soon as I asked about the cause of his father's death.

'I hope you understand that it is still a very painful subject for me and I would rather not go into great detail,' he said, with some reservation.

We sipped our tea in silence; then he leaned forward towards the table and carried on.

'My father was, as you perhaps know, a very rich man and a respected pillar of the community, well known beyond the boundaries of his parish. I was his only son and the apple of his eye. No one has had a better father, and he was my greatest idol throughout my childhood. The 1930s were hard, even in Oppland, but I never saw anyone leave my father's farm empty-handed, whether they needed charity or not. In retrospect, I remember those childhood years as the happiest period of my life.'

He suddenly lowered his eyes to the table, and his lips tightened for a moment before he continued.

'Then one day when I was twelve years old, the war broke out. My father fought for the king and government in April 1940 and immediately took a leading position in the Resistance movement in the district, following the occupation. On 12 January 1941, my thirteenth birthday, of all days, five German soldiers came to arrest him. It was a terrible shock for us all, but perhaps worst for me, the youngest, having admired my father more than anything in the world. This may sound strange, but what I remember most about it all was a young German soldier. He was no more than five or six years older than me and did not seem to like the situation any more than I did. He whispered to me that hopefully everything would get sorted and I would have my father back home again soon. But that is not what happened. I saw my beloved father for the last time that day, being escorted away by soldiers. He was shot a week later. I lost my childhood innocence and much of my belief in humanity the day the Germans shot my father.'

Andreas Gullestad paused and sat lost in his own thoughts. Then he picked up the thread again.

'Losing my father during the war should perhaps be less of a tragedy for me than for many others. After all, he left us money, a forest and land, so we did not suffer any hardship, and the local people were touchingly supportive and sympathetic. It did not take many months after liberation in 1945 before I unveiled a statue in memory of my father. But believe me, it is not always easy to grow up as the son of a statue. It seems that I never quite got over the shock. My father was such a great man, so reliable and robust – I don't think I had ever imagined I would lose him. I managed well in school and my final exams, but then later I could never decide what I wanted to do. I lived in my own world and tried to work out which direction my father would have wanted me to take. And then there was my mother's sorrow, illness and death. Now I can blame everything on the traffic accident, but the sad truth is that my life had already been on hold for a long time. I have been back as little as possible since then. I know only too well that the people there had expected better things of Hans Storskog's only son.'

He finished his cup of tea.

'So perhaps you can understand why I felt it was appropriate to change my name after the accident and why I would rather not talk too much about my father and the war. People are so different. Some think it is easier to talk about things, but I have come to the conclusion that it simply makes things worse.'

As I left his flat, I realized that Patricia's concept of the human fly was a perfect description of Andreas Gullestad. The old psychological wound inflicted by his father's death seemed to cause him more pain than the physical injury from the traffic accident. But neither of these had any direct relevance to my murder case – not for the moment, as it turned out.

VII

On Sunday, 7 April 1968, my working day drew to a close when I telephoned Patricia from my office around seven o'clock to give her a brief account of the day's findings. This proved to be more complicated than expected. Patricia showed great interest in various details, particularly when we broached the topic of the relationship between Kristian Lund and Sara Sundqvist. The call soon extended to half an hour. However, we then agreed that there was not much more that could be done on a Sunday evening. Our conclusion for the time being was quite simply that the case was increasingly complex and the number of potential murderers was rising. Konrad Jensen's position as main suspect was now facing stiff competition from not only Kristian Lund, but also Sara Sundqvist and Darrell Williams. The caretaker's wife had thus far proved to be a liar and to have accepted bribes and was burdened by experiences from the Second World War, as was Andreas Gullestad.

Patricia finished by saying that, given the current stakes, it might be a good idea for me to keep her informed should any new information crop up that I was uncertain about. I said that she was right, and then drove home deep in thought. And so ended the fourth day of the investigation.

DAY FIVE

A Diary and Its Secrets

I

My day started at half past eight on Monday, 8 April 1968 with a phone call to Oslo's main hospital. They recommended that I come as soon as possible if there was anything of importance to discuss with Anton Hansen. I thanked them and asked them to let him know that I would come by in the course of the day.

The history student Bjørn Erik Svendsen was at the top of my list for the day. I did not need to wait long. At twenty-five to nine, he was standing in front of me, out of breath, and apologized profusely that he had not got there sooner, thanks to a late bus. I realized it was Bjørn Erik Svendsen the history student as soon as he appeared in the doorway. His slim body, the spectacles on a chain round his neck and obligatory rucksack, as well as the Beatles hairdo and anti-war in Vietnam and pro-Socialist People's Party badges could almost be one of the identikit drawings of 'wanted' students that I and a couple of younger colleagues made to entertain ourselves in lunch breaks. His handshake was firm, and his friendly voice picked up pace as soon as Harald Olesen's name was mentioned.

The story of Bjørn Erik Svendsen's acquaintance with Harald Olesen was simple and credible. Three years previously, he had started work on a thesis about the relationship between the Resistance movement and the communists, and after working on it for a year, he had tried to contact a handful of central figures from the Home Front. This had not been an entirely positive experience: Jesper Christopher Haraldsen and several other leaders had been rather arrogant and dismissed him, whereas Harald Olesen had immediately agreed to meet him, and despite differences in age and politics, the two had hit it off. Svendsen explained their friendship with the fact that Olesen had a considerable intellectual capacity. He swiftly added that it may also have been because Olesen had no children himself, and as a widower, his days were long and lonely. The thesis was redefined with a much clearer focus on Harald Olesen's role. Olesen had himself read the first draft with great interest and had immediately agreed when Bjørn Erik Svendsen had suggested writing a biography about him. His thesis had now been with the examination board for assessment for four months, but Svendsen was so inspired at this point that he had already started to write the manuscript for the book project.

When I asked for a short presentation of Harald Olesen's activities during the war, Svendsen immediately launched into a mini lecture. Olesen's involvement in the war was interesting not least because his cover had never been blown, despite his considerable and complex involvement. He had for a period been one of the leaders of the Home Front, and had organized sabotage operations as well as civil-disobedience campaigns, and had himself smuggled refugees over the border. However, the greatest revelation in the manuscript was something that had happened in the final months of the war and the years immediately after. In close cooperation with American agents in Norway, Olesen had gathered information about the Norwegian communists that had later been leaked from the CIA archives. Consequently, Olesen was not only conspicuous in his role as a hero from the Resistance, but also for his role in the government's cooperation with the USA after the war.

Svendsen firmly believed that his life story would generate great interest, even before his sensational murder. His knowledge of the murder case was limited, so he had as yet not formed any 'theories as to the cause', but based on his own findings, he could suggest several possibilities. Both paranoid American intelligence agencies and old Nazis seeking revenge had possible motives. When asked, he agreed that the same would be true of old communists, although he personally felt that an attack from those quarters was far less likely. He also thought Olesen's political career was not likely to give grounds for murder. As a cabinet minister and in his other roles, he had been well respected by people both in and out of the party. He had never caused a stir in any of the major political debates during his time as cabinet minister, and indeed had ended his political career without any great conflict. The war had been his greatest and most dramatic success. He admitted himself that he had never been a shining star as a cabinet minister. Olesen had said that he had eventually asked for the prime minister's permission to resign, in the knowledge that he would otherwise soon be pushed aside.

Inspired by his theories regarding American intelligence and old Nazis, I read the names of the other residents out to

Bjørn Erik Svendsen and asked him whether he knew any of them from another context. He replied that he had already noted the names during one of his visits to Harald Olesen, but had never seen any of them anywhere else. He thought it was an 'incredible coincidence' that an American diplomat lived next door, but did not recognize his name from his source material. Nor had he ever heard Olesen say anything in particular about his neighbours. Svendsen had himself spoken only briefly to the caretaker and his wife in connection with some questions about Olesen's activities during the war. The caretaker was very obviously an alcoholic and not in a good way, but had answered the questions with impressive clarity. The caretaker's wife had found the situation awkward and had left the room shaking her head when her husband started to sniffle.

Svendsen had little to tell about Harald Olesen as a private person. Olesen had been devoted to his wife and had on several occasions mentioned that one of his greatest sorrows in life was that they had not been able to have children. His relationship with his siblings had been close, whereas his relationship with his niece and nephew seemed to be increasingly sporadic and strained. Olesen had once sighed when he spoke of them and said that, given his long career, surely he must deserve better-qualified heirs. However, he made no mention of this again, and Svendsen was not aware of any potential dramas in connection with the will.

The greatest surprise in the course of the conversation was when Svendsen me told that Harald Olesen had kept a regular diary in his later years. When asked where these diaries were now, he immediately produced two spiral-bound notebooks from his rucksack, marked '1963–4' and '1965–6', which he had borrowed in order to work on the biography. He added, apologetically, that there was not much to be gleaned from them regarding the murder. Harald Olesen had not taken any great chances in lending out his diaries from those years. His entries consisted of concise factual information about his everyday life. He wrote in a tidy hand about letters and telephone calls from old friends and acquaintances, and had made short notes about current affairs. His niece and nephew were mentioned in only a couple of places, and the neighbours barely at all.

Svendsen had read through the diaries again following the murder, but had found only one thing that might possibly be of relevance. Under the date '17 November 1966', there was a brief note that was conspicuous in part due to the fact that Olesen did not write the full names of the people concerned, and in part due to the dramatic nature of the content: *Unexpectedly bumped into S, accompanied by the ghastly N. S is ill and a shadow of what I remember from all those years ago, but still aroused strong memories. A very unsettling encounter.*

I read the short entry four times and the feeling that this may be of great significance became more pronounced each time. Without any further indications of the time and circumstances of this meeting with S, it was difficult to know who it was and what this was about. Neither S nor N were mentioned anywhere else in the diaries, I heard Bjørn Erik Svendsen say. He immediately added that it would be interesting to see whether S or N was mentioned again in the most recent diary, which covered 1967 to 1968.

I was staring at the three mysterious sentences from 17 November 1966 and must have looked either very threatening or completely baffled when the significance of this new piece of information finally sank in. Bjørn Erik Svendsen certainly hurried to say that he should perhaps have mentioned it straightaway, but he had assumed it had been found when the flat was searched. He had on several occasions when he was visiting seen Harald Olesen leafing through a new diary marked '1967–8', which he had refused to give to him along with the others. By way of explanation, he had said that he was still writing in the diary, and he needed to think hard about whether to divulge some of the information. Svendsen had seen the diary lying on the sitting-room table during one of his visits. When the diary was out, Olesen always kept an eye on it, but Svendsen had absolutely no idea where it was kept.

I replied truthfully that no trace of any such diary had been found in the flat. We now lacked not only the weapon with which the murder was carried out, but also a diary that might contain the solution to the murder mystery.

I asked Bjørn Erik Svendsen to leave the diaries with me and to wait by the reception. Reminding him that this was a murder investigation, I explained that he would have to wait there while I read the diaries. He expressed his full understanding and added that the murder mystery was of course of great relevance to his book, then left the room without further ado.

I believed the biographer when he said that the entry was the only thing of any interest in the two diaries and put them down on the desk in front of me. After twenty increasingly frustrating minutes of attempting to use my own grey cells, I reluctantly gave in and grabbed the phone. While I waited for an answer, I amused myself by wondering what Bjørn

Erik Svendsen would have said if he knew that I was calling a direct line to the White House.

II

Patricia listened with silent concentration to my ten-minute briefing on the new information from Bjørn Erik Svendsen. She acknowledged the news of the mysterious diary entry and missing diary with a tut.

'So, what would you advise me to do now?' I asked.

This was followed by a tense ten-second silence and then a very short and clear recommendation.

'I advise you to take Bjørn Erik Svendsen with you to Harald Olesen's flat in 25 Krebs' Street as soon as possible.'

This was fortunately followed up swiftly with some further instructions. It was not immediately obvious to me why I had to take Bjørn Erik Svendsen to 25 Krebs' Street.

'The diary may prove to be a vital source. There are two possibilities here. Either the murderer knew about the third book and has taken it or destroyed it there in the flat, which is perfectly plausible. Getting hold of the diary may in fact have been the motive for murdering Harald Olesen in the first place, if the murderer knew about the diary and that it contained something important. But Harald Olesen was obviously very concerned that the diary should not fall into the wrong hands, so it is also perfectly possible, and highly likely, that the murderer never even saw the diary, that he or she did not know of its existence and therefore did not look for it. In which case, the diary is still where Harald Olesen hid it in the flat.'

I made a feeble protest on behalf of the police.

'Please do not completely underestimate us! We have searched the flat and would of course have acted immediately had we found a handwritten diary.'

Patricia had a ready answer.

'Of course, I have absolute confidence in the police. But firstly, you had no idea that there was a diary to look for, and secondly, a diary is relatively easy to hide. Again there are two possibilities: Harald Olesen may have hidden it in a secret compartment in his bedside table or wardrobe or suchlike—'

I interrupted her with an indignant protest.

'I would like to see such a compartment: we have knocked on and measured every wall in every room!'

Patricia still did not seem entirely convinced, but changed tack.

'In that case, the question is whether you checked the best hiding place for a diary.'

She on purpose said no more, thereby forcing me to ask.

'And where do you think is the best place to hide a diary?'

Her answer was followed by delighted laugher.

'Why, in the bookshelf, of course. I should imagine that you made a list of all the book titles, but did any of you check that none of them contained a diary?'

I had to admit to myself that we had done neither, but I did not say a word, just made a mental note that we should look through the bookcases and the rest of the flat again, given the news of the missing diary. We agreed in all haste that this was what I should do and then go to see her at around seven. I spontaneously said 'yes, please' to a light supper. She asked me to take the diaries with me and any other papers that might be relevant, and to go and see the caretaker in hospital on the way. She then assured me that it would not be a problem if I was late: she had no plans to go anywhere today. I could still hear her slightly smug laughter ringing in my ears as I gathered up my papers and the diaries and headed for the door.

III

Bjørn Erik Svendsen was more than happy to be driven in a police car to Harald Olesen's flat, but repeated several times en route that he had no idea where the diary was hidden. We were quickly able to confirm that there was no sign of it on the desk or any other table. The idea that it might be hidden among the books appealed to Svendsen. He asked whether there was a compulsory methodology course for aspiring policemen. I replied that policemen were also allowed to think creatively. He nodded enthusiastically and immediately got started on the right-hand section of Harald Olesen's bookshelves. I myself started on the left.

I must admit that my enthusiasm for Patricia's theory gradually waned as I ploughed my way through the first hundred books. I counted routinely, so that, if nothing else, I could later impress my colleagues with details of my thorough work. I was just about to put back book number 246 when an excited yelp from Bjørn Erik Svendsen broke the silence in the flat. With shaking hands, he lifted from the floor a notebook of the same type as the two previous ones. It had fallen out from the generous covers of Volume 2 of *The Great War*. He held it out to me, triumphant. The dates

'1967–8' glared at me from the front cover, even though they were written in lead pencil in an old man's hand.

I confiscated the book on the spot and refused to let the history student read over my shoulder. He initially objected that it might contain important historical source material that would be of significance for the biography, but soon accepted the situation when I assured him that he would of course be given access to the diary as soon as the murder investigation had been closed. I swiftly added that any knowledge of the diary's contents could in fact be dangerous. He promptly agreed to leave the room and wait in the kitchen in case I had any questions for him once I had read it.

The start of the diary year 1967 was relatively uneventful for Harald Olesen. January and February passed with nothing more than short, undramatic entries with full names. However, the entry for 20 March 1967 was short and mysterious, which could bode ill given the one from the year before: *N has made contact. Told that S was dead and had confessed in the end. N was angry and demanded money.*

The remainder of March and April comprised only short factual entries about anniversary dinners and letters received from old acquaintances. In March, he had written some brief comments regarding the news that Stalin's daughter had gone into exile in the USA, and in April, he recorded the deaths of the writer Johan Falkberget and the former German chancellor Konrad Adenauer. But on 2 May, N suddenly appeared once more: *N has contacted me again. Demanded money and threatened to tell.*

The problem with N appeared to settle again later in May. Harald Olesen expressed his concern about the situation in Greece following the military coup and uncertainty as to how

Norway should respond. N was not mentioned at all again for the rest of May. Instead, a new mystery letter cropped up on 15 May: *D came to visit – actually came into my flat today. Once inside the door, D's face changed completely. Was glad to still be alive when he left. Know only too well what D is capable of. A bad night – got up twice to check that the safety chain was on.*

June and July passed with only short entries about people he knew, a couple of longer passages about the Six-Day War in the Middle East and the riots in the USA. Harald Olesen spent a considerable amount of time keeping himself informed of what was going on in the world, via the news-papers, radio and television. But his personal problems returned with a vengeance in the autumn. In August, there were suddenly two short entries, separated only by a note on the USA's increasing military involvement in Vietnam.

12 August: N still hounding me for money. Where will this end?

27 August: Another aggressive conversation with D. My illness is getting worse and therefore also my dilemma. I want to speak out, but D rejects this point blank – and is now threatening me.

It was clear that Harald Olesen's situation was deterio-rating rapidly, and also his health. Through September there were more and more brief entries about pain and appoint-ments with the doctor. The local elections at the end of the month were dealt with in only a few lines. And two new letters appeared, only a few days apart.

21 September: O, whom I have not seen for over 20 years, contacted me. O was extremely concerned that our activities and those of others from back then remained secret forever. I agreed and said that I would sort out the papers.

29 September: J has also contacted me now. Arouses sympathy.
Impossible to sleep afterwards. Great dilemma.

Olesen appeared more or less to lose his appetite for world affairs in October and November. The much-discussed deaths of Che Guevara and the last emperor of China were given no more than a line each, as were that autumn's Vietnam demonstrations in Oslo. Instead, there were a growing number of entries about health problems. These culminated dramatically in the middle of Advent.

12 December: Dramatic conclusion following another
examination by the doctor. The end is only months away.
The thought of death is light as a feather, whereas the greatest
decision of my life weighs on me like lead.

This stood as the final gripping entry for 1967. The entries for 1968 were few and far between, and they were exclusively in connection with Harald Olesen's personal problems.

18 January: Bad day. Stayed in bed with pains all morning.
N wants even more money, in my will too, now. Powerful
emotions after a conversation with J yesterday. And the
menacing figure of D looms constantly in the background . . .

22 January: O got in touch, was worried about my health.
I promised to take all our secrets with me to the grave. Evil
shall with evil be expelled! O looked through the papers and
then we burned them in the stove. We did not talk about
personal differences, but O seemed remarkably relaxed about
it all.

28 January: Intense physical pain, but the psychological pain is
worse. Cannot see a solution. Massive doubts regarding the issue
of the will.

14 February: Frightful conversation with D, who suddenly went into a rage, as he often does. D does not want money, but wants eternal silence – and the old hate for me is growing ever stronger. No person on earth frightens me more than D. May the Lord I have never believed in soon open His gates and grant my soul mercy!

19 February: Short conversation with O, who thanked me for what I have done and promised not to bother me again. But can I believe that?

1 March: J desperate and impatient, threatening to go to the press. Cannot bear to think what D might do then – either to me or J. Managed to persuade J to delay, but the ground is burning beneath my feet, and the pain is searing my wretched old body.

12 March: Still alive, if only just. J vacillates between tears and rage, could break and do something rash. D did not get angry during our last conversation, but rather was threatening and ominously calm, as only D can be . . . N constantly pestering for money. I fear D more than I despise N. Tussle with hugely mixed feelings regarding J. N and J may possibly know about one another now. Only hope that neither of them knows about D, and that D does not know about them. Or else all hell might break loose in Torshov!

20 March: Changed the will under considerable duress. A debt must always be paid, after all, no matter how loathsome the creditor.

25 March: After several sleepless nights on the edge of my grave, I have changed my will again. Everything shall be sacrificed on the altar of my greatest sin!

30 March: Pressure increasing from all quarters. Could bump into J, D and N at any moment. All three are threatening and erratic. The evil spirits from my past are crowding me into my grave. Will let the will stand as it is and hope that it will bring happiness to the one I have failed the most. In desperation, have called a final meeting on Thursday evening, despite the obvious risks.

With this entry, the diary stopped abruptly. All the remaining pages were blank.

Harald Olesen was shot during a meeting in his home on the evening of 4 April, which was the first Thursday after 30 March. But I did not know if he had arranged this meeting with D, J, N or O, or who any of them were. None of the initials D, J, N or O fitted the names of anyone in the building. Unless 'J' quite simply stood for 'Jensen'.

I went into Bjørn Erik Svendsen and asked if he had ever heard Harald Olesen mention the initials D, J, N or O, or come across them in any other context. He shook his head without any hesitation. In pure desperation, I read a couple of the entries out loud to him, but this did not help to reveal the identity of the people in question. However, the colour did still drain from Bjørn Erik Svendsen's face and he told me that in all his conversations with Harald Olesen, he had never heard mention of the words 'fear' and 'terror'. It was therefore a shock to hear just how scared the old Resistance hero had been in the last months of his life.

I ordered Bjørn Erik Svendsen not to say a word about the existence of the diary, something he swore to. I then asked him to remain in town and to contact me immediately should he remember anything that might be of importance regarding the identity of D, J, N or O – or the investigation in general. He assured me that he would, and asked me twice not to mention that he knew about the diary.

A minute later, I saw Bjørn Erik Svendsen almost running along the pavement below the window. I realized how profoundly the murder would affect his life, and even more so, the other residents of 25 Krebs' Street. It was strange to think how very different the situation would have been for them, as it would for me, if Harald Olesen had been allowed to die from his illness a few days or weeks later.

I sat there alone leafing backwards and forwards through the diary for an hour, but was none the wiser. I desperately missed Patricia's voice and was several times about to drive to her home unannounced. But when I later got into the car, I headed not towards Erling Skjalgsson's Street, but towards the hospital. There was a man waiting there who had been given a message to say that I would come today whom no one dared believe would live another day.

IV

Sadly, his wife had been right. There was not much left of Anton Hansen in 1968, compared with the handsome, dark-haired groom in the photograph from 1928. Forty years later, the same person was a worn and grey bag of bones lying in a white hospital bed. I would have guessed his age to be no less than seventy-five and his weight well under nine stone, despite the fact that he was still at least five foot ten. His hair was grey, his skin pallid, his breathing laboured and his mouth toothless. He had one tube in his left arm and another up his nose, but as he was constantly coughing, they were constantly in danger of falling out.

In other words, Anton Hansen the caretaker appeared to be precisely what he was: a man who had lived a hard life and who was now dying as a result. His eyes lit up when he saw me, but his face and body both remained heavy and, somehow, disillusioned. He gave an almost imperceptible nod in welcome. He lifted his hand from the bed in greeting, but his handshake was without energy or will. There seemed to be something strangely deformed about his hands. It took a couple of minutes before I realized that not only did he lack teeth, he also lacked nails.

'Detective Inspector Kolbjørn Kristiansen. I am here, as I am sure you understand, in connection with the unsolved murder of your neighbour Harald Olesen.'

He nodded again. His voice was weak but friendly.

'I thought I was going to die myself when I heard about the murder. Harald Olesen is one of the people I have admired most in this world, and I never imagined that I would outlive him. I had hoped that he would come to my funeral and still have many years before him.'

He gasped for breath and coughed at the same time, but continued remarkably quickly.

'During the war, everyone who knew his identity worried that he would be shot any day. But now, so many years later . . . it came as a shock, and I cannot imagine who would want to kill him. Not anymore.'

His head fell back on the pillow. I discreetly stood up and moved closer to the bed so he could see me without lifting his head. He nodded gratefully.

'I admired Harald Olesen during the war, of course, but it

was actually later that I fully understood just how strong he was. Harald Olesen was a man of action, someone who could always distinguish what was important and what was not, who always looked to the future. He managed to carry on, even though he must have seen things far worse than I did during the war.'

He coughed again, this time so violently that I looked around for a nurse, but then he carried on speaking.

'My problem was that I remembered everything so clearly, and then you get caught up in what happened and it is impossible to move on – especially when the experiences are as powerful as those I carried with me from the war.'

It seemed to me that Caretaker Anton Hansen was intellectually fitter than he was physically. But now I was impatient to know more about what happened during the war and about his neighbours, before it was too late.

'It must have been very peculiar for you and Harald Olesen, as former Resistance fighters, to have a convicted NS member as a neighbour.'

A small smile slid over Anton Hansen's face, but then quickly gave way to a grimace.

'Well, yes, but Konrad Jensen has not harmed a fly since the end of the war. I never asked Harald how he felt about having a former Nazi as a neighbour, but it was not a problem for me. In a strange way, it felt as though Konrad and I shared a fate. We were both small, weak men who tried to dance with the big, strong men like Harald Olesen during the war. And we paid for it dearly in later years, each in our own way.'

'Can you remember any particular events or people from the occupation that may be of significance?'

He heaved a heavy sigh – and then had to gasp for air.

'My problem is that I remember too much. So much happened during those years, and most of it was secret, so I am not sure what might or might not be important. I remember the happy moments: Liberation Day and the return of the royal family. And I remember the first refugees who we hid in our cellar. There were four of them in 1942 to 1943, and all made it over the border to Sweden. While they were with us, I will never forget that tension. If the Germans had come while they were there, both my wife and I would have been shot along with our guests. We lived together for a few days, with the threat of death hanging over us. The youngest of these guests was a petrified lad of only sixteen or seventeen who spoke both Norwegian and German. He came back ten years later with his wife and child to give us gifts in thanks for our help. That is one of my best memories from after the war.'

Anton Hansen smiled for a moment, until he was once again overwhelmed by a coughing fit.

'And then there were the three last ones . . . and they were not quite so lucky.'

I moved even closer into his range of vision and indicated impatiently that he should continue.

'A young couple with a baby who came to us in February 1944. Dark-haired, attractive and well dressed, but terrified by the danger hanging over them. They scarcely dared to let one another or the child out of sight for a moment, and I heard them crying and whispering together in a foreign language every night. They spoke Norwegian, but their intonation was odd and they used lots of strange words, so I realized that they came from another country and had somehow found themselves behind enemy lines in Norway.'

He was seized by an extreme fit of coughing. I was afraid that Anton Hansen would die in the middle of the very interesting story, but his eyes were still shining when his chest calmed down.

'Harald Olesen had an almost supernatural power in critical situations. He could smell danger like a predator – by instinct more than intellect. On the third afternoon that they were with us, he came and said that he had a feeling that there was an acute danger, and out of consideration to both us and them, he could not let the refugees stay in town any longer. So he came to collect them in his car around two in the morning. It was a hasty farewell. I remember the tiny baby shoe that was left behind on the floor.'

Anton Hansen's head fell back on the pillow again. I took the opportunity to fire a question.

'Can you remember what kind of car Harald Olesen was driving?'

He nodded weakly, without raising his head from the pillow.

'He was driving his black Volvo 1932 model that evening, as always.'

I smiled, hoping to encourage both him and myself.

'Good, good. And what happened to the refugees after that?'

First a fleeting smile and then a sharp spasm passed over Anton Hansen's face.

'I'm afraid I don't know much about that. We were never told their names or anything else about the people who stayed with us, or which route they followed from here. I never saw them again, but I don't think it ended well. I asked Harald Olesen about it once, later. He suddenly looked extremely grave and said that they had been very unlucky and that I must never ask again. It would be best if I didn't know more, he said. So I never asked again. I had the utmost respect for what Harald Olesen said, but I often wondered about it. Images and memories have dogged me through the years. I presume that none of them survived the war.'

He paused briefly, coughed a couple of times and then carried on.

'On the other hand, one thing I know for sure is that Harald Olesen's instinct saved both me and my wife that time. Somehow we'd been found out or someone had informed on us. The following morning, I was woken by five soldiers from the Gestapo kicking down my door and tearing the flat apart. The baby shoe on the floor was one of the things they asked about, but luck was with us and it fitted our youngest son.'

There was another short pause. The memories were obviously potent and his voice got weaker.

'But I was arrested all the same and locked up in Grini Prison Camp. As I was escorted out of the flat that morning, I was sure that it was the last time I would see my wife and children. I was questioned and beaten up for four days before they let me go. On the third day, they said that I would be shot if I didn't tell them immediately where the refugees had gone and who had gone with them. I said my final farewell to life. But it was just a bluff – they lined me up and pulled their triggers without having loaded the guns. That convinced them that I had nothing to confess. The next day, they let me go. I came home minus three teeth and ten nails, but that did not bother my wife and me. If that had been the worst damage, I guess we would have lived happily ever after. My involvement in the Resistance ended there and then. Harald felt that it was too dangerous for us, and them, to hide any more refugees, and I didn't protest.'

Anton Hansen was on the verge of tears now. The memories from after the war seemed to be more of a burden than those from the war. His voice was almost a whisper and trembled when he finally continued.

'Later, I have often thought that I should have said no the first time that Harald Olesen asked if I wanted to work for the Resistance and hide a refugee. I bitterly regret it now when I see the consequences it has had for my wife and children. But if Norway were to be occupied again and Harald Olesen was standing by the kitchen table asking me to help my country by hiding refugees, I still wouldn't say no. How could I?'

I nodded with as much sympathy as I could muster.

'Of course not. You made a great contribution to this country and its people, and no one could have foreseen what the consequences would be.'

He smiled for a moment, but this was followed by another spasm and a shadow once again fell over his face.

'It's strange how differently we cope with things. No one can predict it. There were children and young women who came home after years in a concentration camp and apparently managed to deal with it easily. They are still happily alive today. Whereas I, a big mature man, never got over those four days in the prison camp. Even here in the hospital, I can be woken in the middle of the night by the Germans storming in, or knocking out my teeth, or I am standing in front of the firing squad. Faces come back to me constantly, whether I am awake or asleep. And often it is the terrified young couple with the baby.'

His persistent use of the word 'baby' reminded me of an unresolved question.

'Do you know if the child was a boy or a girl?'

He gave a feeble shake of the head.

'Neither my wife nor I was certain about it afterwards, strangely enough. It was important to know and remember as little as possible. The child was only a few months old and in nappies, so it wasn't easy to tell. I think it was a girl, but I am not sure.'

'And you have no idea where Harald Olesen drove them?'

He moaned quietly and shook his head.

'No. Unfortunately, he didn't say. We were not supposed to know that sort of thing, but I think . . .'

He was seized by a coughing fit again. I felt guilty about pressing the skin-and-bones man in the bed for any more now, but could not leave without hearing the rest of the story.

'I don't think he intended to go straight to the border. The Germans kept a strict guard on the roads and there were lots of soldiers in the border region, so the shortest way was often the most dangerous. And it wouldn't be easy to smuggle two adults and a baby through the roadblocks. I think rather that he took them out into the forest, on foot.'

'But this was in winter – was there not snow on the ground?'

He nodded weakly, twice.

'It was the middle of February. They left us on the night of 14 February. It was a difficult situation. Either Harald Olesen had to find a safe hiding place for two parents and a baby of two or three months or they had to get out the skis. I think he had planned the latter. The day before they left, he said in

143

passing that it seemed that he and Deerfoot had to take a trip to the mountains.'

I looked down at the emaciated man on the bed, my question no doubt clear on my face. He smiled disarmingly and then sometime after spoke again with great effort.

'I understood from what he said that this Deerfoot was some kind of guide whom he used when he took the refugees over to Sweden. I have always imagined in later years that Deerfoot was a young man in his twenties or thirties, but I have no idea where Deerfoot came from or how old he was, and certainly not what he was called. I don't even know which route they took, as there were many possibilities. They might, for example, have driven east towards Østfold, or north to Hedmark or Oppland. What puzzled me was that Deerfoot was mentioned several times in 1942 and 1943, but never again later. I mentioned him one time after the war, but Harald replied dismissively that things had gone awry for Deerfoot. So without knowing anything for certain, I have always presumed that something terrible happened on that trip, and that as result, Deerfoot and the three refugees died that winter in 1944.'

It certainly did not sound implausible, but I was not going to let this new character in Harald Olesen's life go that easily.

'Did you by any chance see this Deerfoot when Olesen came to collect them?'

He shook his head as firmly as his strength allowed.

'No, no. Harald was alone when he came, and only had the couple and the baby with him when he left. I have never seen or spoken to Deerfoot. That much I do know.'

Then quite suddenly his strength left him. Anton Hansen lay listless on his bed for several minutes, gasping for air. I patted him gently on the shoulder, thanked him so much for his help and told him to rest. He nodded with the ghost of a smile on his lips. But just as I was leaving, he mustered his strength and waved for me to come back.

'If you see my wife, then tell her that it is perhaps just as well if she doesn't come here again, but do say . . .'

His voice faded out, but carried on in a whisper after a pause.

'Say that I still love her very much and am very sorry for everything that has happened after the war. Please can you tell her that?'

I nodded, despite a niggling doubt that I would ever have the heart to fulfil my promise. Then I mumbled a farewell and said thank you again. I was at a loss as to what more to say and suddenly had a strong desire to leave the hospital before I was accused of causing the death of Anton Hansen the caretaker.

I caught a final glimpse of the caretaker from the doorway as I left. He had already fallen asleep. I dutifully stopped a passing nurse and asked her to see to him. Then I walked through the long corridors to the exit with the feeling that I had just seen a dying human fly and it was an incredibly sad sight. It also occurred to me that in the end human flies are human beings as well.

The caretaker's good memory, which had plagued him so, had given me plenty to think about. In addition to the familiar faces of the other residents, I now also had to look for a refugee family that had disappeared and a faceless ghost from the war. There were – as Patricia had already intimated yesterday – an increasing number of threads that needed to be tied up that all led back to the dark days of the war.

V

The clock in reception showed half past four by the time I left the hospital. There were still two and half hours to go before my dinner appointment with Patricia. I was unsure for a few minutes as to what I should do: should I go back to the station or go and talk to the deceased Harald Olesen's neighbours? I decided on the latter in the end. I wanted to know whether the caretaker's wife had anything to add to her husband's story from the war. What is more, a rather alluring idea was staring to form in my mind. The fact that I should not mention the discovery of the diary to any of the residents was absolutely clear. But in the course of my journey, I changed my mind at least eight times as to whether or not I should confront the neighbours with the name Deerfoot and the initials D, J, N and O.

The caretaker's wife was at her post when I arrived. She could confirm her husband's story from the war, but had nothing of importance to add. She remembered well the young refugee from the war who had returned ten years later with gifts and thanks. It was also one of the highlights of her post-war years. She had never seen the other refugees again, and her memory of them was more hazy. Nevertheless, she could confirm that a young couple with a baby had been hidden there for a few days, and that Harald Olesen had collected them the night before the Gestapo showed up at the door. She thought she had heard her husband mention the name Deerfoot, but could not remember Olesen talking about him.

The caretaker's wife hesitated when I thanked her. Then

from her pocket she produced a folded sheet with something akin to awe.

'A telegram boy came here today. It has happened before – it's not that. Harald Olesen received a great number of telegrams when he was in the government. But this one was for me!'

She held it out to me with a trembling hand. The text was short:

TO MRS RANDI HANSEN 25 KREBS STREET OSLO IN
ACCORDANCE WITH THE WISHES OF THE DECEASED
HARALD OLESEN YOU ARE ADVISED TO BE PRESENT
AT OUR MEETING ROOM IN 28B IDUN STREET ON
WEDNESDAY 10 APRIL AT 12 NOON STOP THIS IN
CONNECTION WITH THE READING OF MR OLESENS WILL
STOP RØNNINNG, RØNNING & RØNNING LAW FIRM

I nodded with interest and asked if the other residents had also received such a telegram today. To which she nodded, slowly.

'Yes, yes – they all received one. The American was out, so the telegram boy went on to the embassy. Konrad Jensen did not want to open the door until he heard my voice, so I had to go up with the boy. I am sure it means nothing special, except that it's the first time anyone has sent me a telegram. But still, I thought . . .'

The caretaker's wife suddenly blushed like a schoolgirl and averted her gaze. A minute passed before she smiled apologetically and continued.

'Well, we all have our little dreams . . . Harald Olesen was such a kind man, you see, who always remembered to give us Christmas presents and the like. And my husband did help him during the war, after all, and I have done his cleaning for him for many years. So I thought that maybe there was a slight chance that he had left us a small amount in his will.'

I said nothing. This obviously made her nervous, so she hurried on.

'Yes, I know – it's terrible to think like that, but it's so easy to drift off into daydreams when you've had as little as I have for so long. If it was three hundred or five hundred kroner, that would be a small fortune to me . . . Two thousand would be enough to keep me in coffee and Christmas and birthday presents for my children and grandchildren until I turn seventy and get a pension. I would be eternally grateful to Harald Olesen. It would never be that much, of course. But he was kind and rich, so maybe I can hope for a couple of hundred. I have started to pack my belongings, as I will have to move out as soon as Anton dies, and then I will stay with one of my daughters; they will have to keep me out of charity for a few months each. It's always nice to see the children and grandchildren, but it will be awful to sit there and not have the money to buy anything for them.'

She looked down and then up again.

'Forgive me, but I just had to tell someone,' she said very quietly.

I was more than happy to forgive; then I thanked her and left. I could not bring myself to say anything that might give her false hope. However, I had to admit that the telegrams in no way diminished my confusion regarding the case – or my curiosity regarding the will.

The telegrams were decisive with regard to my decision to test out the name Deerfoot on all the neighbours. Everyone was at home at this time in the afternoon, but the findings were meagre pickings all the same.

Darrell Williams was once again in a benevolent and diplomatic mood. He roared with laughter and commented that it was a very creative code name, but that he had no idea as to who or what was behind it. He associated the name Deerfoot with some Red Indian books (were they not written by James Fenimore Cooper?) that he had read at some point in the 1930s. He had, to his surprise, also received a telegram advising him to be present for the reading of the will. He could not understand why, but it was less mysterious now that he knew that everyone in the building had received one. He would of course go, out of curiosity and politeness.

Kristian and Karen Lund were eating supper when I knocked on the door, and their son was sitting in a highchair at the end of the table. The perfect family. They confirmed that they had received a telegram and were also terribly curious as to why. She was just as phlegmatic as she had been the last time, and he was far calmer. I hoped that it meant he was not hiding any more from me, but did not presume to take that for granted. They were taken aback by the name, but did not recognize it.

Sara Sundqvist hesitantly opened the door a crack with the safety chain to begin with, but then lit up when she saw that it was me. She had also received a telegram and was not sure whether to attend or not, but promised that she would when I told her that the others were probably going. I jokingly added that I would be there myself, so she would be perfectly safe. She immediately gave me a charming smile and leaned forward in her chair. I understood why Kristian

Lund was so attracted to her and caught myself wondering whether perhaps she should concentrate more on the theatre.

Sara Sundqvist gave a start when I mentioned Deerfoot, but quickly regained her composure and said that she did not associate anything with the name. In her softest voice, she asked where the mysterious name came from, and nodded with understanding when I said that I could not reveal that at present. I thought it a suitable moment to take my leave.

Konrad Jensen opened the door as cautiously as before, but seemed to be slightly calmer. He had come to terms with the loss of his car, but the future still looked bleak without it. When the telegram boy had showed up at the door, he had thought that it was someone trying to deceive him, but had opened the door when the caretaker's wife came and told him that she had received a similar telegram. He still did not see the point of it all. The very idea that Harald Olesen would leave something to him was ridiculous, and why the old Resistance hero wanted him to be there was a mystery. The whole thing might be a plot to lure him out onto the open street. He had no plans of going, and in fact had no plans of going out at all.

The name Deerfoot spawned a new sceptical sneer, but nothing more. Konrad Jensen thought he had heard the name in a story or a book when he was young, but it could equally have been a film. He was not aware of any association with Harald Olesen or the building. I gave him a clue and mentioned the war, but he continued to shake his head uncomprehendingly. With a hint of optimism, I also intimated that we had found some new clues and hoped that the case would soon be solved. He smiled gingerly at this and wished me luck before hastily closing and locking the door.

Andreas Gullestad nodded with recognition as soon as he heard the name Deerfoot, even though he quite 'decidedly' remembered that the books were written by Ellis and not by Cooper. But he had no further association with the name, either from the war or after. He had also received a telegram and equally could not understand why, but would of course be there if that was what the deceased wanted. The caretaker's wife had already promised to help him with the wheelchair, and had explained to him that she and the other neighbours had also been notified of the reading of the will.

The contrast between Konrad Jensen pacing nervously around in the neighbouring flat and Andreas Gullestad, who sat here completely relaxed in his wheelchair, was striking. However, he had little of any interest to tell. At ten to seven, I extracted myself from the flat, muttering something about an 'important meeting'. Which was a small white lie. I reluctantly had to acknowledge that the many meetings I had had that day had provided plenty of new information, but very few conclusions as to the way forward.

As I walked down the street, I looked back at 25 Krebs' Street. I felt a warm rush in my chest. The reward was just as I would have wished, had I had the choice. Harald Olesen's windows were of course dark and empty, as were Darrell Williams's. Konrad Jensen had the light on, but the curtains were firmly closed. Mrs Lund was to be seen moving around in the Lunds' flat with the baby in her arms. Andreas Gullestad's window was lit but empty. But in the sixth window stood the tall and beautiful silhouette of a woman, unmoving. However it was to be interpreted, Sara Sundqvist was watching me with increasing interest.

VI

Patricia's large desk was set for two when I was ushered in by the maid, five minutes late. Not unexpectedly, a 'light supper' proved to be a rather sophisticated affair in the Borchmann household. The first course – a beautifully prepared asparagus soup – was already on the table when I arrived. I complimented Benedikte on the soup and Patricia of course had to correct me straightaway.

'First of all, the maids do not make the food in this house. The cook has to do something to earn her salary. And second, that is not Benedikte.'

I looked at the maid, bewildered, as she was in every way identical to the girl I had met on my previous visits. The maid smiled timidly at my confusion, until Patricia's voice rang out once more.

'That is her twin sister; this one is called Beate. They each work for two days at a time and then have two days off. It is a practical arrangement, as I can basically have the same maid with more or less the same good and bad habits all the time, and they have a manageable working week. That way, both girls also have time to enjoy the company of some relatively intelligent and not-too-bad-looking young men.'

Beate's mouth held a brave smile, which understandably did not reach her eyes. I refrained from saying anything, but my thoughts were so loud that I was afraid she might hear; the way in which Patricia used her intellectual capacity was not always entirely engaging.

Once the mystery of the maids had been cleared up, we proceeded to eat slowly. I told Patricia in detail about the lives of Bjørn Erik Svendsen and the caretaker, as well as about the discovery of the diary and its contents. This time she was an impatient listener and constantly interrupted me with astute, detailed questions.

After the soup, Patricia cheerfully refused to let the main course be served until she had seen the diary. This did not involve any great delay. Patricia truly devoured the pages with her eyes and was done with the entire book within five minutes or so. Safely locked away in her own small kingdom and away from the dark streets of Oslo, Patricia appeared to experience none of the alarm that both Bjørn Erik Svendsen and I had felt regarding the diary in Harald Olesen's flat. But her fascination with it was no less. A few minutes of thoughtful silence followed while we tucked into the superb tenderloin, served with vegetables and roast potatoes. Patricia chewed slowly, but undoubtedly thought fast. The minutes of silence were at irregular intervals interspersed with frantic blinking.

'Rather a good day's work,' she said finally, when the dessert was on the table and the loyal Beate had left the room. 'We have made some great strides in the investigation and have gathered what is surely very important information.'

I nodded smugly.

'Yes, thank you. It does feel like that. But I still do not see any obvious way to resolve the case.'

Patricia gave one of her mischievous smiles.

'That is not so strange – I can scarcely see it myself. We still lack some key information, which means that we cannot have a clear picture of the murderer. But both the diary and the caretaker's story have contributed some new details to this picture.'

Patricia paused for thought before she continued.

'The letters in the diary must have a meaning and could be of crucial importance. Harald Olesen is not likely to have chosen letters from a known letter system, as he would in that case have started with A or X. He has used letters that have an immediate association for him, with either a name or title that he might associate with the person in question. That way, they would be instantly recognizable for him, but are an extremely difficult crossword puzzle for the rest of us. He seems to have made it deliberately difficult for his biographer, relatives or anyone else who might get hold of his diary later. I am fairly certain that he has not used names for the key people, D, J, N or O, but rather titles or words that he associates with those people. O seems to operate alone and is seen to be less of a problem, even though he and Harald Olesen have obviously had secrets and conflicts in the past. D, J, and N, on the other hand, seem to be connected in some way.'

'J could be Konrad Jensen,' I suggested, in the hope of contributing something that was not too idiotic.

Patricia shook her head lightly.

'I have of course considered that possibility, but then the text makes little sense. It would appear that J is someone who instils sympathy and a sense of guilt in Harald Olesen. And even though one can never know what lies hidden in the past, it does seem rather unlikely that an ageing Nazi would fulfil that role.'

Patricia suddenly put down her dessert spoon and thought very hard. I could almost hear the creaking in her brain. Then equally suddenly she fired a completely unexpected question at me.

'I am sure that you have already checked this; however,

I am not so sure that you have told me . . . What was the name of Kristian Lund's dead mother?'

I had never been told, and nor had I asked. On the other hand, I had remembered to take with me the papers from the census records that she had requested, and quickly found the sheets that related to Kristian Lund. A thought struck me as I leafed through the papers and I looked up at Patricia in surprise.

'But Kristian Lund's mother was already dead when Harald Olesen started to write about D, J, N and O.'

There was a hint of irony in Patricia's voice when she replied: 'Precisely!'

I had a swift look through the papers in the hope that I would not appear to be as slow as I felt.

'Kristian of course has her surname, as his father was unknown. Her first name was Nathalie.'

Patricia frowned and shook her head and gave a deep sigh.

'I am afraid that the name Nathalie Lund is not of much help to us . . . Did she perhaps have a middle name or a nickname that she used or was known by?'

I looked at the sheet from the census records, and then the two pages about her trial for treason.

'No known middle name, but in a subclause here in her case papers it mentions that she was often called Sonja during the war, as she apparently looked like the film star Sonja Henie.'

It was silent for a beat. When I looked up, I discovered that Patricia had fixed me with an accusing telescopic gaze.

'You could have spared us the delay by telling me that immediately! That fits perfectly with the obvious scenario. We still do not have the murderer, but we have at least identified the mysterious N as the shop manager Kristian Lund, whose address is 25 Krebs' Street.'

I looked at Patricia as if she were a green Martian on roller skates, not a white woman in a wheelchair. She rolled her eyes.

'Given the information that "S" could stand for "Sonja" and that this plays on her resemblance to the beautiful and famous actress, the rest is rather elementary, my dear Kristiansen. The whole sequence is then almost too perfect for it to be a coincidence. Konrad Jensen was right when he claimed to have seen Harald Olesen picking up a young woman from an NS meeting in Asker in 1939. She came from Drammen and had a relationship with Harald Olesen. Which he absolutely did not want to be reminded of later, for various reasons I hope I do not need to explain. So "S", who is mentioned briefly in Harald Olesen's diary, stands for "Sonja". He would naturally still use a pet name for an old love, which means that the N Harald Olesen met unexpectedly with S, and who later tried to extort money from him, is of course her son. In which case, it is not so surprising that Kristian Lund did not want to let you see his bank statements.'

I had remembered the story with the car when I visited the caretaker, but then quickly forgotten about it again. Which annoyed me, so I moved swiftly on.

'What does "N" stand for, then?'

Patricia furrowed her brow with impatience.

'That is a relatively minor question that I cannot answer with any certainty yet, and that we may perhaps never have a definite answer to, but my guess would be that "N" stands for something à la "Nazi child". More importantly, it would seem that he is in fact Harald Olesen's own son.'

This was too much all at once. The room began to spin around me, but Patricia's voice was just as clear and convincing when she continued.

'It is of course possible that Kristian Lund was blackmailing Harald Olesen purely on the basis of his knowledge that Harald Olesen had had a relationship with a woman who supported the NS. But the reasons would of course be greater, and emotions far stronger, if Harald Olesen really was his father. It also fits well with the chronology, if we assume that Harald Olesen was in a relationship with his mother as late as 1939, and Kristian Lund was born in winter 1941. If the child was conceived in May or June 1940, it would be no less disastrous for Harald Olesen. What is more, it might explain certain similarities between the potential father and son. Both are obviously intelligent and energetic. And both have a talent for the immoral, particularly with regard to getting into the knickers of beautiful young women without their naive wives noticing!'

The latter was accompanied by a particularly unsympathetic teenage giggle. Patricia's views on love struck me as being rather cynical. However, I saw no reason to waste time discussing this, as the main thrust of her reasoning was both highly convincing and important.

'Which leaves Kristian Lund in a bit of a fix.'

Patricia immediately stopped laughing and was promptly very serious and earnest again.

'Yes and no. Yes, in the sense that he quite obviously is not only unfaithful to his wife, but has also blackmailed his father. Yes, in that he is not only a liar, but a rather conniving pathological liar. He has possibly already gone well beyond the penal boundary with regard to false evidence. But no, in the sense that it is still an open question as to whether it was he who shot Harald Olesen. In terms of the diary, N is of course a potential murderer, but so are J and O, and certainly D, in every sense. And what is more, there may also be a fifth person, who is or is not associated with one of the four, whom Harald Olesen knew nothing about. You should absolutely interview Kristian Lund again, but in the meantime, we must try to identify D, J and O. And as yet, I only have enough information to form some very insubstantial theories.'

I waited half a minute in the hope that she would share her hypotheses on the identity of D, J and O with me – insubstantial or not – but instead, she asked another unexpected question.

'The limitation period for murder in Norway is still twenty-five years, is it not?'

I confirmed this, but added swiftly that I sincerely hoped we could close the investigation into the case before then. Patricia laughed politely, but was soon serious again.

'I am thinking of the past and not the future. This may perhaps be influenced by the fact that I recently read a novel by the great Belgian–French crime writer Simenon in which the limitation period for an old murder suddenly spawned several new murders. And it may be of great importance to us too. The events that the caretaker talked of took place in winter 1944. If we now say hypothetically that one or more murders that Harald Olesen knew about, to which this Deerfoot and other living people may be linked, took place around this time . . . then they are still a criminal offence, but in one year from now they will be time-barred.'

I nodded gravely and asked whether she thought this might be decisive to the case.

'Again, yes and no. I have an increasingly strong feeling that something major and serious happened during the war that is crucial to our case now. I think that it is to a large extent a matter of emotions and the like, but the legal implications may still be important. Particularly when we consider that someone has a very strong wish that Harald Olesen should remain silent about something that happened during the war – preferably forever, but certainly until the limitation period has expired. Which also happens to fit in rather neatly with the notes in the diary.'

Patricia sat deep in thought for a moment. Then she managed once again to ambush me with a totally unexpected question.

'As you are so tall and, what is more, able to stand, could you take down my almanac for 1967? It may actually prove to be very important to the case, and should be easy to find. It should be number eight from the right on the top left-hand shelf of the bookcase behind me.'

I got up mechanically and, as instructed, counted my way to her almanac from 1967. I was unable to resist the childish temptation of mentioning that the book was in fact number ten, not eight, from the right. I immediately regretted having said anything. Patricia's face darkened, and as she reached for the almanac, she muttered something about Benedikte and Beate and reprimanding them for creating the confusion when spring-cleaning. She looked determined and a touch triumphant when she raised her eyes to meet mine, having quickly glanced in the book.

'Well, the position of the book is strictly irrelevant. I was right, however, about what is now the only important thing in this almanac and that is that Whitsun fell on the weekend of 13 to 15 May last year.'

After a minute of intense thought, I had to swallow the bitter pill and admit that I had no idea why Whitsun last year was of any significance to the murder this year. Patricia replied in a saccharine voice and with a glorious smile.

'That is perfectly understandable. There are so many unusual facts involved in this case that it requires an exceptionally good memory to see the significance of this. But it may be of great importance all the same.'

In that moment it struck me that people who appear to be very understanding may sometimes in fact instead be extremely sarcastic. Fortunately, my irritation quickly gave way to curiosity and she immediately proceeded to provide me with the explanation.

'The first time that D is mentioned in Harald Olesen's diary is when he wrote that D had visited him in his flat on 15 May 1967. Andreas Gullestad, who incidentally seems to have a memory that is worth noting, claims it was Whitsun last year when he saw the mysterious person in the blue raincoat in the building. In other words, we cannot know whether D was in 25 Krebs' Street on the evening the murder took place, and thus even less whether it was D who murdered Harald Olesen. The same is true of the person in the blue raincoat. However, it is highly likely that the person in the blue raincoat is the very same D and he did visit Harald Olesen on 15 May 1967. Which then becomes of even greater interest when we consider that a blue raincoat was discovered in the rubbish bin on the evening that Harald Olesen was murdered. Or is there something elementary that I have overlooked?'

There certainly was nothing elementary she had overlooked. I, on the other hand, had overlooked much that was not entirely elementary. However, there was one simple thing that I had understood, and which I had held back.

'In which case, what happened to D? Could D perhaps be the same as Deerfoot?'

We were definitely on to something again. Patricia gave a couple of quick nods and then continued eagerly: 'I have given considerable thought to two obvious but important questions. D could of course stand for many more conventional names or words: Dag, Danielsen, Danger – or Deerfoot. If it stands for Deerfoot, it could fit nicely with a person who entered the building on 15 May to meet Harald Olesen and who did not want to risk being recognized. But as yet we know nothing about this Deerfoot whom Harald Olesen knew during the war. We have no suggestion of a name or face, and have no idea where he came from or what he did – in fact, we cannot even rule out that "he" might in fact be a "she". The identity of Deerfoot and whether or not he or she is still alive may be of little relevance, but could also be the key to unlocking the mystery. Do ask Bjørn Erik Svendsen, Jesper Christopher Haraldsen and anyone else who may have heard about Deerfoot, next time you meet them. But if "D" does stand for "Deerfoot", and the same D reappeared from the past on the night in question to murder Harald Olesen, we not only have to explain how he or she managed to escape afterwards, we also have to find out how he or she got in without being noticed in the first place. Unless . . .'

Patricia sat staring straight ahead, deep in thought.

'Unless . . .' I said eventually, in the hope that I might prompt her. I had come to understand that Patricia did not like to say things that might later prove to be wrong. She hesitated for half a minute, but then launched in.

'Unless D did not need to get either in or out, because he or she lives in the building and was there all the time. In which case, D is someone you have already met. The Lunds and Sara Sundqvist were all born during the war, Ivar Storskog, aka Andreas Gullestad, was still just a boy when his father was shot during the war, and Konrad Jensen we can safely say was not active in the Resistance. But Darrell Williams was a young man, who was in Norway and did take an active part in the fight against the Germans. It does seem unlikely that an American would be used as a guide in Norway, but the circumstances surrounding all this are still unclear. Some loose circumstantial evidence might be that Darrell Williams was probably lighter on his feet back then, and Deerfoot is after all a well-known name from American children's literature. To be more specific, from Edward S. Ellis's books.'

'I thought it was James Fenimore Cooper,' I said.

Patricia shook her head firmly – with a slight blush on her cheeks.

'It was definitely Ellis. I don't have the books in here, of course. I read them in the lunch breaks in second or third grade. But there is no mistake about the name; the silly boys in my class certainly talked enough about his Red Indian books later.'

'Darrell Williams thought it was Cooper,' I argued with caution.

A sudden silence fell in the room.

'How did you discover that Darrell Williams thought that?' Patricia exclaimed, in an almost accusatory tone, following a minute of tense silence. Her pale face suddenly appeared to be chalk white, and something akin to a fearful wonder shone in her dark eyes.

I told her straightaway that I had already tested the name Deerfoot out on the caretaker's wife and the other residents in the building, but without great success in terms of reaction.

On this news, Patricia's face blanched further. It struck me that behind her self-assured demeanour and steady voice, she was after all still a young girl with nerves.

'I understand your motives, and it was a bold move in this great chess game. You of course thought that if anyone in the building was in fact the murderer or in cahoots with him or her, which is almost certainly the case, then the pressure would mount when he or she realized that the investigation was progressing. If the mysterious Deerfoot had anything to do with the case, the pressure and likelihood of suspicious activity would also increase.'

I nodded. That was no doubt more or less what I had subconsciously thought.

'The problem being, however, that you are absolutely right in this assumption, and therefore the risk of further dramatic events has now doubled!'

I held up my hands in defence.

'I have posted reliable armed policemen on both sides of the building. It would be quite a feat to escape without any of them noticing.'

Patricia nodded, but did not smile.

'Very good, but it is not the murderer making a dash for

163

freedom that I am afraid of. In fact, we might even hope for that: it would identify the murderer without causing any of the others harm. I am far more concerned that something dramatic might happen in the building itself. We still do not know who the murderer is, but judging from what we do know, we are hunting for an unusually cunning and determined predator.'

Patricia fidgeted uneasily in her wheelchair for a couple of minutes. It was obvious that the situation had now taken an uncontrolled turn that she did not like, and was no longer simply an intellectual game to her.

'I would urge you to arrange immediately for a policeman to stand guard on each of the three floors in 25 Krebs' Street from tonight,' she said abruptly. 'But that is of course a decision you must take yourself,' she added in the same breath.

I looked at the clock – it was a quarter past nine – and gave her an honest answer: that it was difficult to justify such drastic measures at such short notice, and what is more, we may not be able to find a further three police officers who were available right now. Indeed, the case was confusing and alarming enough as it was without us starting to see ghosts in broad daylight.

This calmed Patricia down somewhat. She apologized if she had overreacted and repeated that it was difficult decision that only I could take. However, she did ask that I at least sleep on it and evaluate the possibility in the morning. It was as though the fear and mystery in the diary had touched Patricia as well, albeit a few hours later, and despite the fact that she was so safe where she was.

The atmosphere was tense when we said our goodbyes shortly after, just as her clock struck ten. I thanked her for the food and good advice, but the only response was a cautious smile. Patricia seemed to be somewhat pacified when I promised to consider increasing security in the morning, and to let her know immediately if there were any important developments in the case.

There was a strange little incident as I got up to leave and looked around, past the bookshelves, expecting to see the ever-loyal Beate. Patricia suddenly became very concerned about how late it was and that she must not keep me any longer than necessary. She rang immediately for Beate and asked her to show me out as quickly as possible.

However, the little mystery was cleared up without any help, thankfully, when I followed Beate down the steps onto the street only a few minutes later. It also confirmed for me that Patricia had of course been right once again, and that Darrell Williams had either intentionally or unintentionally misinformed me about the Deerfoot books. They were written by Edward S. Ellis. Despite her efforts to hide the fact that they were there, I had caught a glimpse of four of the books on Patricia's bookshelf.

Once out in the night and dark again, on my way to the car, my thoughts turned quickly to the seriousness of the murder case. Even though the identity of the murderer was still unknown, I felt that with Patricia's help, we had made some important breakthroughs. When I later opened the door to my flat and collapsed on the bed, my last clear thought was that Tuesday, 9 April would probably be another dramatic day for the investigation. And I was blissfully unaware of just how dramatic it would turn out to be.

DAY SIX

A Mysterious Death

I

On Tuesday, 9 April, my working day started at the main police station at half past eight. I had Kristian Lund lined up as my first stop of the day, but I tried to be rational and asked my secretary to arrange three important meetings that I had postponed for too long: with the ambassador of the USA, Supreme Court Justice Jesper Christopher Haraldsen and Party Secretary Haavard Linde. My secretary smiled and commented that it should be possible to arrange the first in the course of the day at least. I looked at her in surprise. She pulled out a telegram that had come earlier that morning, which immediately sent a shiver down my spine.

> THE AMBASSADOR OF THE USA REQUESTS A MEETING
> AS SOON AS POSSIBLE WITH DETECTIVE INSPECTOR
> K KRISTIANSEN STOP IN CONNECTION WITH THE
> INVESTIGATION INTO THE MURDER OF HARALD OLESEN
> STOP SUGGEST MEETING IN THE EMBASSY TODAY AT 1PM
> IF POSSIBLE STOP IMMEDIATE RESPONSE DESIRED STOP
> EMBASSY COUNSELLOR GEORGE ADAMS

With a measured voice, I said that should be fine and asked my secretary to send a reply straightaway to say that I would meet George Adams at one o'clock. She then tried to set up meetings in whatever order later in the day with Jesper Christopher Haraldsen and Haavard Linde, in connection with the ongoing investigation into the murder of a former government minister and Resistance leader. I sat there for a while wondering why the American Embassy had contacted me of their own volition and requested an urgent meeting. I did not come to any conclusion – other than that it probably had something to do with Darrell Williams, and that was hardly good news from my point of view.

At nine o'clock, I telephoned the sports shop to see if Kristian Lund was at work yet. When the chirpy voice on the other end told me that he had just arrived, I politely announced my arrival in the course of a few minutes and immediately went out to the car. I needed something else to think about in advance of my meeting at the embassy and had to admit that any breakthroughs in the investigation before that time would be an enormous relief.

Kristian Lund had obviously been warned and was sitting ready in his office with a broad smile on his face when the secretary showed me in. I briskly thanked the secretary and demonstratively closed the door as soon as she had gone out. The smile on the shop manager's face had given way to a visible disquiet by the time I sat down.

'The good news for you is that we no longer need any details about your bank account.'

He nodded in anticipation. This inspired an offensive attack on my part.

'The bad news is that this is because we already know that you were blackmailing Harald Olesen.'

Kristian Lund remained impressively calm, so for a moment I wondered whether we had made a mistake. Then he nodded gravely.

'I had thought of telling you the whole story later on today . . . Denying you access to my account was a panicked reaction that would only arouse suspicions about serious matters. Yes, it is true that I have received a considerable amount from Harald Olesen on a couple of occasions in the past year, but I would not call it blackmail. It would be fairer to say I asked for and got what he should have given me a long time ago.'

I inwardly thanked Patricia for yet another bullseye and quickly followed up on this success.

'Because he was your father. That is perhaps also why you moved to 25 Krebs' Street?'

He unexpectedly shook his head in response to the latter, which was in fact an improvisation on my part.

'Believe it or not, moving into the same building was more or less pure coincidence. I may perhaps have thought that it would be exciting to live in the same building as a former Resistance leader and cabinet minister, and that may have influenced our choice, but at the time, I had no idea that he was my father. In fact, it was the other way round: I found out that he was my father because we moved in there. But yes, you are right – he was my father. And I hope that you will soon also be able to conclude that my financial disagreement with my father had nothing to do with his death.'

I was not willing to draw any conclusions straightaway and demanded an immediate and honest answer from Kristian Lund regarding how and when he discovered the relationship. He was silent at first, but then he started, following a short and bitter laugh.

'I'm more than happy to tell you; it was a strange coincidence. As you no doubt remember I told you, I had badgered my mother for years to get her to tell me who my father was. Well, I had reached the stage where I had more or less accepted the fact that it would forever be a secret. It felt less important now that I had a good job and my own family. And what is more, Mother was seriously ill, so nagging her any more felt wrong. But then came that fateful day in late autumn, about a year and a half ago. It was the last time that my mother managed to visit us, and I had to more or less carry her out of the flat in Drammen. I have often wondered later how different things might have been if she had not been able to come that day. But I cannot imagine that it had anything to do with the murder . . .'

He nodded pensively, lit up a cigarette and then carried on.

'I had parked the car and was about to help Mother in. She coughed and coughed and hung round my neck like a sick child. We were on our way up the stairs when suddenly I noticed her face freeze in a look of surprise and devotion I had never seen before. I looked up and discovered that we had bumped into Harald Olesen, but I barely had time to recognize him as he more or less stormed back up the stairs and into his flat. I immediately thought it very odd, as he had been on his way out when we met on the stairs. I did not manage to see his face. My mother said nothing and I did not like to ask. But she seemed distant and strange for the rest of the day, and my suspicions that there was some kind of connection between her and Harald Olesen only grew stronger.'

Kristian Lund blew some smoke rings out into the room as he pondered, but then picked up the story again.

'And so once more I spent a considerable amount of time pondering the great mystery of my childhood. One day, I went to the library and found some books with pictures of him from the war. I look more like my mother, so our faces were not that similar, but the eyes and ears were so alike that it seemed to confirm what I thought. It was a difficult dilemma. My mother was hovering between life and death, and I did not want to do anything that would make the burden heavier for her. But at the same time, the uncertainty surrounding my father's identity burned inside with increasing intensity the closer Mother came to death. Then they called from the hospital in Drammen one evening to say that Mother was not likely to live through the night and I made up my mind. I drove straight there and sat by her side from eight in the evening until she finally let go of the pain at around six o'clock in the morning. That night, she nodded in answer when I asked if Harald Olesen was my father. She had thought that no one would believe us and that everything would just get worse if she said anything, she told me. Those were her last words. I said that I forgave her and held her hand tight until all the warmth had left it. Then I walked through the empty hospital corridors alone, feeling a deep love for my mother, and a passionate hatred for my father because he had let us both down for all those years.'

My impression was that Kristian Lund's love for his mother was deep and sincere, in a life that was guided by few other values and an otherwise cynical attitude to women. This impression was strengthened when he continued.

'It was a hectic and difficult time. I became a father three days after I lost my mother, and buried her four days after that. I was anxious to see whether Harald Olesen would at least do her the honour of coming to her funeral, but he did not make an appearance. So I went up to the second floor and knocked on his door. He blanched when I confronted him, giving me the confirmation that I needed. But my first meeting with my father was not as I had hoped. He still managed to say some nice things about my mother – that she had accepted the consequences of her errors during the war and had not talked about it later. But me, his only son, he addressed scornfully simply as "NS boy". I pointed out that I had never had anything to do with the NS and asked how he, if he was so morally pure himself, had ended up in bed with an NS woman after the outbreak of war. At that, he asked me never to speak to him again and slammed the door in my face.'

Kristian Lund shook his head in exasperation, and to be fair, it was easy to understand why.

'This insult made me even more determined. I sent him a letter in which I wrote that I could not force him to see me, but I did have the right, as his only child, to an inheritance – and that I intended to get what was mine, even if it meant I had to go to the national papers and the supreme court. I had grown up poor because he had never cared about me, his only son, and did not want to risk that either I or my young son would ever be in that position again. He told me that he had burned the letter, the next time I knocked on his door. But he was calmer this time, no doubt as he was now ill himself. He would be more than happy to give me some money on the quiet if I would be satisfied with that and not make any more demands. In the end, he gave me two payments of a hundred thousand kroner, one last autumn and one in February just past. But he would not promise me anything in terms of his will. So there you have it: I pressured him to give me my well-deserved inheritance, but still do not know whether I succeeded. If you asked me whether I feel like a good son, the answer would be no, but my father did not deserve a good son either.'

Given that the story that Kristian Lund had just told was close to the full truth, then it was hard to disagree with his conclusion. I made a quick note that 'N' in the diary in all likelihood stood for 'NS boy' and that the explanation given by Kristian Lund was in line with what Harald Olesen had written in his diary. I then asked if he had anything more to add in relation to the murder. He repeated that he had an absolutely clear conscience. He sounded convincing enough, but my trust in Kristian Lund had been steadily eroded. So I said that it would have been more credible if he had told us straightaway, but that we would of course take his story seriously and keep all options open. In response to my final question, whether he was still in touch with Sara Sundqvist, he replied that he had broken off all contact and had no intention of renewing it. The murder now stood between them like a wall.

I left the sports shop at half past ten on Tuesday, 9 April with the feeling that I had more than enough to deal with at the moment. The weight of expectation increased further when my secretary back at the main station beamed and told me that she had indeed arranged two meetings, one with Jesper Christopher Haraldsen at eleven o'clock and one with Haavard Linde at midday. I had to scramble in order not to be late for the meeting with one of my childhood idols.

II

It can be a strange experience suddenly to stand face to face as an adult with one of the great heroes of your childhood and youth. Which is precisely how I felt when I was shown into Jesper Christopher Haraldsen's office on Youngstorget on 9 April 1968. In my youth, I had been interested in his work both as one of the country's leading lawyers and as a cabinet minister who had held several important posts for various governments. However, my youthful fascination with him had been spawned by the heroic stories of his efforts as a leader of the Home Front during the occupation. And I have to admit I was now excited not only about what he would have to tell me about Harald Olesen, but also about being able to see a living legend in the flesh.

The man who stood up behind the vast, orderly desk was just as I had imagined: upright, powerful and dynamic in his movements, with a firm handshake and a brightness in his eye. Patience did not appear to be one of his strengths, even though he was now well over fifty. He interrupted my attempt to give a brief outline of the case after only two minutes, with the comment that he still read the papers and could I please get to the point.

In his reply to my question regarding Harald Olesen's contribution and importance during the war, Jesper Christopher Haraldsen briskly said that both were great, but not quite in the national league to which he himself belonged. Harald Olesen had been involved in various actions, as well as smuggling refugees across the border, and for a time functioned as the regional leader for the Resistance in Hedmark and Oppland. Jesper Christopher Haraldsen mentioned intelligence, self-control and luck as his best qualities in his work for the Home Front. I was taken aback by the last, but just had to take note of the supreme court justice's very firm opinion that luck was a good quality that some people had – and Olesen had it in ample supply.

Haraldsen dismissed the suggestion that there may have been some form of internal strife in the Home Front that may have resulted in someone bearing a grudge against Harald Olesen. He had far more belief in the theory that it might be a somewhat postponed revenge killing by the Nazis, without linking it to any particular event or person. Haraldsen frowned for a minute or two in response to my question about a man who worked for the Resistance and went under the code name Deerfoot. He then answered that he had never heard of this person and that it sounded like a rather unlikely code name for a Norwegian Resistance fighter. Haraldsen was visibly rattled, but I found it difficult to discern whether this was due to something he knew or something he felt he ought to know. According to Jesper Christopher Haraldsen, Olesen had been a sound and well-intentioned cabinet minister, but never one of the leading lights. He had rarely dealt with the most important issues in government.

When I asked about possible connections with the American intelligence services, Jesper Christopher Haraldsen leaned forward over his desk and his voice took on a steel edge. He found it inappropriate that such convoluted conspiracies against our most important ally were triggered by the mere fact that there was an American diplomat living in the same building. He also felt that it was illustrative of the younger generation that they did not view a convicted Nazi who also lived there with the same suspicion. He claimed to have no knowledge as to whether Olesen had had any significant contact with the American intelligence services. And added that I could be certain that if such had existed, he would most certainly have known and remembered.

As far as Haraldsen knew, Harald Olesen had always been a forward-thinking man in terms of foreign policy and was therefore a loyal friend of the USA. It was utterly unthinkable that the Americans would participate in any form of political assassination in Norway. And what was more, it was even more inconceivable, if possible, that they would then target an old friend who no longer held a position. Anyone of more than average intelligence must realize that. If he, based on his own long experience, were to give me some advice, it would be to look for the perpetrator in marginalized extremist circles, be that far right or far left. Far-right and far-left dictators were equally insane, and he was sorry to say that he would have to be in court shortly for an important case. I took the hint, shook his hand and beat a hasty retreat.

I now had definite proof that the rumours regarding Haraldsen's forceful character and intelligence were true. But I also had to admit, somewhat unwillingly, that the rumours about his arrogance and obstinacy were not without basis. In terms of the investigation, I noted grimly that nothing had come to light that might indicate a link with either the victim's work as a cabinet minister or as a leader of the Home Front in the Oslo area.

I descended the stairs from Jesper Christopher Haraldsen's office and made my way to meet another of the idols from my youth, whom I hoped would be able to cast more light on Harald Olesen's political history and the possible significance of the USA lead.

III

Although my parents now belong to the upper class, and the family on my mother's side is decidedly bourgeois, both my father and my paternal grandfather were former representatives of the Labour Party. My own political affiliation also lay here, though it went no further than a party membership and a low-level position in the police union. I had grown up with stories about the party's great leaders. And among them, the now ageing Haavard Linde held a special position, thanks to his former far-sighted fight against dictators and for military rearmament in Norway. So I was fraught with anticipation when I entered the Labour Party's offices to meet this party legend. It was obvious that he was still held in high esteem by the employees. The middle-aged secretary who came to meet me lit up when his name was mentioned and assured me that he would do his best to help me.

I entered Party Secretary Linde's office with some trepidation: he too had a reputation for being a temperamental man. I was, however, pleasantly surprised. Haavard Linde was casually dressed in jeans and a checked shirt, and was apparently in a very good and relaxed mood. He beamed and squeezed my hand, and to my surprise knew immediately who I was talking about when I mentioned my father. 'Now there's a good man!' he exclaimed enthusiastically. He was even happier when he realized that I myself was a party member and union official. Without hesitation, he intimated that it was young people like me that the party needed in these critical times. I had no desire to know precisely what he meant by that and moved the conversation promptly on to the murder investigation.

Haavard Linde's expression saddened when Harald Olesen was mentioned. For a moment I thought I saw tears in his eyes, but his voice was firm when he carried on speaking. Harald Olesen had been a 'good man' who had done so much for the party over the years, and his death had been a shock. It had to be said that he was past his prime when he became a cabinet minister, and that his performance there was not his greatest achievement. But he was still someone you could rely on and who had helped form the country and party into what they were today.

The very idea that anyone in the party may have wished to kill Harald Olesen was inconceivable to Haavard Linde. Olesen had never been a divisive politician, was well liked by everyone and had not been part of the disagreements that had so blighted the 1960s. The thought that anyone in the party would want to physically harm someone else in the party seemed equally ludicrous.

In answer to my question whether someone in politics outside the Labour Party might have harboured a deep hatred of Harald Olesen, Haavard Linde had little to say. He thought about it and said that one never knew with the communists and the various groups attached to them. But he could think of no reason why they should hate Harald Olesen and so could not name any person or group who might be responsible. The old communist party was on its last legs. And he simply sneered at the new communist party, which he called the Socialist People's Party, but did add that given their anti-military stance, they could hardly be suspected of an armed attack.

As soon as we touched on the USA, the hitherto pleasant conversation abruptly gathered pace. When I asked whether Harald Olesen had had any special contact with the Americans, Haavard Linde instantly replied that he had never heard of any such thing. However, his curiosity was piqued by this and he wondered from where I had got such a strange idea. I answered that so far it was not based on anything concrete, but was still a possibility that was being considered. Not least because of the strange coincidence that an American diplomat was living in the same building. Saying this to Haavard Linde was like turning the knob on a hotplate – the temperature rose fast. Within five seconds he had launched into a long and increasingly passionate tirade about the Americans being our friends and most important allies, and that I could dismiss any suggestion that they in any way had anything to do with the murder.

A minute later, I was told that the very idea that American intelligence would do any such thing in Norway was unthinkable, and we youngsters must never for a moment believe anything else, no matter what the communist propaganda machine churned out. And furthermore, he had himself met Darrell Williams on a couple of occasions and he was a good man whom no one could accuse of wrongdoing. Haavard Linde's voice got louder and louder, his face got redder and redder, and his movements more and more animated. I quickly realized that it would be impossible to continue the conversation, but remained seated, intrigued, and listened to his impassioned lecture.

There followed a rather chaotic, but nevertheless extremely interesting, fifteen-minute tour of the interwar period, the Second World War and the Cold War. Then all of a sudden, Linde burned out and collapsed onto his chair. He was perhaps not in such good shape as he had been in his heyday in the 1940s and 1950s, but he still looked impressively dynamic. I gingerly gave my thanks and left the party office in a bit of a rush.

My conclusion was that there were clearly no grounds to believe that anyone from the Labour Party or wider political circles would have had any desire to bump off Harald Olesen. On the other hand – despite his great passion and charisma – I could not simply accept Haavard Linde's categorical denial of any connection with the American Embassy. Rather, my feeling that there was something combustible hidden here – though not necessarily a motive for murder – got stronger as I drove away.

IV

I smelt a rat as soon as I was shown in to Counsellor George Adams's office. The man who was waiting for me behind the mahogany desk was nearly six foot six, slim and bald, dressed in an alarmingly neutral black suit and could have been anywhere between thirty-five and fifty-five years old. Both his words and voice were those of a shrewd, super-power diplomat – of the sort who can talk and be friendly, but be holding a large club behind his back all the while. As I sat down, I was reminded of what Professor Borchmann had said about how it felt to meet someone who was always one step ahead of you. This embassy counsellor reminded me of a cobra, with his slimness and length, as he more or less coiled himself round to tower over me, while keeping steady eye contact.

Once he had shaken my hand and shown me to a chair that was lower than his own throne behind the desk, George Adams did not beat about the bush.

'Let me first say how grateful we are that you were able to respond so quickly to our request for a meeting, and that we have heard great things about you, that you are a detective inspector of rare talent and have a very promising career ahead of you. We therefore hope that our concerns regarding this case can be dealt with swiftly.'

I was very curious as to who had said such great things about me, but he brusquely waved this off.

'Now, to clarify the starting point, as I am sure you are aware, there have been some well-organized and extremely exaggerated reactions to the unfortunate consequences of the ongoing conflict in Vietnam. These are to a large extent organized by Norwegian communist sympathizers, but are, at the moment, having a regrettable influence on some Norwegian newspapers and public opinion. However, this does not mean there has been any change to our relationship. The USA is Norway's most important ally and the only real guarantor for Norway's survival as an independent state. Fortunately, most of the leading politicians and senior public officials both know and appreciate this.'

Once again, I wondered if he had any particular names in mind, but contained myself and indicated that he should continue.

'Given this background, we would like to express a degree

of concern that you, as far as we understand, appear to suspect a highly valued American diplomat of murder.'

I looked at him, perplexed. Now I really had no idea who he had been talking to.

'Who has said that I do?'

He graced me with a forced smile.

'It has not been said explicitly, but it is hard to interpret otherwise the fact that you asked the person in question to remain available for questioning and have even requested information regarding his financial situation. We find this to be a very unconventional approach, and should the wrong voices in the media get wind of this, it could result in some very negative attention, both in Norway and the USA, which in turn could have very unfavourable consequences for the diplomat in question and key people in the incumbent presidential administration in the USA. But also for those officials involved in Norway . . .'

This was feeling more and more like a threat. I tried to play the diplomat in the hope of steering the conversation onto a more positive track.

'I would like to stress that the person in question is not officially a suspect, but is one of a large group of people who were present in the building on the night of the murder and have therefore been asked to remain available for questioning. What is more, I am not under the impression that he has any particular desire to leave Oslo.'

George Adams nodded, but still did not smile.

'We of course understand that such availability might be desirable. However, it is doubtful that the press would appreciate such subtleties in a situation in which an American diplomat has been ordered to stay in Oslo against his own wishes and those of his employer. Furthermore, we have also been led to understand that you have in fact already had several conversations with the person in question and that he has nothing more of any interest to add. Unless there are grounds to believe that he may in some way be linked to the murder. But such a theory would require strong evidence, and if such exists, it would only be reasonable that the embassy was informed of what this might be . . . Unless such material can be provided, we are of the opinion that the best way to avoid any unfounded suspicions is that the person in question is given permission to leave Oslo. And I confirm this is his personal wish and that of his employer.'

The man's voice was still seductively friendly and it was tempting to give him this right straightaway. However, I broke into a sweat when I imagined the possible scandalous headline: 'Norwegian Detective Allows American Embassy to Take Over Murder Case.' This was quickly followed by another: 'American Murder Suspect Allowed to Leave Oslo: Police Chief Apologizes and Detective Resigns.' I was frantically trying to think of a suitable response, but came up with nothing better than the platitude that I unfortunately could not release any material from the investigation, nor could I allow key witnesses to leave the country, for fear of the public reaction. But I swiftly added that I would certainly reassess the situation and hoped we could find a mutual solution soon.

To the extent that I had hoped that Adams would say that he was happy with that, I was disappointed. He replied that the embassy obviously had to assess this, but underlined that a prompt explanation would be desirable in a situation in which the journalists could at any moment become interested in the case and misunderstand things.

I had actually just got up to leave when I made an error of judgement that I found hard to understand later on in the day. Instead of accepting this short though undefined delay in the investigation, I asked a critical question.

'I also have a question, and I hope that the answer may help the investigation: is it normal that senior American diplomats are accommodated in private flats in Torshov? And if not, was there any particular reason why Darrell Williams was placed there?'

George Adams's head shot up and forwards across the desk, and he fixed me with gimlet eyes. For a moment I was afraid that he would lean right over and sink two venomous fangs into me. Instead, he whipped me with his silky voice.

'First of all, it is highly unusual for the USA's embassies in any country to be asked to give comment to the police on the choice of diplomats' accommodation. Secondly, it is even more unheard of for detective inspectors to suggest that certain named individuals have been placed somewhere by the embassy with the intent of committing serious crime. I assume that as you are asking such questions, it is because you have very concrete and well-reasoned suspicions that you can share with us?'

There was total silence in the room. I had been outmanoeuvred by George Adams and could not think of anything to say that would not make my position even more exposed. I had the acute feeling that there was no smoke without fire, but could not even guess what it might be. And so I just stood there without saying a word – and hoped that this deeply uncomfortable meeting would soon be over. It felt as though the floor beneath me was shaking when George Adams very efficiently closed the conversation.

'In that case, I will not take up more of your time, but I hope that the investigation will be concluded in the near future in a way that is satisfactory for everyone concerned.'

I took the hint and hurried out of the room without making any attempt to shake his hand. Later, I could not even recall how I got out. It felt more like I had fallen than walked out. What I did remember, however, was that I fortunately met no one on my way out of the American Embassy.

V

I have always seen myself as a rather balanced and calm man, but it has to be said that on the afternoon of 9 April 1968, behind my mask, I was in a very sombre and agitated frame of mind. Despite the discovery of the diary and other advances the previous day, I was still far from arresting anyone in the case – something that more and more newspapers were calling for, according to the pool of secretaries. The day's three clashes with George Adams, Jesper Christopher Haraldsen and Haavard Linde had hardly increased the chances of finding a solution to the murder mystery. To the contrary, they had quite clearly increased the danger that the head of the investigation might encounter problems both in completing the investigation and keeping his position. And I must come clean that an hour after lunch, I was thinking more about the threat to my own position than about the possibilities inherent in the continued investigation. Another hour passed before I realized that I had, in fact, not eaten lunch. In the meantime, I had the wildest thoughts about what influences the American Embassy, Jesper Christopher Haraldsen or Haavard Linde might have and use against me. The fact that the country had a centre-right government who were unlikely to obey orders from someone in the Labour Party, and especially not in connection with a murder investigation, was not something I thought about at the time.

At one point, I was convinced that a phone call from the government calling for my resignation was imminent and wondered whether it would be the minister of justice, the foreign minister or the prime minister himself who called. My defence in terms of the anticipated phone call was nothing more than a couple of sentences along the lines of that I was responsible for investigating the murder of a former top politician and was therefore duty-bound to hold all options open, also in relation to foreign nationals. No doubt they would ask how I could even think of accusing an American diplomat and whether this had been cleared in advance with the Ministry of Foreign Affairs, or at the very least with the chief of police in Oslo. And to that, I had no good answer.

My pulse started to slow after the first long hour and then another hour that was almost as long without anyone storming in – and without the telephone ringing. It did, however, rocket again when it started to ring at twenty-five past two – despite orders to the switchboard that only important messages should be put through. I swore out loud twice before I picked up the receiver with a shaking hand.

'Detective Inspector Kristiansen,' I said, as firmly as I could, and then shrank back from the expected tirade. Which never came. To begin with, there was silence on the other end of the line. Then some heavy breathing and a small sigh. Followed not by a furious man's voice, but by a thin, frightened woman's voice.

'I do apologize if this is a bad time to call. They said it had to be very important, but I said it was about the murder, and that I was calling about a horrible situation at the scene of the crime. It's me, Randi Hansen, the caretaker's wife from 25 Krebs' Street, where Harald Olesen was killed, if you remember me.'

The enormous weight lifted from my shoulders with a shudder. I answered with real joy that of course I remembered her, and that of course she had done the right thing in calling.

'It won't take long. It's probably just me being a bit fearful and overly cautious after the murder, but I decided that I had to ring because now I'm starting to get very worried about one of the other residents here.'

I snapped to attention. The faces of the surviving neighbours ran through my mind and it has to be said that it was Sara Sundqvist's smiling face that remained. Fortunately, the caretaker's wife carried on regardless in her stuttering voice and another, less dangerous face replaced it.

'It's Konrad Jensen. He was so beside himself and terrified yesterday, you see. Poor Konrad didn't even dare set foot outside his door, and did not open it until he had checked three times that it was me. I was going to do some shopping for him and knocked on his door to deliver it at midday today. He made a great deal of fuss about it being midday, so he could know it was me. I got there at twelve on the dot. I rang the bell several times, but he didn't open, so I started to get worried. At first, I thought that maybe he had just fallen asleep, or that he had somehow snuck by me when I was out. But it's well past two now and he is not answering his phone or responding to the doorbell or to knocking, so I am really worried that something terrible has happened to him. I have a key, but don't want to go in before you say that I should. And Lord only knows if I would dare go in by myself, even if you say that I should, because I don't like this one bit!'

Her voice rose to soprano pitch, then fizzled out and the heavy breathing returned.

I took a few seconds to gather my thoughts, and once again saw the tortured face of Konrad Jensen from the evening before. I could not imagine what powers on earth could have got him to leave his flat for several hours today. And I also desperately wanted to get away from the tele- phone and the office. So I heard myself saying that she should just stay at her post with the key; I would personally drive over and we could go into the flat together. She could not thank me enough, and said again what a good person I was, and assured me that she would not leave her post for one second until I arrived. I promised to be there as soon as I could and put down the receiver. Thankfully, the telephone remained silent as I rushed out of the office.

It was only when I reached my car that I realized that I did not have my service gun with me. I hesitated for a moment, but then sneaked back past the phone to get it. I was not ex- pecting a shootout in Konrad Jensen's flat, but said to myself that if I was armed, it might have a reassuring and calming effect on the caretaker's wife and the other residents. The truth was that the caretaker's wife had infected me just a little with her fear. I did not want to venture into the building unarmed, far less into Konrad Jensen's locked flat.

The caretaker's wife was sitting anxiously at her table when I arrived at 25 Krebs' Street. She bobbed with relief and mumbled her thanks. I tried to reassure her, and to a certain degree managed. However, my own pulse was starting to race. I asked her to try calling him again, which she immediately did. I took the receiver and stood listening to ring after ring without anyone answering. After twelve seemingly endless signals, I put the phone down and nodded for her to follow me up the few steps to the ground-floor flats.

We rang the bell three times with no response. I knocked so hard that I thought the door might break, and shouted as loudly as I could. This only succeeded in alarming Andreas Gullestad, who rolled out of the neighbouring flat, and Mrs Lund, who came running down from the floor above with her son on her arm. But there was still no sign of life from Konrad Jensen's flat.

I eventually said what we all were thinking: that there was no other option than to let ourselves in. I called for PC Eriksen to come from his post by the corner outside and asked him to stand guard at the door while I went in. He stayed there, standing beside Andreas Gullestad and Mrs Lund, who was still holding her young son. We were all gripped by the tension, neither of them wanting to return to their flats until the drama was over, despite my request. Mrs Lund went to her flat to put her son down in the cot, but then came running back down. I asked the caretaker's wife to unlock the door and then wait while I went in. She nodded frantically and fumbled with the lock for some time until she managed to open it.

I went into Konrad Jensen's flat alone, with my service gun

in my hand and all my senses on full alert. I noticed straightaway that the ceiling light was on, which was strange if he had gone out. But apart from the light, there was no evidence of anything suspicious in Konrad Jensen's hallway. His shoes stood by the door, and his worn grey overcoat hung there on a hook. There was nothing else of any interest to see, and certainly no people.

It sounded like a thunderclap in the loaded silence when I shouted: 'Are you there, Konrad Jensen?' I could almost hear the constable and two neighbours jump outside the flat, but all remained quiet inside. Deathly quiet, it occurred to me.

Other than myself, there was not another living soul in the flat. But Konrad Jensen was there all the same. I saw him as soon as I went through the door into the living room. The light was on there too.

Konrad Jensen was slumped in his threadbare armchair by the coffee table. His eyes were closed, but the bullet wound between his eyes was very much open. His features had frozen into a twisted grimace when the bullet hit. Even in death, Konrad Jensen looked bitter about life.

It took no more than a glance to confirm that Konrad Jensen was dead. The bullet had gone straight through his head and was embedded in the back of the chair behind him. And I could confirm that he had been dead for quite some time when I gingerly touched his left hand. All human warmth had left him. His hand hung heavy and useless down the side of the chair. On the floor below lay a gun, which I quickly identified as a Kongsberg Colt .45. Everything fell into place, even before I spotted the BIC ballpoint and white paper on the table in front of him. The sheet had obviously been folded about two-thirds of the way up, but now it lay open in front of him, with the writing facing up. I read the letter with agitation and increasing relief.

> The undersigned, Konrad Jensen, hereby confesses that
> it was I who shot and killed Harald Olesen last Thursday,
> in revenge for his involvement in the fight against Nazism
> during the war. I now regret my crime and have therefore
> ended my unworthy life rather than serving the sentence
> that could be expected following my imminent arrest.
> May the Almighty have mercy on my soul!

The text was written on a typewriter, but the signature, Konrad Jensen, was written in ink just below.

I nodded to myself, as I stood there alone in the flat with a dead man and a signed suicide note. It was a huge relief, but also strangely disappointing. The most obvious solution had in fact been the truth all along: the hero of the Resistance had fallen at the hands of an avenging small-time Nazi. All the creative and advanced theories that Patricia had mooted and that I had allowed myself to believe in had, despite their brilliance, been of no practical relevance to the case.

The circumstances surrounding Konrad Jensen's death prevented me from feeling any sympathy for him. If anything, I was annoyed because I had been fooled long enough to allow him to commit suicide before an arrest. And I have to admit that I immediately started to think about how I would present it to the press and my superiors. On the positive side, the case had been solved and the investigation could be closed. The wild sidetrack involving the American Embassy could be buried now without further ado.

As I stood there lost in my own thoughts, it suddenly

dawned on me that I was no longer alone in the room. PC Eriksen had come as far as the threshold to the living room, closely followed by the caretaker's wife and Mrs Lund. A short distance behind came Andreas Gullestad in his wheelchair. I gave a friendly nod and held up the letter for them to see.

'It was him! He has written a confession and then killed himself!'

There was a moment's silence, and then the caretaker's wife whispered: 'Thank goodness for that!' which immediately broke the mood.

PC Eriksen was the first to shake my hand, closely followed by the others. I was somewhat surprised by this positive reaction, but true to form, I played along with it. My attempts to say that it was not *just* thanks to me were, much to my relief, immediately dismissed.

'Of course it is thanks to you,' exclaimed Mrs Lund ardently. 'I said to Kristian only yesterday, after you had been here, that we could expect an arrest soon. And Konrad Jensen must have realized that as well and so put an end to his life rather than be arrested. Because it was him you suspected all along, wasn't it?'

I grasped this branch without it being too obvious and said something diplomatic about it never being good to make a hasty arrest in cases like this, and that we had indeed made some important breakthroughs in the investigation, and that Konrad Jensen had always been the prime suspect. The caretaker's wife shed tears of relief that the murderer had been caught and they were all safe again. Both Andreas Gullestad and Mrs Lund nodded in agreement and said that none could have handled the case better and more professionally than I had done.

I got nervous for a moment when I saw Darrell Williams coming down the stairs. If he had heard about my set-to with the embassy counsellor earlier on in the day, it did not in any way affect his behaviour. He also spontaneously gave me his hand and congratulated me sincerely on the successful conclusion of the investigation. However, Sara Sundqvist's reaction was an even greater relief. At first, she seemed confused, but then beamed when I repeated what she had already heard, that Konrad Jensen was dead and had confessed to the murder in a suicide note. In a rush of joy, she embraced me warmly. When I felt her soft body pressed against mine, I thought for a moment that perhaps I was getting too close to the residents. But as there were no journalists or photographers present, I allowed myself to be infected by their relief.

It was nearly four o'clock in the afternoon by the time I returned to the station. My boss was waiting for me with flowers, and my colleagues more or less queued up to congratulate me. It was clear that, while it had not been obvious, the case had been an increasingly aggravated sore point for the rest of the station as well. The fact that the murderer had confessed in writing and then shot himself was, in the words of an overworked police lawyer, 'the perfect solution'. And several of my colleagues also commented that the case had been solved with almost perfect timing, with one more newspaper edition to go before the Easter holidays. It started to dawn on me just how fortunate I had been, and that with the help of the statements from the residents of 25 Krebs' Street, I could well benefit hugely from this case, both in terms of the newspapers and from my superiors.

The only thorn was my persisting anxiety that there may be further complications with the American Embassy, and I saw my opportunity to save face when I was invited into my boss's office. I mentioned that one of the people who lived in the building was an employee of the American Embassy, and that I had made it clear to the embassy that he was in no way a suspect, but that until an arrest was made, he was requested to remain available for questioning as a witness. My visibly relieved boss immediately supported me in this, and added the American must surely understand that in such situations it was important to work with the police in allied countries. He thanked me for upholding the integrity of the force and for preventing any unnecessarily critical questions from the press. If anything more was said about it, I should just refer it on to him and demand that Americans in Norway comply with the murder investigation. He would have no problems in stating this to the national broadcasting services, the Ministry of Foreign Affairs and the Norwegian press, should it be necessary.

There was nothing to cast a shadow on my joy after this. My boss and I congratulated each other a further three times on our excellent success, before I practically floated into my own office again.

VI

All alone in the middle of my desk lay a simple small white envelope, addressed with a neat hand and a stamp. The letter was brief.

7 April 1968

To Detective Inspector Kolbjørn Kristiansen,

The only person in 25 Krebs' Street who has told you
the truth is Konrad Jensen.

Patricia Louise I. E. Borchmann

It was impossible not to burst into laughter at the short, solemn text. I had forgotten young Miss Patricia in all the excitement following Konrad Jensen's death and the happy resolution of the murder mystery. I quickly recognized that she should be informed that the case was closed, out of respect, before hearing about it on the television and reading about it in the papers. And I would also have to point out that her more circumstantial explanations were redundant. With a considerably lighter heart than on previous days, I lifted the receiver and dialled her number, which I now knew by heart. I saw no reason whatsoever to ration the good news when she answered the phone.

'I have just found Konrad Jensen dead. He was locked in his flat with a bullet wound to his head and a .45-calibre gun on the floor beside him. On the table in front of him was a suicide note in which he confessed to the murder of Harald Olesen.'

Patricia's reaction was intense, but not at all the positive one that I had hoped for.

Her 'Damnation!' exploded in my ear.

Then there was silence for a few seconds. When she spoke again, it was more muted.

'Excuse my French. I am not angry with you, but furious with myself. Because exactly what I feared would happen has happened: the murderer felt pushed into a corner and struck again. And I had reason to believe that Konrad Jensen would be the one, but did not want to say anything for fear of being wrong. Damn, damn – but we will solve both the murders!'

I smiled smugly to myself and spoke in a patronizingly kind voice: 'But my dear Patricia, there was only ever *one* murder and it has now been solved. Konrad Jensen shot Harald Olesen and then himself. We have his written and signed confession, and there is no evidence of anyone else having been in his flat.'

There was silence for a few moments again; then Patricia's sharp voice returned.

'I agree that we are dealing with a particularly cunning murderer and another exceedingly sophisticated murder. But with all due respect, do you really believe what you just said?'

I was starting to get irritated now and fell for the temptation of an arrogant answer.

'Of course I believe what I just said, and so does everyone else here. You see, we are police officers – and live in the real world.'

More silence, but Patricia obviously still had no intention of giving up.

'In which case, there are certain simple things from the real world that you might simply be able to explain to silly little me, who sits locked away in my ivory tower. Number one: what about the blue raincoat? Who wore it, and why was it thrown away on the night of the murder? Number two: what about the diary? Who are the J and O that Harald Olesen writes about, not to speak of D, of whom he was so frightened?'

It was only when she fired these questions at me that I, for the first time, got the uncomfortable feeling that there was indeed something amiss and that perhaps our conclusion was wrong.

'I am aware that there are still things that we have not cleared up, but there are many possible explanations. D, J and O could be half the town, as could the man in the blue raincoat, and do not necessarily need to be involved in the murder in any way. "J" may even stand for "Jensen", as I suggested. But now we have the murder weapon and a confession from a previously convicted Nazi who was in the same building on the night of the murder and has since committed suicide. That seems clear enough to me.'

Patricia said nothing; for a moment she seemed to be in doubt, but then her voice returned.

'I admit that it is all extremely clever, but that is exactly what makes it so odd. Just think of Konrad Jensen – a small-time Nazi of average intelligence who never really used it to any success and was weak and self-centred by nature. It is unthinkable that he could devise such a sophisticated plot for murdering an old Resistance hero like Harald Olesen. What makes it even more absurd is that he so obviously would be the first person to be suspected and the target of any reactions. Can you imagine Konrad Jensen thinking up the clever plan with the stereo player and then shooting Harald Olesen in cold blood? I obviously do not have enough imagination.'

And neither did I, truth be told. I felt I was on shifting ground, but defended my triumph resolutely.

'It is not easy to imagine, no. I also doubted that it could be him, but the combination of the murder weapon and a typewritten confession are pretty persuasive.'

The voice at the other end of the line was silent for nearly half a minute. Then it came back – echoing more disbelief than before.

'Typewritten? Did you really say that his confession was typewritten?'

When I heard the depth of scepticism in Patricia's voice, I got that extremely frustrating feeling one gets when one realizes that something is far from right – without knowing exactly what.

'Yes. The body of Konrad Jensen's suicide note was typewritten, but the handwritten signature underneath is definitely his!'

Silence again. Patricia's voice was steely when she replied.

'But surely Konrad Jensen barely knew his way around the alphabet, let alone the keys of a typewriter. And you have never mentioned that he had a typewriter in his flat. Does he?'

The question hit me like a boxing glove in the stomach. I myself had gone through the few things in Konrad Jensen's flat after the murder of Harald Olesen, and I had gone through all the rooms again today and there was not a typewriter to be seen anywhere.

'If there is no typewriter in the flat, how on earth could Konrad Jensen type the suicide note himself when he has not dared set foot outside the door for days? Let us hope you have a good answer to that, in the event that a journalist with even a below-average IQ should show up – out there in the real world.'

This time it was a knockout. I allowed myself to be swallowed by my swivel chair and was suddenly very glad that I was alone in my office.

When Patricia eventually asked if I was still there, I answered that I was, but that I would very shortly be on my way over to see her. She said she would be waiting for me, and reminded me to bring both the murder weapon and the suicide note, and then put down the phone. I took the hint and more or less ran along the corridors out into the real world.

VII

Patricia was obviously both piqued and motivated by the news of Konrad Jensen's death. She sat leaning across the table, impatient, while I told her about the day's meetings and the events leading up to the discovery of Konrad Jensen's body. To my relief, she just shook her head and waved me on when I tentatively indicated that I perhaps had been a bit harsh on the embassy counsellor regarding Darrell Williams. My narrative consumed us both. The coffee cups that Beate had put out were still untouched when I finished and leaned back in my chair.

'I agree that the question of the typewriter is an important argument and that he probably did not commit suicide, but surely it is not absolutely impossible?' I ventured, once I had finished my update.

She shook her head, but did try to humour me.

'I believe that it is out of the question, but agree that in theory it is a possibility that we do have to take into account. Konrad Jensen may have typed the suicide note before murdering Harald Olesen, or may in some way have managed to get it in at some later point. But that seems to be as unlikely and absurd as me being selected by a football team. Nevertheless, the combination of the gun and a signed suicide note is of course impossible to ignore. Konrad Jensen must have been extremely willing to cooperate if he signed a suicide note before he was shot. Typewritten suicide notes are not uncommon, as such. Would it be possible to see this remarkable document?'

I nodded and put the letter on the table.

'The signature is definitely his own. The caretaker's wife recognized it straightaway, and it is the same as the one on the rental contract he had in the flat.'

Patricia nodded, but did not look as though she was listening to what I said. She was staring at the letter in fascination. When she spoke again, her voice was tense.

'Now think carefully, because this is really important. Was that crease there when you found the letter, or is it a result of you or someone else folding the letter later?'

Patricia pointed impatiently to the crease two-thirds of the way up the sheet.

'We do have some procedures for securing evidence. The crease was there when I found the letter lying on the table in Konrad Jensen's flat, and I was the first person at the scene.'

Patricia suddenly smiled broadly and handed back the letter. Her voice was relaxed again.

'Excellent. Well, that then solves the otherwise bothersome mystery of why Konrad Jenson signed his own suicide letter. Fold it carefully along the crease and you will understand what happened.'

I did as she said – and suddenly understood what she meant. If one folded the letter in this way, the typed text disappeared, but Konrad Jensen's signature did not.

'In other words, Konrad Jensen signed his own death sentence, presumably with a gun to his head and without knowing what he was signing. One might wonder whether the murderer let him see it afterwards or simply fired the shot as soon as he had signed it. The latter is more likely, as there was an obvious risk that Konrad Jensen would cause a commotion if he saw the text.'

Suddenly, I could picture it all. It was a ghastly scene. Konrad Jensen sitting in the threadbare chair by his own coffee table, terrified and shaking, signing the letter with a gun to his head – only to be shot the moment he put down the pen. Annoyingly, the only thing I could not picture was the face of the person holding the gun. The faces of Sara Sundqvist, the caretaker's wife, Andreas Gullestad, Darrell Williams and the Lunds all flickered past, but I was unable to get any of them to fit.

Patricia's voice was slightly more optimistic when she continued.

'But this was really rather sloppy work. A crease in the middle of the paper would hardly have been worth a mention, but an obvious crease two-thirds of the way up the page would cause any astute person to wonder. Let us hope that this means that our otherwise extremely calculating murderer is now starting to feel that we are breathing down his or her neck. Alternatively, he or she continues to underestimate us. Whichever it is, it is good news for the investigation.'

I let her comment about any astute person pass without remark. Instead, I asked her if she had got anything more from the letter. She shook her head apologetically.

'The text says nothing to me, other than that if Konrad Jensen had written it, he was better at Norwegian grammar than I thought. You should of course check the script against any typewriters that the other neighbours might have, though

I would be very surprised if that leads to anything. And do not think for a moment that our murderer is the sort to leave fingerprints all over the flat either, though naturally that should be checked as well.'

I nodded. It would be easy to justify both things as routine following a murder and a suicide in the very same building.

'I am afraid there is nothing more to be gained from the letter. However, the gun is obviously of considerable interest. What kind of gun is it?'

I laid it on the table.

'The most common model of a standard Kongsberg Colt .45, probably produced just after the war, with a silencer. The serial number has been filed off. It is a relatively powerful and efficient handgun. The shot to Jensen's forehead killed him instantly. A Kongsberg Colt has a seven-bullet magazine, and there are five bullets left, so that tallies with one bullet for Harald Olesen and one for Konrad Jensen.'

Patricia studied the weapon pensively.

'The bullet count obviously tallies with what the murderer wants us to believe. Only a very considerate neighbour would use a silencer to shoot themselves. The reason could of course be that the silencer had not been removed after the murder of Harald Olesen. Quite apart from the fact that we still have no explanation as to where Konrad Jensen hid the gun in the meantime.'

Patricia sat glaring at the revolver with ever more threatening eyes, but it remained silent and obstinately refused to give up the great secret as to which hand had been holding it when the fatal shot was fired.

'In other words, if – I mean when Konrad Jensen was murdered, the question remains as to why the gun was left behind this time and not after the murder of Harald Olesen. Because in that case, even I would have easily accepted that it was a suicide.'

Patricia eventually gave up trying to get the gun to speak and instead looked up at me.

'Could you please have one of the forensic technicians check whether the bullet that killed Konrad Jensen today and the one that killed Harald Olesen were both fired from this gun? I have a theory as to why the gun was not left after the murder of Harald Olesen, and I will not rest until I have it confirmed.'

I nodded. Once again, I did not understand entirely what she was thinking. But it was a natural routine procedure that would hardly cause a negative response.

'Otherwise, I have had Konrad Jensen sent to the pathologist, but have not yet received confirmation of the time of death. The most obvious guess is that he died sometime in the morning.'

Patricia nodded.

'That sounds logical, but does not help us very much. If he died before Kristian Lund went to work and before the caretaker's wife was at her post, any of the residents could have shot him. And the fact that the murderer managed to get out is no mystery, as the door has a snib lock and there was no one outside. How the murderer managed to get in is, however, a puzzle. I assume that you looked for any visible signs of a break-in through the window, or marks on the door?'

I nodded – and promised myself I would check both options carefully the next time I was there. But I had seen nothing that would indicate a break-in, so I asked Patricia what that told us.

'Well, there are three alternatives: the murderer was the caretaker's wife, or the murderer was someone who got hold of the caretaker's wife's keys, or the murderer was someone who Konrad Jensen let into the flat.'

'None of those options sounds immediately plausible,' I replied.

Patricia nodded in agreement – and gave a bitter smile.

'But one of them has to be right, all the same. Check the caretaker's wife's keys and in the meantime I will discuss the case with myself. The most obvious option is that Konrad Jensen let the murderer in himself. Given what you have told me, he had no doubt barricaded himself in behind two locks and a safety chain, which would make it no easy feat to get in against his will.'

I nodded, but did put up a feeble protest.

'But that means you are taking it for granted that Konrad Jensen was murdered, and I am not entirely convinced of that yet. You have good arguments, but still have to get past the revolver and the suicide note. And again we lack a motive and an explanation as to how the murderer got in. Everyone is happy with the case as it stands. It will not be easy to justify extending the investigation.'

Patricia gave a deep sigh. She sat in silence, slapping her small hands against the table in irritation. The cold coffee sloshed around dangerously in her cup.

'And the murderer is very happy with the situation as it is, I can promise you. While I am utterly convinced that we are talking about not just one murder, but a double murder, and the person responsible is still at large. Probably sitting comfortably in 25 Krebs' Street rubbing his or her hands.

But I do understand your problem as well: it is not an easy situation.'

Patricia sighed again twice and continued in a resigned voice.

'I do not think we are going to get any further tonight. You think about it and do what you believe is best. But do at least make the checks we have talked about, and give me twenty-four hours more before closing the case. You do not need to do any more than that for the moment. There is no need for extra security any longer. The murderer feels safe now and will not do anything that might risk exposure.'

I nodded. I felt a deep sympathy for Patricia, who, despite her brilliant reasoning, might still find that the case was closed without a murderer being arrested. Nevertheless, she had been able to convince me that things were not so clear-cut as I and the other neighbours had believed when we found Konrad Jensen. There were still several questions that screamed for answers, and I did not know what I would say should some critical journalist ask them.

When I commented that we had at least solved the mystery of the missing money from Harald Olesen's account, Patricia remarked pensively that there was still an unsolved mystery. It was clear that most of the money had been paid to Kristian Lund, but if he had received two payments of 100,000, a total of 50,000 was still missing.

We called it a day at around seven o'clock, in a tense and sombre mood. I promised her that I would ponder the case until tomorrow and would as far as possible check the things that she had mentioned. I also promised to go to the reading of Harald Olesen's will. Naturally, I was very curious as to what was in the will, having read Harald Olesen's diary. She said goodbye without so much as a smile. It was clear that the day's events had made an impression on her. A gnawing thought at the back of my mind was starting to bother me. If Konrad Jensen really had been murdered this morning, it was reasonable to assume that his life could have been saved if I had ordered increased security yesterday.

As I stood in the doorway, ready to leave, Patricia suddenly laughed again, cynically. I looked at her in surprise.

'I'm sorry – another murder is not funny at all, but it really is quite a murder case, when we still have Konrad Jensen as a prime suspect after he himself has been shot!'

I smiled sheepishly and gave her the last word. So our ways parted on a relatively jolly note after all, even though it was black humour. On the way out, I noticed that the four Ellis books that I had seen in Patricia's bookshelves the evening before had now been discreetly replaced by a new three-volume work on British politics in the twentieth century.

VIII

I stood undecided outside the White House for a moment. In the end, I drove to the main police station. Three journalists surged forward the minute I got out of the car. They followed me in, furiously taking down notes. I confirmed in brief that one of the residents, who had previously been convicted during the treason trials after the war, had been found dead in his flat. A .45-calibre revolver and a signed suicide note, in which he confessed to the murder of Harald Olesen, were found by the body. I then added that there were still some technical examinations to be carried out and a few details to be clarified, but there was much to indicate that the case was closed. One of the journalists asked if I could confirm something that one of the other residents had said earlier in the day, that it would seem that the murderer had killed himself because he realized that there had been important breakthroughs in the investigation and an arrest was imminent. I emphasized that one always had to be careful when speculating about the reasons for suicide, but that I could confirm that the investigation had made some major breakthroughs and that the deceased had been one of the main suspects from the start.

I waited with a pounding heart for the critical questions that were never asked. All three congratulated me on solving the murder and assured me that the story would be given good and very favourable coverage in the morning papers. One of them jokingly suggested 'K2 Scales New Heights' as a possible headline. Back in my office, I composed a press release, the content of which was more or less what I had told the journalists.

The ballistics expert had gone home for the day. I did, however, manage to speak to him on the phone and pointed out that even though the case now seemed to be cut and dried, the gun from Konrad Jensen's flat should be examined in relation to the bullet that was found there and the bullet from Harald Olesen's flat. He agreed with me and promised to see to it in the morning. He also congratulated me on a successful investigation. As did the fingerprint expert when I called him afterwards and asked him to examine Konrad Jensen's flat the following morning.

After I had put the receiver down, I sat on my swivel chair

and reflected for a few minutes on the likelihood of these congratulations still holding strong tomorrow. Then I called it a day and left the office, but did not go home quite yet. Instead, I headed for 25 Krebs' Street.

The caretaker's wife had retired to her flat but opened the door as soon as I rang the bell and beamed when she saw it was me. I hastily assured her that these were simply routine measures in connection with my reports, but there were still a couple of things I needed to ask of her.

With regard to the keys, the caretaker's wife was categorical that no one else could have got hold of them. She carried the keys with her all day, and at night they lay on her bedside table. She had slept alone in her flat with the door locked and could swear and cross her heart that no one had been in her bedroom. She said the latter with a gentle smile. When I told her that there were a few more examinations to be done in Konrad Jensen's flat, she immediately produced the key and let me in.

To my relief, I found what I had said to Patricia to be true. There were no marks or signs on either the door or the window to indicate that someone had broken in. When I got there, I had only a vague idea as to what else I was looking for. After my conversation with Patricia, I had just wanted to look over Konrad Jensen's flat again and to think the situation through by myself.

For many years Konrad Jensen had lived alone, a surly and bitter man. The flat was imbued with his spirit, even after his death. He had obviously been scared even to open the windows for the past few days. The cigarette smoke was in the walls. Konrad Jensen had not left many personal belongings behind. Two days of dirty dishes stood piled up in the kitchen.

An out-of-focus, yellowing confirmation photo hung on the wall in the living room, but other than that, there were no pictures to be seen anywhere. This was the flat of a man who had not only lived without a family, but without friends.

Konrad Jensen had an old wireless, but no television. It did not look like he subscribed to any newspapers, but instead bought *VG*, *Dagbladet* and *Aftenposten* on particular days. Last month's newspapers were stacked on the floor. Several of them were folded at the sports pages. The bookshelf boasted a worn Bible and a fairly random selection of other books. In a drawer in the kitchen, I found a collection of car pictures cut out from magazines together with a bank book and some other personal papers. A small pile of football-pools coupons lay abandoned and it seemed that Konrad Jensen did not spend much time on them and had never been particularly successful either. Eight right was the highest he had ever achieved, according to his own notes.

I found myself wondering what the dead man had done in all the thousands of hours that he must have spent here over the years – in addition to eating, smoking and cursing his fate. It struck me that perhaps no one other than him had been in the flat for years, before this murder case forced me on him. The questions remained: had Konrad Jensen been on his own here when he died this morning, or had another person been here with him?

Konrad Jensen's bedroom was equally sparsely furnished and impregnated with smoke. A half-full ashtray stood on the stool that he had positioned to act as a bedside table. I wondered whether a woman had ever shared the bed. There was much to indicate that if one had, it was many years ago.

There were two pairs of trousers and two jackets hanging in the wardrobe, as well as three shirts and three sets of underwear. An old black suit lay crumpled on a shelf on its own. It was very possible that it had not been used for a good few years. No one was likely to invite Konrad Jensen anywhere he might need to wear a suit, and he was even less likely to go to such places of his own accord. I despondently picked up the suit jacket – and jumped when something fell out of it.

It was a quite large and thick brown envelope. There was nothing written on the outside. Inside, there was a sheaf of white papers with blue text, handwritten by Konrad Jensen. I immediately took them with me out to the table in the living room. I sat there for almost an hour looking through the fifty pages or so left by the man who had died here in his chair this morning.

It was not what I would have expected to find in this flat: it was an attempt to write a book.

Having had years to ponder his fate in silence, Konrad Jensen had obviously decided to write down his thoughts. There were around twenty pages about his childhood and youth, and about twenty pages or so about the war. Having ploughed my way through it, it was with some disappointment that I had to accept that there was no information here that was of any use to the investigation. Not a word was said about Harald Olesen, nor was there anything about Deerfoot. It was a very self-centred and self-righteous story of a young man who had felt misunderstood all his life and found it hard to accept his lack of success.

My suspicion that Norway had not lost a great literary talent with Konrad Jensen's death was confirmed before I had even finished the first page. The structure was chaotic, it was unfocused, and the punctuation and grammar were appalling. Paragraphs and headings appeared to be unknown quantities to Konrad Jensen. This attempt by an unknown and menial member of the NS was hardly a project that any publisher would dare to take on, by an author no one would spend tuppence on. But Konrad Jensen had put a lot of work into it. The dates of writing were jotted down in the margin, and he had written nearly every day since November last year. The last section, about the end of the war, was dated 3 April – the day before Harald Olesen was murdered.

I put the papers down with the reinforced feeling that Patricia had been right and that Konrad Jensen had been murdered. How pathetic it all was that Konrad Jensen had died and left behind a life lie, as described by Ibsen, one of our greatest writers – a project that he was working on and had great hopes for. But I was also aware that this was entirely based on my intuition and would hardly stand up in court or the media.

As I was about to put the papers back into the envelope, the first sentence caught my eye: 'I Konrad Jensen hearby start my life story that I do not regreat.'

I sat staring at this single sentence.

Konrad Jensen had only a couple of months ago written by hand and misspelled the words 'hereby' and 'regret'. In the typewritten letter, both words were spelled correctly.

It could of course be the case that he had learned to spell both words correctly later, but Konrad Jensen's manuscript was written without a comma and with frequent misspellings of the simplest words. This was also the case with the last notes, made only a few days ago. Patricia had been absolutely right in her assumptions about his writing. It was simply not possible to imagine that the same man had written a suicide note on a typewriter with perfect spelling and grammar.

I put the papers down on the table with care. Then I went out into Konrad Jensen's kitchen and washed my face with ice-cold water, twice. Afterwards, I was still convinced that Konrad Jensen had been murdered – and still furiously determined to catch this incredibly cold-blooded and cynical murderer. I picked up the manuscript that was his testament and quietly left Konrad Jensen's flat, asking the caretaker's wife to make sure the door was locked behind me.

Then I drove home and phoned Patricia. At half past nine in the evening, she was immediately alert when she heard the news. It was a short and optimistic conversation, in sharp contrast to the long, pessimistic one we had had earlier in the day. I promised not to close the investigation – certainly not until after the Easter weekend. She promised me that with our combined efforts, we would definitely catch the murderer.

I went to bed on the sixth day of the investigation in an invigorated mood, my mind teeming with thoughts. It was two o'clock in the morning before I closed my eyes, but the final hours of the day brought no breakthrough. My last thought before I fell asleep was about what Harald Olesen's will might hold. The last face I saw before I fell asleep was, for a change, that of Konrad Jensen. He stared at me, grim and unhappy as usual. I looked at him questioningly, without getting an answer. It seemed to me that his expression was particularly malcontented, and he shook his head without saying a word when I said something about recording his death as suicide. But by then I was no doubt fast asleep.

DAY SEVEN
A Will – and Its Impact

I

The first two hours in the office on Wednesday, 10 April were fairly uneventful and involved a lot of gratifying reading in the papers. At twenty-five past ten, however, there was a loud, impatient knock on my door. Outside stood an unusually breathless ballistics expert with a very bewildered expression on his face.

'The report is ready, but I must warn you that the conclusion is perhaps not what you had hoped,' he blurted out.

I was prepared and indicated that he should continue, expectant. He carried on in an unsteady voice.

'The bullet that killed Konrad Jensen came from the .45-calibre revolver that was found in the flat, the last Kongsberg Colt model from 1947. But . . .'

The ballistics expert paused for a moment. I kept a straight face and helped him by finishing the sentence.

'But the bullet that killed Harald Olesen came from another, possibly older .45-calibre gun, so we are still missing the murder weapon.'

He nodded, dumbfounded, and looked at me in admiration.

'As you perhaps understand, I had reason to believe that was the case, so it is excellent that you could confirm it so quickly. Can you tell me any more about the missing revolver?'

He nodded eagerly and hurried to continue.

'It is also a Kongsberg Colt, but as you said, an older model. It is hard to say how much older. The first model was mass-produced from 1918 until the war, but very few were actually produced after 1930. So I would guess that the gun that killed Harald Olesen was probably from around 1920. The .45-calibre Kongsberg Colt was used a lot in those days, not least by the army. There were still a considerable number of these guns in use during and just after the war, but this early type then became less popular.'

I nodded thoughtfully and said that that fitted very well with one theory. Which it no doubt did, only I unfortunately had no idea what the theory was.

The pathologist phoned shortly after. His results were less dramatic, but not without interest. The exact time of death was still uncertain, given the temperature of the room. However, it was clear that the fatal shot was fired later than first assumed. It was not before nine or after one, so was presumably fired sometime between ten and twelve.

The typewriter lead I could check myself, and as expected, it had not led to anything. Konrad Jensen's suicide note was written on one of the most common typewriters on sale in Norway. According to the itinerary from the first house searches, there were three typewriters in the building: the Lunds' typewriter was of the same model as the one that the suicide note had been written on, whereas Sara Sundqvist's and Andreas Gullestad's were not. But there was not much to be had from this, as the model in question was so common that it could be found in practically any office. The same typewriter might be used in an embassy, a sports shop or a university.

Having given it some thought for a good ten minutes, there was really only one person who I could not imagine had written the letter on a typewriter in the course of the past few days, and that was Konrad Jensen. The realization that he had not shot himself dug deeper and deeper into my conscience. And my desire to find the cold-blooded man or woman who had weaselled his or her way in to this lonely man's flat to kill him grew ever stronger.

At a quarter past eleven, my impatience drove me to call the fingerprint expert, who had just returned from Konrad Jensen's flat. He had found my own prints on the door, as well as those of the caretaker's wife and Konrad Jensen, but that was all. I thanked him for his work, and made a mental note that technical evidence would not be enough to catch the murderer in this case.

II

A tense atmosphere already prevailed when I arrived at the conference room of the law firm Rønning, Rønning & Rønning in Idun Street fifteen minutes before the will was due to be read. Neither Rønning Junior nor the will was to be seen in the room, which held six rows of chairs with table arms, as well as a small podium with a lectern. A good number of the deceased's neighbours and relatives were already present. Mr and Mrs Lund were sitting on their own to the far left of the front row, and Harald Olesen's niece and nephew were sitting in the third row. The caretaker's wife had just pushed in Andreas Gullestad in his wheelchair and seated herself considerately behind him in the fourth row. She swiftly packed her worn winter coat away in a nylon net bag.

All of the residents who were present nodded or waved to me when I came into the room. I did a quiet tour and shook them all by the hand. The caretaker's wife was excited but controlled. Andreas Gullestad was as calm and smiling as ever: he did not have anything to get excited about. Mrs Lund seemed a little uneasy about the situation and kept looking around the room, whereas Kristian Lund kept a stiff upper lip. I found myself admiring his stoicism, which quickly broke when Sara Sundqvist came in at ten minutes to twelve. She sat down demonstratively on her own to the right of the back row and seemed to avoid looking at the Lunds.

At four minutes to midday, the doorway was suddenly filled with the handsome figure of Darrell Williams. He arrived at full speed, wearing a fur coat, and sat down without any pleasantries in the back row, on the chair nearest the door. All of those there turned round instinctively when they heard the door, and the other neighbours gave him a brief nod. I noticed that the Olesen siblings positively stared at him, and that the niece in particular looked at him for a long time before turning back round. I did not find this in the slightest bit strange, as they were unlikely to have seen him before. Furthermore, the arrival of Darrell Williams was shortly overshadowed by the arrival of a slightly smaller, much thinner man, who three minutes later stepped up onto the podium with a large sealed envelope in his hands.

It had already occurred to me that Mr Rønning Junior was likely to milk the situation for all it was worth. He did not disappoint. At exactly one minute to midday, the young man had entered the room with a pince-nez, an unusually self-conscious expression and an undoubtedly extremely expensive suit. He would have fitted into 1920s Norway without raising any eyebrows, and this impression was reinforced when he then opened his mouth, as his language was extremely conservative and precise. However, the man's immaculate and irritating image was upstaged by the large sealed envelope he held in his hand, which he opened with deliberate, slow movements as soon as the clock started to strike twelve. A profound silence reigned in the room until the twelve chimes were over.

'On behalf of the deceased Harald Olesen's estate, I would firstly like to thank you all for taking the time to be here, as requested in an appendix to the aforementioned will. Furthermore, we can confirm that all those invited are present, with the exception of Mr Konrad Jensen, who is unable to attend as he died yesterday, as I am sure you are all aware.'

The room was so still you could hear a pin drop. I stared at the lawyer with horrified fascination.

'Harald Olesen died a widower with no living parents or known heirs. In this situation, he was legally free to divide his estate and assets as desired in a will. These comprise his flat in 25 Krebs' Street and contents, with an estimated value of 70,000 kroner, and a cabin outside Stokke in Horten, which his nephew has used for the past few years, with an estimated value of 40,000 kroner. He also had cash holdings in a bank account that amount to 1,122,434 kroner, when the lawyer's fee and other fees and taxes have been deducted. And finally, the sum of 263 kroner and 75 øre was found in cash in his wallet.'

The lawyer took the first opportunity for a dramatic pause and solemnly looked around the room. This did not increase his already tepid popularity with the audience. He carried on unperturbed.

'Only days before his death, Harald Olesen expressed the explicit wish that his will should be read as now, six days after his death. It was somewhat more unusual that he requested that earlier versions of the will should also be made known to those present.'

With this detail, the atmosphere in the room suddenly changed. Harald Olesen's niece and nephew looked at each other anxiously. I thought I saw a fleeting and triumphant smile play on Kristian Lund's lips, which was echoed by a more guarded smile from his wife. Rather distastefully, both couples brought me in mind of vultures.

'The will has undergone several changes, but has nonetheless always remained relatively simple, with a main heir who will essentially inherit all of Olesen's estate and assets. One not so insignificant exception has been made, in favour of Mrs Randi Hansen, the wife of the caretaker in the building where Harald Olesen had his residence.'

For a moment all eyes turned to the caretaker's wife, who sat alone and silent on her seat. She was sitting on the edge of the chair with trembling lips. A single tear ran down her cheek as she waited to hear the amount.

'For many years Harald Olesen had left a sum of thirty thousand kroner to Mrs Hansen in his will.'

There was a quiet gasp from the audience. I thought I

could detect disapproval in the faces of the niece and nephew, and Kristian Lund. The caretaker's wife, on the other hand, looked as if she was about to faint on her chair. She instinctively hid her face in her hands, but still could not stop the tears that now flowed down both cheeks.

'However . . .'

As if at the stroke of a wand, there was silence in the room again.

'However, a few days before his death, Harald Olesen requested that the amount left to Mrs Hansen be changed substantially. The final amount that she will inherit from his estate is now . . .'

The man must have been a born sadist and then honed his craft carefully. There was a full ten seconds of breathless silence before he completed his sentence. I seriously feared that the caretaker's wife, who was still sitting with her face hidden beneath her hands, would die of a heart attack in the meantime.

'. . . one hundred thousand kroner.'

This time there were several gasps and a couple of loud groans of disappointment. I did not manage to locate where they came from, but then it was doubtful that anyone else did either. Rønning Junior was not affected in the slightest by this and stuck to his planned staging. He took three steps forward across the floor and informed Mrs Hansen that the money would be deposited in her account as soon as she came to the office with her bank book. Mrs Hansen did not answer. She had more or less collapsed in a heap on her chair, her eyes wide open, unable to say a word. Rønning Junior seemed somewhat put out not to receive a reply, but continued nevertheless after another dramatic pause.

'With regard to the remainder of Harald Olesen's property and assets, for many years the will was formulated as follows: "The remainder of my estate I leave to my nephew, Joachim Olesen, and my niece, Cecilia Olesen, out of respect to my deceased brother, Bernt Olesen."'

The way this was formulated and the reason given could hardly be described as affectionate towards the two heirs, but they nodded in agreement, only to freeze when it became obvious that the lawyer had not yet finished.

'However . . .'

There was little doubt that this was his favourite word and that he knew exactly how to use it.

'However, some weeks before he died, Harald Olesen requested that this extremely important point of his will be amended. The text as it stood was to be removed in its entirety and be replaced by the following: "The remainder of my estate I leave to my neighbour Mr Kristian Lund, with apologies for the pain that I have caused him and his deceased mother."'

Kristian Lund was a former athlete, and certainly not a gentleman. He rejoiced, triumphant, with his hands above his head, as soon as the new text was read out. His wife stared at him in astonishment, but then joyfully threw her arms round his neck. They both started, as I and everyone else did, when there was a loud bang in the room just seconds after. This fortunately proved to be no more than the sound of Harald Olesen's nephew's briefcase falling to the floor for unknown reasons.

'However . . .'

All eyes turned back to Rønning Junior. Harald Olesen's nephew picked up his briefcase with a thunderous expression on his face, whereas an expression of terror was now visible on that of Kristian Lund. His wife looked from him to the lawyer in total bewilderment.

'However, not long before he died, on 25 March to be specific, Harald Olesen requested a further change in the wording of this crucial point in his will. The earlier text was once again to be removed in its entirety. It was then to be replaced with the following wording, which thus is the final will: "The remainder of my estate I leave to my neighbour Miss Sara Sundqvist, with sincere apologies for the great pain I have caused her and her deceased parents."'

Time stood still for a short moment. Then everything erupted into noise and movement. Joachim Olesen and his briefcase ran out of the room. His sister remained seated for a short while, then stood up and ran after him. Darrell Williams rolled his eyes and roared with laughter. Andreas Gullestad remained sitting in his wheelchair, naturally enough. However, he was nodding with unusual vigour, and tried without much joy to catch the attention of his assistant, the caretaker's wife, who meanwhile sat on her chair paralysed by emotion.

Mrs Lund collapsed into a heap, but the look that she sent Sara Sundqvist was one of pure hatred. The most dramatic reaction, however, was that of Kristian Lund. He leaped to his feet and first waved his fist at Sara Sundqvist. Then, from the depths of his despair and powerful lungs, he shouted: 'May you roast in hell, Father! Not only did you let me down when you were alive, you have also let me down now that you're dead!'

Rønning Junior snapped out of his trance and looked around with interest – I dare say for new clients. I myself had spontaneously stood up, without having any idea as to whom I should arrest or what I should otherwise do.

The only person in the room who did not stir was, in short, Sara Sundqvist, the new millionairess. She sat there, more beautiful and more like a princess than ever, as unmoving as a pillar of salt in the middle of all the chaos around her. For what seemed like an eternity, her face remained static, as if hypnotized. Then the tears started to run down her cheeks.

'I had no idea at all about this – it really was not me who killed him,' she suddenly blurted out.

That was when I managed to pull myself together enough to proclaim in as steady a voice as possible that no one was to leave the room until they had given a new statement.

III

It turned into a long and demanding afternoon in an improvised interview room at the offices of Rønning, Rønning & Rønning. Rønning Junior immediately protested against the 'highly irregular and unnecessary requisition of legally acquired premises', but quickly vanished when a far less straight-laced Rønning Senior appeared and was promised extraordinary rental fees for use of the conference room. Rønning Senior was roughly twice as old and twice as heavy as his junior, and certainly seemed to be twice as pragmatic. A small side room was swiftly converted into an interview room, so that those waiting could spread out in the generous conference room and reception area.

Sara Sundqvist nodded, in a state akin to shock, when she was told that she would be the first to be questioned, and followed me meekly into the side office. Her face brightened once we were sitting alone, and she gave me a timorous smile as she left, but otherwise I found it hard to imagine that anyone could show less joy at inheriting a million. With deep despair, she claimed repeatedly that she had never asked Harald Olesen for money and knew nothing about his murder. She did, however, confess that she had been in both contact and conflict with Harald Olesen prior to his murder. I was then promptly given the background to this.

An old uncle in France had told her that the last sign of life from Sara Sundqvist's parents was a postcard sent from Oslo at Christmas in 1942. It seemed that they were living under a secret identity as Norwegians. Sara herself had then turned up in Sweden as a child cleared for adoption in summer 1944. The story in between these two points was unknown. Her desire to find out what had happened to her parents was one of the driving forces in her choice to study in Oslo. When she discovered that she was living in the same building as an old Resistance leader, she had mustered her courage a few days later to ask if he knew anything about the matter.

She had rung the doorbell and asked him straight out – without much hope of anything other than a polite no. To her surprise, Harald Olesen's face had blanched. After a long silence, he had mumbled something about there having been so many tragic stories during the war, but he was not familiar with this one. Then he slammed the door in her face and had not opened it again, even though she had rung the bell several times. It had of course been impossible for her to leave it at that, and she had on many occasions stopped him in the hallway or knocked on his door in attempt to find out more. Each time he had denied any knowledge of the story, but had nonetheless looked so guilty that it was impossible to believe him. The inheritance had never been mentioned by either him or her. She had no idea who had shot him, and herself had grieved his death. Though she had to admit that this was largely because the hope that she might find out what had happened to her parents had died with him.

In answer to the next question, as to whether she had been aware of Kristian Lund's relationship to Harald Olesen, she immediately replied that she had had no idea when she embarked on the affair. However, she had at a later point understood that Kristian Lund believed he was Harald Olesen's son and had also realized that he was pushing him to acknowledge this and thus to ensure his inheritance. She had agreed with him that it was only reasonable, and had been led to believe that he had finally been promised this. This morning, when she came to the reading of the will, she had fully expected him to be the main heir. That her name was then read out instead came as a total shock. If she really was going to inherit the flat and the money – which still seemed incredible – it would of course open completely new opportunities for her. But at the same time, she had naturally felt anxious that she would be suspected of being involved in his murder in some way. And on top of it all was the powerful emotional response when the reference to her 'deceased parents' was read out. The fact that Harald Olesen had seemed to know her parents' story but had not said outright that they were dead had rekindled the latent hope that they might still be alive somewhere in the world.

We concluded the interview there. I allowed her to go home, but asked her to stay there and under no circumstances to leave Oslo without my permission. She agreed to this, and added that she would be eternally grateful if I could help her to find out what had happened to her parents. If I had any further questions, I was more than welcome to knock on her door at any time. She gingerly placed a hand on my arm when she said this. And without being able to explain why, I remained standing by the window until I had seen her pass on the street, heading in the right direction.

The next person was, of course, Kristian Lund. He was involved in a heated discussion with Rønning Junior when I came out, and only with great reluctance joined me. 'She is not going to get a single penny!' was his first comment when we were alone. 'First, she seduces me and tries to get me to leave my wife because she believes I will shortly inherit a million kroner. Then she goes behind my back and convinces my father that she should inherit the money herself. She is not going to get a single penny! I still have the right to my inheritance if I can prove that I am the son of the deceased Harald Olesen; even Mr Rønning had to admit that. And I will happily go to court to prove it!'

The latter was said with great emotion, but then he suddenly calmed down. Kristian Lund was a man capable of quick turnarounds.

'I apologize for my outburst, and lying earlier on in the investigation, but it really has not been an easy situation. It was an enormous relief when I finally managed to get the stubborn old goat to give me what was my right. And how could I know that he would change it again?'

Kristian Lund could confirm that Sara Sundqvist had pressed Harald Olesen to tell her what had happened to her parents, but did not appear to know about the relationship between him and Olesen until he told her sometime in

March. They had both been of the opinion that the old man looked ill and troubled, and had discussed the likelihood that he was suffering from a terminal illness. His death was therefore not unexpected, but the fact that he had been murdered had naturally come as a shock. When asked if he had shot Harald Olesen himself, Kristian Lund threw open his hands in exasperation and answered no, demonstratively. When I asked if he thought Sara Sundqvist might have committed the murder, he replied somewhat more cautiously that he still did not believe so.

Despite the gravity of the situation, there was somehow nothing more to say. Even in light of his late father's betrayal, Kristian Lund was showing himself to be increasingly unpleasant and egotistic. But I had to admit that his explanation tallied well with the previous one. And it was good to be reminded that we, thus far, only had Sara's word that she had not blackmailed Harald Olesen. So I allowed Kristian Lund to leave, with the order that he stay within reach. He assured me with a bitter smile that he would only be going out to get himself a damn good lawyer, but other than that had no plans except to look after his family and work.

It seemed natural to call in Mrs Lund, after her husband. My curiosity as to whether she was more than just the kind, pretty and not-so-bright housewife she appeared to be was definitely satisfied within the course of the conversation. The Karen Lund who answered my questions succinctly and effectively was very solemn indeed. My impression of her shifted from simple and quite naive to simple and very wilful. Yes, she had known about her husband's relationship to Harald Olesen and the possibility that he would inherit. He had told her about it as soon as he had discovered it. Yes, she was also aware of her husband's extramarital affair. Her suspicions had been aroused one day when they met Sara Sundqvist in the hallway and she had noted a look of triumph on Miss Sundqvist's face and simultaneously felt a prick of conscience in her husband's hand. This suspicion had been confirmed when she later phoned her husband at work one day only to be told that he had just left, yet he did not come through the door until an hour and a half later.

It had been an extremely difficult situation for her, especially because of her young son. She was neither willing nor able to confront her husband with clear evidence. Her response was therefore to be as kind and dutiful as she possibly could in her roles as wife and mother, which was something she could do, and in this way fight to keep her husband. And she was now quite sure that she had succeeded. If he still had any feelings for that devious Swedish woman, they had no doubt died the moment the will was read out. She herself believed that her husband deserved the money, given the shameful way in which his father had treated him, and she would support him if he went to court to secure it. But the question of the will was of less importance to her than whether he stayed with her and their son. Because Harald Olesen had treated her husband in the way he had, she had felt no particular grief when he died, though the fact that he was murdered had been a shock. But she still slept beside her husband every night secure in the knowledge that he had not killed anyone and was not likely to do so.

I could not help myself asking whether, notwithstanding his infidelity, she had ever re-evaluated her marriage. To which she simply shook her head. Yes, she had been jealous and even angry with her husband, but she understood that it was hard for him too, and that he had been seduced by the dark-eyed beauty. He had now also admitted it to her himself, and with tears in his eyes had begged her to forgive him. Which she of course did. Because he was her husband, the father of her son and the love of her life, whom she could not live without.

I thought to myself that Karen Lund had probably had a very conservative upbringing and had read a few too many romantic magazines, but the situation felt easier now it was clear that she knew about her husband's affair. Her personal choices were none of my business, and her explanation was frank enough. So I commented that it would perhaps have been better if she had told me before, but added that I understood that she was in a very difficult situation and thanked her for being so honest now. She shook my hand with relief before she left, and nodded obediently when I requested that she stay at home in case of further questioning. I watched with mixed feelings as the Lunds passed outside the window shortly after, on their way home. They were holding hands and, if one did not know any better, looked for all the world like an ordinary young couple without a care in the world.

I called in Harald Olesen's niece and nephew together. They were both upset by the fact that they were to go home without so much as a krone, having come in the belief that they were the main heirs. However, they had quickly got over the initial shock. Joachim Olesen started by apologizing for his behaviour during the reading. He pointed out that neither he nor his sister had any financial worries, and added that the will should not really have come as a surprise.

I sent him a questioning look, but it was his sister who answered. Harald Olesen had been a generous uncle to them since they were small, but he was also strict and distant. As he had no children of his own, he had often had strong opinions about their choices in life, and in their youth had expressed his views on their choice of education and sweethearts quite clearly. In later years, they had both had their own families to prioritize, and Harald Olesen had not exactly encouraged contact. After his wife's death, he had more or less kept himself to himself. The niece and nephew both felt guilty for not having looked after their sick uncle more in the last months of his life, but there were old underlying tensions, and Harald Olesen had basically become a stranger who did not arouse much sympathy. When they phoned him, he was curt in his response. This seemed to tie in well with the possibility that something serious from his past had been plaguing him over the last few months, but they had no idea what it might be. The family had not known that Harald Olesen had a son from an extramarital affair. The name Deerfoot did not mean anything to them, but that was not so strange. Harald Olesen had been reluctant to talk about his experiences during the war, even to his brother when he was alive.

It all sounded credible enough. I let the Olesen siblings go, with the assurance that they would be informed of any significant developments in connection with the murder of their late uncle and his will.

The remaining interviews were much swifter. Darrell Williams had viewed the spectacle from his place in the back row with sardonic humour. He was still chuckling when he commented that it was the most exciting reading of a will that he had ever experienced and 'the greatest show' he had seen outside the USA. It had all been entirely unexpected to him, but given the reactions in the room, he had immediately sympathized with the beautiful young lady. Andreas Gullestad was of the same opinion, in direct response to the reactions of the Olesens and Kristian Lund. But his sympathies were overwhelmingly with the caretaker's wife, who had truly earned this acknowledgement after many years of toil and worry. Both Darrell Williams and Andreas Gullestad denied any knowledge of Harald Olesen's family connections, including the fact that Kristian Lund was his son.

And as for the caretaker's wife, two hours later she was still overwhelmed by her sudden fortune. She asked me repeatedly if it was true that she was going to get the money and I answered, as Rønning Junior had also done many times, that her share was secure, no matter who inherited the rest. If Kristian Lund won his case, he would receive the lion's share of the estate, but she would still get her 100,000 kroner. She apologized that she had not noticed the reactions of the other people in the room. But from what had been said, she did not think it was wrong that Sara Sundqvist had been left the money, even though she did not understand why.

I told her in all honesty that I could not say why yet either. Then I congratulated her on her inheritance, which I felt was well deserved after all her years working for others.

I smiled quietly to myself as I watched the caretaker's wife pass below the window in her worn, grey coat. I realized that she had always walked with heavy steps before, whereas now she was so light of foot that I feared she might suddenly lift off and float away over the city. It was a pleasure to imagine her coming back here with her little red post-office savings book so that the balance could rocket from 48 to 100,048 kroner. If nothing else, the murders of Harald Olesen and Konrad Jensen had helped to make one person happy.

But there was little else to smile about. The day had thrown up a good deal of new information, but still no solutions. Ensconced back in my office, I quickly dialled Patricia's number. As soon as she heard who had been named the main heir, she invited me to visit her immediately.

IV

'So, I still do not know who the murderer is, but I am starting to get a pretty clear picture of who J might be.'

The time was twenty-five to six. I had had longer to mull over the case than Patricia, who had just heard my account from the reading of the will, so it was once again disappointing to discover she was ahead of me in the game all the same.

'No bonus points for this one. "J" is clearly an abbreviation for Sara Sundqvist. I guess that the "J" stands for "Jewish child" or "Jewess".'

I replied that I had also guessed that, and also come to the conclusion that it had to be one of the two, the latter being more accurate than the former.

'Of greater interest, and almost as obvious, is the fact that she must have been the small child who was hidden in the caretaker's flat with her parents until Harald Olesen came to collect them that evening in February 1944. Thus far, the connection is clear. But what on earth happened between then and when she pops up in an adoption agency in Sweden a few months later? This historical mystery is now one of the investigation's most burning issues.'

I nodded quickly in agreement. I had not thought this far yet, but when she said it, it was of course obvious. Patricia was on fire and continued immediately.

'Now, who might know more about this? My best suggestion is that you send a telegram to your colleagues in Sweden and ask them to investigate immediately the circumstances surrounding Sara Sundqvist's adoption. If she arrived as a refugee from Norway during the war, then someone must have carried or driven her across the border. And it must have been registered in some way by the Swedish authorities.'

I nodded. After today's events, it sounded like a very sensible suggestion.

'Otherwise, the most interesting thing about Sara Sundqvist's reaction today was her spontaneous outburst that she did not kill Harald Olesen. What would have been a very logical reaction yesterday morning is now illogical, as everyone assumes that Konrad Jensen is the murderer.'

I had to agree with this too. I also asked myself critically if I had consciously or unconsciously suppressed this uncomfortable fact.

'It may have been the shock, of course, but what she said to you later, in less fraught surroundings, would indicate that she does not believe that Konrad Jensen is the murderer. In which case, there are only two alternatives: either that she murdered Harald Olesen herself or she suspects that someone else may have done it and does not want to give voice to her suspicions. We have to keep both options open for the moment.'

I rather reluctantly had to agree. My heart rebelled against Sara Sundqvist being a cold-blooded murderer, but my mind insisted that it was a possibility that I had to face.

'As for the Lunds, there is not much more to learn there, as is true of both Andreas Gullestad and the caretaker's wife. But today's events have bolstered my theory relating to Darrell Williams and the Olesen pair.'

I gave her a puzzled looked – and was no doubt unable to hide my surprise.

'It may of course still be coincidence, but the reaction of the niece and nephew, and what they have said about their uncle, fits remarkably well in terms of chronology if . . .'

She fell silent and looked at me expectantly. I said nothing and stared back at her expectantly. We sat there in what resembled a standoff. In the end, it was me who gave in.

'I have no idea what you are implying. What chronology are you talking about?'

Patricia grinned, not without a hint of glee.

'The war chronology, but a different one from that of Sara Sundqvist. Harald Olesen's niece would have been eighteen or nineteen years old at the end of the war. Darrell was twenty-two and in Norway. Around this time, he had a Norwegian girlfriend whom he refuses to name, for reasons unbeknown to us. The niece and nephew both said that they had a somewhat strained relationship with Harald Olesen in later years because he had used his authority to interfere with their lives when they were young, among other things in relation to their choice of sweetheart. Therefore it seems natural to assume, first of all, that Darrell Williams's Norwegian girlfriend was in fact Harald Olesen's niece, and second, that Harald Olesen played a role in the breakup of that relationship. A dream romance with an American prince whom she subsequently lost might still cause considerable pain to this day, especially given that her later marriage did not last . . .'

I gave a limp nod. It might be coincidence, but I would be very surprised if it was. The way in which the niece and nephew reacted when Darrell Williams appeared fitted in perfectly with this theory.

'If I were you and could walk, I would go to visit Cecilia Olesen this evening and ask her about it directly. If she says yes, then call me before you talk to Darrell Williams.'

'Asking Cecilia Olesen outright sounds eminently sensible, but why on earth should I call you afterwards?'

Patricia's smile was secretive and slightly coquettish.

'Because I have a linked theory that you also need to confront Darrell Williams with, but I do not want to tell you until I have had the relationship confirmed. If it is not the case, then my creative imagination has spun a little too far.'

I nodded again. Patricia helped me to take such great leaps that I had to bear with her more eccentric and conceited behaviour.

'But I believe that is as far as we will get with the logic of Sherlock Holmes, so now we need to apply the Agatha Christie method and see how far we can get by focusing on the motives of the remaining neighbours.'

Once again, she was right, so I started with the obvious ones.

'Andreas Gullestad and Darrell Williams still have no motive for the murder, do they?'

Patricia nodded, but somehow managed to shake her head at the same time.

'Certainly, with the addition of "as far as we know at the

moment". I have a suspicion that both of them may have things of interest that are buried in the past. We touched on Darrell Williams just now. He could have felt extremely bitter towards Harald Olesen after the breakup from his niece, if the theory is true, or in connection with something else from his stay in Norway.'

'We will follow that up immediately. But what about Andreas Gullestad?'

Patricia frowned.

'That is even less clear, but there may be something in connection with his father's activities in the Resistance and subsequent death, even though that was early on in the war and we still have no link with Harald Olesen. Has it also struck you that there are very few mountains in Østfold?'

Once again, Patricia managed to ambush me with a totally unexpected question. I really did not see the relevance of geography here. She noticed the scepticism on my face and promptly continued.

'If what you told me is correct, the caretaker said that Harald Olesen planned to take the refugees on a trip to the mountains. Then he mentioned Østfold or Hedmark and Oppland, which were both known routes for smuggling refugees into Sweden. But Østfold is as flat as a Danish pancake, which could mean that they took the route via Hedmark to Oppland. Harald Olesen was also a leader for the Home Front there. And it is not so far from where Andreas Gullestad grew up, and from where his father, a couple of years earlier, had been shot for his part in the Resistance. It is tenuous, but I would not strike Andreas Gullestad from the list quite yet. Double-check with Harald Olesen's niece and nephew whether there might be a connection there.'

'Fair enough. And even though I do not for a moment believe that it was the caretaker's wife, she now also has a motive.'

Patricia nodded gravely.

'I too have serious doubts about the caretaker's wife playing the cold-blooded murderer, but this has become more feasible in view of what has transpired today. She was the only one with keys to Konrad Jensen's flat, and she also had his full trust. And a hundred thousand kroner is a more powerful motive than many of us might imagine for a person who has struggled and constantly lived in financial straits and now faces old age with only forty-eight kroner in her post-office savings account. Remember that she also put through Harald Olesen's phone calls. If she knew that a substantial sum had been left to her in his will, and had realized that the will was being changed a lot, then she had a very strong motive indeed.'

Now it was my turn to nod gravely.

'Sara Sundqvist has the strongest motive of them all – if she knew that Harald Olesen had changed the will and left her a million kroner.'

Patricia agreed without hesitation.

'Obviously. We only have her word for it that she knew nothing, and we also only have her word for it that she knows nothing about what happened in 1944. There might be a powerful motive there too. The will clearly implies this: Harald Olesen obviously had a very bad conscience when it came to her. In fact, it is interesting just how much the lady does not know. I advise you to keep an eye on her, but also to keep her at a good arm's length for a few more days at least.'

This last piece of advice was rather obscure, but I did not feel the need for an explanation of what Patricia meant. Therefore I asked what she thought with regard to the Lunds instead.

'Kristian Lund has had an obvious motive for as long as he has believed he was the heir, particularly if he was aware of the danger that the will was to be changed. In addition, he has also openly expressed his hatred for his deceased father and lied so many times that I have lost count, despite my good maths. His wife could have the same motive as far as the will is concerned, and the same need for revenge. As well as a more advanced but equally plausible motive, linked to another person . . .'

My face must have been a question mark.

'This is a rather tenuous but all the same captivating theory. It would naturally be every jealous housewife's dream to see her husband's mistress publicly convicted and locked up for years, only to be let out when she is approaching forty, without children or friends. Especially if in the meantime you could use the inherited millions that she was denied . . .'

And she was right – it was a possibility. Mrs Lund's hatred had risen to the surface and made an impression today.

'The late Konrad Jensen also had both the opportunity and a possible motive. In short, after one week's investigation, we still cannot exclude anyone who was in 25 Krebs' Street when Harald Olesen was shot.'

Patricia nodded glumly.

'We have made considerable progress and know far more, but still do not have a clear picture of the murderer. All the neighbours could have had the opportunity, and they all have at least one possible motive – some even have more. Kristian Lund and Sara Sundqvist are on the shakiest ground, but I advise you not to trust anyone other than me. And to make Harald Olesen's niece your next port of call.'

I accepted this advice and got up to leave.

V

Cecilia Olesen lived in a spacious two-bedroomed flat in Ullern. She opened the door herself when I rang the bell and asked me in straightaway. As could only be expected, she did not seem particularly overjoyed to see me, but nor was she particularly hostile. A freckled girl of around ten years old poked her head inquisitively round the door to her room, but was immediately ordered to return to her maths homework. The ten-year-old protested that she had already finished her homework, but was not heeded.

I was shown into a comfortable living room and served coffee on a traditional painted tray and it all felt far too pleasant to ask the difficult question that I now had to ask regardless.

'I do apologize for disturbing you again, but there are still some circumstances that need to be clarified in relation to your uncle's murder.'

She nodded – and sighed.

'So I am afraid I have to ask if you knew one of the other people present today slightly better than you may previously have intimated . . .'

No more was needed. Cecilia Olesen's apparently staunch facade cracked and the tears started to fall.

'You are absolutely right. I have been thinking about it ever since. But it was all such a shock – first to see him again, then the will and then discovering an unknown cousin. I could not gather my thoughts until I came home.'

I gave her a charming smile, and all the time she needed. Her voice had steadied when she carried on a couple of minutes later.

'I knew that he might come, but prayed and hoped that it would not be too upsetting. I suppose I hoped that he would in some way be different – older, greyer and fatter – but he was almost just as I remembered him. A bit heavier, of course, but just as tall, just as dark, just as powerful and irresistibly confident. I almost fell off my chair when he came through the door.'

I gave her an understanding look.

'So it is as I thought: you are the young Norwegian sweetheart that Darrell Williams has refused to name.'

She looked genuinely surprised when I said this, but hurried on.

'That is so typical of Darrell, not to give my name in order to protect me. He was my first and my greatest love. I knew that the first time I saw him one autumn day in 1945. A day has not passed since when I have not thought about him.'

'And yet it never amounted to more than young love?'

Her bright face darkened abruptly into something that resembled hate.

'No, and that was my uncle's fault. He was against the relationship from the start and successfully exerted his influence on my parents. It was so easy to fall in love when you were nineteen, he said, but nothing would ever come of it; he was an American soldier, after all – said he who himself worked closely with the Americans both during the war and after. So things got more and more difficult for us. Then one day in spring 1948, Darrell came to tell me that he had been ordered home with only a few days' notice. I have always suspected that my uncle used one of his contacts to arrange that recall order. I still remember every detail of the day Darrell left. I stood at the very end of the harbour in Oslo and waved to him for as long as he was visible on deck, and we have not seen each other since until today. When he came into the room . . . it was almost as if I was young again and back in 1948. As if the ship had suddenly turned round and docked again, and my Darrell had come back to me – but then stopped a few feet away.'

Cecilia Olesen sat in silence, staring into the past.

'I married a very nice and bright man, whom both my parents and uncle approved of, but it was our parents, and not us, who wanted it. I knew that I was standing with the wrong man when I said yes in the church, and it became very obvious as early as our honeymoon. But our wonderful daughter came out of it, if not a lot else. We stayed together for five years, and that was at least four too many. I never forgave my uncle. If he ever regretted it, he never managed to bring himself to ask for my forgiveness.'

It was easy to feel compassion. I nodded and then got up to leave a couple of minutes later when it became evident that she did not want to say any more.

There was something unsaid in the air when she followed me out to the door. She hesitated until the last moment, but then finally spoke as I stood in the doorway.

'I have to ask you . . . I know nothing, and have wondered

every day for the past twenty years. Do you know what Darrell has done in the meantime? He has obviously made a good career for himself, but does he have a wife and children? If I've understood correctly, he is alone here in Oslo?'

The last question was almost whispered, with an undercurrent of hope. I nodded calmly.

'He told me that he had been married in the USA, but they had had no children and the relationship broke down after only a few years. So his story is very much like your own, only without children.'

I had hoped that this would comfort her, but instead the information unleashed a new torrent of tears.

'Oh, I'm so glad, but the thought of him having no children is so, so sad. You see, he was going to have one in 1948. I found out the day after he sailed away.'

Her words winded me and pierced my heart.

'You found out – that you were carrying his child?'

She nodded, swallowed and managed to stammer out the rest.

'It was a scandal, of course, and the only solution was an abortion. My uncle knew some doctors and everything was arranged quietly and discreetly. It took several weeks before I could write to Darrell about it, and I have never known if he received that letter. I have always wanted to believe that he did, but that sorrow and disappointment prevented him from answering.'

I did not know what to say to this unexpected twist. So I stood there in silence for a minute or two before I gently put my arm round her shoulder. I thought to myself that the more unpleasant aspects of Harald Olesen's past were now rising to the surface. And that Darrell Williams also had a strong revenge motive vis-à-vis Harald Olesen – particularly if he in fact had received that letter twenty years ago.

VI

I left Cecilia Olesen as soon as I could, and did not want to ask if I could use her phone. So instead, I made a stop at the office and called from there. Patricia answered immediately and sounded relieved that I had phoned. She whistled appreciatively when I told her about Cecilia Olesen.

'The possibility of an abortion had in fact occurred to me, but I thought that was perhaps too much detail to mention. But this lead is of increasing interest. You should confront Darrell Williams about not only this, but also the papers that he and Harald Olesen burned. Because I am pretty certain that Darrell Williams is the O that Harald Olesen writes about in his diary. It fits well with the timeline when he moved in, the unspecified personal issue that Olesen writes about, and also suspiciously well with the letter itself.'

I had not thought about this possibility, but had to admit that it fell into place rather well. But I still had to ask what the letter 'O' fitted so suspiciously well with. The answer was to the point.

'"O" stands for "OSS agent".'

I nodded – and whistled. The OSS was the forerunner the CIA, and had been active in Norway both during and after the war. I had even mentioned it to Darrell Williams myself, without considering a possible link to the O in Harald Olesen's diary.

'You should question Darrell Williams again as soon as possible. Call Bjørn Erik Svendsen to find out about the OSS. But first send a telegram to the Swedish Police. Even though the US lead is of increasing interest, it may in fact be the Swedish lead that is the right one.'

Patricia hesitated for a moment, but then continued in a slightly shaky voice.

'So, now we have established that N in the diary is Kristian Lund, J is Sara Sundqvist, and O is Darrell Williams, but we are still no closer to identifying D, who is the most interesting and frightening, if what Harald Olesen writes in his diary is to be believed. Unless he has used two different letters for the same person, which seems highly unlikely, the one he feared most is not one of our three main suspects. So keep your eyes peeled for a possible terrifying fourth person who might be D – both inside and outside 25 Krebs' Street.'

I promised to do that, but had to apologize when Patricia asked and admit that I had forgotten to ask the niece if Harald Olesen had had any contacts in the Gjøvik area. We then ended the call and I composed a telegram to the Swedish Police.

IMPORTANT URGENT CASE STOP IN RELATION TO
INVESTIGATION INTO THE HARALD OLESEN MURDER
STOP REQUEST INFORMATION REGARDING SARA
SUNDQVIST BORN 1943 AND ADOPTED IN GOTHENBURG
SUMMER 1944 STOP MAY HAVE COME TO SWEDEN WITH
HARALD OLESEN OR SOMEONE CALLED DEERFOOT STOP
PLEASE TELEGRAM IMMEDIATELY ANY KNOWLEDGE AS
TO DEERFOOTS NAME STOP KOLBJØRN KRISTIANSEN
MAIN POLICE STATION OSLO

The investigation was becoming nothing short of an obsession. I was extremely curious as to what Darrell Williams would say regarding the information from Cecilia Olesen.

But first I followed Patricia's advice and phoned Bjørn Erik Svendsen to find out what he knew about Harald Olesen's contact with the OSS. And this was certainly not insignificant. Harald Olesen had apparently been the contact person for several OSS agents in Norway during the war. It was probably via these channels that he communicated information about Norwegian communists after the war, which then later ended up in the CIA's archives. It was possible to get a fairly good idea of who these communists were from the documents. However, the names of the American agents were not known, or which other Norwegians had been involved in this information-gathering or known about it, or what else they might have done. Harald Olesen was the only one to be identified so far, but there was reason to believe that more people had been involved. It was possible that some of them might today hold key positions in Norway and/or the USA. This was one of the points that Harald Olesen had not wanted to discuss with his biographer, Bjørn Erik Svendsen told me, so he would be eternally grateful for any supplementary information I could give him.

I did not feel inclined to talk to Cecilia Olesen again following her emotional outpouring no more than a couple of hours earlier, so instead I called her brother to ask if he knew whether Harald Olesen had any close friends in the area around Gjøvik. And rather unexpectedly hit bullseye. He answered straightaway that his uncle had had lots of contacts in the area, but the first to spring to mind was a wealthy farmer whom he had visited several times in the years running up to the war. The nephew had even gone with him once. He could not remember his Christian name, but his surname was easy to remember, as he had owned a considerable amount of forested land: Storskog. He immediately replied: 'Yes, of course!' when I asked if this friend of Harald Olesen was perhaps called Hans. I quickly thanked him for the information, threw down the phone and ran out to the car.

VII

It was almost nine o'clock by the time I arrived at 25 Krebs' Street, but the lights were still on in all the windows, except the two flats left empty by Harald Olesen and Konrad Jensen.

Darrell Williams opened the door slowly when I rang the bell and nodded pensively when he saw it was me. I caught a hint of acknowledgement in his eyes as we briefly shook hands.

I was starting to feel tired after a long day and was secure enough in my case to get straight to the point.

'You perhaps understand why I am here. I worked it out by myself. She did not say anything and still only has fond feelings for you.'

He gave a curt nod and pointed me into the living room. We sat down in the armchairs. I got the impression that it had been a tough day for Darrell Williams as well, and this was reinforced when I saw the bottles and glasses standing on the coffee table.

'I now know that you had a relationship with Cecilia Olesen from 1945 until 1948 and that her uncle vehemently opposed it. However, I do not know if you received the letter she sent you a few months after you had to leave Norway in spring 1948.'

Darrell Williams sat deep in thought for a few moments, then poured a drink from one of the bottles on the table. He held the bottle up to me, but put it down as soon as I shook my head.

'Sadly, I did, but I have not yet managed to write the reply,' he said brusquely.

He emptied his glass, then started to talk quickly in a controlled voice.

'My feelings for Harald Olesen were anything but sympathetic for many years after that. But over the years the intensity has diminished. At the time, in 1948, I felt like I could kill him, but I most certainly did not now, in 1968. It was easier to meet him again than I had expected and feared. But today was worse – seeing her again, that is.'

I had no difficulty believing him.

'Which is why you arrived so late and sat by the door. And why you laughed so loudly and criticized her and her brother so strongly – to disguise the fact.'

Darrell Williams said nothing, but shrugged his confirmation. I immediately followed up on this success.

'One more thing. It seems unlikely that you were sent to Oslo and accommodated in the same building as Harald Olesen because of this old personal conflict.'

He shook his head firmly.

'Of course not. That was never an issue for my employers.'

I nodded and carried on swiftly.

'But it is still no coincidence that you ended up here. You came here because Harald Olesen had some papers and information that your employer was keen to ensure would not fall into the wrong hands either before or after his death.'

Darrell Williams sighed deeply.

'You are putting me in a very difficult situation now. These are things that I cannot confirm or deny without permission from the highest level.'

'Let me then simply state that this is the case and that you can neither confirm nor deny it.'

He nodded silently.

'I will also state, then, that these papers included information about certain Norwegians and Americans who today hold very senior positions, and whom Harald Olesen knew had been actively involved in highly sensitive campaigns against the communists and individuals who were assumed to be communists for no given reason. And it would be extremely detrimental to these individuals, and perhaps also to relations between the USA and Norway, if this became known. And it would appear that you are still unable or unwilling to deny any of this.'

Darrell Williams's sigh was even heavier, and his nod even more silent.

'And I would find it very hard to persuade you to give me the names of these people?'

He smiled, but it was a sombre and almost twisted smile.

'If such persons exist, it would be impossible for me to give you their names.'

'But they are of no particular relevance to my investigation – so long as you are not the murderer.'

Darrell Williams spontaneously held out his hand.

'You are quite clearly a very good and intelligent policeman. And it is my sincere hope that you will also manage to put together the remaining pieces in this case, so that I can finish up and leave Norway. The situation was awkward enough to begin with, but my emotional ballast now makes it unbearable.'

I wanted to offer him an olive branch.

'I have reason to believe that everything will fall into place within a couple of days now. And in the meantime, I hope you understand that I must ask you to stay put.'

Another curt nod. Then he got up. I took the hint and followed him out into the hallway. In the spirit of cooperation, I added that an anonymous OSS agent, whom I believed was him, was mentioned in Harald Olesen's diary. He thanked me for this information and concluded that I probably would not have needed to ask him about the names if they had been in the diary.

It certainly felt as if we understood each other and were working for the common good – two officials on important missions from different countries. I left Darrell Williams with the feeling that he had now told the truth and was not the murderer. But I still could not strike him from the list.

As he opened the door for me, Darrell Williams sheepishly asked me a final question.

'One sometimes wonders . . . Do you know how Cecilia's life has been? Does she have a family and the like? I noticed that she still had the same name and that she came with her brother.'

I nodded reassuringly.

'She has a daughter from a short and unhappy marriage, but is now divorced.'

He thanked me quickly for this information and asked me to give Cecilia Olesen his regards if I saw her again. He then seemed to dab his eyes. Darrell Williams was a strong man. He did not cry. Certainly not before he had shut me out of his flat without further ado. But I thought I heard a muffled sob as the door closed behind me. Perhaps it was just my imagination. It had been a long and dramatic day for us both.

VIII

My final stop for the day had to be Andreas Gullestad on the ground floor. He greeted me with his usual friendliness and offered me coffee and a wide selection of teas. However, his face darkened quickly once again when I said I had to ask a question about his father.

'I should have realized that you would find out. It occurred to me after your last visit,' he said, visibly agitated when I asked if it was definitely the case that he had never met Harald Olesen before moving in here. However, he quickly regained his composure.

'I realized suddenly after the murder that my neighbour Harald Olesen must be the same Harald that my father talked about with such respect, and whom he counted as one of his close friends. In which case, I had met him a couple of times when I was a child, when he visited my father before the war. I should of course have phoned you straightaway to amend my statement, but I would rather not talk about any memories connected with my father – the old grief cuts through me like a knife every time I hear his name. I have no particularly good or bad memories of Harald Olesen's visits to the lost paradise of my childhood. In fact, it was only after his murder that I remembered he had come. I certainly hope that you do not believe that I pushed myself up to the second floor in my wheelchair and shot him because he visited my father a couple of times when I was a boy?'

I assured him that of course I did not. But it did strike me that even this friendly man on the ground floor had withheld information several times and that he too was proving to be more complex and less likeable the more I got to know him.

I took a potshot and asked if he could remember any younger men in his father's family or circle of friends who might possibly have worked with Harald Olesen during the war. Andreas Gullestad dutifully gave it some thought, but then shook his head apologetically. His father had been an only child and so had neither younger brothers nor nephews. And given that he himself was only a boy at the time, he could not remember any younger men who might fit that description from among his father's staff or friends. The code name Deerfoot still meant nothing to him.

Andreas Gullestad apologized profusely that he could not help me more, and was as friendly as could be when I left him some minutes later. But I did note that I no longer trusted him. Which, depressingly, was the case with all the surviving residents of 25 Krebs' Street, with the possible exception of the caretaker's wife in the basement.

Once again I went to bed alone that evening with the feeling that we were getting closer and closer to the solution, but I also felt increasingly impatient. The murderer was still not in sight. It helped that the public thought that the case had been solved with the death of Konrad Jensen. But I could feel the strain of the seven-day investigation, and dearly hoped to be able to catch sight of the murderer on the eighth day. All ideas of taking a holiday over Easter this year were definitely off the cards, but the thought that there would be no newspapers for two days and fewer colleagues at work was a relief.

DAY EIGHT

A Disappearance – and a New Clue

I

On 11 April, Maundy Thursday, I enjoyed a good breakfast in peace, but the moment I got into work at nine o'clock, the drama started. At five past nine, the phone on my desk started to ring. At the other end, I heard the loud and determined voice of Supreme Court Justice Jesper Christopher Haraldsen, but to my enormous relief, he sounded unusually friendly.

'Good morning, Detective Inspector. I thought I would just call to wish you a good Easter and to congratulate you on the swift conclusion of such an apparently complex murder case!'

I thanked him – and with a rising pulse waited for him to continue. I suspected that this was not the only reason that Jesper Christopher Haraldsen had interrupted his Easter holiday to phone me. And this promptly proved to be the case.

'I, of course, also wanted to make sure that the case really has been solved, and to say that I am still available should you need any further advice. But when a convicted Nazi commits

251

suicide and leaves behind a written confession in the very building where a Resistance hero has been found murdered, there is perhaps not much need for any further advice?'

Not only was my pulse evident now, but also my sweat. Following a lightning review of the situation, I decided to humour him a bit, but at the same time be diplomatic.

'There is certainly no other suspect at the moment, but a number of very peculiar circumstances have come to light, and as a result of that, the investigation has not yet been closed.'

There was silence at the other end for a moment. Followed by the inevitable question – in a slightly sterner voice.

'Well, I must say that sounds quite alarming, my young man. What sort of peculiar circumstances would merit a review of such compelling evidence? I do hope that this is in no way connected to the unfortunate coincidence that a representative of the American Embassy rents a flat in the same building?'

I sidestepped the question.

'I hope that you, as a supreme court justice, will understand that I cannot go into details regarding the investigation at this point. But please rest assured that the option that the deceased Nazi was the murderer and therefore committed suicide is being thoroughly assessed. However, other crucial information has now come to light that means we must still keep all options open over the weekend, at least.'

Again there was a silence at the other end for a few seconds. Then he let me have it, in a voice that assailed my ear like a machine gun.

'Well, then I certainly hope that there is at least another

murder over Easter, or you may find that there is a new head of investigation after Easter.'

He slammed down the phone without giving me a chance to comment. I sat there paralysed for a moment. Then I rushed over to my boss's office with unusual speed. Fortunately, he was in his office, and when I asked if it was possible to speak to him immediately, he was more than happy to do so. I jumped when the phone rang while we were sitting there and nodded in appreciation when he commented that he would not take any calls until we were finished.

I gave him a detailed account of the investigation and why I had chosen to continue it. He agreed with me and praised my discerning conclusions and my work so far. My boss told me he was relieved to hear me say that it was not likely that the American was involved in the murder, but fully supported my wish for him to remain in Norway until the case had been solved. We also agreed that for the moment it was probably best if the public and the rest of the force thought that the case had been closed following Konrad Jensen's death, but that the investigation should continue to look for other potential murderers.

II

However, despite the support of my superior, it was hard to prevent the voice of Jesper Christopher Haraldsen from buzzing in my head for the next hour. At around half past eleven, I decided to phone Darrell Williams to try to establish whether or not he knew Haraldsen. The caretaker's wife promptly answered the phone. I asked if all was well with her and she said that things could not be better. The money was due to be deposited in her account just after Easter. In the meantime, she was celebrating by planning how she was going to surprise her children and grandchildren with gifts.

The caretaker's wife transferred me to Darrell Williams, but the phone just rang and rang. This made me feel uneasy. I called back the caretaker's wife and asked her to go and ring on Darrell Williams's doorbell. She did this and came back to say that there was no sign of life from inside the flat. Which was very odd, she said with audible anxiety in her voice. She had not seen the American leave the building, so if he was out, he must have left very early, or in the few minutes when she had not been at her post.

I said that I would ring again in half an hour and asked her in the meantime to go out and check whether there were any lights on in Darrell Williams's flat. A nerve-tingling thirty minutes followed. When I rang back at twelve, the caretaker's wife did not sound so happy anymore. She had now been out to have a look and the lights were on, but there was still no sign of life from Darrell Williams's flat.

There was silence on the line for a moment. We both remembered only too well our discovery in Konrad Jensen's flat two days earlier. The lights were the deciding factor. I asked her to be ready with the keys and immediately went down to the car to drive over there.

A quarter of an hour later, I was once again standing with a nervous caretaker's wife outside a locked door. Once again I was armed with my service revolver. And once again there was not a sound to be heard from inside, even though I rang the bell and knocked on the door several times. At twenty-five past twelve, I asked the caretaker's wife to open the door and crossed the threshold with trepidation, my gun ready in my hand.

The lights were on in all the rooms. There was no apparent difference from the day before. The furniture was all in the same place, the books and papers were untouched, and there was some washing-up left from his last meal in the kitchen, but his fur coat was no longer on the coat stand by the door. And most importantly, Darrell Williams himself was nowhere to be seen, not in the hall, not in the bathroom, not in the bedroom or the kitchen. I left the living room until last and half expected to find Darrell Williams collapsed in a chair – just as I had found Konrad Jensen two days earlier on the floor below. But fortunately, all the chairs were empty. Between the bottles on the table lay a short letter with a brief attempt at an explanation.

> *Honourable Detective Inspector Kristiansen,*
>
> *I apologize sincerely that I am duty-bound to follow a new order from my employer and to leave Norway immediately without being able to inform you in advance. I would like to reiterate my assurance that I have no knowledge of the circumstances surrounding Harald Olesen's death, and leave the country confident that you will find his murderer without my cooperation within the next few days.*
>
> *With my deepest respect,*
>
> *Darrell Williams*

I read the letter four times. The first two times with increasing disbelief, the last two with increasing anger. I went out to reassure the caretaker's wife that there had not been another death, but that Darrell Williams had had to go away at short notice. Then I went back down to the car and drove faster than the speed limit and traffic permitted to the American Embassy.

III

My anger at Darrell Williams's disappearing act survived the journey remarkably well, just as it did my meeting with the building's facade and the American Embassy staff. I informed the receptionist briefly, and possibly a touch too curtly, that I was Detective Inspector Kristiansen and was investigating the murder of Harald Olesen and that I would wait here until Embassy Counsellor George Adams had the time to meet me. It was a bold strategy. Behind my bravado, my heart pounded for the endless, long-drawn minutes that followed until someone came to tell me that 'Mr Adams' was in his office and would be happy to see me immediately.

The desk was just as big, the handshake just as firm, the face just as void of expression and the voice just as drawling as on my last visit.

'What a pleasure to see you again, Detective Inspector. Congratulations on your breakthrough in the investigation, which was reported in the papers yesterday. Now, how can we help you today?'

I studied him, without seeing any cracks in his diplomatic armour.

'Well, to begin with, you can explain to me why Darrell Williams has disappeared and then tell me where and why he has gone.'

George Adams rubbed his hands.

'"Disappeared" is perhaps the wrong word. I can confirm that Darrell Williams has left the country, and we of course know where he is. There is no drama attached to the situation. As Mauritius has become an independent state, the USA has established an embassy there and Mr Williams was asked to assume the position of ambassador.'

I nodded grimly; it was about as audacious as I had expected.

'In which case, why did the embassy not find it necessary to inform me or the police of this?'

George Adams rubbed his hands even harder and looked even more smug.

'We of course apologize if such notification should have been given, but we saw no grounds to disturb such an important person as yourself in a situation where we had every reason to believe that the murder case had been solved in the best possible way, without Mr Williams being involved at all. Furthermore, we had no reason to believe that you would appreciate being informed at midnight on Maundy Thursday.'

I quickly realized that any display of anger or irritation was pointless and decided to play the diplomat myself. This time, I fortunately had a far better card up my sleeve than before.

'I am afraid there appears to have been a regrettable breakdown in communication. I informed Darrell Williams late last night of a dramatic development in the murder investigation that made it necessary for all the residents of 25 Krebs' Street who were there on the night of the murder to remain in town until after the Easter weekend.'

George Adams gave an apologetic shrug and smiled blithely.

'I am very sorry to hear that. As you say, there appears to have been a regrettable breakdown in communication. Might I add that there is a simple explanation as to why Mr Williams did not mention this at the time. He was called to Mauritius by telephone at two o'clock this morning and left Norway on a six-o'clock flight. Obviously, the opportunity to become an ambassador was so unexpected and attractive that he immediately forgot everything else.'

I gave an even more exaggerated shrug and smiled even more blithely.

'These things happen, and obviously no one is to blame, but the misunderstanding is indeed very unfortunate as it may trigger unwarranted anti-American reactions from politicians and the press in Norway. That was what I had hoped to avoid by telling Mr Williams yesterday.'

It felt for the first time like I had hit a weak point in George Adams's armour. He kept his friendly smile, but his movements were more tense.

'The embassy would naturally do whatever necessary to avoid such a development. Would you be able to explain what the problem is?'

'With pleasure. I have no reason to believe that Darrell Williams is in any way involved with the murder, but a situation may arise over the weekend in which the press once again turns a critical eye on the investigation and I may be obliged to ask some important questions of all the witnesses. If Mr Williams is no longer here, it would of course give rise to suspicion and possible speculation. The press would then ask if I had informed Williams that he was not allowed to leave the country and as a guardian of the law, I would have to tell the truth. And that in turn could easily lead to unfortunate rumours and more speculation.'

George Adams gave a sharp nod to indicate that he understood the problem and then leaned forward over the desk. It was clear that he was wracking his brains to find a solution. I still had an ace of spades up my sleeve and saw no reason to save it, given the way things had gone.

'However, the misunderstanding is all the more regrettable as I have, in the course of the investigation, got wind of information that could indicate a degree of cooperation between Harald Olesen and American intelligence agencies in the past, which may also have involved certain leading politicians in both Norway and the USA. There may be details of activities in Norway and lists of who was involved. As far as I can tell, this is of little significance to the murder investigation, and I had hoped that it would be possible to exclude it from my reports. But should the press decide to take a more critical look at the case, this may be difficult. And that would be extremely unfortunate, given the upcoming election in the USA and the already excessive anti-American feeling abroad in Norway . . .'

I had obviously hit the jackpot. George Adams's head immediately dropped noticeably, and his gaze was almost fearful. It was impossible not to be impressed at how well he continued to express himself even though the tension in his voice was now obvious.

'The embassy would like to thank you for informing us immediately, and we will of course do our best to avoid a situation in which sensitive personal information falls into the wrong hands and creates any extreme reactions. Could you please advise us on how best to avoid such a situation?'

I nodded with exaggerated willingness.

'Well, let us hope first of all that Mr Williams has not yet boarded the flight to Mauritius and that it will be possible to get him a return ticket to Oslo as soon as possible. If he was back in his flat in Oslo by four o'clock tomorrow afternoon, for example, we should be able to control the situation. Otherwise, the situation could become very dramatic and uncomfortable should it be necessary to issue a warrant through Interpol. It is only reasonable to assume that enemies of the USA here in this country and elsewhere would soon notice such a warrant for an American diplomat. In which case, the situation could quickly spiral out of control in both political circles and the press. In the worst-case scenario, a list of Harald Olesen's contacts in Norway and America and information about what they have done may get out.'

George Adams immediately nodded three times, his head sinking with every nod. By the third, his chin almost hit the desk.

'Then I won't take up any more of your time and will myself immediately review the situation and investigate ways in which to get Darrell Williams back to Oslo as soon as possible in order to avoid any further complications. On behalf of the American Embassy, I would once again like to thank you for your goodwill, and I will inform you immediately when we have an overview of the situation.'

This time the embassy counsellor's hand was definitely sweaty. I managed to keep a straight face until I had left the building and was back in my car driving away – but no longer.

A new howl of laughter was triggered that afternoon in my office when a secretary came in at half past two with an urgent telegram from the American Embassy. The message was short:

> DARRELL WILLIAMS LANDING AT FORNEBU TOMORROW
> 2.30PM AND WILL IMMEDIATELY BE·DRIVEN TO HIS FLAT
> STOP THANK YOU FOR COOPERATION AND AGAIN
> APOLOGIES FOR MISUNDERSTANDING STOP GEORGE
> ADAMS

My irritation at Williams's disappearance had definitely now turned into joy at the way the case was progressing. I was filled with childish delight and pride at the fact that I had forced the mighty American Embassy to retreat. Just then, my secretary came in with another urgent telegram. I asked, not without trepidation, if it was also from the embassy, but was told that it was from the Swedish Police. I ripped open the telegram immediately. It was longer than the one from the American Embassy, and even more dramatic:

> SARA SUNDQVIST TAKEN IN CHARGE AT A SMALL POLICE
> STATION IN SÄLEN FEBRUARY 1944 STOP CHIEF OF POLICE
> HANS ANDERSSON STILL IN SERVICE AND REMEMBERS
> MANY DETAILS STOP HAS MET HARALD OLESEN AND
> DEERFOOT BUT DOES NOT KNOW HIS NAME STOP
> ANDERSSON ASKS YOU TO COME TO SÄLEN IN PERSON AS
> SOON AS POSSIBLE STOP SWEDISH POLICE STOCKHOLM

I looked at my watch and saw that as it took four to five hours to get to Sälen, it was too late to drive there and back today. So I hastily wrote a return telegram in which I confirmed that I would get to Sälen around lunchtime tomorrow.

And then I phoned Patricia to hear if she had any good advice to help me on my way.

IV

My afternoon meeting at the White House lasted no longer than an hour – even though it included an excellent three-course meal of onion soup, salmon and rice cream. It felt a little as though we were celebrating the imminent closure of the case. However, the atmosphere was far from riotous. Patricia laughed, as I had hoped, at the story of my new and far more productive meeting with the embassy counsellor, but soon became deadly serious again.

'Well, let us hope that your intuition is right and that Darrell Williams is not the murderer. Otherwise it may in fact be difficult to avoid a public scandal.'

A piece of potato got stuck in my throat.

'I think it is safe to say that he is not. I did seriously start to wonder if Darrell Williams was the murderer when he was given help by the embassy to leave the country. But in that case, they would hardly have agreed on the spot to have him sent back . . .'

Patricia chewed her salmon thoughtfully.

'This is a slightly risky situation. Darrell Williams is a truly cold-hearted player if he did commit the murders and comes back all the same, and there is already much to indicate that he is a cool player. What has happened is that the embassy now trusts you, and you trust the embassy. Your successful tactic today more or less knocks one of the remaining theories on the head, namely that Harald Olesen was murdered by Darrell Williams because of the old information and things that had to be kept secret. Which in turn reinforces the impression given in the diary that the situation had already been resolved and the papers burned before Harald Olesen was murdered. But the embassy must have totally misjudged the situation and believed that if Darrell Williams disappeared from the scene, the negative focus would not be as great. Or they knew about his old conflicts with Harald Olesen and were afraid that he may have actually murdered him. Which cannot be entirely ruled out, can it?'

For a moment I lost my appetite and pushed the rest of the delicious salmon to one side. We could unfortunately not rule this out, and it would be a very embarrassing scenario, especially given my performance at the American Embassy today. I comforted myself with the thought that if Darrell Williams should prove to be the murderer, the situation would be more embarrassing for the embassy. Practically everything I had said or done in the course of the investigation could be justified in relation to the general public and my superiors. However, the idea of being accused of hoodwinking the embassy of Norway's most powerful ally in connection with a murder case was not an attractive one, it had to be said. I hastily replied to Patricia that it seemed highly unlikely and she gave a sombre shake of the head.

'There are several other theories that would imply other murderers that I, at present, find more plausible. But this one is still not impossible. Hopefully, we will be in a better position to judge this tomorrow evening – if you are able, in the meantime, to establish whether Deerfoot is Williams or not.'

Patricia pushed her plate out of the way and leaned over the table towards me.

'Above all else, there are two things you must try to establish in Sweden, both of which may be decisive. First, note down all the known details regarding Sara Sundqvist and what may have happened to her parents. And second, everything you can find out about Deerfoot, which may help us to discover his identity. Now that we finally have confirmation of his existence and had found someone who has actually met him, it will be interesting to see where it leads.'

We raised our glasses to that and ate our rice cream in comfortable silence. Before I left, Patricia asked me to phone her from Sälen if she could be of any help and to come here as soon as I returned to Oslo. I promised to do so with a light heart. I did not like to say so, but thinking about where the investigation might have been today without Patricia's vision was a terrifying thought. If I would ever have managed to work out how the murder was committed was an open question. A creeping minor worry was the extent to which Patricia might want her role to be highlighted, but thus far she had said nothing to indicate a desire for public recognition.

What had dominated until now was the increasing desire to find the murderer. I recaptured some of the excitement from my first hare hunt when I was a youth and felt an ever more obsessive drive to lock the handcuffs round the wrists of this mysterious person who had taken the lives of both Harald Olesen and Konrad Jensen without being noticed. Because Konrad Jensen had also been murdered, I no longer doubted that for a minute. In fact, it was almost shameful to think that I had resisted accepting Patricia's reasoning for so long.

Before leaving, I said to her that I would do a final check

of the building before driving to Sälen. She nodded her approval. It was perfectly reasonable to ask the residents to keep themselves available for questioning from Friday afternoon over the weekend. However, she strongly advised me not to tell them where I was going in the meantime. Any references to Sweden or Sälen might alarm one or more of the residents. We parted in high spirits, full of optimistic expectations for what tomorrow would bring.

V

The evening round at 25 Krebs' Street was without drama. The building seemed to be poised in the calm before the storm, and now that there was life in only four of the seven flats, it did not take long. It was raining heavily outside, and the prevailing atmosphere was grey and heavy.

The caretaker's wife was in her flat in the basement, and nodded with relief when she heard the news that Darrell Williams was on his way back, and promised to make a note of when he arrived. Otherwise, she largely answered yes to all my questions. Everything was tranquil in the building now.

Andreas Gullestad opened his door almost as soon as I rang the bell, with his usual smile and offer of coffee and cake. He said that he had registered, with some anxiety, my visit earlier on in the day and that the lights in Darrell Williams's flat had not come on later in the evening. He thanked me when I told him that Williams would be back the next day and assured me that he would be here and waiting for the final interviews over the course of the weekend. 'I seldom go anywhere at the weekend, anyway,' he commented, with his jovial smile and a chuckle. This sounded very familiar, but it took a couple of minutes before I realized that Patricia had made exactly the same point a few days earlier.

Mr and Mrs Lund came to the door together when I rang the bell, and proclaimed more or less in chorus that they had nothing more to say. Both appeared to be relieved when I told them that it looked as if the investigation would soon be over, and they promised to be available over the weekend. They informed me that they no longer dared to have their young son at home in the building and had therefore sent him to his grandparents in Bærum for Easter. Kristian Lund was in relatively good humour, having found a lawyer who thought that he had a strong case in terms of the will. His wife nodded in agreement, but added that the most important thing was that they still had each other and their little boy. Kristian Lund then said in a loud, clear voice that he deeply regretted having betrayed his wife and that he would never see Sara Sundqvist again. His wife put an affectionate arm round his waist and kissed him on the cheek. They seemed to be happy, and I really wanted to believe them. Yet I could not, completely. They had lied too much and failed to tell too much early on in the investigation.

I saved my visit to Sara Sundqvist until last. She opened the door a crack, with the safety chain still on. But when she heard my voice, she opened up and embraced me warmly. Sara was visibly tense. Her hands were shaking, and her heart was beating quickly: I could feel it through the thin material of her dress. She promised to stay at home all weekend, and had nothing new to tell me. Again, I really wanted to believe her, but no longer dared to take anything for granted in her case either.

There was a dramatic end to my visit, though, when Sara Sundqvist suddenly grabbed me by the arm and pointed out of the window.

'Do you see that person in a dark trench coat down there on the pavement?' she asked.

I started and looked to where she was pointing, and true enough, in the shadow of the neighbouring building stood a figure in a raincoat with a hood. Even though the light was dim, the coat was undeniably blue. It was either a man or a tall woman, but it was difficult to tell through the dark and rain.

Sara Sundqvist was either frightfully nervous or extremely good at pretending. It was apparently a great relief to her that I could also see the mysterious street guest in a raincoat.

'Thank goodness it is not just my imagination running wild. Maybe it is merely a coincidence. It does seem rather strange that . . . that person has been standing there for several hours this afternoon. It wasn't wrong of me to mention it to you, was it?'

I gave a reassuring shake of the head. It was definitely worth checking out. It may simply be someone from the neighbouring building who happened to be waiting there, or a journalist, or an overzealous newspaper reader. But it was undoubtedly odd that the person had been standing there for several hours – and, above all, was wearing a blue raincoat.

The person in the raincoat was standing still by his or her post when I took a final look out of the window with Sara. But when I then swung out onto the street following a hasty goodbye, the entrance to the neighbouring building was suddenly empty. I glanced briefly either way and caught sight of a figure in a raincoat and hood heading briskly towards the nearest bus-stop. I thought to myself that it was either a woman or a very light-footed man. Egged on by the thought that I may have caught sight of Deerfoot, I gave chase. The person in front of me noticed and picked up pace into a sprint. Just then, the bus pulled into the stop. The person in the raincoat ran for the bus and I ran after the person in the raincoat. As I closed in, I became certain that it was a woman running in front of me. A couple of moments later, the pursuit ended in confusion when she ran into the bus and I ran into her.

The bus drove on without the woman in the blue raincoat. A moment before she pushed down the hood, apologizing profusely, I recognized her. The long, fair locks of Cecilia Olesen tumbled into view.

She apologized for running away, and then for standing outside 25 Krebs' Street, but it was nothing to do with anything criminal, she assured me. The reading of the will and then our conversation yesterday had rekindled old feelings and memories. She could find no peace at home, so she had asked a friend to babysit for the evening. And had stood here alone on the pavement, despite the rain, and stared at the building in the hope of catching a glimpse of Darrell Williams. She became more and more anxious as the hours passed and the flat remained in darkness. Then she panicked when I came out and started to follow her. Because it was dark, she had only recognized me when we collided at the bus – she said. She assured me that she had not been inside the building, neither today nor previously this year, either with or without a blue raincoat, which she maintained she had had for many years.

I told her not to come again tomorrow and promised that

I would ask Darrell Williams to contact her later if he was innocent. She gave me a spontaneous hug and waved to me with gratitude when she got on the next bus a couple of minutes later. My hair was dripping when I walked back to my car and drove home. I had a long drive and a very interesting conversation in store for the ninth day of the investigation. In anticipation of my expedition to Sweden, pictures of all the surviving residents were still on the cards, as well as a joker card for the ever-evasive Deerfoot.

DAY NINE

On the Trail of a Light-Footed War Ghost

I

My working day started earlier than usual on Good Friday, 12 April 1968. By ten to eight, I was at the office, where, to my relief, nothing of any note had happened. At eight o'clock on the dot, I got into my car, ready to start my solo expedition to Sweden. I went via 25 Krebs' Street, where everything still seemed to be calm. But it definitely felt like something was brewing when I left Oslo.

My journey progressed at a steady pace. There was not much traffic, and the roads were clear of snow until I was well up into the mountains. Even though the snow was melting, I drove through a beautiful Norwegian winter landscape on my way up to Trysil. The border control with Sweden was symbolic. A customs officer saluted and waved me through without any further formality as soon as he saw the police car. There were no border guards to be seen on either the Norwegian or the Swedish side. It struck me that the control here would have been much stricter and far more frightening for those who fled occupied Norway in fear of their lives during the war. It was a strange feeling to be looking for tracks in the snow that had long since disappeared in pursuit of a mysterious border guide and two refugees who had vanished some twenty-four years earlier.

Once on the Swedish side, I drove for miles without seeing anyone. Then all of a sudden, the police station appeared, round a bend. It was just after one o'clock. The turnoff was marked with a police sign, and there were two unmistakable Swedish police cars parked outside. The station itself was more like a simple two-storey family house, and lay at the foot of one side of a long valley.

Chief of Police Hans Andersson had coffee and cakes waiting for me in his office. He was more or less as I had imagined: a slightly greying man in his sixties, about half a head shorter than me, but a bit heavier all the same. His back was still straight, his eyes still bright, his handshake firm and his smile friendly. But his voice was gentler than expected, and his first sentence even more unexpected.

'Welcome. Always nice to get a visit from a fellow countryman!'

He chuckled at my surprise and explained.

'Once upon a time, it was Hans Andersen from Norway – I started my training there. But then I met a beautiful young girl from these parts one Easter holiday and life turned out the way it did . . . I trained as a policeman in Gothenburg and have served here ever since.'

He quickly leaned over towards me and lowered his voice when he continued.

'It has not always been easy. The dissolution of the union was only a couple of decades old and the older generation still harboured a good deal of prejudice against the Norwegians. My father-in-law said very early on that he could accept a

Norwegian as his son-in-law, but he could not accept his grandchildren having a Norwegian surname. So Hans Andersen became Hans Andersson.'

He paused and chewed pensively on a bun.

'Things got better for a while, but then the war broke out and it all got more complicated again. In the first two years of the war, there was considerable sympathy for the Germans, and a firm belief that they would win the war. You know, perhaps, that the Norwegian foreign minister Koht came to Sälen in 1940 only to be told that he was not welcome here and that the king could risk being imprisoned if he came to Sweden.'

I nodded and signalled that he should continue. I realized that this was going to be a long and interesting conversation.

'Fortunately, the mood soon changed in 1942 to 1943. News of the executions and arrests in Norway drew more attention and it became increasingly obvious that the Germans were on the defensive. The orders from Stockholm came through that refugees coming from Norway should be welcomed and well looked after. We adopted a very pragmatic approach to the situation. The refugees were first registered properly here in the office on the ground floor. Then they were taken up to the living room in my flat upstairs to celebrate with coffee and food. More than once we put them up overnight in one of the guest rooms. There were many great moments, as I am sure you can imagine. I saw some of the happiest people I have ever seen in my life outside this building during the war.'

'Do you remember when it was that you met Harald Olesen for the first time?'

He nodded and smiled happily.

'I remember the date very well, because it was the day before Christmas Eve 1942. They had walked through the night and came down the side of the valley shortly after breakfast. We had just started decorating the Christmas tree when they came. I found out what his real name was much later. During the war, he was called Hawkeye here on the Swedish side. The name is from a Red Indian book and is very fitting. Harald Olesen's profile resembled a hawk, and he had better eyesight than most. He was nearly fifty by then, but looked much younger. I have thought about it later – the code names were perhaps rather risky, even though we seldom used them. The name Hawkeye was well suited to Harald Olesen, and Deerfoot fitted his partner remarkably well. I once mentioned it to Harald Olesen, but he just laughed and said that no one would suspect Deerfoot of anything, and that in fact the name Catpaw would have been even better. Which was true. Deerfoot was in many ways a remarkable young man. He was incredibly light on his feet. In both summer and winter, Deerfoot seemed to float, and we often joked that he did not leave any tracks, not even in newly fallen snow. Never before or since have I seen a person dance so lightly over the snow as Deerfoot. It was always as if he was tightly sprung, ready to pounce. Like a featherweight boxer, if you see what I mean.'

I had seen some boxing matches and knew exactly what he meant. I had also understood quite quickly that Hans Andersson was not a fast storyteller and had a penchant for melodrama.

'Very interesting. And was Deerfoot there the first time that you met Harald Olesen?'

He nodded eagerly.

'Yes, both then and every time after. It was an interesting story. Harald Olesen always struck me as being a very intelligent and capable man. I was not at all surprised when he became a government minister after the war. But as a member of the Resistance, he had one real weakness, which he controlled because he was well aware of it. He told me on the third or fourth time that he was here, and I certainly had never noticed it. Harald Olesen had almost no sense of direction. If he had gone out into the mountains alone with the refugees, they may never have found their way anywhere. He would often call Deerfoot his map and compass. As I understood it, Deerfoot knew the mountains well from before the war, and also had a keen sense of direction.'

He paused and politely waited for me to finish writing my notes. I waved him on impatiently.

'There were many refugees who benefited from Deerfoot's infallible sense of direction, and who were openly grateful. We raised the flag here every day as a discreet signal to any refugees who might cross the border. There was great excitement here many a time when the people making their way down the side of the valley saw the flag and realized that they had finally arrived safely in Sweden. I remember the first time especially well, because one of the refugees they had with them was so young. He was only sixteen at the time, in 1942. He told me himself when he came back ten years later with his wife and child to thank us and give us presents.'

I nodded in recognition. It was a touching story, but I had heard it before. It was clearly the same refugee who had been hidden by the caretaker and his wife, in the basement of the building in Oslo where Harald Olesen was later shot. It now felt like we were getting very warm and Deerfoot would soon be in sight.

'This is all very interesting, but I would like some more details about this Deerfoot. As far as I have understood, you never knew his real name. But what else can you tell me about him? His age, where he came from and suchlike. And did he have an American accent by any chance?'

Hans Andersson shook his head apologetically.

'Deerfoot spoke Norwegian without an accent, and as far as I can remember, without any distinct dialect either. He could have come from anywhere in eastern Norway. He was cagey and said very little about himself. But I have actually found an old photograph of him!'

I watched dumbfounded as he got up and went over to the desk and pulled an old black-and-white photograph from a drawer with something akin to awe.

'I don't remember taking the photograph, but we must have done at the time. I was given it by the young refugee when he came back years later, and I dug it out again after your telegram came. So it must be from 23 December 1942. The young refugee is on the right and Deerfoot on the left.'

He slid the photograph that held the secret across the table, face down.

'You will perhaps understand what Harald Olesen meant when he said that no one would suspect Deerfoot of anything – and why I said that he was a remarkable young man,' he commented, with a mischievous smile.

I flipped the photograph over in a flash and immediately understood what he meant.

The theory that Darrell Williams was Deerfoot could be shelved.

The refugee was an extremely happy, smiling dark-haired youth of sixteen in the yellowing picture from 23 December 1942. He was clearly not yet fully grown, but was still the taller of the two youths in the picture.

There was a flash from a silver pendant round Deerfoot's neck, but no trace of a smile on his face. The youth who stared at the camera from underneath a dark fringe was very focused and serious. In December 1942, Deerfoot had been a lean and dark young lad, with not even a hint of facial hair. I would estimate his age to be thirteen at the least and fifteen at the most.

Hans Andersson smiled momentarily at my surprise and carried on speaking before I could ask a question.

'I don't know what Deerfoot was called, or where he came from, or how old he was. The first time I asked about his age, he just laughed it off and joked that he was ten and big for his age. I never got a proper answer later either. He grew a little in the year that I knew him, but I cannot imagine that he was any older than sixteen the last time I saw him, in winter 1944.'

He came over to me and pointed at the photograph.

'I never saw him without that pendant. It seemed to be a kind of talisman that he always wore. You can see how serious and grown-up his face is in the photograph. That was the one we saw most. He was very deeply affected by growing up in the war, but he also had a younger, jocular face that sometimes appeared. He was not an easy person to get hold of.'

I had no trouble in believing that. Deerfoot was certainly not an easy person get hold of, and even less to arrest. His facial features were very vague on the photograph and did not remind me of anyone I had met thus far in the investigation. Which was all the more irritating because I increasingly had the feeling that this serious boy in the photograph from 1942 in some way held the key to solving the murder of Harald Olesen now in 1968. This prompted me to think of an important question.

'What was your impression of the relationship between the two of them – Harald Olesen and Deerfoot, that is?'

Hans Andersson nodded pensively.

'Good question – I have often wondered about it. In 1942 and 1943, it seemed to be a good old-fashioned father–son type of relationship. In fact, I even heard Deerfoot talk about Harald Olesen as "father" several times, and Harald Olesen accepted this with a smile. But Deerfoot was clearly not Harald Olesen's son. Harald Olesen once told me that he sadly had no children of his own, which was confirmed in the papers after his death. I thought that perhaps for that time during the war, Deerfoot was somehow the son he had always wished he had had. So I imagined that Deerfoot was an orphan, especially as he never spoke about his family. But that may of course also have been because he was being careful.'

Despite his young age, it seemed that Deerfoot had also been remarkably good at covering his tracks after the war. Which gave immediate associations to the mysterious murder in 1968.

'So the last time you saw Deerfoot was here in winter 1944. Was that also when Sara Sundqvist came here?'

He nodded again, but was very sombre all of a sudden.

'Yes, but to hear that story you need to come outside with me.'

Hans Andersson got up without waiting for an answer,

picked up some binoculars that were waiting on the desk and walked ahead of me down the corridor towards the main door. I picked up my notebook and followed him.

II

Hans Andersson and I stood together looking up at the sides of the valley, which were still covered in snow.

'The valley here is beautiful on good days like today, but the mountains can be hell when the winter storms are blowing,' he reflected.

I nodded in agreement, in the hope that he would continue. I was becoming increasingly impatient to hear more about the young Deerfoot's war experiences, and about Sara Sundqvist and the fate of her parents. He noticed this perhaps and picked up the thread.

'You will hear the story shortly, but the valley and the weather are actually very important factors. As you can see, the pass is extremely steep over there.'

That was certainly no exaggeration. The main path down the side of the valley was as steep as a ski slope and ended in a small cliff that dropped about sixteen feet. Scree could be seen sticking up through the white snow below. Hans Andersson pointed at it with a warning.

'That is the fastest way down from the mountain, but you take it at your own peril. When the snow is at its thickest, it is possible to jump off the cliff if you know how to land. But even then it is a very risky route. It is said that that is one of the reasons that a police station was built here in the first place, to make sure that no young hotheads decided to give it a try. The first time that Harald Olesen and Deerfoot were here, just before they left, I noticed Deerfoot staring up at the cliff as if enthralled. I was quick to say that he must never try jumping off it, unless he had the devil at his heels and it was a matter of life and death. He nodded soberly and promised me not to.'

Hans Andersson was quiet for a while and then pointed far up the mountainside.

'People still come down from the mountains from up there. That is where I always spotted the small groups of refugees coming down during the war, with Harald Olesen and Deerfoot at the helm. It was as great a relief every time. When they appeared up there, they were already well into Sweden, so all danger was past. We used to say they walked as quickly as they could in Norway and as slowly as they wanted to in Sweden. The final stretch through the woods up there was simply a victory parade. Deerfoot always walked in front to show the way.'

The path came down where the side of the valley was least steep, down the slope through the woods. Even someone who was exhausted and not used to being on skis would be able to come down there without any danger of accidents. I waited with growing impatience to discover what the local topography had to do with the story. Fortunately, Hans Andersson soon started on his tale.

'We had established quite a routine with the refugees by the last couple of years of the war. Everything had gone well up until then, so we had perhaps become a bit careless. I had an uncle in Elverum who lived on the refugee route and helped to get everything organized. He would call me when he had seen refugees passing, and in among all the talk of family and farms, he would slip in a message that would tell us who was on their way and how many were in the group. We would then sit up with food and refreshments and wait for them to arrive. These messages were coded, of course, in case the phones were tapped. But it has plagued me in later years that this was maybe how the tragedy started.'

He stood for a moment and stared despondently at the mountainside. Then he continued, but was in no rush.

'It was early on the evening of 20 February 1944 when my uncle called, with a message that Deerfoot and his father had passed with two large sacks and one small one. This meant that Harald Olesen and Deerfoot had two adult refugees and a child with them. No more than an hour later, my uncle called again and sounded extremely agitated. The message was that a pack of six wolves had just passed outside the window. And so our greatest nightmare became reality. Harald Olesen and Deerfoot were by now in open terrain with the refugees, and a German military patrol was following their tracks.'

Hans Andersson was really slowing down now. Powerful memories were obviously pressing in.

'And then . . .' I prompted.

'And then the worst winter storm of the year blew up,' he said, with a heavy heart. 'I had been up since five in the morning, but still did not get to sleep until four that night. I went out several times with my binoculars, but it was impossible to see anything on the mountain in the dark and whirling snow. The storm was a double-edged sword. The weather would make things very hard for their pursuers, but at the same time, it would be hell on earth to be out there with the German soldiers on your tail – especially with a screaming baby. The wind and cold were dangerous enough at night. When I finally went to bed at four, I was sure that I had seen Harald Olesen and Deerfoot for the last time. My wife woke me at ten in the morning to tell me that the wind had dropped, but that there was still no sign of life on the mountainside. I more or less gave up hope there and then.'

Hans Andersson did not say anything for what seemed like an hour. He stood staring up at the mountainside.

'I still remember the morning of 21 February 1944 in detail. The wind had dropped completely over the space of a few hours. The sky was blue and the air was clear, but still treacherously cold and dry – the thermometer showed minus twenty-five degrees. So I waited in my office that day with dwindling hope. I have never really believed in God, but around two that afternoon, I experienced what perhaps might be called an epiphany. I suddenly felt very strongly that I had been given a kind of order to go outside to see if there was any sign of movement on the mountainside. It was impossible to remain in the office after that, so I grabbed my binoculars and went out.'

He handed me the binoculars and said firmly: 'Look up at the top of the mountainside.'

I did as he told me. The weather was clear, but I still saw no sign of any people up there. He nodded.

'The mountainside was just as deadly still that perishingly cold day in February 1944. Then all of a sudden I saw a slight movement through the binoculars that made me start. It turned out it was just a hare. But it seemed to be frightened, running from something in a way that made me wonder if there was more movement up there. Then a flock of ptarmigan was startled into the air. And suddenly he came sailing down from the mountain and the cold. A solitary man on skis – and he was going hell for leather like he had the devil at his heels!'

'Harald Olesen?' I asked. The grim possibility that he and little Sara were the only two who had come out of it alive suddenly struck me.

Hans Andersson shook his head.

'That is what I thought at first. But I recognized the lightness of foot before I could even see him clearly through the binoculars. It was Deerfoot who came flying down over the seas of snow.'

I held the binoculars close to my eyes and could almost imagine Deerfoot skiing down the side of the valley from the mountain. I waited in breathless anticipation to hear the rest of the story of the time when he actually had.

'At first, I hoped that I would see Harald Olesen and the other refugees coming up behind him. And then I started to fear that our worst nightmare was upon us and that the German soldiers in their desire to catch the guide had crossed the border and come into Sweden. An old fear was awakened. In the first years of the war, we had discussed what on earth we would do in such a situation and had never found a better answer than that we would immediately ring Stockholm. I remember thinking that they would have to appear soon if they were to keep him within shooting range. But there was no one behind him, neither friend nor foe. Normally the guide came with a small party, but this time Deerfoot was guide to no one. And still he kept pace like I have seen no champion do. I could not comprehend it and started to fear that he had lost his mind. Especially when I realized which path he planned on taking.'

I lowered the binoculars and looked at him, wide-eyed. He gave a sombre nod and pointed to the cliff.

'My relief at seeing Deerfoot soon gave way to desperation as I watched him speeding towards the cliff. It would be treacherous even to try jumping it at the end of February. The scree was bare at the bottom and then gradually got covered by snow. It was simply madness that Deerfoot, exhausted as he must be after coming over the mountains and with the wrong skis on, would even dare to attempt it. I tried to wave to him to stop, but he was already mustering strength and speed for the jump.'

There was no one to be seen on the mountainside or by the cliff today, and yet, as I listened to the story, I could see it so clearly, Deerfoot sailing over the edge.

'It was the most terrifying moment of my life, standing here watching him launch himself over the edge of the cliff. At first, it looked as though he was heading straight for the stones. But he had obviously jumped on skis before and leaned forwards over his skis as he cut through the air. The skis just grazed the last big stones. He landed safely on the snow and remained crouching until he lost speed, and then he stood straight up again, pushing himself to get here as fast as he could. I thought he had lost his marbles. But when I was able to see his face clearly in the binoculars, there was no sign of fear or panic, just the manic determination to get down to me as quickly as possible. Once down in the valley, he fair flew along, his arms moving so fast that you could scarcely see them.'

He stopped abruptly and shook his head.

'It's still incredible that I did not understand what was going on. Do you?'

I shook my head slowly, without even thinking about it.

'I still did not understand when he was down here on the fields and only yards from me. Then the world around me stopped when he pulled a lifeless baby, bundled up in a scarf and a woolly sweater, from inside his anorak.'

I looked down at the snow for a moment, and possibly admitted to myself that, like him, I should have realized. Fortunately, he immediately carried on.

'If there is one dramatic event in my life I will never forget, that is it. Deerfoot slapped the baby on the cheeks twice, without any reaction, but still did not give up hope. "There's still warmth in her," he said, in a remarkably calm voice. Then he handed the baby to me and told me to put her in warm water. I was still paralysed and stood there without moving for a few seconds. Deerfoot told me again in a louder voice that I had to get her into hot water immediately. It almost sounded like an order. But it was only when he reached out to take the little girl back that I came to life and ran up the stairs with her.'

Despite the gravity of the situation, a broad grin slipped over Hans Andersson's face.

'Fortunately, my wife was bathing our son right then. You can imagine what she must have thought when I came charging in with another baby and threw her into the water, clothes and all. But she quickly understood the situation and tried to give her mouth-to-mouth resuscitation. For several minutes there was no sign of life. Then there was a spasm in one of her tiny hands. And she started to howl.'

'So little Sara came down from the mountains alive?' I said.

He nodded solemnly.

'Little Sara came down from the mountains alive – but only in the nick of time. Five minutes later, it may have been too late, the doctor who examined her said. But I tend to believe my wife, who says that even two minutes later would have been too late.'

'How did Deerfoot react?' I asked.

Hans Andersson pointed at the snow just by the wall of the house.

'He lay there absolutely exhausted, flat on his back on the snow, and was still breathing heavily when I came out again. It was only then that I fully understood how physically gruelling the ski run over the mountains must have been. All the same, he was strangely relaxed and clear in the head. When I asked him whether he had prayed to God, he whispered that he no longer believed in God. And when I then said that the child would survive, he nodded and whispered that it gave the whole tragedy meaning after all. He stayed lying on the snow for some minutes more, but quickly bucked up after a cup of hot coffee. I jokingly said that he must never think of jumping the cliff again. He replied with a cursory smile that he had no intention of doing so. But then he added, gravely, that it had been a matter of life and death, and that the devil had indeed been at his heels. He had felt confident for the first part of the journey, so long as he heard the baby crying and felt her movements. But this was followed by a stage where he only heard the odd whimper, and then he heard nothing. She lay quite still against his stomach and he could feel her getting colder. He had quickly recognized the danger and skied as though possessed to get her to safety as fast as possible.'

Hans Andersson frowned and rolled his eyes.

'I said, as did my wife and the doctor when he came, that what Deerfoot had done was truly a heroic deed. A new Birkebeiner endurance test was what the doctor called it. I did not know what he meant and had to look it up in a history book to discover the story of how King Sverre's supporters carried the little Prince Håkon over the mountains in the winter of 1206. But Deerfoot smiled as soon as that was mentioned, and said, as was only too true, that there were several Birkebeiners so they could at least take turns in holding the baby. This, and other small comments that he made, reinforced the impression I had that he came from a well-to-do home and had a good education.'

This seemed like a reasonable assumption. My curiosity about Deerfoot was considerable, but at that moment was overtaken by my curiosity regarding his companion.

'What about Harald Olesen? What had happened to him? He was obviously still alive.'

Hans Andersson nodded.

'When Deerfoot recovered again, to my great relief he told me that Harald Olesen had survived and was on his way over the mountains. They had been caught in a very dramatic situation up there. Three of the German soldiers had turned back with the onslaught of the storm, but the three others had continued. After sheltering from the storm overnight in the mountains, there had then been an exchange of fire that had left the three German soldiers and two refugees dead. Harald Olesen had stayed behind to bury them, while Deerfoot had taken the little girl and gone ahead. He hoped that Harald Olesen would be able to find his way here by following his tracks. Which he did, three or four hours later. He had obviously taken it slower and chosen the less risky path through the woods. The story he told was the same as that Deerfoot had told. Once the storm had died down around dawn, they had been caught in an exchange of fire, and whereas he had managed to shoot the three German soldiers, he had not been able to prevent the two refugees being shot. He had laid the five bodies out at the back of a cave and then followed Deerfoot's tracks. I made a short account of events for the record and contacted Stockholm. As far as I understood, the exchange of fire had been on the Norwegian side of the border, and Stockholm soon lost interest once they established that no Swedish citizens were involved.'

There was another short pause before Hans Andersson carried on.

'By the evening, the baby was doing well and crawling around on the rug with our little son. It warmed your heart to watch her. But otherwise, the atmosphere was oppressive. Harald Olesen and Deerfoot stayed the night in separate rooms. Both seemed to be troubled. I thought to myself that it was not so strange, given what they had been through. I asked tentatively if they thought it wise to return to Norway after this, but they were both adamant that they would set off again after breakfast the next day. But I was in for another shock before they left.'

I was following his words with intense interest.

'It was a complete coincidence that I witnessed this. I had opened a window upstairs to throw out my shaving water when I saw Harald Olesen and Deerfoot. They had gone out and were standing by the house wall just over there by the corner. I could not hear what they were saying, but quickly realized that it was an emotionally charged conversation. If you have been a teenager yourself and have had teenage children, you will certainly have experienced a few serious confrontations. But this was still one of the most dramatic conversations I have ever observed. Deerfoot, who otherwise was always so calm, was suddenly beside himself with rage. He pointed a threatening finger right in Harald Olesen's face, and his other hand was balled into a fist, which he waved around, and he was talking fast and hard like a machine gun. Harald Olesen himself barely said a word. He was leaning against the wall, his face drained of colour, and was shaking so much that I was afraid he would faint at any minute. It was quite an unbelievable sight. I had never seen either of them like this before. When I bid them farewell half an hour later, everything was as normal. Deerfoot had his mischievous smile again and fooled around with the little girl for a while before he left. It almost made me wonder if what I had seen was a strange dream of some sort. But it was not. Once they had left, I came over here to the wall. There were obvious signs that they had been here, and Harald Olesen's shoes had sunk deep into the snow.'

I nodded. The fact that Deerfoot had got angry and threatened Harald Olesen would seem to fit relatively well with what had happened twenty-four years later.

'Was that the last you saw of them both?'

Hans Andersson nodded.

'Yes – that is to say, almost. Neither of them came back here during the war, and I have not seen or heard of Deerfoot since then. But I did meet Harald Olesen again some years after the war. I happened to be visiting my family in Oslo when he was giving a lecture in town. I went up to speak to him afterwards. He recognized me and thanked me for all my help during the war, but was obviously busy and not inclined to chat. Over the years I had often wondered what had happened to Deerfoot, so I tried to ask. But he just mumbled in a quiet voice that it was a sad story. Then he excused himself, as he had to be somewhere else, and made a dash for it.'

We were both silent for a while. It was clear that Harald Olesen did not want to talk about the disastrous trip and his guide, and no doubt he had his reasons. I wracked my brains to think what these might be, and who, now that Harald Olesen was dead, might know more about it and about Deerfoot.

'The refugee who came with Deerfoot and Harald Olesen in 1942 – do you know where we might find him?'

Hans Andersson gave an apologetic shake of the head.

'He was the son of an Austrian refugee and was called Helmut Schmidt. He lived in Vienna the last time I heard from him, but I doubt there is much to be gained there. Helmut was not with them that night, and when he came here after the war, he did not know what Deerfoot was really called, or where to find him. Helmut would gladly have travelled to the ends of the earth to give him more than a token of his gratitude, he said. He would never forget that cold and pitch-black night when Deerfoot miraculously guided him safely over the mountains to freedom. They had set off together after he had been dropped by a car on a country road near Elverum. Deerfoot had appeared on his own, out of nowhere, on skis. It was impossible to say where he came from.'

I cursed silently. This Deerfoot really was frustratingly good not only at showing the way, but also at covering his own tracks.

Hans Andersson and I stood without saying anything for some minutes, looking up at the snowy mountainside in silent understanding. We were no doubt both thinking that the strange story of the young Deerfoot's war efforts was in some way of great significance to the murder of Harald Olesen, but it was not easy to fathom how. Whether Deerfoot was still alive twenty-four years later or not, and where in the world he might be, remained an unsolved mystery. I had at last caught a glimpse of this mysterious figure here in Sälen, only to lose sight of him again. Deerfoot had, light-footed as ever, gone back up the snowy mountainside one freezing-cold day in 1944 and all trace of him stopped there.

Hans Andersson and I exchanged looks. He understood what I was thinking and pointed up to the mountain pass.

'Deerfoot followed some way behind Harald Olesen when they set off for the mountains again that morning. I stood here with my binoculars and watched him disappear over the pass. I have no idea what happened to him after that, but I still wonder every year when I stand here and see the first signs of spring.'

I promised to let him know if I found out any more about Deerfoot, and then asked what had happened to Sara Sundqvist afterwards.

'That too is a sad story, though of course it was a wonder that her life had been saved. She was the sweetest little girl and played happily here on the floor with my son for several weeks. My wife and I often talked of adopting her, but that did not happen in the end. From the information that Harald

Olesen gave about her parents, it was clear that they not only were refugees, but also Jews. When he heard this, my father-in-law was beside himself. So we gave up the idea of keeping the little girl and sent her to the adoption agency in Gothenburg. Which caused us great pain. For many years we had no idea what had happened to little Sara. But apparently she was taken in by good people, and despite such a difficult start in life, things are going well for her now.'

I suddenly felt the icy claws of suspicion grip my heart and asked perhaps a little too quickly how he could know that, and this time his answer was short and swift.

'Because she came here and I told her the story too. It must have been a couple of years ago now. It was apparently the first time she had heard her parents' names and been told how she came to be adopted in Gothenburg. She was naturally very interested in Harald Olesen, and even more so in Deerfoot.'

He realized that something was amiss and shot me a questioning look.

'I called the head office to check before I told her anything. But they were of the same opinion as me: that she had a right to know what we knew of her story. It was all such a long time ago, and did not involve anything criminal, certainly not here in Sweden.'

I found it hard to disagree, but that did not prevent me from feeling a surge of anger and disquiet. Sara Sundqvist had lied to me again – and this time the discovery did not put her in a good light at all.

I said that he had done the right thing, to help put his mind at rest. Then I asked without further ado if I could borrow his office to make an important phone call to Oslo.

III

As I dialled the number, I imagined Patricia sitting alone waiting by the phone in the White House. As expected, she answered on the second ring, and listened with bated breath to my short version of Hans Andersson's story. To my slight annoyance, she guessed that the child was inside Deerfoot's anorak long before he had made it down from the mountain, even though he took considerably less time in my version than in Hans Andersson's. Nor did the news that Sara Sundqvist had beaten us to it and already been here seem to come as a great surprise.

The line was quiet for a moment when I finished the story. Then Patricia was off again.

'Congratulations on making such good progress in the investigation. So Deerfoot was a child soldier with severe mood swings during the war, who was probably left scarred by memories and had a deep hatred for Harald Olesen. An undeniably strong starting point. But we still must not take it as given that he is the murderer. I really only have one question for Hans Andersson. Did he ever see what kind of gun Deerfoot and Harald Olesen had with them?'

I should of course have remembered to ask that myself. I put the receiver down on the desk and stuck my head round the door into the side room to ask Hans Andersson the question. Barely a minute later, I was back on the line.

'No. He always assumed that at least Harald Olesen was armed, and possibly also Deerfoot, but he never saw any guns and never asked about them either. So we do not know whether they were armed or not, and if they were, with what.'

Patricia's sigh could be heard all the way from Oslo.

'Of course they were armed. It is extremely unusual to win in a shootout with three German soldiers without having a gun yourself. As Hans Andersson never saw any guns, it would be fair to say that they had handguns of some sort or another. But the million-dollar question is what kind of revolver or pistol they had. If Hans Andersson had known, you might have been able to arrest the murderer this evening. But now there are several real possibilities, even though one seems to be the most likely. There will be overtime for us tonight, but I hope I can encourage you with the prospect of an arrest tomorrow. Come here as soon as you get back to Oslo and I will ask Benedikte to prepare a simple supper. Eight o'clock should be doable?'

I said that I thought so and we put the phone down at the same time. I thanked Hans Andersson for all his help and promised to keep him updated on any developments, then hurried out to the car.

Crossing the border back into Norway was just as unproblematic as it had been going out, but I was still very perplexed. It was clear that Sara Sundqvist would have difficulties explaining herself. She now had a much clearer revenge motive, given that she knew that Harald Olesen had been present when her parents died, though it remained unclear whether he was responsible for this or not. I was buoyed by the fact that Patricia was clearly still working with several alternatives, which included the persistently mysterious Deerfoot as a possible murderer.

That Deerfoot could be the man in the blue raincoat was an obvious possibility. However, it seemed to me that we were still a long way from arresting anyone. Deerfoot's identity and abode today were still unknown, as it was now absolutely clear that it could not be Darrell Williams. The positive side of this was that I could relax, as the danger of a public scandal and new confrontation with the American Embassy had as good as evaporated.

It was only when I was halfway between Trysil and Elverum that it dawned on me that the discovery of Deerfoot's age allowed for a possible new protagonist who thus far had remained on the periphery. But the impact of this was so powerful that I and the car almost ended up in a ditch. Despite my eagerness to get back to Oslo, I made an unplanned stop by the side of the road and looked through my papers. I was suddenly unsure of how old Harald Olesen's nephew, Joachim, was. Was he older or younger than his sister? The tension grew when I saw in the census records that he was eighteen months younger than his sister, and was born in July 1928.

In February 1944, Joachim Olesen would have been fifteen years old. That fitted well, as did the close relationship he appeared to have had with Harald Olesen at the time. The relationship had clearly become more estranged latterly, which seemed reasonable if Harald Olesen had let his nephew down badly in winter 1944. Joachim Olesen could possibly have wanted revenge in relation to both his own and his sister's experiences. What is more, he also stood to gain from the expected inheritance. And he had demonstrated that he had a quick temper and mood swings at the reading of the will.

I realized that an obvious possibility was that though the 'D' in Harald Olesen's diary stood for 'Deerfoot', in reality it was his own nephew who stood behind the code name. The fact that Joachim Olesen had been present as himself in several other situations did not mean that he was not the man in the blue raincoat whom Andreas Gullestad had seen. And it fitted well that the raincoat had been found at 25 Krebs' Street on the evening of the murder. It would be hard to place any more importance on the fact that his sister had more or less the same type of blue raincoat. But it did strike me as relevant and possible that the siblings might have bought the same type of raincoat, without her being aware of the significance.

However, the not-quite-so-minor practical problem remained as to how Joachim Olesen had managed to get in and out of the building on the evening of the murder without being seen. But as everything else seemed to fit so well, I felt that it was a problem that could be solved, for example if he was in cahoots with the caretaker's wife or another of the neighbours. As for the murder of Konrad Jensen, I thought it was quite possible that Joachim Olesen had managed to sneak both in and out of the building unnoticed, either first thing in the morning or when the caretaker's wife was out shopping.

By the time I passed Hamar, I was almost convinced, and as I approached Oslo, I had to stop myself from driving straight to Joachim Olesen to take a statement. But the practical problems remained, which meant that I kept my dinner appointment at the White House.

I made a brief stop at the office, where there were still no important messages waiting. The public seemed to have accepted that the case was closed following Konrad Jensen's death. I made a quick telephone call to the caretaker's wife in 25 Krebs' Street, to make sure that everything was all right.

Darrell Williams had come back at five to four in a taxi that sped up to the entrance, and had made a very odd comment to her about just having made it, despite the plane being delayed. Fortunately, I managed to thank the caretaker's wife and put down the receiver before I released a smug laugh.

IV

I made my dinner appointment with a ten-minute margin and arrived in an optimistic mood. Patricia, on the other hand, seemed to be more pessimistic. She played with the asparagus soup and, in between the first mouthfuls, looked sceptically at the photograph of Deerfoot from 1942. She was not able to get much from it either. The boy in the picture was young, and the image was also blurred. His hair was obviously dark, but the colour of his eyes and skin was not clear. Then she asked me to tell her the story from Sweden again, but more slowly this time and in some more detail. This took us through the rest of the soup and halfway through the roast pork.

It occurred to me that at times it might seem that Patricia had drunk too much cold water in her life. This impression was further bolstered by the fact that she drank six glasses during the course of the meal. At one point, I jokingly commented that Deerfoot, with his cross-country skiing, off-piste, combined and jumping, had covered half the Olympic programme. But this only raised a half-smile from Patricia, who added that the big question now was whether he was also a biathlete or not – and if he was, what, then, had he shot with?

In the middle of the main course, she asked a simple question, which was if I had at any point in the investigation seen a silver pendant similar to the one Deerfoot had round his neck in the photograph. With the proviso that I so far had had no reason to look for such a pendant, I told her that I could not recall having seen anything of the kind. Then I swiftly added that finding such a pendant so many years later might also be a shaky means of identification. She agreed with me, but then made the short and mysterious comment that the pendant may still be extremely important.

I asked Patricia what she thought might have happened on the fateful trip in 1944. She replied that it was difficult to know the details at this point, but that the bigger picture was relatively clear. From what they had been told, three soldiers and Sara Sundqvist's parents had been killed during an exchange of fire. As was shown by his will, Harald Olesen had been dogged by guilt about this incident, both during and after the war. Following his death, Deerfoot was presumably the only person in the world who knew what had happened. The precise details were not so important at this point.

'But I can more or less promise that Deerfoot will tell you all the details when we find him,' Patricia added, with a glum and very serious expression on her face.

I noted straightaway that she had said 'when' and asked if that meant that she was sure that Deerfoot had survived the war and was still alive. She nodded firmly.

'Despite his young age, Deerfoot appears to have been an unusually vigorous young man, even in 1944. To my knowledge, there is only one reason why a guide would choose to follow up at the rear, and that is when he fears being shot in the back. When Deerfoot agreed to go back with Harald

Olesen, he took precautions. It would seem that any trust between them had been destroyed. I am now convinced first of all that the "D" in Harald Olesen's diary really does stand for "Deerfoot", and second, it is he who has been running around in the infamous blue raincoat these past couple of years. I also have little doubt as to his identity and address.'

I nodded in agreement. It was true – this fitted well with my theory about Joachim Olesen.

An oppressive silence followed, with close to ten minutes of expectant chewing. Ironically, it was only when ice cream was served for dessert that Patricia eventually thawed.

'Please excuse me if I appear to be pensive. You have made great progress today. The murderer is just ahead of us now and we are catching up. By this time tomorrow, I hope that it will all be over, and I have a clear favourite as to whom it is who will be arrested. But we still lack answers to a few very important questions. It is such a frustrating situation to be so close yet not quite there. As you may have noticed, I hate drawing conclusions that may be wrong. I will therefore continue to mull on this theory in anticipation of the answers we will get tomorrow.'

Patricia paused for thought yet again and had an almost melancholy expression on her face when she continued.

'The whole situation is so sad. Harald Olesen had done so much for his country and its people, both as a Resistance hero and a cabinet minister, and yet in the last year of his life, after his wife's death and his retirement from public life, shadows from his past dominated. And in those final months he almost became a human fly himself. A group of human flies swarmed around him, with very intense feelings towards him linked to the past, all of whom could have had the motive and opportunity to murder him. In fact, at the time of Harald Olesen's death, all of the residents of 25 Krebs' Street could be described as human flies for different reasons. It is very depressing indeed.'

I interrupted this unhappy train of thought to ask if she had any suggestions as to how we might finally solve the murder. To my relief, she carried on in a far more optimistic voice.

'The problem that remains is that some of the neighbours in 25 Krebs' Street saw something on the evening of the murder, or to be more precise someone, and for various reasons still do not want to tell us about it. We need to force the answers from them in order to eliminate potential murderers until we are left with only one possibility. And this is how we will do it: you will go there tomorrow, armed with your service gun and two sets of handcuffs. You will call me once you are there and I will tell you who to talk to first and what questions to ask. Either the answers will make it perfectly clear to you who the murderer is and you can then make an immediate arrest, or we will have to move on to the next flat with more questions. In which case, telephone me if you are in any doubt as to what you should do or what you should ask.'

I looked at her with scepticism.

'How many flats will I have to visit before I find the murderer?'

Patricia shrugged apologetically.

'In the worst case, five. They could all be housing a murderer, or at the very least someone who is hiding vital information.'

I was very glad that we were so close to catching the

murderer in 25 Krebs' Street, but the plan that Patricia proposed was less attractive. I suddenly thought of something that would be a vast improvement, and laughed in a jocular manner before I spoke.

'That all sounds very complicated. It would be pretty hopeless if the head of investigation had to borrow a telephone to put a call through to an anonymous friend before making the next move. I accept the need to confront the various parties at the scene of the crime tomorrow, but we need to make one practical adjustment . . .'

Patricia looked at me warily. It was the first time I was ahead of her in the game and she seemed genuinely uncomfortable with the situation.

'You have to come with me!'

The moment I said those words, a powerful shudder went through Patricia's thin body. She sat staring at me from her wheelchair, not saying a word. I hurried on.

'Not only is it the best solution, but also absolutely necessary. Various situations might arise where I simply cannot reach you in time by telephone. And what is more, it is entirely doable in practical terms. Andreas Gullestad manages to move around the building in his wheelchair, so why would you not be able to? We can give you a pen and paper and say that you are my secretary and have an injury. And just think how interesting it would be for you to be there when the case is concluded and to meet all the people you have spent so much time analysing over the past week . . .'

Patricia remained uncharacteristically silent in her wheelchair.

'The fact is, it is very difficult to find a rational counterargument,' she said in the end, with a serious face. Then her sardonic humour cut through and she laughed.

'And I am not exactly spoilt for choice with invitations to do exciting things at the weekend anymore . . . All right, I will come with you!'

I spontaneously held out my hand before she had time to change her mind. Patricia's hand was shaking, but was warm and full of enthusiasm. When I added that she should perhaps get her father's permission first, she gave me a wry look and commented that 'the fossil' had only too often said that she should get out more. And in any case, he could no longer decide where she went and with whom. She did, however, promise to 'let him know what he needs to know'.

Patricia insisted that I collect her myself, in an unmarked police car. In answer to my question as to why the latter was important, she chuckled and replied that the staff and neighbours would possibly celebrate and be only too happy to snap pictures of her being driven away in a police car. But then she switched in an instant and became deadly serious again.

'And you must have two reliable armed officers posted by the outer doors tonight. I am still slightly unsure as to who the murderer is, but I am in no doubt that he or she is an exceptionally cold person who is capable of anything. And not only do we still not have the murderer, we do not have the murder weapon either . . .'

I nodded my consent.

The possibility that Joachim Olesen was the murderer still seemed the most plausible solution to me – except perhaps Sara Sundqvist, but I did not want to believe it was her. It worried me in every way that Patricia's attention was so obviously focused on the building, even though that did not necessarily mean that the murderer was physically there.

'The chance for a happy ending might perhaps increase if I asked Harald Olesen's niece and nephew to come to 25 Krebs' Street? I am sure that they could wait in the entrance or with the caretaker's wife in her flat, in case we need to talk to them.'

For a moment Patricia looked confused. Then suddenly she burst out laughing again.

'*Now* I understand what you meant. A happy ending, what a brilliant way of putting it. By all means ask them. And who knows, some questions may crop up that they might be able to answer. And aesthetically, it does feel fitting that we do a Poirot and gather all the surviving parties together before the arrest.'

I felt that this minor success could indicate that the ever-secretive Patricia was thinking along the same lines as me and suspected the nephew. We were both in good spirits when we agreed that I should collect her at half past eleven, so that we would be ready to start at Krebs' Street by midday at the latest.

On my way out, I was unable to contain myself and asked one final question.

'Have you decided which flat we should start with tomorrow?'

The answer was what I had expected, but not what I had hoped for.

'I think we should start by seeing what Sara Sundqvist has to say in her defence this time.'

She may have seen the disappointment on my face, for she continued briskly.

'Much depends on what she can tell us, and what she wants to, but it is by no means certain that we will end there.'

I carried my hope with me out into the dark. I made a quick stop at the now quiet police station to make three brief telephone calls. The first was to Cecilia Olesen, who this time sounded far happier to hear my voice. She cheered up even more when I told her that Darrell Williams had returned and that we expected to close the case over the course of the weekend. That said, she immediately and almost enthusiastically agreed to my request to come to the scene of the crime at a quarter to twelve the next day.

I was of course more curious about her brother, Joachim Olesen. His voice was measured, but by no means eager. I had a strong feeling that I could now see the murderer's face clearly for the first time when he held back and said that he had already promised to prepare a balance sheet for the ministry on Saturday. He was silent for a while when I emphasized that it would be to everyone's advantage if he was available for questioning in the final stages of the investigation. He gave in with a quiet sigh and said that in that case he would of course make himself available for the police.

The final telephone call was to the caretaker's wife, who told me that all was peaceful in the building. She promised to be waiting with the key to each flat at a quarter to twelve, and to be at her post early to make sure that all the residents were at home.

In the end, I made a fourth call and ordered a constable to keep an eye on Joachim Olesen's flat, and to follow him should he go out before he was due to meet us. I did not want to be missing a key witness in the grand finale of my first major murder investigation – and especially not the one who was my prime suspect.

When I finally fell asleep around two o'clock in the morning, I could still see the nephew's secretive face in my mind's eye. All the same, I thought carefully about each of the others who would be there. The face of the ever-elusive Sara Sundqvist was the last I pictured before I dropped off. If nothing else, I would be able to establish on the tenth day of the investigation whether she had become involved in the murders by sheer misfortune or whether she was a particularly devious murderer.

The Story of a Human Fly

I

Saturday, 13 April was not only the day before Easter; it was also the investigation's tenth day. For me, it started like any other Saturday. I had a lie-in and ate breakfast on my own at around ten o'clock. By half past ten I was in my office and could to my relief confirm that nothing new or of any note had happened there. After a quick telephone call to 25 Krebs' Street at eleven o'clock, I knew that all the residents were at home. The caretaker's wife was also informed that Harald Olesen's niece and nephew would be coming, and she promised to put out a table and a couple of chairs for them.

At a quarter past eleven, I left the main police station in an unmarked car. Patricia, dressed in a simple green dress, was sitting waiting for me in the hallway when I arrived at Erling Skjalgsson's Street. For a moment I was afraid when I saw Professor Ragnar Borchmann towering beside her, but he gripped my hand enthusiastically and happily gave me leave to borrow his only daughter 'for up to four hours'. As Patricia wheeled herself out in front of us, he commented in a hushed voice that he had not seen her so cheerful and focused since the accident.

Our journey got off to a slow start. Some of the streets we had to pass were blocked off in honour of one of Oslo's more recent signs of spring: another demonstration against the war in Vietnam. This was not a particularly big or well-planned protest and was dominated by a group of around twenty to thirty angry students. Patricia watched them soulfully through the car window when we were finally able to pass. It struck me that I had no idea what she thought about the war in Vietnam or other major events. I could imagine her both opposing and supporting the war, and being a supporter of both the Conservative Party and the Socialist Party. But I found it hard to believe that she would not have strong opinions about the Vietnam War and Norwegian political parties.

Patricia and I were both affected by the solemnity of the moment, and by the fact that within a matter of hours we could expect to be face to face with an unusually calculating double murderer. She commented later that I had apparently asked three times in the course of the journey whether she was sitting comfortably, and twice said that spring was definitely here now. After which it was a great relief to her when I finally asked a more relevant question that had been bothering me all of the previous evening. It was in connection with her observation that each of the residents in Krebs' Street were human flies. Based on the revelations of recent days, I could accept that the description was to a greater or lesser extent suited to the caretaker's wife, the now dead Konrad Jensen, as well as to Darrell Williams, Kristian Lund and Sara Sundqvist. The description might also possibly fit Andreas

Gullestad, given his father's early death and his own accident. But I found it hard to see the fat cat's daughter, Karen Lund, in this light.

Patricia had to agree with me in part, but she believed, all the same, that as Mrs Lund's fate was so intertwined with that of her husband, she could also be seen as a human fly, by virtue of her marriage. She added that if Kristian Lund now proved to be the devious double murderer, it was impossible to imagine that his wife was not a conspirator. She would, in the first instance, have given him a false alibi for the murder of Harald Olesen. As for the murder of Konrad Jensen, Kristian Lund was apparently at work when the shot was fired. In which case, it must have been his wife who killed him. Unless he of course was in cahoots with another neighbour, she added without specifying anyone.

I nodded and acknowledged that there was still every reason to suspect all the residents. A minute later, we stopped outside their front door.

II

The caretaker's wife welcomed us and shook my hand with great warmth. Not unexpectedly, our reception from Cecilia and Joachim Olesen was somewhat more restrained, but both of them were there, as promised. It was with some relief that I noted that Joachim had come without a bag of any kind and was dressed in a simple suit, so it would be hard to hide a gun. Cecilia Olesen had obviously put more time into preparing herself. She was beautifully made up and dressed in an elegant, if somewhat old-fashioned dress. I noticed that Patricia tried to hide a small smile when she saw her.

All three were taken by surprise when Patricia was wheeled in, but they greeted her with a friendly smile and I introduced her as my young secretary, Patricia Pettersen, and added that she was temporarily confined to a wheelchair as a result of a skiing accident. It must be said that Patricia had put considerable thought into the role. She had a clipboard, a thick notepad and five different-coloured pens in her lap, and dutifully took notes from the moment she was wheeled into 25 Krebs' Street.

I asked the caretaker's wife and Cecilia and Joachim Olesen to wait by the entrance and then wheeled Patricia into the lift and we went up to the first floor.

Patricia's brief instruction on our way up was: 'Just tell her that you know that she has lied and that she was given money by Harald Olesen, then ask if she has anything to add to her statement from the night of his murder. Now, this is important – always position my wheelchair just inside the door and you yourself stand or sit opposite the person you are talking to, if possible diagonally across from me,' she added in a quiet voice, as the lift stopped.

I nodded and felt the tension percolating through my body. I suggested that Patricia should tap her pen on the pad twice when she wanted to move on to another flat. This time she nodded and immediately tapped her pad with her pen twice and smiled.

About thirty seconds later, we rang the doorbell of Flat 2A.

Sara Sundqvist was lightly made up and wearing a black dress that flattered rather than hid her bust. When she opened the door, she leaned over the threshold to give me a hug and said how happy she was to see me again. I wondered what Patricia was writing down at that moment and had to admit to myself that Sara's demeanour was impressively relaxed if she was in constant fear of being revealed as a murderer. She was naturally rather taken aback when she saw Patricia, but immediately shook her hand when it was explained to her who Patricia was.

'I have been to Sälen and spoken to the chief of police there, and apparently someone else has been there too . . .' I started.

No more was needed for her front to fall and the tears to run. With a dramatic shrug, Sara Sundqvist threw open her hands and apologized for not telling me that she had been to Sälen. She was frightened that she would become a suspect if it was discovered that she knew about this episode from Harald Olesen's past and had hoped that she would never be found out. She knew the story about Deerfoot and had tried, without success, to get Harald Olesen to tell her about him. She dearly wanted to meet Deerfoot if he was still alive, partly to thank him for having saved her life, and partly in the hope of finding out more about what happened to her parents. But Harald Olesen had dismissed the question and spoken in a way that might indicate that Deerfoot was dead. If Deerfoot was alive, she had no idea who he was or what he was called.

I then asked if she had blackmailed Harald Olesen and omitted to tell me. She admitted that she had been given money by him, but denied that she had blackmailed him. One day when she had knocked on his door to ask about her parents and Deerfoot, he had handed her a thick envelope, which, to her shock, contained fifty thousand-kroner notes. She had gone back with the envelope the following day, but he had asked her to keep the money and forget the whole thing. She put the money in the bank, but could not forget the whole thing. It had only served to strengthen her impression that Harald Olesen knew more about her parents' fate than he was letting on.

When I asked if she would like to amend her statement from the night of the murder, she looked confused and stammered that she had nothing to add. She apologized over and over again for lying to me in pure desperation, but she knew nothing more about who had murdered Harald Olesen and had nothing to do with it herself. She had never asked for the 50,000 kroner, and the will had been a shock.

I glanced over at Patricia, who just then tapped her pad with her pen twice. We thanked Sara for her time and asked her to stay in the flat and not to let anyone else in. She slouched in the chair and whispered that she had not murdered Harald Olesen and that she would not let anyone in other than me. She repeated this twice, like an oath, as I wheeled Patricia out of the flat.

III

'She still knows more than she is letting on,' Patricia said, as soon as we were in the lift.

I had to admit that this chimed well with my own gut feeling.

'So, what do we do now?' I asked.

Patricia looked determined.

'Well, we can hope that if she has some time on her own to think, things might improve. She is terrified of something. I am tempted to say that it is either something she has done herself or something she has seen. But she is so frightened and tense that we need more information before we can push her any further. And perhaps we will find that where we are going now.'

It sounded so convincing that I just nodded and asked where we were going.

'To the second floor,' Patricia said, and impatiently stretched out her arm and pressed the lift button.

Patricia looked so small and thin in her wheelchair in the confines of the lift, but her voice was just as clear and firm as at home in the big library in the White House.

'Start by welcoming him back and be nice, then ask him if he was at all sad when Harald Olesen was murdered. Remind him of his old conflict with Olesen and suggest that he moved here because of it, and that he had more than one gun in the flat when he first arrived. And finally, ask him who he saw coming towards Harald Olesen's flat on the evening of the murder. My hope is that this will prompt some new and interesting information. Now, remember where to position me!'

Patricia's mood was constantly switching from serious to sardonic. Suddenly she smiled and chuckled quietly.

'To a certain extent, I understand why Kristian Lund was tempted into an affair – I felt almost jealous of her natural beauty and consummate technique. And by the way, she is, if nothing else, definitely guilty of being unhappily in love.'

My heart beat a little faster when she said that, but I did not want to be distracted by the topic for all manner of reasons. Fortunately, the lift stopped at that moment on the second floor. I pushed Patricia out and rang on the bell of the flat next door to Harald Olesen's.

IV

Darrell Williams was truly a diplomat through and through. He smiled as soon as he saw me, shook my hand and apologized that his work had forced him to leave the country temporarily. He looked at my companion with greater scepticism, but reluctantly accepted my explanation about an injured secretary. It helped when I assured him that nothing from our conversation would be recorded in the official reports and that the notes were for internal use only.

I parked Patricia in the middle of the floor, while Darrell and I sat down on the same armchairs that we had sat in a few days before. This time, the gravity of the situation was clear. Our host was sober, and there was a large carafe of water on the table between us. I noted a tense nervousness behind our host's smile that I had not experienced on previous occasions.

'Welcome back. You no doubt understand that your disappearance, which was contrary to my orders, almost caused a very unfortunate situation.'

He looked at me without answering, waiting for me to carry on. Which I quickly did.

'That being said, it is a pleasure to see you again, and we all hope that the case can now be concluded without any further complications. But that rather depends on you now giving us, better late than never, complete and truthful answers to our final questions.'

Darrell Williams nodded and leaned forward in concentration. I did not have the feeling that I was sitting opposite a human fly, but rather a lion or a bear or some other beast.

'First question: did you feel any sorrow whatsoever when you heard that Harald Olesen had been murdered?'

Darrell Williams laughed briefly, then shook his head.

'Absolutely not. He was a great man but not a good man. The story of his will, his son and his relatives only goes to show that. But I was surprised that he had been murdered. I have no idea who shot him and was definitely not there when it happened.'

He hesitated for a moment, but said nothing more. It gave me no choice other than to push him a little further.

'But you were accommodated here in the flat next door to Harald Olesen in order to ensure that certain names and information did not get out. In the first months that you lived here, you kept two guns in the flat. Did you or your employer at any point consider murdering him as an option?'

Darrell Williams smiled bitterly and I got the impression that he almost nodded before he answered.

'I am afraid that I can neither confirm nor deny that kind of question. I would like to reiterate that my accounts with Harald Olesen, both personal and professional, had been settled by the time he died. As you yourself saw when you searched my flat, the guns were no longer here at that point. And from what I understand, neither of them would be compatible with the bullet that killed Olesen in any case.'

I gave a cursory nod.

'But if I am now to believe that you are innocent, and that you and the embassy had nothing to do with the murder . . . could you please think carefully through the evening of the murder one more time and inform us if there is anything you may have forgotten to tell us that might help to track down the real murderer.'

He gave an apologetic shrug.

'Yes, there is, and I should have thought about it earlier. I saw one of my neighbours heading towards Harald Olesen's flat shortly before the murder. There are several reasons why I have not mentioned this before. The first was that I did not want myself or the embassy to become any more involved than necessary, and I could of course not be sure that the person I saw passing was in fact the murderer. And later my antipathy towards Harald Olesen intensified. The palaver with the will must have been deeply upsetting for the son.'

My patience was dangerously close to breaking.

'We want the truth on the table now. So this person whom you saw going towards Harald Olesen's flat shortly before he was murdered was . . .'

He nodded and picked up the thread.

'His son, Kristian Lund. It was very unusual to see him up here on the second floor, so I remembered it. It was not long before I went for my evening stroll. I cannot say the exact time, and of course do not know whether he was the one who fired the shot or not. As far as I could tell, he was not carrying a weapon, but he was wearing a winter overcoat that could hide pretty much anything.'

I swiftly glanced over at Patricia, whose eyebrows were knitted so tight that it was clear she was thinking furiously. Then she gently tapped her pad with her pen twice.

On the way out, I mentioned in passing that an old friend of his was down on the ground floor and that she would no doubt be very happy if he went to see her. This triggered first a smile and then a final defence – said with pure American pathos.

'Despite the unfortunate circumstances surrounding our first meeting, please do not judge me too harshly. I have lived all my adult life fighting dictatorship – first against the Nazis during the war and then against communism after the war. And in all these years, I have carried a great loneliness after losing my first love. It can make you a bit of a loner, even though you might at heart be a good person.'

He hesitated for a moment, then took out his wallet and from a pocket at the front produced a white folded sheet that he held out towards me.

'This is the letter that you asked about. You can read it if you like,' he said abruptly.

I looked over at Patricia, who quickly shook her head and tapped her pen on her notebook. I got the very strong feeling that Darrell Williams had carried the letter wherever he went for the twenty years since he received it – and that it possibly was the first time that he had asked someone else to read it. But I no longer had any reason to doubt his word that there was nothing more in his past that was of any significance to Harald Olesen's murder. He seemed to both understand and appreciate this. We shook each other by the hand before the door closed behind Patricia and me.

V

Patricia was in a good mood and giggled as we went into the lift. I looked at her sternly. She shrugged.

'In the middle of all this tragedy, there is a really sweet love story. I think it is better to have a happy ending twenty years too late than never at all. She is still younger than my mother was when she had me. You must promise to tell me how things work out for those two.'

I promised to do that – on the condition that she would soon tell me who the murderer was. She was immediately serious again.

'I do not know for certain quite yet. What he told us was not what I had expected, so we are still missing a link. I can, however, tell you where we are going now, and that is the first floor.'

I was not very impressed. That was exactly what I had just thought myself.

'And this time to Mr and Mrs Lund?'

Patricia smiled.

'Of course. This should be relatively simple. Confront him with the fact that he was in Harald Olesen's flat on the night of the murder, and her with the fact that she is lying when she says that he did not go out. Leave me just by the door as usual, and make sure that you can see them both at the same time.'

I agreed that it sounded like a good plan of action and pressed the button for the first floor.

VI

The Lunds came to the door together. They also accepted my brief explanation about the injured secretary. They asked us in without any protests or obvious pleasure. I positioned Patricia just inside the door, sat down on one side of the coffee table and indicated to the Lunds that they should sit together on the sofa opposite. They automatically did as I told them. When they were seated, Mrs Lund reached out for her husband's hand. He squeezed hers gratefully.

I started by emphasizing how serious the case was.

'The investigation has reached a critical stage and we now have every reason to believe that Konrad Jensen did not kill Harald Olesen. Much of what has been said earlier can be forgiven, if we now get the full truth.'

They nodded at the same time and moved almost imperceptibly closer together.

'So, I will start by saying that I have clear indications that you, Kristian Lund, lied when you said that you had not spoken to Harald Olesen on the evening of the murder. I also have reason to believe that you, Karen Lund, lied when you said that your husband did not leave the flat after he had come home on the evening of the murder.'

Their reactions were very different. She blushed deeply and frantically shook her head, whereas his face lost all colour and he nodded. She was the first to speak.

'I don't know who it is who has been lying, but you are on the wrong track now, Detective Inspector! My husband was here with me from the time he came home until we heard the gunshot.'

It was said with such passion that I found it hard not to believe her. The ashen-faced Kristian Lund, who was now cornered and almost unrecognizable, resolved the situation.

'She is telling the truth,' he said in a low voice. 'I am the one who lied again,' he added, even closer to a whisper.

All three of us stared at him. Fortunately, he quickly continued with the explanation.

'I went up to the second floor and spoke to Harald Olesen

on the night of the murder. But it was before he was killed. I went directly from Sara's flat and was only there for a minute or so. Then I came back down here and was together with my wife until we heard the shot ring out.'

I gave him a stern look.

'And what happened during your final meeting with Harald Olesen?'

His smile was twisted.

'There and then it was pleasant enough and I felt pleased when I came back here afterwards. He opened the door as soon as I rang the bell, but looked surprised when he saw it was me. He said he was expecting someone else for an important meeting and did not have time to talk. I said that it would not take long, as all I wanted was confirmation that he had changed his will as I had asked. He thought about it for a moment or two, then smiled and assured me that he had changed his will. I thanked him and said that I was glad, then left. And I took his word for it until I heard the final will being read out. The old swine had neglected to tell me that he had changed the will yet again, thereby denying me my rightful inheritance!'

I thought quickly through what had happened at the reading of the will – Kristian Lund's reaction and the other facts that I knew – and realized that it all fitted very well with this last explanation. But I could not remember just then if this was his fourth or fifth version.

I looked questioningly over at Patricia. She held my eye but did not tap her pen. There was a short silence before Patricia did exactly what I had hoped she would: spoke.

'We can almost definitely conclude that you did not commit the murder. But you are still covering for the person you met on the way down from Olesen's flat on the evening he was murdered.'

No one was taken aback by the fact that Patricia had spoken. Kristian Lund's reaction was too dramatic for that. He lost what little colour he had left in his face, dropped his wife's hand and collapsed back on the sofa. I immediately seized the opportunity to take command again.

'Exactly who was it you saw on the evening of the murder, and why are you covering for them?'

I fixed Mrs Lund with a beady eye, but her attention was taken up by her husband and her husband alone. Kristian Lund swallowed three times before he managed to say anything. The silence was crackling by the time he finally croaked a short, tiny and devastating word.

'Sara.'

The name exploded like a bomb in the static silence between us. Mrs Lund's voice a few seconds later resembled a machine gun.

'I do not believe it! Have you known all this time that it was her who killed your father and not said a word to me? You could have sent that witch to prison over a week ago! And instead, you have lied to me and the police in order to protect her. Is that really the truth?'

Kristian Lund nodded almost imperceptibly and then looked up at me with pleading eyes, not daring to look at his wife.

'We had not arranged it, and I certainly did not expect it. I had just come down to the first floor when I bumped into her at the door. We smiled briefly at each other as we passed. It was only when I had opened the door that I realized that she had gone up the stairs, not down. I did not think anything more of it at the time, but obviously it become more significant after the murder and then the reading of the will.'

I held his gaze and hurried to say something before the increasingly red Mrs Lund beat me to it.

'But you are still not telling us *why*.'

Kristian Lund's voice was barely audible, but was clear all the same in the tense silence.

'Partly because I was such an obvious suspect myself. I had been to his door too. If she said that and claimed that he was dead when she arrived, who would you believe then? I think we both realized what a fateful web we were caught in. So we met as soon as we could for a minute out in the hallway the day after the murder. She had the door ajar when I came home. We agreed not to betray each other, and that was it.'

Then he stopped himself. I coaxed him on.

'So it was partly because you were scared of your own situation and partly because you still had feelings for her and could not bring yourself to hand over the woman you loved to the police. Is that right?'

He nodded. That was when Mrs Lund slapped her husband across the face in an outburst of fury. Fortunately, the slap seemed to wake him up. The healthy red colour returned to his cheeks; he straightened himself up and was more alert when he looked at me.

'We have pursued you from pillar to post for nine days now, Kristian Lund. Is there anything else of importance that you still have not told us?'

He shook his head firmly.

'I have passed the point of no return now and am teetering on the edge. I have nothing more to add other than that I deeply regret what I have done and apologize profusely – to you and even more to my wife.'

I had my doubts about this apology and it looked like his wife did too. He noticed this and immediately added: 'When you arrest Sara, send her my greetings and tell her that I never want to see her again. I will send my lawyer to talk to her in prison regarding the will.'

I instinctively felt nothing but contempt for Kristian Lund and was about to reply that he could tell her himself when he was serving a sentence for perjury and hampering a murder investigation. However, I realized in time that it was perhaps just as well not to aggravate the situation any more right now. His wife seemed to calm down marginally after this last statement, but she was still one of the most furious young women I had ever seen – which sadly is not saying much. The situation felt more and more depressing. And then in the background I heard a strange sound. I eventually realized that it was Patricia, who was tapping her pen for the fifth time. We found our own way out, without turning round.

VII

Patricia did not hold back. As soon as we were in the lift, she burst out laughing.

'Thus far you have provided me with good and interesting entertainment. So she could forgive him for lies, blackmail, infidelity and possible murder, but not for loving and protecting another woman. I desperately wanted to stay and see what happened, but we still have a ruthless murderer to catch.'

I nodded, slightly bewildered, and stretched out to press one of the lift buttons.

'Which floor are we going to this time?'

Patricia smiled.

'Why, this one, of course. But it is useful to be able to talk for a couple of minutes without being disturbed. We are going to see Sara Sundqvist again, and this time she better have a very good explanation if a remand cell at 19 Møller Street is not to be her next stop. Just confront her with Kristian Lund's latest version, keep your eye on her and listen to what she has to say. I will intervene if necessary.'

I nodded, but my voice was thick when I asked my short question.

'She really is on thin ice now, isn't she?'

Patricia mulled it over for a while before answering.

'Today, her situation has gone from bad to worse. But the day is not over yet, and I am loath to give up on my main theory. So I am very interested to hear what she has to say in her defence, now that her former lover has pushed her to the edge ahead of him. There really is only one thing she can say now to stop herself from falling – and that has to be the truth.'

I replied that I understood what she meant. This was a pure lie, which I later could only justify to myself by saying that the whole situation had been so confusing.

VIII

Sara Sundqvist's smile was just as friendly as before when she opened her door. I was so impatient to solve the case that I forgot everything that Patricia and I had agreed about positioning and started to talk as soon as we were in the hall.

'I am deeply disappointed, Sara. You have lied to us again.'

She looked at me uneasily, but clearly did not understand.

'Kristian Lund has told us that he went up to see Harald Olesen on the evening of the murder and that he saw you on your way up there as he came down. We have every reason to believe that it is the truth.'

An expression of horror flooded her face. Her voice was distant and hesitant when she spoke.

'I never dreamed that he would dare. Has he really broken his word and betrayed me?'

I nodded gravely, and my frown deepened.

'He asked me to tell you that he never wants to see you again, that he is looking forward to you being arrested and that he will send his lawyer to meet you in prison to demand the return of his rightful inheritance.'

It was as if Sara Sundqvist's slim frame had been struck by a triple blow in the boxing ring. She swayed perilously and had to steady herself against the wall. I resisted the urge to reach out and support her.

'But . . . I don't understand! That he wanted to maybe, but that he dared . . .'

I have to admit that I did not understand it all myself. As Sara Sundqvist was unarmed, unsteady and leaning against the wall, there seemed to be little danger, so I glanced quickly over at Patricia. She looked as though she understood more, but was watching Sara Sundqvist like a hawk.

'But . . . it is a relief. Because now I can tell you everything I have wanted to all along!'

I thought it better not to comment on this statement, but indicated impatiently that she should continue. Which she did – and managed to say an impressive amount without drawing breath.

'It is true that I went to see Harald Olesen that evening. I decided to go up and ask him once again about Deerfoot and my parents. I did not know that Kristian had gone up there already, but realized that he had when I met him on his way down. We just smiled at each other and carried on our separate ways. When I got to Harald Olesen's flat, he was still alive, but refused to let me in. We argued at the door for a few minutes. He said he was expecting an important guest at any moment, but asked me to come back in the morning. I felt that it was a step forward and left. It was obvious that his health was deteriorating, and he was clearly anxious about his guest. In fact, he was frightened. I remember that it made me feel anxious as well, because he was so secretive and his hand was shaking so badly. But it was not me who killed him. It must have been his mysterious guest, whom I met on the way down.'

Suddenly, Sara Sundqvist seemed to be frightened herself. Her voice trembled when she continued with the story.

'It was all very alarming. I realized that something was amiss when I saw the man whom Harald Olesen was expecting. His very appearance chilled me and inspired fear and secrecy. He was wearing a blue raincoat with a hood, and had a scarf wrapped round his head so that it was impossible to see his face. I had a strong premonition of catastrophe; it felt like Judgement Day to be honest. I ran down the stairs and buried myself under the duvet with a pillow over my head and hoped for the best. It was no shock when I heard the gunshot, and even less when you came to the door to tell me that he had been killed.'

I gave her a hard and threatening stare, but was met only with pleading, terrified eyes.

'Do you have any idea who he was?'

Sara shook her head in distress.

'Until now I have thought . . .'

She looked down and fell silent. I had to cough a couple of times before she continued.

'Well, the legs were definitely a man's legs. He was about as tall as me, but it was not possible to see much more because of the raincoat and hood and scarf. At first, I thought he was a stranger who had come from outside, but then you came and said that the murderer must have come from inside the building. And that scared me even more. Konrad Jensen was too short, Darrell Williams too tall, and Andreas Gullestad cannot walk. So that meant there was no one it could possibly be other than Kristian, who had returned in disguise so he would not be recognized.'

The argument was reasonable enough, unless of course the nephew or someone else had managed to get in from outside. But I no longer dared to take anything as given in this case.

'Could it perhaps have been Konrad Jensen in high boots or something similar?'

She shook her head again.

'No, no. There was something to indicate that he came from inside. The man in the raincoat was not wearing shoes – he only had black socks on his feet.'

Silence fell in the room. Sara was trembling, which was not hard to understand given what she had told us about her experience, and now I instinctively put my arm round her. She immediately leaned against me, warm and trusting, and seemed to calm down a bit. But the bliss only lasted for a second or two before Patricia's voice filled the room for the first time. I quickly came to myself and instinctively stepped away from Sara's dangerously warm and soft body.

'Was there anything else about this man that was alarming?'

Sara stared straight ahead and nodded several times, gratefully.

'Yes. The man in the raincoat was light as a feather and danced more than walked – like a cat or a boxer. He seemed to glide down the corridor. It made me think about Deerfoot. But as he did not live in the building, the only possible explanation that I could find was that it was Kristian who was walking like that on purpose so he would not be recognized.'

'Eureka!'

This outburst was completely unexpected and hung in the air for a moment. Sara and I looked at each other, bewildered. The next thing we heard was Patricia hitting the pad with her pen again and again, as if the pen were a drumstick.

'Brilliant – that is just what we needed! You are obviously innocent. The man in the blue raincoat shot Harald Olesen shortly after you saw him. And I know where to find him!'

At first, Sara looked like she might float up and away. And then she did – and landed beaming with her arms round my neck. I could hear some clucking sounds in the background, which meant that Patricia was enjoying the spectacle. The chuckling stopped mysteriously as soon as Sara came to her senses and sheepishly lowered her feet to the floor again.

I have to admit that my first thought was that it was Kristian Lund who was going to be arrested, after all. My second thought was that I did not object to that in any way. However, Patricia's next words quickly put an end to that theory.

'So, now we can finally go and meet this Mr Deerfoot. And if you would like to meet him too, Sara, please join us.'

Sara looked at me and then gave me a quick hug when I said that of course she could come. We all rushed out in convoy to the lift.

IX

'Are we going down to the ground floor, then?' I asked.

Patricia nodded quickly and Sara looked as if she would follow us to the ends of the earth without protesting.

When the lift door opened, we were met with a delightful scene. Darrell Williams and Cecilia Olesen were sitting opposite each other talking as if they would never stop. The caretaker's wife had discreetly retired, and Joachim Olesen was looking pointedly out of the window. Darrell Williams was unrecognizable. Suddenly, he was the world's most amusing and charming man, even from a distance. Just as we emerged, he leaned forward and kissed her tenderly on the mouth. Patricia clucked contentedly again and pulled at my hand.

'It really was a good idea to get the niece and nephew to come here too,' she said, with a smile.

When I started to move towards them, she held me back firmly by the hand.

'Wait a while – we can talk to them later. Don't disturb

their bliss. Let us rather pay a visit to the one neighbour I have not yet met.'

It was in fact Joachim Olesen whom I had expected to talk to, but I quickly gave this up as Patricia was pointing eagerly at the first door on the right.

X

Andreas Gullestad opened the door with his usual jovial smile and immediately invited all three of us in. He accepted my explanation of Patricia in the wheelchair without question and added with self-irony that it was good to meet a wheelchair user who still wanted to contribute to society. I caught a wry smile passing between them.

While Gullestad went out into the kitchen to get some cups and to make coffee, I installed Patricia by the door. Sara and I sat down by the table in the living room. Our host came in again from the kitchen with the coffee and poured us all a cup. I was still impatient to prove my theory that Joachim Olesen was Deerfoot and could not understand what new information Patricia expected to find here.

It was only when Andreas Gullestad had settled and then asked what he could help me with today that I suddenly realized that something was wrong – very wrong indeed.

It came quite literally in a flash, when the ceiling light caught something silver that our host was wearing round his neck.

Either he had not been wearing the necklace on previous visits or I had simply not noticed. I sat there staring at the pendant as if hypnotized. Andreas Gullestad, meanwhile, looked annoyingly relaxed and not in the slightest bit threatening as he sat there in his wheelchair.

'I am afraid that I have a number of difficult questions to ask you today . . .'

Andreas Gullestad looked up at me in surprise, and his face stiffened. But he replied, with a friendly smile, that he would do his best to help me – whether the questions were difficult or not.

'Do you still maintain that the name Deerfoot is unknown to you?'

If I had hoped for some kind of breakthrough, I was disappointed. Andreas Gullestad furrowed his brows. He did not blink, and his voice was just as friendly.

'I am afraid I am going to have to disappoint you again there. I may perhaps have heard about this person by another name, but the description you have given me so far is still a bit hazy. Do you have any more details that might jog my memory?'

I was more than happy to provide these.

'Deerfoot was a young guide who helped Harald Olesen when he had to cross the border into Sweden during the war. They made several trips together, the last of which was in February 1944 and ended in tragedy in the mountains between Trysil and Sälen. Not only were three German soldiers killed, but also two Jewish refugees. Deerfoot heroically skied over the mountains with their baby under his anorak and thereby managed to save her life. Does that ring any bells?'

Andreas Gullestad shook his head firmly.

'No, I am afraid I do still maintain that this Deerfoot is unknown to me. I grew up not so far from there and heard many credible and incredible stories about what went on in the area. I cannot guarantee that I still remember them all, but I would have remembered that one if I had heard it. Do you have any questions from the more recent past that I might be able to answer?'

I nodded and made a swift decision to attack from a different angle.

'Absolutely. We can instead talk about the mysterious man in the blue raincoat whom you said you had seen here in the building over the Whitsun weekend last year, but not since.'

He nodded pensively, with some reluctance.

'If I was to say that he was seen wandering the corridors again on the evening that Harald Olesen was murdered, and that if you saw him last year you must have been looking in a mirror, and that it was you who threw a blue raincoat out in the rubbish . . . what would you say then?'

Andreas Gullestad pulled himself up slightly in his chair, put his right hand to his thigh and lifted his left hand to point at something.

'Then I would say there has been a terrible misunderstanding that I hope can be resolved immediately. I do have a blue raincoat, but as you can see, it is still hanging on the coat hook by the door!'

He was pointing towards the door behind Patricia. Instinctively, I turned round, but could not see a blue raincoat. Nor could I see any coat hooks that the raincoat might hang on. Instead, I saw the shock on Patricia's face. But it was only when I heard a loud whimper from Sara, followed by a strange thud that I could not place, that I spun my head back round. But it was too late.

It was a very different room that I saw. The friendly, harmless Andreas Gullestad had vanished, and his wheelchair had toppled back onto the floor. In the middle of the room stood a man of around my height, his legs like a panther ready to pounce. His face was so changed that it took a few seconds before I recognized him. Andreas Gullestad's relaxed expression was gone. Despite the different hair colour and rounder cheeks, I could now recognize the young Deerfoot's intense and focused face from the old photograph. However, the biggest and most worrying change was that I was looking straight down the barrel of a .45-calibre Kongsberg Colt.

XI

'This is my father's old army pistol, and it was hidden in a pocket inside the cushion in my wheelchair. I have literally been sitting on the murder weapon for ten days!'

He said this with a shadow of a smile on his lips, but in a voice that was very different and could hardly be described as jolly. It was tense and serious – and threatening rather than friendly. Andreas Gullestad had become a totally different person when he threw back his wheelchair and pulled out a gun. I did not doubt for a moment that this was a man who had shot people before – and was willing to do so again. His finger was ready on the trigger. The only positive thing was that he appeared to be prepared to talk. And with a racing heart, I threw myself at this opening.

'I know that it is the gun that killed Harald Olesen, but how many people did it kill during the war?'

He nodded in acknowledgement.

'Four. It was me who shot all three soldiers during the incident in 1944. I could live with that, even though they still haunt my dreams from time to time. War is war, and occupiers are occupiers. What was far worse was that I also shot the mother of your young Swedish friend.'

There was another whimper from Sara. The twitch in Deerfoot's face was like an echo. It was obvious that he was reliving painful old memories. I tried desperately to encourage him to continue.

'I had a feeling that Harald Olesen's report in Sweden was misleading . . . but what actually happened?'

He shook his head slowly.

'The report was about five minutes from the truth. If it had been right, everything would have been different. The fact that there was an exchange of fire and three German soldiers were killed is true. What is not true is that the refugees we had with us were shot at the same time. We had shot them ourselves a few minutes before.'

Sara's whimpering increased. Deerfoot's hand trembled slightly and he continued in an unsteady voice.

'It has haunted me every hour of the day for the whole of my life since – and it was Harald Olesen's fault, all of it. He took their lives and ruined mine at the same time. And he had to die for his sins.'

I said nothing more for fear of provoking him. Fortunately, he was still delving deep into his memory.

'It was hell on earth, and I have relived it every day since and almost every night . . . The endless journey with those hopelessly slow refugees who had never used skis before. Harald and I could easily have escaped from the Germans, but we could not leave the refugees behind. At one point, he said to me that all hope was lost and that I should escape while I could, but I told him that I would stay with him and with them to the bitter end. We hoped that we might be spared when the storm blew up and three of the Germans turned back, but the other three carried on and were getting closer by the hour. We thought that we could hide at the top, but they were gaining ground as we hauled the refugees up with us. They fired at us from further down the mountainside when we finally got to the summit. Then it soon became impossible to see anything, and almost impossible to carry on in the storm. I knew exactly where we were – a matter of miles from the Swedish border – but we would not be able to make it with the refugees in a howling snowstorm. We hid behind a rocky outcrop, with the two increasingly desperate refugees and a crying baby, for the rest of the night, knowing full well that our pursuers might find us at any time. Hour after hour we sat there, each with a gun in our hand, ready to shoot if we suddenly came under fire. Finally, we dared to carry on in the morning once the storm had dropped. Harald hoped that the Germans had turned back, but I had my doubts. It is hard to give up the hunt when you have come so far and are so near. We were all together, exhausted and nervous, when it happened.'

We listened with bated breath. He swallowed several times before he continued.

'I still do not know exactly what happened, but suddenly, Harald Olesen and the man we had with us were arguing in raised voices. Then there was a shot. And Harald Olesen stood there, paralysed, with a smoking gun in his hand, staring at a dead man in the snow. Then I saw the wife of the fallen refugee screaming and waving her fists at Harald.

So I gave it a moment's thought, then shot her in the head. I have since often wondered why I shot her. I looked up to Harald, not just as a leader, but also as a father figure. My instinct was to protect him under any circumstance. But then, she was unarmed, and I knew that she was. So the answer has to be that I was scared that her screams would let them know where we were, and I was sick and tired of being held back by her and therefore wanted her dead.'

Deerfoot swallowed again before carrying on, but his feet were still dancing – and his finger was still on the trigger.

'So there I stood. Both refugees lay dead in the snow, and the mother still had a crying baby at her neck. Harald Olesen stood as if petrified, looking down at them. Then I heard the sound of voices and skis from around the crag. For a moment I thought about killing myself, but then decided to risk the small chance that I had to survive. I ran over to the nearest snowdrift and threw myself down behind it. I was lying there when they appeared. Harald Olesen was still in his own world. I realized that my only hope was to kill all three of them by myself – and I only had six bullets left in the gun.'

Deerfoot's story was almost as tense as the situation we now found ourselves in, and very frightening indeed. He blinked a couple of times, but his hand was now steady and his finger remained on the trigger.

'The three soldiers were young: two were around twenty-five, and one was barely a day over twenty-one. An unexpected sight awaited them: two dead refugees in the snow and Harald Olesen standing there, out of his senses. I was not that far away from them and kept my aim as long as I dared. But when one of them pointed to my tracks in the snow, there was no time to think anymore. So I fired at the one who was closest, then quickly moved my aim to the next. The first one fell straightaway, and the second before he could pull his gun, but the third managed to do this and fired at me several times. Twice I just managed to throw myself to the side in the snowdrift before the bullets hit the spot where I had been. In the end, I stood up and aimed at him. My first shot missed. He spun round and aimed. We shot at each other at the same time. I felt the pressure as the bullet sliced past my ear, but my bullet hit him in the cheek. He stood there and swayed for a moment, with his gun trained on me, but then fell, the blood shooting up into the air. When I fired again, I hit him in the middle of the forehead. The scene that met my eyes when I came out from behind the snowdrift was gruesome. Five dead people in the snow. The only man standing was Harald Olesen, and he was apparently still paralysed.'

A hard expression slipped over Deerfoot's face. His story was dramatic and it struck me that it was possibly the first time he had told it to anyone. His eyes were fixed on me – and the gun was still alarmingly pointed at me.

'Do you remember the young German soldier I mentioned to you, the one who had tried to comfort me when they came to get my father? He was one of the three who had pursued us now – the second one to be shot. He was still alive when I went over to him. He tried to say something to me. "*En...*" He started twice without managing to say the word. I have later thought that he was perhaps trying to say "*Entschuldigung*" – that he was trying to apologize to me, who had shot him. It was an awful situation; he was not much more than a boy himself. I put my gun to his head and looked away while

I pulled the trigger. He still comes back to haunt me – only last night I was woken by the sight of his face.'

Once again Deerfoot's eyes became glazed, but they were still looking straight at me, and I was in no doubt that he would shoot me immediately if I so much as took a step towards him. I nodded as calmly as I could in the hope that he would continue the story.

'The worst shock was still to come, though. After I had fired my final shot, I looked up and saw that Harald Olesen had raised his gun and was aiming at me. He said something vague about me having seen him kill a refugee so I had to die. I expected him to pull the trigger and kill me at any moment. God knows what I said. My guess is that it was probably that he had seen me kill her and that it was our shared secret. And that he would never find his way back on his own and that the baby would freeze to death in the cold without me. I think it was the latter that made him finally lower his gun and hand me the child. In which case it was the baby who saved me, and I then saved her in turn. You apparently know the rest of what happened. He stayed behind to bury the dead in a nearby cave. I skied for my life all the way to Sälen, first to get out of Harald Olesen's firing range and then to save the baby's life. It became an obsession: having killed her mother, I at least had to do something to save her life.'

Deerfoot was back in the present and reacted immediately when I carefully raised my hands.

'Stay still! Both I and the gun have killed before!'

His voice was controlled, but had a dangerous undercurrent of desperation. I nodded as soothingly as I could. It was hard to see how we would get out of this alive. The only hope was to keep the dialogue going. Suddenly, Sara's soft voice came to my aid.

'Thank you for saving my life. I forgive you for killing my mother – you were young and you were in a situation in which you feared for your own life. Finally knowing what happened will help to ease the burden of grief. Do you remember where the cave is?'

Deerfoot cast half a glance in her direction. A tear twinkled in her eye as she spoke. But he continued to keep his focus on me – and his finger itching on the trigger.

'I know exactly where the cave is. But you will only find remnants of the clothes and bones of the five people who were fated to die there together one winter day in 1944. I have never been back, but have never managed to move on from there all the same. I was a wreck in 1946 and 1947, when the papers were writing about the two border guides who killed the Feldmann couple. And in later years I have lived with the memories, every hour and every day – and with the fear of being discovered one day and ending up as a new Feldmann murderer on the front of every newspaper.'

He fell silent. His finger started to tremble on the trigger.

I carried on talking, out of sheer desperation.

'Why did you not leave the pistol behind when you killed Harald Olesen?'

A painful expression flooded Deerfoot's face.

'That was my initial plan: the perfect murder camouflaged as suicide. The problem was that I then began to wonder how easy it would be to trace the army pistol back to my father's time in the army. If it could be traced back to him, I was finished. I thought about procuring an unregistered weapon, but Harald Olesen was at death's door and was under considerable pressure from the young Miss Sara here. He wanted to ease his conscience and tell her the truth before he died. So in the end, I did not dare wait any longer. It had to be the perfect murder without a murder weapon at the scene of the crime, instead of the perfect murder with the weapon at the scene of the crime. As for Jensen, buying an unregistered weapon would not have been easy, as I could not go out. The solution was to buy a more recent model from a half-witted childhood friend, who both before and after the murder accepted my explanation that I needed it to feel safe in Oslo. I had to go to Gjøvik to arrange it, hence my trip home last weekend.

'When you have already killed several people at a young age and then used the rest of your adult life trying to live with the memories and hide the truth, you become a bit of a lone wolf. It is all about survival and protecting yourself from possible dangers. Harald Olesen's death does not upset me so much now. After all, he did not have long to live. And it was largely his betrayal that made me the monster I am. But in the end, it was my fear of being exposed that made me pull the trigger; I shot him when he told me that he had finally decided to tell Sara the whole story. So in a way, I shot him in self-defence, having tried every other means. But I admit that there was also a latent need to avenge my broken life.'

He stopped and let his finger play with the trigger. His story was finished. I immediately tried to extend it.

'Then you committed another murder, to avoid the risk of being arrested for the first?'

He nodded brusquely, twice, and then blinked his eyes furiously.

'That has plagued me far more than the murder of Harald Olesen. No matter how repulsive Konrad Jensen was, and no matter how dismal his future prospects, he should have been able to live out the last years of his life here in peace, with all his bitterness and complexities. But your investigation seemed to be making dangerous progress. A scapegoat was needed, and as a former Nazi, he was clearly the best candidate. I made the plan even before I murdered Harald Olesen, and wrote the suicide note for Konrad Jensen when I was in Gjøvik last weekend. He was terrified of everyone and everything after the murder, but also desperately lonely. And he could not imagine, like other greater men, that a friendly and sophisticated cripple could be a murderer. So while the caretaker's wife was out doing the shopping, I knocked on his door. He was wary at first, but then opened up when he saw that it was me and all I wanted was a cup of coffee and a chat in these uncertain times. He signed the suicide note with the gun to his forehead, without having any idea of what he was signing, and died without pain only seconds later, without ever knowing. It was a sad end to a tragic life. But Konrad Jensen became the necessary sacrifice for a greater and more important cause – that is, my life, my freedom and my honour.'

He stopped talking; a deathly silence fell in the flat. I made a final attempt to stop him from shooting.

'I have four armed policemen standing guard on the street outside. You will be caught without much trouble – and your punishment will be worse for every murder you commit.'

He nodded, but did not smile – nor did he show any sign of desperation or weakness.

'I guessed that that would be the case. So I really am back in that snowdrift in 1944 that I have revisited in my dreams so many times since. I have to try to shoot my way out, against all odds, and I have nothing to lose in trying. There are too many corpses in my wake for me to turn back now. Four policemen in a town does not feel that hopeless when you have survived against three soldiers in the mountains at the age of sixteen.'

His answers were becoming shorter, and his tone harder. My brain was frantically trying to come up with new questions to keep the conversation alive – and finally found one.

'But how on earth did you manage to convince the world that you were crippled?'

He suddenly smiled, and a hint of pride glowed in his face.

'The traffic accident was real and unpleasant enough. I was run over one day when I had suddenly been overwhelmed by memories from the war in the middle of a crossroads. For a while the doctor feared that I would be left in a wheelchair. I understood myself that things were improving and that I would recover again. But it struck me that keeping the wheelchair would be the perfect camouflage – certainly until my score with Harald Olesen had been settled. It was not so difficult. Who doubts the injuries of a man who has been in an accident and has received treatment, who is still a wheelchair user and does not ask for any money from the State? But you should have studied the signature more, because it is a fraud!'

He broke into a smile again – this time, a terrible, twisted, triumphant smile that sent a chill down my spine.

'Never underestimate a man who appears to be a cripple. Harald Olesen once gave me that advice during the war. That was your only mistake in the investigation, but it was a fateful one.'

And then suddenly our conversation was over. For a couple of torturous seconds Deerfoot improved his aim at my chest. It was a terrifying feeling, watching the finger curl round the trigger right in front of you. I would not wish it on my worst enemy. The fear was paralysing. But suddenly a new sound filled the room. It was Patricia's blessed strong and determined voice.

'I am aiming at your head, Deerfoot. You can shoot him, but then I will shoot you. Your flight is over now. The best thing you can do, not only for yourself, is to hand him the gun.'

Deerfoot started and for an eternal moment seemed to be paralysed too. He glanced to one side, towards the door, to make sure that there really was a gun pointing at him. Then he focused his attention on me again.

We probably stood like this on the edge of eternity for no more than ten seconds, but it could as well have been an hour. I was only feet away from Deerfoot and was now ready to pounce myself. The instinct to try to knock the gun from his hand if he lowered it or looked to the side again grew stronger. Deerfoot's eyes once again glazed over. He seemed to be lost in his own world. But the gun in his hand was still pointing at my chest, and his finger was still on the trigger. I felt that he really was back behind that snowdrift in 1944 and was dithering between giving himself up, turning the gun on himself or trying to shoot his way out.

Then he seemed to make his decision. Very slowly, he lowered the barrel of the gun to the floor. I took a step forward as soon as it was no longer pointing at me. I did not have time to think when Deerfoot, without warning, danced two steps to the side, hunkered down and in a flash aimed the gun towards the door. It was pure instinct, and the fear of seeing Patricia die, that made me throw myself towards him.

I hit him with full force just as the shot was fired. The bullet flew upwards and hit the ceiling above Patricia. Again, on pure instinct, I hit out at his firing arm. The gun flew out of his hand, bounced along the floor and fortunately slid under the sofa.

The next thing I heard was Patricia's hardest and iciest voice: 'Stay exactly where you are *now* and do not move, Deerfoot – and hold out your hands in front of you. Or I will shoot you in the leg!'

I expected even more high drama in the next few seconds, but as if by magic, Deerfoot changed instantly. He was once again the relaxed and friendly Andreas Gullestad. He calmly held both his hands out in front of him and appeared to be almost relieved when I eventually managed to pull out the handcuffs and put them on him. Suddenly, it seemed that he had accepted his fate.

'Do not underestimate a woman who really is a cripple either!' Patricia exclaimed, as we passed her wheelchair on the way out. I hugged her as soon as I could once I had thrust our captive out into the hall. And I experienced my last shock of the day. In stark contrast to Patricia's level voice and calm face, I could feel the emotion in her body. I had never felt such a racing and pounding pulse in anyone. The heartbeat in her tiny thin body was thundering and furious.

XII

Out in the hallway, Andreas Gullestad had apparently once again regained his composure. When I eventually thought to inform him that he was under arrest for the murders of Harald Olesen and Konrad Jensen, he added voluntarily: 'Do not forget the murder of a refugee and being an accomplice to the murder of a second refugee, plus the attempted murder of a police officer and two other people today. This will cost me dear.' Out in the entrance, he praised me for having positioned a lady sharpshooter, disguised as a cripple, out of sight by the door.

When I came out with the handcuffed Andreas Gullestad, it caused quite a stir among the people waiting by the front door. Especially when he calmly reassured them that the case had now definitely been solved and the murderer had been arrested, and then went on to congratulate me on a successful investigation.

The neighbours queued up to congratulate me once the murderer had been driven away by two constables and the circumstances had been explained to them. Darrell Williams was particularly heartfelt in his congratulations when he pumped my hand and thanked me for all my help. On seeing him and Cecilia Olesen standing together smiling, I felt for a moment something of what Deerfoot must have felt when he saved young Sara's life in 1944 – it truly was an ill wind that blows no good.

This feeling did not diminish when, a few seconds later, I saw a smiling Sara Sundqvist coming down the stairs towards me. She embraced me warmly and whispered that

Patricia wanted to leave the building and go home as soon and as discreetly as possible. We were able to do this fifteen minutes later, once I had with some authority cleared the hall of residents with vague references to 'wrapping up the investigation'.

I was naturally relieved and on top form when I finally got into the car with Patricia, but still I noticed that things were remarkably quiet in the back seat. Even though Patricia was the one who had kept her head during the arrest in Andreas Gullestad's flat, on reflection she now seemed to be the one most deeply affected by the day's drama. She sat in complete silence for the first part of the journey. Then she interrupted my attempts to make contact with a cursory comment that she was tired and needed time to digest what had happened. She suggested that I pop in to see her at noon the following day, when I would be given a decent lunch and the answers to any remaining questions. In the meantime, she advised that I only talked about the case in broad brush-strokes and that I played down her role in the investigation as far as possible, particularly with regard to the media. I of course promised with a light heart to do just that.

We said goodbye in an unusually subdued mood. However, when Beate opened the door and took charge of the wheelchair, Patricia gave a fleeting smile and thanked me for 'a particularly interesting and eventful trip into town'.

The rest of the evening was spent informing my police colleagues and journalists of the sensational development. I ignored any requests for details of the actual arrest and instead gave a quick presentation of the murderer's confession and a rough outline of his story. I was showered with compliments and words of praise, in particular for the fact that I had continued the investigation in secret following the murder of Konrad Jensen. I gave my boss a fifteen-minute report, in which Patricia's role had been minimized to the extent that I did not even mention that she was present during the arrest. He told me I was a credit to the force and shook my hand three times. It was the night before Easter, and I finally got to bed around twelve, full of optimism for my future in the force and what the papers would say on Tuesday.

DAY ELEVEN

Tidying Up and Conclusions

I

As the more observant, older reader will perhaps recall, there was never a big court case following the murders in 25 Krebs' Street. I was woken early on 14 April 1968 by the telephone – despite the fact that it was a Sunday, and Easter Sunday at that. It was barely eight o'clock. The call was from Oslo Remand Prison, where Andreas Gullestad had just been found dead in his cell.

I drove straight to the prison, where the governor informed me with deep regret of what had happened. The prisoner had been extremely cooperative on arrival and not given reason for any special measures to be put in place. He had asked for some paper and a pen in order to write a more detailed confession, which he hoped might help the investigation. He had obviously sat up late writing, as three tightly spaced pages and a two-page map had been left on the table. But he himself was lying dead on his bed with a smile on his lips when his breakfast was brought in to him in the morning.

On the table lay a letter that said the following:

Oslo, 13 April 1968

To Detective Inspector Kolbjørn Kristiansen – and anyone else he may wish to share this with,

In order to save the legal system unnecessary costs, I hereby confirm that it was the undersigned who shot and killed Harald Olesen in 25 Krebs' Street on Thursday, 4 April this year. My motive was revenge and a strong desire to prevent him from revealing details of a criminal incident in 1944 that is detailed below. In order to disguise the murder of Olesen, I then killed Konrad Jensen at the same address on Tuesday, 9 April this year.

I also confess to the killing of the refugee Anna Maria Rozenthal by the Swedish border near Trysil on 21 February 1944. I am, however, not responsible for the murder of her husband, Felix Rozenthal, who had been shot and killed by Harald Olesen in my presence only a few seconds earlier. For further details of these four murders, I refer to the oral statement I gave to you in the presence of witnesses earlier today.

I would like to congratulate you on your perfectly executed investigation into the murders of Harald Olesen and Konrad Jensen. In the course of the past ten days, you have not only solved these two murders, but also two further murders that you had never heard of until the investigation was opened. It was my great misfortunate that you were appointed to lead this investigation. It was an unpleasant surprise to see how quickly you were on my trail, as a result of some very astute conclusions in the days immediately after the death of Harald Olesen. However, your manoeuvre following the death of Konrad Jensen was even more elegant, when you officially stopped the investigation, but in reality stepped it up. I recognized how dangerous you were when you asked me once again about my deceased father's connection with Harald Olesen before the war, the following day. But it was really only on Friday, when I received the order to remain available for questioning over the weekend, that I realized that the danger was not over and that the investigation was in fact on my tail again and making progress. And finally, you fooled me again during my arrest today by placing a lady sharpshooter disguised as a handicapped secretary in a position where I could not see both of you at once.

In hindsight, I would also like to thank you for saving me from myself – to the extent that your arrest prevented me from adding any more deaths to my already heavy burden. I would like to apologize sincerely to you and to the young Miss Sara Sundqvist for the deeply upsetting events that I hope you will understand were only set in motion through sheer desperation. I also, to the extent that this now is of any interest, declare myself guilty of the attempted murder of a policeman.

I must also apologize deeply to Miss Sundqvist for my role in the death of her mother. I still see this as my greatest crime. I hope that my subsequent effort to save Sara Sundqvist's life in some way makes up for it. As I now understand that she has a strong wish to see her parents' grave, I leave with this letter a hand-drawn map that may possibly help her to find the cave in question.

I know only too well that the loss of a parent can never be compensated fully with money, but hope it will be of some comfort that I hereby leave Sara Sundqvist half of my estate. The other half is left to my sister, again with profound apologies for the distress that the revelation of my crimes will cause her and her family. Following the example of Harald Olesen, I leave my flat in 25 Krebs' Street to the ever-helpful Mrs Randi Hansen.

It is my hope that this will help you to understand my imminent death, which will now prevent me from attending a court case. I admit that my suicide is primarily driven by egoism. The prospect of a long court case in which the details of the murders that I have committed are unfolded is for me more painful than the long sentence I would no doubt have to serve. However, I hope and believe that my death prior to any such court case will be a relief not only for me and my family, but also for Sara Sundqvist and the surviving residents, as well as the friends and family of Harald Olesen and Konrad Jensen.

As I have previously told you, I lost my faith on that day in January 1941 when I received the message that my father had been shot by the Germans. I have never been able to rekindle my belief in a good and almighty God. I therefore die happy in the belief, given the circumstances, that there is no heaven or hell on the other side, just a vast emptiness, in which I can finally find peace from the memories and overwhelming feelings of guilt that have hounded me every day and as good as every night of my adult life.

And finally, in order to solve the mystery of my own death, I have committed suicide by swallowing a capsule of poison that I took with me into the cell. You will no doubt know that many members of the Resistance had suicide pills hidden on their bodies throughout the war. On my trips across the border with refugees during the war, I carried my suicide pill in a silver necklace, disguised as part of the chain. I started to wear this necklace again following your instructions on Friday. It is my hope that I am the last person in Norway to carry one of these suicide pills from the war, and that on finishing this letter, I will be the last to swallow one.

With my deepest respect, Andreas Gullestad
(christened Ivar Storskog and better known by the code name Deerfoot during the war)

The prison governor's relief was tangible when I voiced my understanding for the fact that the necklace had not been taken from the prisoner. I had to admit that I myself would not have imagined that it was hiding a deadly secret.

As the news of the investigation's successful conclusion spread, telegrams and flowers flowed into the office. The murderer's suicide in prison did not detract from the fact that the case, in terms of the investigation, had been perfectly handled – and certainly did not seem to put a dampener on the praise. I also realized very quickly that various potentially uncomfortable questions relating to details were no longer relevant.

II

I got a slight shock when I was shown into Patricia's living room at five to twelve on Sunday. This was the first time that Patricia and I were not left alone after the maid's hasty retreat. Sara Sundqvist sent me a friendly smile from her seat next to Patricia.

Patricia winked merrily at me and held out her hand towards her guest.

'I took the liberty of inviting another guest to my home today. I understood that the young Miss Sundqvist would naturally also be interested in hearing an explanation of certain points.'

It struck me as somewhat comical that 'the young Miss Sundqvist' was patently at least six years older than the young Miss Borchmann herself. However, Sara nodded in agreement and looked at me with pleading eyes. I tried to give a friendly nod in return and sat down with forced calm in my usual place on the opposite side of the table. It must be said that my spontaneous feeling on seeing Sara was one of excited joy. However, this was soon replaced by one of growing unease. For all manner of reasons, I did not want Sara to discover just how much of the investigation's success was thanks to Patricia. However, the damage was already done, as she had been present during yesterday's drama.

And there was more drama in store, as I had to start by telling them about Andreas Gullestad's suicide. I then put the letter and map that he had left down on the table. Patricia seemed to be neither particularly surprised nor disappointed by this news. Sara, on the other hand, reacted with great emotion when she read the letter and burst into tears. Despite all the crimes he had committed, she would always be grateful to Deerfoot, who had competed with death when he skied over the mountains to save her life. I suddenly felt a great sympathy for Sara and reluctantly also had to admit that I felt a slight ambivalence towards the now deceased Andreas Gullestad.

Patricia appeared to be in far better and lighter humour than the evening before. 'So, what else is there that we still have to discuss regarding the successful conclusion of this case?' she asked playfully, when lunch was on the table. We raised our glasses to each other and to the fact that the dramatic murder investigation of the past ten days was finally over.

Once Sara had dried her tears, she had a number of easier and more complex questions. I was delighted that in her answers, Patricia always highlighted my efforts as far as possible. Inspired by this, I myself sought to answer more and more of her questions. I was slightly annoyed by the fact that I had several questions I dearly wanted to ask Patricia but could not ask when Sara was present as they would reveal my own inadequacies. However, I did get indirect answers to some of them.

In reply to Sara's question as to when we had started to suspect Andreas Gullestad, Patricia said that he had quickly become of interest when Konrad Jensen was murdered. When my discovery in Konrad Jensen's flat showed that he could not have written the suicide note, the number of suspects was narrowed down following a critical comparison of the two murders. All the residents in 25 Krebs' Street could in theory have murdered Harald Olesen, but only four of the neighbours would have had the opportunity to throw away the blue raincoat after the murder: the caretaker's wife, Andreas Gullestad, Karen Lund and Sara Sundqvist. And of them, Sara was the least likely murderer, largely because it was not probable that she would have got into Konrad Jensen's flat. It was hard to imagine a situation in which the terrified Konrad Jensen, with his deep suspicion of the Jews, would let her in.

Of the three remaining, Andreas Gullestad was clearly the most likely murderer, as soon as the initial 'D' in the diary had been linked to the story of Deerfoot. The picture became clear when my trip to Sweden revealed that Deerfoot had been very young during the war – and when it became obvious that this Deerfoot had an intense hatred for Harald Olesen as a result of something he experienced during the war. Gullestad's weekend in Gjøvik fitted in well with the theory that he was then able to write the suicide note and get a new gun with which to kill Konrad Jensen. The last pieces fell into place when Sara's statement confirmed that the man in the blue raincoat had visited Harald Olesen on the evening of the murder and walked with Deerfoot's characteristically light step. Up until that point, there were other possible explanations that had to be tested, even though they appeared to be less and less probable.

In retrospect, Andreas Gullestad had always been a realistic option with both a motive and the opportunity. It did, however, require that you were far-sighted enough not to be misled into believing that simply because someone is in a wheelchair, they cannot move around without it. The fact that none of the other parties involved in the case were particularly light on their feet made it natural to focus on the one person who had never been seen walking. It was also interesting that Andreas Gullestad could remember the day on which he had seen the man in the blue raincoat, especially when the caretaker's wife also claimed to have seen such a man in the building. But this in no way disproved that Andreas Gullestad could himself have been the man in the blue raincoat.

I nodded in agreement with her reasoning, and to my relief saw that Sara was impressed, but did not ask any more specific questions. She swiftly moved from asking about the investigation to apologizing for her own offences. Sara was almost in tears when she leaned over the table towards me and asked me to forgive her for holding back important information in the case. Even though everything was over between her and Kristian Lund after the murder of Harald Olesen, she had felt obliged to keep their agreement until he broke it himself. She was also terribly afraid that she would herself be suspected of the murder, as she had been up to see Harald Olesen shortly before he was murdered, but could not prove that he was alive when she left. She realized now that giving in to Kristian Lund's emotional blackmail and agreeing to cover for him was a hysterical response to female anxiety. She could only put her hand on her heart and apologize for this unforgivable blunder. I noticed a twitch in the corner of Patricia's mouth and saw that she was swallowing hard, which indicated that she was trying to control a fit of laughter, so I sent her such a threatening look that she managed to pull herself together.

At twenty to two, lunch was suddenly over. Patricia was quiet and reflective and answered only with single-syllable words, which became increasingly evident to Sara and me. Patricia then asked Sara abruptly if she had any more questions. As the answer was no, she told Sara that they were finished with lunch, then. Patricia said that she was starting to feel very tired and that there were a couple of strictly confidential things that she had to discuss with the detective inspector. This all seemed very impolite to me, given that she was the one who had invited Sara there herself. However, Sara took it well. She thanked Patricia effusively for the lunch, said that she had to get ready for an important meeting later in the afternoon, then followed Benedikte out without protest. I felt a stab of jealousy and wondered who it was she was going to meet later on.

III

'She is a beautiful and charming young lady who undoubtedly has not had an easy life,' I said, slightly exercised, when the door had been closed behind Sara.

Patricia looked at me with a crooked smile and chuckled.

'What you say is absolutely true. But what I say is also true: she is a good actress and a crafty player. What she said about Kristian Lund blackmailing her was such an out-and-out lie that her nose almost started to grow. From what I have understood, she initiated the agreement with Kristian Lund herself and covered for him to very end, even though she thought he was the murderer. It is clear that she has changed her allegiances drastically since then, but three days into the investigation, she told you openly that she hoped to keep him. And by the way, she has just drawn out the lunch for forty minutes longer than I suggested to her yesterday. You never know where you are with ladies like her, until you find yourself lying on top of them!'

I hurriedly asked Patricia if she had at any stage suspected Harald Olesen's nephew, Joachim. I intimated vaguely that I 'at a much earlier point' in the investigation had thought that perhaps the nephew might have been Deerfoot, as he had a possible motive and age-wise it could fit. Patricia pulled a face and shook her head firmly.

'The thought did cross my mind a couple of times, but was quickly forgotten. After the murder of Konrad Jensen, it was totally unfeasible that the nephew was the murderer. One problem was how he had managed to get out of the building without being seen after having murdered Harald Olesen. But it was a complete mystery as to why he would murder Konrad Jensen, and even more incomprehensible how he had done it. If the nephew had shot Harald Olesen, he would not have had reason to think it was necessary to kill someone else. After all, you had only told the neighbours about the investigation's progress, which proved to be the trigger. He did not know the habits and routines in the building, and the likelihood of Konrad Jensen letting in a stranger would have been around zero.'

Patricia suddenly looked at me with scepticism.

'When did you say you considered this utterly illogical possibility? The fact that his age fitted well with Deerfoot was something we only discovered after your trip to Sweden, which was three days after the murder of Konrad Jensen.'

I mumbled that I had of course never really considered it to be feasible, but that one had to check all possible options in a murder investigation. Then I hurriedly moved the conversation on by saying that I now suspected that a certain person had foreseen that the necklace was in fact a possible means of suicide. Patricia became very serious and cocked her head before she answered.

'Well, I have to say that I am partially guilty. I did not know that the necklace concealed a suicide pill, but definitely had my suspicions. It was difficult to see why he would suddenly start to wear it again in the final stages of the investigation, unless he felt an imminent danger and needed an escape route.'

My face and body language may possibly have shown that I was not entirely happy that she had not told me this before. Patricia squirmed a bit and glanced down at the suicide letter.

'I have to be honest and say more or less the same as he did. Egoism is probably the reason that I did not mention my suspicions to you. I was dreading being wheeled into the court as a witness if there was a case. But I also thought that it would actually be better for all parties if there were not a long trial. As for reporting to the public and honouring those who deserve it . . .'

I nodded and looked at her expectantly. And once again she did not disappoint.

'Surely the best solution must be that you publish his letter. It is a gripping document that will be of great interest to both the press and the public. And it gives an excellent summary of the case that we both agree is correct.'

Her smile when she said the latter was somewhat bitter.

Following this clarification, I no longer had any pressing questions that I needed Patricia to answer. She, for her part, sat and mulled over the murderer's letter for a few minutes, without wanting to say what it was she wanted to talk to me about.

'Bloody hell,' she said suddenly, very loudly, as she threw the letter down on the table.

My surprise at this outburst was promptly followed by another that was no less shocking. Patricia took out a packet of cigarettes and, with a shaking hand, lit one of them from the candle. A few minutes of tense silence followed while she blew smoke rings up towards the ceiling in deep contemplation.

'I did not know that you smoked. When did you start?' I asked quietly. This development was far less to my taste.

'Yesterday evening. But I do not intend to take it up and will stop again soon,' Patricia replied, with an even more twisted smile. She demonstratively stubbed out the half-smoked cigarette in her dessert bowl, but then only seconds later lit another one.

'What I wanted to talk to you about was this. The story of Harald Olesen's last year, when he himself had become a human fly, and was surrounded by other human flies, is tragic enough in itself. And it was not remedied in any way by the arrest. It struck me even before I had met Andreas Gullestad that he was one of the most intelligent men I had ever come across. What he later told us and what this letter confirms is that not only was he an unusually intelligent man, but also a person with many other great talents. Just look at the map he drew.'

I looked at it and realized what she meant. The map was both informative and elegant, even though it must have been drawn in a rush. It was clearly the work of a person with an excellent geometric memory and considerable artistic skills.

'The very idea of leaving a map also shows that Andreas Gullestad was not a completely evil person without feelings. But despite all his talents and good intentions, as a sixteen-year-old he still killed the mother of a small child, partly because of the war and partly because of Harald Olesen's betrayal. And for the next twenty years, after the war, he lived as a human fly. Despite his many talents, all he ever really did was hide his dark secret from the war, tussle with his memories of the event and fight against his urge to seek revenge on the man who had made him a murderer. In the end, in his loneliness, he could not take the pressure and ended up killing first two more people and then himself.'

Patricia paused and with resignation blew some more smoke out into the air between us.

'Do not misunderstand me. Not only was it right but it was also absolutely necessary that he was caught and arrested. Murder must never be left unsolved and go unpunished in any civilized society. But the fact that it ended as it did for this extremely gifted youth who volunteered his services to the Resistance during the war after his father's death is in reality a greater tragedy than the end of Harald Olesen's life.'

I sat in silence and did not contradict her. I did not have much to say – and suddenly longed to get out into the fresh, smoke-free spring air.

Patricia, however, was far from finished.

'But all this is probably said out of frustration and disappointment in my own inadequacy.'

This time I had to protest.

'That is enough. It was actually your incredible efforts that helped us to establish who the murderer was and then arrest him.'

Patricia smiled quickly, but then held her hand up to stop me.

'Thank you for that – and for letting me be part of a very exciting and interesting case. But this welcome confirmation of my own intellectual capacity does not make the bitter truth that I have become a human fly myself any easier.'

I was dumbfounded. She took two drags of the cigarette and then carried on.

'It did not happen yesterday, so it is in no way your fault. I was already a human fly, but only really realized it fully yesterday. Sitting here, I like to think that my mind is just as sharp, and that everything is as it was before the accident. But it is not – and never will be. I felt like a tortoise yesterday: clear in my thoughts, but physically handicapped and ridiculously unable to save myself if something did not go according to plan. Despite all the interesting experiences and people that I met, it was a nightmare from the time that I left this room until I got back here. I relived the confrontation in Deerfoot's flat three times last night, and each time the ending was not a happy one. The first two times, I was shot. In the third, I was roasted in my wheelchair when the building went up in flames and everyone else ran out.'

Patricia stubbed out the second cigarette in her dessert bowl, but twice reached out to take a new one, before she hesitantly continued without.

'I asked my father to call you that morning eight days ago because I still thought and hoped that I could make an important difference to someone out there. And I now know that I can. But I also had my fears confirmed: that I no longer belong out there in the real world. So I will just have to sit here in my unreal world – and hope that every now and then an opportunity will crop up for me to take part in your life and influence what goes on out there.'

I looked at her bewildered. She lit yet another cigarette and made some more smoke rings before explaining.

'I will never come out with you again, but if you should get involved in a new case in which you think that my advice might be of help, you are always welcome to phone me or knock on the door. The only condition is that I do not want any kind of official recognition, and you must say as little as possible about me and my advice to anyone out there.'

I shook her hand on this. It was worse than I had hoped, and far better than I had feared. It had for a moment dawned on me that I might have considerable problems defending my newly won reputation as an ingenious investigator if I could not seek Patricia's advice at a later point. Having seen the miracles that Patricia had performed in this case, I found it difficult to imagine a case that she could not solve. But the fact that her role should not be discussed in public, I have to say, suited me rather well.

We sat in silence again for a few minutes following this little explosion. Then Patricia rang for Benedikte – or was it perhaps Beate who was working that Sunday? I had lost count of which of them was working when. On the other hand, I had come to understand that having two taciturn twins as maids was a means of ensuring that Patricia's environment was controlled and stable.

I got up as soon as the maid came in, but Patricia immediately put up a hand to stop me. Once again, her face went through a rapid change of mood. She stubbed out her cigarette in disgust, thrust the rest of the packet deep into a pocket and suddenly flashed me one of her more mischievous smiles. She whispered something to Benedikte, who gave a quick nod and immediately left the room.

'Please be seated for a moment or two more. I still have an amusing little theory that I want to test out with some help from Benedikte, before I can say that I am finished with the case.'

We waited in anticipation for a couple of minutes. Though I wracked my brains, I could find no explanation as to what this might be. Benedikte returned, as solitary as when she left, and whispered a short message in Patricia's ear. The reaction was both explosive and unexpected. Patricia's fit of laughter lasted for almost a minute.

'What is it that is so funny?' I eventually asked – no doubt with some irritation in my voice.

Patricia had to dry her eyes on a napkin before she could answer.

'Just that I have had my theory confirmed that people, when you get to know them a little, are in fact a very predictable race,' she replied, with a cheerful smile.

I suddenly got that uncomfortable feeling you always get when you realize that someone is laughing at you without yourself knowing why. I stood up again to leave. This time Patricia did not try to stop me. She just gave an apologetic shrug – and carried on laughing. As Benedikte opened the door to show me out, there was a final piece of advice from the wheelchair.

'By the way, my last piece of advice to you for now as you go back out into the real world . . . Remember, if you want to play in the kitchen, you have to put up with the heat!'

It sounded like a pubescent or childish twist on the well-known saying, the sort of thing that one has to be either five or fifteen to come up with. I was slightly worried that the drama of yesterday really had knocked Patricia's mental balance off-kilter. Unless she was even more complex than I had understood so far. Whatever the case, I thought it better simply to grin and bear it, and gave her a friendly wave and smile as I disappeared out through the door. Patricia's laughter was fortunately cut short when the door closed behind me.

IV

I managed to follow Benedikte quietly and obediently down one and a half flights of stairs on my way out. But then I could not stop myself from asking what her mysterious message had been that had made Patricia laugh so much. It was the first time that I saw the otherwise serious Benedikte smile – and the first time I heard her voice. And it was just as I had imagined it: simple and easy to understand.

'Miss said that you would ask me on the way out and I was to tell you the truth, that I had looked out of the window to check and that you would understand soon enough. Miss has a sharp tongue now and then, but it is her mind that is sharpest, you see. She can even predict the future sometimes.'

I nodded pensively, but still had no idea what this was all about and so asked cheerfully how soon I would know what it was that I would know. The loyal Benedikte replied, with a very gentle smile, that it would be no bother.

I did not understand until I was standing outside the White House and looked down Erling Skjalgsson's Street. But then I understood very quickly – and could agree that it did not bother me in the slightest. I could very happily live with the situation out in the real world.

The sun was shining, and the sky was blue, and it was an unusually delightful spring day. And by my car, an unusually beautiful young woman was waiting impatiently for me to come. Two long, slim legs, dressed in tight jeans that emphasized her lovely curves, stamping impatiently on the pavement to keep warm.

She nodded and gave me the most irresistible smile when I came up to the car. I smiled back, got in behind the wheel and indicated that she should get in beside me. Then we drove off together – as if it were the most natural thing in the world.

Fortunately, it was only several decades later, when the great Miss Patricia Louise I. E. Borchmann was no longer with us, that I heard about a comment she made later that day, on Sunday, 14 April 1968. She chuckled and commented to the twin sisters, Benedikte and Beate: 'Detective Inspector Kristiansen undoubtedly has many good qualities, but I am still not certain that intelligence is one of them.'

Afterword

When working on this historical crime novel, I have used my background and experience as a historian, and have tried as far as possible to be true to context in terms of events both in 1968 and the Second World War. But it is nonetheless the literary author Hans Olav Lahlum, and not the better-known historian of the same name, who wrote this novel. And I too have taken the artistic liberty that authors so often use. The place names and streets names used in the novel are authentic, but most of the actual buildings are a product of my imagination. Thus the particularly keen reader will be able to find both Krebs' Street and Erling Skjalgsson's Street, but not the house numbers or buildings that are described in this novel. Similarly, it is not possible to find a police station in Sälen with the same topographical surroundings or architecture as that described in Chapter Nine.

A couple of the minor characters were directly inspired by historical figures. All the main characters, on the other hand, including the murder victim Harald Olesen, are entirely the product of the author's imagination and are not based on any historical figure from either 1968 or the Second World War. And for those few minor characters inspired by historical figures, it must be emphasized that the literary depiction is not based on any historical involvement with a criminal investigation.

The Feldmann case, which is mentioned briefly, was a widely discussed court case from 1946 to 1947 in which two former border guides were acquitted of the murder of a Jewish couple during the war on the grounds of self-defence. This has been used as historical background in the novel, but has no direct parallel with the plot or any of the characters. However, several of the characters were inspired fully or in part by people I know today – including myself.

The head of fiction at Cappelen Damm, Anne Fløtaker, has been my most important adviser in terms of both the content and writing of this novel. I have also received useful feedback from the publisher, Anders Heger, and editor, Marius Wulfsberg. I would also like to give two thousand thanks to a group of personal advisers who read all or parts of the manuscript and gave me constructive comments about the content and/or language. This includes my sister, Ida Lahlum, and my good friends Ingrid Baukhol, Mina Finstad Berg, Ingrid Busterud, Anne Lise Fredlund, Kathrine Næss Hald, Hilde Harbo, Kristin Hatledal, Bjarte Leer-Salvesen, Torstein Lerhol, Espen Lie, Ellisiv Reppen, Jane Iren Solbrekken-Nygård, Karen Thue, Arne Tjølsen and Katrine Tjølsen. Ellisiv and also Mina both deserve a special mention for their continued interest in this project and for their practical help in connection with the final rounds of proofing and editing the manuscript.

Only time will tell whether my first crime novel will also be my last or if it will be the start of a historical crime series. However, I can only hope that *The Human Flies* will be as exciting for some readers as it has been for the author. Readers who have any comments or questions for the author can quite simply email them to hansolahlum@gmail.com or post them on the book's Facebook page.

Gjøvik, 27 June 2010
Hans Olav Lahlum

About My Late Aunt, Dagmar Lahlum
– and My Novel, *The Human Flies*

As was stated at the beginning of this book, this novel is dedicated to my late aunt Dagmar Lahlum. It therefore seems natural to close the book with a short account of her life, and its relevance to this novel.

Dagmar Lahlum was born in Sørumsand on 10 March 1923, but grew up in Eidsvoll in the 1930s. Eleven years younger than her sister, she was very much her mother's baby. Her father, who was fifty-one at the time of Dagmar's birth, had grown up in poverty, as did his two sons from an earlier marriage, who went to stay with their grandparents following their mother's premature death. As a rural shoemaker, Dagmar's father no doubt struggled to feed his second family during the crisis years in the 1920s and 1930s. His youngest daughter was said to have had a hot temper as a teenager, and clearly voiced her dissatisfaction with the situation. For the rest of her life she was to demonstrate both a taste and greed for fancy clothes and luxury goods.

A few weeks before the German invasion on 9 April 1940, Dagmar arrived in Oslo, at the age of seventeen. She did a modelling course and earned a living working as a seamstress and hotel receptionist, among other things. It has not been possible to establish whether she was involved with the Norwegian Resistance movement. In April 1943, she started a whirlwind romance with Eddie 'Zigzag' Chapman, a British MI5 agent who was in Norway under the cover of working for the Germans. It seems that Dagmar believed Eddie was a German soldier when she fell in love with him. As a result of this romance, Dagmar also took on the role of a double agent for the remainder of the war, helping Chapman with his missions at the risk of her own life. The extent to which the MI5 saw her as an enlisted agent is not apparent from the archive documents that have now been released, but it is clear that they were aware of her role. Eddie is recorded as her fiancé in 1943 and 1944 and some sources indicate that Dagmar also fell pregnant and had an abortion.

Eddie Chapman left Norway in spring 1944, still in his role as a German officer. Dagmar had never been a member of the NS, the Norwegian fascist party, but because she worked for the German censoring authorities in the final months of the war, and possibly because she was rumoured to be a German's tart, she was arrested by the Norwegian police on 19 May 1945 and sent to Bredtveit Women's Prison.

In a written statement from prison dated 15 June 1945, Dagmar refers to her contact with Eddie. She claims that her sympathies had always lain with the Resistance and the British, and that her job as a letter censor for the Germans had been cleared by Eddie, who had promised to come back for her as soon as the war was over, if he was still alive. If he was unable to return, he had assured her that if she contacted his employers in British intelligence, they would help her. Consequently, Dagmar was escorted to a meeting with official British representatives in Oslo on 19 June 1945, but they denied any knowledge of the case and she was returned to Bredtveit Women's Prison.

During the treason trials in Norway in 1947, Dagmar was sentenced to 189 days, exactly the number of days she spent in remand in 1945. She also lost the right to vote for the next ten years. She chose to pay the price, rather than face another trial.

Her motives for doing so are unknown. One likely explanation is that, as an uneducated girl from the country, with no money or contacts in Oslo, she considered her position to be hopeless, having being refused assistance by the English representatives and the Norwegian police. The odds were obviously stacked against her. Another possibility is, of course, that she had dubious motives for her contact with the occupying forces during the war, and so accepted the penalty. Whatever the case, the judgment in the treason trials and her reputation as a German's tart dogged her life for many years after the war. 'Remember your aunt was a Jerry bag!' a neighbour once yelled after Dagmar's little niece in Eidsvoll. Dagmar herself soon returned to the more anonymous streets of Oslo and left Eidsvoll for good when she received a small inheritance from her parents in the mid-1950s.

Dagmar never had any children and lived on her own for the rest of her life, with the brief exception of a short marriage in the early 1950s. She had several lovers – all older, wealthy men – who were able to satisfy her need for material luxury. None of these relationships was ever formalized and none of them lasted. She worked as a secretary and had other office jobs until she retired towards the end of the 1980s, but never applied for any public positions or sought to attract public attention in any way.

Dagmar was probably unaware that her wartime lover, Eddie Chapman, had survived and later married in England, until he contacted her again unexpectedly in the 1990s. Almost fifty years after the war had parted them, Eddie and Dagmar re-established contact. Whether she actually travelled to England and met him again remains uncertain, but it seems that around 1996–7 Dagmar expected that Chapman would soon return to

Norway and make public the story of her war effort. However, if that was his intention, Chapman was unable to fulfil it owing to ill health and he died on 12 December 1997.

The news that Eddie had died without coming to Norway, and telling the truth about her wartime experiences, was probably the last blow for Dagmar's already fragile mind. Her final hope for some kind of vindication turned into just another disappointment. The last years of Dagmar's life were very difficult. She was not only a heavy smoker and an alcoholic, but also suffered from Parkinson's disease and became increasingly socially isolated and undernourished. A tragic shadow of her youthful beauty, she continued to walk alone on her circuit from Vinmonopolet (state alcohol shop) to the bank to her flat with increasingly unsteady steps through the late 1990s.

Dagmar was last seen alive by her only remaining friend, her ever helpful niece Bibbi, at a Christmas dinner on 25 December 1999. Four days later Dagmar Lahlum was found dead behind the locked doors of her flat. As was fairly typical for her life, the exact date of her death and the circumstances remain unclear. She was reportedly found lying on the floor among all her old clothes and empty bottles, in a somewhat unusual and defensive position. However, there was no evidence of violence and a routine police investigation concluded that no one else had been in the flat at the time of her death. I believe that, in the end, my old aunt died alone in her home during a fight against some mental ghost from the wartime years. Obviously no one will ever know whether that is what happened in her final moments.

Dagmar Lahlum was virtually forgotten by everyone and her war effort was still entirely unknown at the time of her death, so very few people came to her funeral. Her story was first made public in 2007, when it received a lot of attention in both Norway and Great Britain following two new biographies about her wartime lover.

Dagmar Lahlum was the youngest daughter of my great-grandfather, Karl Lahlum (1871–1954) and the half-sister of my paternal grandfather, Hans Lahlum (1898–1977). I was born in 1973 and never had the chance to get to know Dagmar. As she had no children herself, Dagmar initially demonstrated some interest in her brother's little grandson and the survival of the family name. From the mid-1970s on, however, she came less and less frequently to family gatherings and kept a very low profile when she did. She spoke about herself and her past as little as possible. Every now and then her eyes would flash – and that was when the war was mentioned. And so it never was. My only childhood memory of my great aunt was an order never to mention the war if Dagmar should come to a family gathering again. She never did.

To the question as to whether my Aunt Dagmar's fate inspired my decision to study history, with the Second World War as one of my specialisms, the answer is a definitive no. I only found out about her wartime story a few years after I had graduated. And given the close family relationship, I have later chosen not to write about her as a historian.

To the question as to whether Dagmar Lahlum's life and fate has inspired this criminal novel, the answer is a definitive yes. In Norway, as in many other countries, the pictures painted of people's fate in the Second World War have often been black and white. This has without a doubt been the right thing to do in relation to some war heroes and war criminals. But there are also many, many stories from the war's 'grey zone' that are both moving and thought-provoking. It remains to be seen whether any new historical research in the future will be able to discover

Dagmar Lahlum's true position in the war's grey zone. However, what is important in this context is that her experiences from the latter years of the war dogged her days for the remaining fifty-four years of her life. From the time of her release in the summer of 1945 until her death during Christmas 1999, my aunt Dagmar Lahlum was a living example of the fate that Patricia Louise I. E. Borchmann describes as 'a human fly' in this novel – which could also describe Patricia herself and several other of the main characters in the book. Thus, I was never in any doubt as to what my first novel should be called, or to whom I would dedicate it.

Gjøvik, 20 September 2013
Hans Olav Lahlum

P.S. About sources and further reading: Dagmar's relationship with Eddie Chapman was first made public in the two Chapman biographies from 2007, Nicholas Booth's *Zigzag. The Incredible Wartime Exploits of Double Agent Eddie Chapman* and Ben Macintyre's *Agent Zizag. A True Story of Nazi Espionage, Love and Betrayal.* Both brought to light interesting material about the case from British archives and other British sources. Four years later, their war story was covered on screen in the documentary *Double Agent: The Eddie Chapman Story,* produced by Walker George Films for BBC2.

Dagmar's part of the story was further investigated in Norway in two lengthy newspaper articles written by the journalist and political scientist Hilde Harbo and published in the newspaper *Aftenposten* (14 Jan. 2007 and 22 Jan. 2008). The first historian to write about Dagmar was Professor Tore Pryser, who included a short portrait in his 2007 book *Kvinner i hemmelige tjenester. Etterretning i Norden under den annen verdenskrig*

('Women in Secret Services. Intelligence Work in the Nordic Countries during World War II'). The highly talented young Norwegian historian Kristin Hatledal then studied the case in depth first in her Masters thesis, 'Krigsheltinne eller tyskarjente? Historia om Dagmar Lahlum – i lys av andre etterretnings-kvinner' ('War heroine or German mistress? The story of Dagmar Lahlum – in the light of other female Resistance fighters') in 2009 and then in her book *Kvinnekamp. Historia om norske motstandskvinner* ('Women fighting. The history of Norwegian female Resistance fighters'), published in 2011.

I have discussed the case with Booth, Harbo, Pryser and Hatledal, and provided them with information needed from the Lahlum family, as well as from the file on Dagmar Lahlum's court case in the national Norwegian archives. I owe many thanks to Dagmar's niece Bibbi for sharing with me both the facts and her feelings about Dagmar's life.

If you enjoyed The Human Flies, *you'll love*

SATELLITE PEOPLE

the second instalment in the K2 and Patricia series
from Hans Olav Lahlum

Oslo, 1969. When a wealthy man collapses and dies during a dinner party, Norwegian Detective Inspector Kolbjørn Kristiansen, known as K2, is left shaken. For the victim, Magdalon Schelderup – a multimillionaire businessman and former resistance fighter – had contacted him only the day before, fearing for his life.

It soon becomes clear that every one of Schelderup's ten dinner guests is a suspect in the case. The businessman was disliked, even despised, by many of those close to him; and his recently revised will may have set events in motion. But which of the guests – from his current and former wives and three children to his attractive secretary and old cohorts in the resistance – had the greatest motive for murder?

With the inestimable help of Patricia – a brilliant, acerbic young woman who lives an isolated life at home, in her wheelchair – K2 begins to untangle the lies and deceit within each of the guests' testimonies. But as the investigators receive one mysterious letter after another warning of further deaths, K2 realizes he must race to uncover the killer. Before they strike again . . .

An extract follows here

DAY ONE

An Unexpected Storm Warning

I

'Good afternoon. My name is Magdalon Schelderup and is no doubt familiar to you. I would like to arrange a meeting with you this coming Monday. The reason being that one of my nearest and dearest is planning to murder me later on in the week!'

The time was a quarter past one. The day was Saturday, 10 May 1969. The place was my office in the main police station in Oslo. And the words seemed to hang in the air for a long time after I had heard them.

I waited for this particularly tasteless joke to be followed by either a loud laugh or the phone being thrown down. But the connection was not broken. And when the voice continued, it was without doubt Magdalon Schelderup's distinctively rusty yet dynamic voice, just as I had heard it many times before on the radio and television. I immediately pictured the legendary businessman and multimillionaire as he was most often photographed for the papers: dressed in a long black winter coat, his furrowed face secretive and barely visible under a brown leather hat.

'And just in case you should for a moment believe otherwise, I am Magdalon Schelderup and I am of sound mind and sober. You have been recommended to me by several acquaintances, and I was singularly impressed by your work in connection with the much-discussed murder case last year, so I thought I would give you the honour of solving this case too. The question is quite simply whether you can spare the time to meet me on Monday in connection with my planned murder, or not?'

I felt increasingly bewildered as I sat at my own desk on what I had presumed would be a very ordinary Saturday shift. It was starting to dawn on me that it was in fact Magdalon Schelderup who had called me and that he was serious.

I replied that I would of course give the case highest priority and suggested that we should meet that very same day, rather than wait until Monday morning. Not surprisingly, Magdalon Schelderup had obviously considered this possibility too.

'The truth is that only an hour ago I thought of driving into town to meet you personally. But then I discovered that three of the tyres on my car had unfortunately been slashed overnight. I could of course have taken my wife's car or used one of the company cars, and I can certainly afford to pay for a taxi, but this episode has made me strongly doubt whether the person I had thought of mentioning to you today is in fact the guilty party.'

In response to this, I asked if there were several people in Magdalon Schelderup's closest circle who he suspected might want to kill him. There was a short burst of dry laughter at the other end of the telephone.

'Absolutely. In fact, my closest circle is made up entirely of people who might be suspected of wanting to kill me. It is incredibly difficult to be both successful and popular over time. And given this dilemma, I have always chosen success. But what is new here is that I have good reason to believe that one of my nearest and dearest not only wants to kill me, but also has concrete plans to realize this sometime next week.'

The situation struck me as more and more absurd, but also more and more interesting. I heard my own voice say that we should then at least meet as early as possible on Monday morning. Magdalon Schelderup agreed to this straight away and suggested that I come to his home at Gulleråsen at around nine o'clock. He wanted to dig a little more and would assess the situation over the weekend, but was certain that he would be able to confirm his suspicions well enough to tell me on Monday.

Still dazed, I wished Magdalon Schelderup a good weekend and asked him to take every precaution against possible danger. He assured me that there was no risk of an attempt on his life before Tuesday afternoon, at the earliest. However, he would stay indoors at home until I came to see him on Monday morning and would do everything necessary to ensure his own safety.

Magdalon Schelderup's voice on the telephone was just as it was on the radio: a grand old man's voice, calm, convincing and determined. I put down the phone without any further protest and scribbled our meeting on Monday morning at the top of my to-do list for the coming week.

II

The remaining three-quarters of an hour of my Saturday shift passed without further drama. It was impossible, however, to stop my thoughts from turning to this unexpected telephone conversation. To the extent, in fact, that I called my boss to inform him about the phone call before I left the office. To my relief, he gave his approval of the way in which I had dealt with the situation.

Back home in my flat in Hegdehaugen, I found the latest article about Magdalon Schelderup in the pile of newspapers. It had been published only three days before. Yet another front page of the *Aftenposten* evening edition was filled with his photograph, this time under the headline 'King of Gulleråsen'. It concluded by saying that if the richest man in Gulleråsen was not already one of the ten richest men in Norway, then he very soon would be. The value of his property and assets was estimated at over 100 million kroner. Only months before his seventieth birthday, the property magnate and stock market king was at the peak of his career. With increasing regularity, financial experts speculated that he was one of the twenty most powerful men in Norway, though it was now many years since he had retired from his career as a conservative politician.

Over the years, newspapers and magazines had used unbelievable quantities of ink to write about Magdalon Schelderup. To begin with, they wrote about his contributions as a Resistance fighter and politician during and immediately after the war. There was then a rash of speculative and far less enthusiastic articles about the contact his family businesses might have had with the occupying forces during the war, and why a few years later he stepped back from an apparently promising political career. Later articles about his growing wealth and business acumen were frequently alternated with other more critical articles. These discussed his business methods, as well as the breakdown of his first two marriages and the financial settlements that they incurred. The interest in his turbulent private life appeared to have diminished following some further articles in the early 1950s when he married his third wife – this time a woman twenty-five years his junior. In recent years, however, there had been more and more articles that questioned the manner in which he kept shop. Former competitors and employees more or less queued up to condemn his methods and he had regularly been taken to court. With little success. Magdalon Schelderup cared not a hoot what the newspapers and magazines said, and with the aid of some very good sharpshooting lawyers, he was never sentenced in any court.

And it was this dauntless and apparently unassailable magnate who had telephoned me today to say that someone close to him planned to kill him next week.

Thus 10 May 1969 became one of the very few Saturdays when I yearned with all my heart for it to be Monday morning and the start of a new working week. I did not know then that the case would develop very quickly and dramatically in the meantime.

DAY TWO

Ten Living and One Dead

I

The following morning, 11 May 1969, started like every other Sunday in my life. I caught up with my lack of sleep from the previous week and did not eat breakfast until it was nearly lunch. The first few hours of the afternoon were spent reading the neglected papers from the week gone by. I even managed to read the first four chapters of the book of the week, which was Jens Bjørneboe's *Moment of Freedom*.

When the telephone rang at twenty-five past five, I had just stepped out of the shower. I made absolutely no attempt to answer it quickly. The caller was remarkably persistent, however, and the phone continued to ring until I picked it up. I immediately understood that it was serious.

The telephone call was of course for 'Detective Inspector Kolbjørn Kristiansen'. It was, as I had guessed, from the main police station in Møller Street. And, to my horror, it concerned Magdalon Schelderup. Only minutes before, they had received a telephone message that he had died in the course of an early supper at his home – in the presence of ten witnesses.

On the basis of what had been reported by the constables at the scene, it was presumed to be murder, but which of the witnesses present had committed the crime was 'to put it mildly, unclear'. The officer on duty at the police station had been informed that Schelderup himself had contacted me the day before. As none of the other detectives were available, the duty officer felt it appropriate to ask whether I might be able to carry out an initial investigation and question the witnesses at the scene of the crime.

I did not need to be asked twice, and within a few minutes was speeding towards Gulleråsen.

II

When I got there at ten to six, there was no trace of drama outside the three-storey Gulleråsen mansion where Magdalon Schelderup had both his home and head office. Schelderup had lived in style, and he had lived in safety. The house sat atop a small hill in the middle of a fenced garden, and it was a good 200 yards to the nearest neighbour. Anyone who wished to enter without being seen would have to make their way across a rather large open space. They would also have to find a way through or over the high, spiked wooden fence that surrounded the entire property, with a single opening for the heavy gate that led into the driveway.

I mused that it was the sort of house one finds in an Agatha Christie novel. It was only later on in the day that I discovered it was known as 'Schelderup Hall' by the neighbours.

There were eight cars parked in the space outside the gate, in addition to a police car. One of them was Magdalon

Schelderup's own big, black, shiny BMW. I was quickly able to confirm that he had told the truth: three of the tyres had been slashed with either a knife or some other sharp instrument.

The other cars were all smaller, but still new and of good quality. The only exception was a small, well-used blue Peugeot that looked as if it had been on the road since the early 1950s. I jotted down a working theory that all of the deceased's guests were overwhelmingly upper-class, albeit with some obvious variations in their financial situations.

It was not a warm welcome. As I made my way to the front door, a cacophony of wild and vicious barking suddenly erupted behind me, and I spun round instinctively to protect myself against the attacking dogs. But fortunately that was not necessary: the three great Alsatians that were straining towards me were clearly securely chained. Nevertheless, the sight of the dogs only served to strengthen my feeling of unease and my conviction that Magdalon Schelderup must have felt safe in his own home. The threat had been in his innermost circle – as he had expected, but it had come two days earlier than anticipated.

At the front door, I greeted the two constables who had been first at the scene and were now standing guard. They were both apparently relieved to see me, and confirmed that despite the death, the mood in the house was surprisingly calm.

I soon understood what they meant when, one corridor and two flights of stairs later, I stepped onto the red carpet in Magdalon Schelderup's vast dining room. At first it felt as though I had walked into a waxworks. The furniture and interior was in the style of the early 1900s. The fact that there were no pictures or decoration of any type on the walls only added to the cold, unreal feeling. There was a single exception, which was therefore all the more striking. A well-executed full-length portrait of Magdalon Schelderup filled one of the short walls.

The host himself was now laid out on a sofa by the wall, just inside the door. He was dressed in a simple black suit, and as far as I could see had no obvious injuries of any kind. His eyes were closed and his lips had a bluish tinge. I could quickly confirm that there was no sign of life when I felt for a pulse in his neck and inner wrist.

A large dark mahogany table set for eleven dominated the centre of the room. The roast lamb and vegetables had been served on porcelain plates and the undoubtedly excellent wine had been poured into the wine glasses. But none of the guests had shown any inclination to eat or drink. They also had champagne, which no one had touched.

What had obviously been Magdalon Schelderup's throne at the head of the table was now empty. The ten guests, silent in their Sunday best, had taken their seats around the table again. They were all looking at me, but no one said a word. A swift headcount informed me that there were six women and four men. I noted a degree of uncertainty and surprise in some of the faces, but saw no evidence of grief in any. Not a single tear on any of the twelve ladies' cheeks around the table.

Eight of the guests I reckoned to be fairly evenly distributed across the age group thirty to seventy. They all looked very serious and impressively controlled. There were two who stood out, each in their own way, and therefore immediately grabbed my attention, and they were the youngest in the party.

In the middle of the right-hand side of the table sat a slim, fair-haired young man in his late twenties, who was by far the most nervous person in the room. An hour had passed since the death, and yet he was still squirming on his chair, his face hidden in his shaking hands. There were no tears here either, only beads of sweat on his temples and brow. It struck me that there was something familiar about the young man. But it was only when he realized that I was looking at him and he took his hands from his face that I suddenly recognized him as the famous athlete, Leonard Schelderup.

I had no doubt read somewhere on the sports pages at some point that Leonard Schelderup was Magdalon Schelderup's son, then promptly forgotten. A year ago, I had myself stood on the stands at Bislett Stadium to watch the Norwegian Championships and seen Leonard Schelderup fly past on his way to winning gold in the middle-distance race, his shoulder-length hair fluttering in the wind. And I had been very impressed. Partly by the manner in which he allowed his competitors to pass, only then to speed up dramatically when the bell rang to mark the final lap. And partly by the almost stoic calm he displayed during the thunderous applause when he passed the finishing line. I commented to the person standing next to me at the time that it seemed that nothing, but nothing, could make Leonard Schelderup lose his composure – which was why it now made such an impression on me to see the same man sitting there, looking up at me with pleading eyes. He was only a matter of feet away and apparently on the verge of a nervous breakdown.

The situation was no less bewildering when Leonard Schelderup then broke the silence, throwing up his hands and saying: 'I don't understand why he chose me to taste his food. It wasn't me who started the tape. I didn't taste the nuts. I have no idea who killed him!'

Leonard Schelderup's outburst seemed to ease the tension ever so slightly. No one said anything else, but there were sounds of shuffling and sighs around the table.

And fortuitously, I caught the first smile in the room. It was fleeting and a touch overbearing, just as Leonard Schelderup fell silent. A few seconds later the smile was gone, and I never found out whether she saw that I had noticed. But I did. My gaze had swung almost instinctively a couple of places to the left to catch the reaction of the youngest person in the room.

At first glance, I thought it was my advisor, Patricia, who had somehow or other managed to sneak both herself and her wheelchair into Magdalon Schelderup's home and had joined them at the dining table. Then I started to wonder if it was in fact all an absurd nightmare. Only, I didn't wake up. The ten guests who remained seated at the table were very much alive. Magdalon Schelderup stayed where he was, lying stone dead on the sofa by the door. The young woman who sat to the right of his empty throne at the head of the table was of course not Patricia, though the girl who was sitting there also had dark hair and the same deliberate movements and held herself in the same self-assured manner.

Only, as far as I could see, this young woman was fully able, and about half a head taller than Patricia, as I remembered her from the previous spring; and also somewhat younger. I had never seen this woman before entering

Magdalon Schelderup's house. But somewhere, I had heard that his youngest child was an extraordinarily beautiful daughter, who left those she met awestruck.

Her gaze was no less bold when her eyes met mine. Another fleeting smile slipped over her lips.

It was in those few seconds that I stood there looking into the eyes of the eighteen-year-old Maria Irene Schelderup that I realized there was only one thing to be done. And that was first of all to gather as much information as possible about the death and the deceased from her and the other guests. Then I would have to hurry home and phone the number without a name at the back of my telephone book. The number to a telephone that sat on the desk of Patricia Louise I. E. Borchmann, the professor's daughter, at 104–8 Erling Skjalgsson's Street. I had, with a hint of irony, written it down next to the emergency numbers for the fire brigade and the ambulance service.